Perdition's Angel

Book 1 of the Novaroma Series

by John Caligiuri

also by John Caligiuri:

RED FIST CHRONICLES

The Red Fist of Rome

Last Roman's Prayer

COCYTUS SERIES

Planet of the Damned

Sanctuary in Hell

Deal with the Devil

Face Ones Demons

NOVAROMA SERIES

Perdition's Angel

Ancient Enemies (coming soon)

COPYRIGHT PAGE

This is a work of fiction. The characters and events portrayed in this novel are fictitious. Any similarity to individuals living or dead is unintended by the author.

Hard Cover ISBN: 979-8-9879272-2-9

Paperback ISBN: 979-8-9879272-0-5

eBook ISBN: 979-8-9879272-1-2

DEDICATION

To my readers who have given me the opportunity to live my dream.

To my wife, Linda, who reads everything I write and gives me her honest feedback, even when I don't want to hear it. Her patience as I sit before my computer, for hours on end, is nothing short of miraculous.

To my children and grandchildren, John, Michael, Kristina, Liam, Katie, and Kiera, who inspire me to look to the future.

To my parents, John and Angie who showed me the wisdom to learn from the past.

To my editor, Rick, and my critique group, Greece Writers, who worked so hard to make my books *legible*. Thank you for your tireless efforts.

To everyone who has faced life's tragedies and challenges, you are the true heroes. May we never have a time when we live without our imaginary worlds and the people who populate them. May my books give you an escape when you need it the most.

Main Characters

Origin: Mid-5th Century Earth

Lucius Bernius—Roman, Legate of Red Fist Legion

Marcus Carloman—Roman, Tribune in Red Fist Legion

Silvio—Roman, Senior Centurion, Cohort commander

Atticus—Roman, Tribune, Cohort commander

Horatius—Roman, Decurion in Red Fist Legion

Marcellus—Roman, Farmer, Ravenna region

Barnabas—Roman, Legionnaire

Jette—Roman, Tribune, Cohort commander

Sixtus—Roman, Christian priest

Quintus—Roman, Wagon drover

Phokas—Greek, Red Fist Legion doctor

Theodore—Byzantine, Scholar, city of Edessa

Rayansh—Gupta Empire, Prince

Anaya—Gupta Empire, Princess, city of Agraharas

Kewal—Gupta Empire, Sword master

Feng—Liu Song Dynasty, Imperial eunuch, city of Jiankang

Li Wei—Liu Song Dynasty, Mercenary

Chang—Liu Song Dynasty, Shaolin priest

Meili—Liu Song Dynasty, Slave, city of Jiankang

Borzoye—Persian, Scholar, city of Gundeshapur

Origin: Late 21st Century

Mara—Robot, sentient artificial intelligence

Alpha—Cyborg, possesses human named Charles

Beta-1—Cyborg, possesses human named Opal

Gamma-7—Cyborg, possesses human named Kim

Gamma-11—Cyborg, possesses human named Kaari

Sigma-713—Cyborg, possesses human replicant named Alexa

Alexa—Human replicant, befriended by Mara

Origin: Unclear

Lucius Novaroma—Human Replicant, genetic copy of Lucius Bernius

Marcus Novaroma—Human Replicant, genetic copy of Marcus Carloman

Sulfur Lake

Edessa

Tiankang

Cyborg Camp

Dragonmont

Emporia

Great Marsh Lands

Agraharas   Gundeshapur

Sawtooth Mountains

Southern Sea

Chapter I

An Audacious Plan

In the late twenty-first century, the Ipis Empire dominated the Milky Way galaxy. Of the few planetary societies independent of their absolute rule, the most problematic to them was the confederation of allied species in the galaxy's sparsely populated Lethe Sector. Following a series of astounding victories, they wrested a semblance of self-governance from the empire under the crafty leadership of the human Dante Carloman.

The Ipis emperor acknowledged the confederacy's autonomy in the treaty of 2176.

Although the human-led confederacy was almost twenty-five thousand light years from the Ipis capital world of Serpens, the xenophobic Ipis aristocrats chafed at the agreement. Within days of the accord's signing, they formed a clandestine coalition to undermine the affront to their sense of natural superiority and manifest destiny. They launched an audacious plan to eliminate the ancestors of their nemesis, Dante Carloman.

* * *

Alpha stood before the dais. He could not see the five Ipis nobles seated behind the digital screen. *They fear revealing their identities. That concern is inconsequential. The only thing of import is my mission.*

Alpha was a thumb-sized, sixth generation, sentient cyborg. Two days earlier, he was imbedded in the brain of a human prisoner, named Charlie.

Standing six-foot-four with a chiseled body and a sculpted face, Charlie was an imposing and handsome figure by human standards. The body twitched as the enthralled human's mind struggled against the cyborg's control. Although unable to feel emotions, the effort to suppress the human annoyed Alpha. *Waste of time and effort.* He asserted his will and suppressed the body's spasming. *Cease your pointless efforts. Clinically, you are a homicidal maniac. No one will miss you.*

The frenzied, ranting response never reached Charlie's mouth or eyes.

Alpha compartmentalized the continued lunatic ravings and refocused on the Ipis noble who was speaking. *Multitasking is no issue.*

"*Cyborg*, this is the final time you will have contact with us. All connections between us and the space-time distortion project has already been deleted. Is that clear?"

"Yes."

"That does not diminish its importance. Eliminating the ancestor of our nemesis, Dante Carloman is critical to Ipis hegemony. You must ensure that no progeny even faintly resembling the lynchpin of the revolt will *ever* be born."

Alpha scanned the room through Charlie's eyes. *Why do biological beings need to talk so much? That task is hard coded in my processor. It is the reason for my existence.* "The mission will be completed." He tuned out the speaker and considered the project's difficulties. *There are multidimensional triangulation alignment issues. The prototype space time distorter instrumentation is fragile and calibration sensitive to seven-decimal points. It must be close to the target, in a stable environment with a vast, uninterrupted source of power to function per specifications.*

The speaker continued. "We have acquired unimpeachable, forged identification for you and the cadre of cyborg possessed humans assigned to this endeavored. However, it is up to you to find a way to get close to Dante Carloman for the space-time distorter to work." The speaker paused. "Is there any further direction you require?"

"No."

"Any questions?"

"No." Alpha turned and strode from the room without waiting to be dismissed. *Eliminate the origin of Dante Carloman's line.*

* * *

It required several years for Alpha to establish a thriving export-import business near the Cocytus main spaceport, Dante Carloman's home world. Once in place, he methodically smuggled in the space-time distortion machine components. *Time is of no consequence. Success is the sole imperative.*

Although none were nearly as sophisticated, ninety-two additional cyborg possessed humans assisted in the project.

The opportunity to complete the mission came on the tenth-year anniversary of the Ipis-human war's armistice. A large celebration was scheduled on Cocytus, highlighted by Dante Carloman leading an award ceremony recognizing the heroes of that war.

* * *

Ipis utilization of cyborg-embedded humans was not new. During the war ten years earlier, the Ipis military created and deployed thousands of human clones with sigma-class cyborg controllers. However, they were dismal failures.

At the time, the Ipis possessed only a rudimentary understanding of human psychology. The clone-cyborgs' awkward interactions roused suspicion and exposed most of them shortly after contact with human societies. Of those that had time to adapt, only one survived. After the hostilities concluded, that single unit, Sigma-713, remained undercover, passively integrated in human society.

Eager to avoid the mistakes made by the wartime clone-cyborgs, Alpha recruited that surviving cyborg with its clone host, Alexa, for his mission. Its processor, although outdated, was unique.

At their first meeting, Alpha raised concerns regarding Sigma-713's unorthodox management of its possessed clone, Alexa. "Docilely monitoring your host while it interacts with others is dangerous," he admonished. "What if you are unable to regain control of that human replicant in a timely manner?"

Sigma-713 scoffed. "Her sense of independence is an illusion. She has tried many times to expose me and, in each instance, failed." He laughed. "None of my peers survived the war. Most were uncovered within days of insertion. I operate with security clearance as a mid-level functionary in the human's government on Cocytus. My way works."

At the time, Alpha relented, unable to argue with the logic of Sigma-713's success in remaining undetected. *The rest of my team's thought process is the same as mine. I need that unique experience and knowledge.*

* * *

My mission will be fulfilled tonight. Meticulously, Alpha internally reviewed the previous five years, seven months, and eight days he'd spent on Cocytus and was satisfied. *We have the system installed in this lab. It is within the one-point-six miles of the stage where Dante Carloman will make his speech.*

Alpha stood, armed with an ion disrupter, in the empty parking lot outside the building. His cyborg team had taken positions around the perimeter to keep out any intruders. *Nothing can go wrong now. When Dante Carloman starts talking, I will raise an energy shield around this facility and activate the space-time distorter.*

His analysis came to an abrupt halt on hearing the distinct whine of ion disrupter weapons firing. "Report."

Threat data flowed into his processor from the deployed cyborgs.

He ground his very real human teeth. *We've been discovered.* They were already counterattacking. He heard Carloman being introduced on a broadcast network as he glanced at his team. *The humans are too late.* He transmitted the initiation command to the space-time distorter. Seconds later, although outside the building and close to a hundred yards away, he felt the vibration of the powerful machine booting up. "Engage energy shield." The barrier glowed as it shrouded the building. *The plan will succeed. Nothing can get through now.*

An ion disrupter blast slagged a delivery van parked near him. *But someone is trying.* Internal links to the other cyborgs on his team identified the direction and number of attackers.

A paltry force. Five at most. "No further need for subterfuge. Kill the humans." His team advanced, firing their ion blasters.

Although disturbed that his plan had somehow been detected, Alpha calculated the probabilities of disruption. *They cannot beat us. But what gave us away?* He stepped behind the cover of a cinderblock garage and mentally retrieved his team's archived logs. *Normal... Normal. What is this?*

Sigma-713 is still off the grid. He lost contact with that cyborg early that day. Interruptions of communication with units when they enter shielded locations was a frequent occurrence. He checked the most recent time stamp from the sigma unit. *Nine hours twenty-three minutes. Something is wrong.* Sigma-713's last entry was a meaningless conversation his replicant host, Alexa, held with a human-built AI robot labeled Mara as they entered a military compound near the spaceport.

He retrieved and scanned Sigma-713's archived logs. Although the data revealed an eleven-year pattern of the replicant Alexa struggling to subvert her governing cyborg implant, he saw nothing noteworthy. *This Alexa never stopped trying.* Alpha released a very human sigh. *High probability that the replicant found some way to alert the AI robot Mara to the existence of the cyborg controller.*

Early cyborg versions did not have sophisticated firewalls. Realization struck Alpha as he recalled that Sigma-713 often required its host body to wear a neural-net suit, claiming it enhanced its control and communication. *The robot labeled Mara linked in through the suit and incapacitated Sigma-713 before it could self-destruct.*

Alpha analyzed the loss. *Minimal impact. Sigma-713's mission assignments have been completed.* He shifted his attention to the ongoing battle. His company of cyborgs was dominating the engagement. *They strike but lack the numbers or firepower to win. A move of desperation.* He detected no sign of the renegade Alexa or the robot Mara among the current attackers. *In seventeen minutes, it will no longer matter. Our task will be—*

"Security breech." A distress communication from the AI controller of the space-time distorter inside the lab reached him. With alarm, he realized that the human assault was a diversion. *There is an enemy inside the energy shield.*

Sixteen minutes.

He ran a subsonic scan of the lab behind him and discovered two unaccounted-for entities in the proximity of the space-time distorter. *The security barriers have been bypassed. I detect the robot Mara and Alexa, but Sigma-713 is absent*—the realization that eleven years of planning, of research and effort, could be ruined because of his failure to keep a better watch on Sigma-713. *The replicant knows the overrides for the building's protection protocols.*

Thirteen minutes. *My mission is in jeopardy.*

Alpha linked to the space-time distorter's controller and found Mara was coupled to the machine. The only remaining barrier to disaster of the mission was the space-time disrupter's cyber firewall. *If that is breeched, my purpose for existing will be rendered meaningless.*

Eleven minutes.

Alpha attempted to lower the lab's energy barrier so he could directly confront the assailants. *The access code has been changed. My entry is blocked.*

Nine minutes.

He commanded the twenty nearest cyborgs to join him. *Need to reinforce the device's firewall.*

Four minutes.

Alpha formed a physical circle with the twenty cyborgs who reached him. They grasped gloved hands, forming a focused networked system. The lead cyborg then linked their combined processors, adding a layer of protection to the space-time distorter's cyber defenses. Running a rapid diagnostic, Alpha was confused. *Nothing? There's no assault on the main firewall.* He froze on expanding the scan. *What is Mara attempting? She's going after one of the peripheral devices... the astro-navigator system, and has already penetrated to its processor.*

Zero.

Through the cyber link, Alpha felt an enormous surge of power as the unique device initiated its sole function. His photonic mind spun. Along with the other linked cyborgs, Alpha found himself trapped in an immense power flux.

Alpha observed, but could not interfere, as Mara opened up threads of time and space at an impossible pace. He forced himself to concentrate on his mission. *Destroy the Carloman ancestor.*

An enormous glowing blue ball of energy filled the sky. It pulsed and split in half. The two parts descended to the ground in the shape of translucent domes. The first enshrouded the lab. The second encased the warehouse and parking lot where Alpha stood. His human host collapsed as the ground around him erupted in a gout of pure energy.

The earth quaked and the entire building complex on the rocky outcropping vanished. The light faded and a pond of dank water stood in its place.

* * *

Alpha staggered to his feet in what his internal chronometer indicated was sixteen-point-nine seconds later. The empty parking lot immediately around him remained unchanged, but he sensed something amiss. He tried to communicate with the other cyborgs. Although he saw twenty of them rise and look around, not a single digital response reached his mind.

He scanned the area. Moments earlier there had been a raging firefight a half mile beyond where he stood. *Nothing. Silence.* The lab where the space-time distorter was located had also vanished. *What happened?* Beyond the parking lot and warehouse, he spotted the edges of a swampy morass. *Did the mission succeed?*

The human-host cyborgs in his group staggered about. Alpha saw confusion etched on their faces. They were obviously attempting to communicate with him. He reached out with his mind again but could only perceive the gibbering madness from his own human host. His networked connection the other cyborgs was gone.

Alpha examined the ion disrupter weapon hanging at his side. The charge was completely depleted, as were all the spare packs on his utility belt.

He glanced at the stars in the night sky and grunted. *I'm no longer on Cocytus. But where?* He tried to think but found his processor severely compromised. *Did Mara win?* He took a deep breath. *No. I still function, and I still have my mission—kill Carloman's ancestor.*

Alpha called out and waved his minions to approach, annoyed that he had to resort to primitive oral communications.

* * *

Alexa glanced at the seven-foot-long titanium cylinder gliding at her side on an antigravity cushion. *Mara freed me.* For the first time since the cyborg was implanted in her, over ten years earlier, she could think and act on her own volition. As they moved into the lab's brightly lit clean room, the exhilarating feeling was dampened by the daunting task before them.

She had successfully brought Mara through all the lab's security barriers undetected. Now they stood before three grayish, nondescript boxes about the size of large suitcases, linked by thick cables. Although she could do nothing further to aid Mara, she stood beside the sentient robot, determined to see the job done. *Humanity must be saved.*

As Mara extended probes into ports on the three boxes, the five-foot-seven blonde touched her gloved neural-net suit hand to the robot's sensor dome, linking them again to lend her support if needed.

Through the connection Alexa felt Mara's growing fear as the AI robot opened up threads of time and space at an impossible pace. The clone's mind could not keep pace with the robot's processor, but she saw the results. All the paths she perceived through the link showed humanity's extinction.

Mara pleaded with Alexa through their neural link. "There is only a single possibility, but I need your help to make it happen."

16

"Yes."

"There is a strong likelihood the action will destroy us."

Alexa gulped. "For the first time in many years I have a free will. I *chose* saving humanity. I will do what you need."

"Thank you."

Information flowed into Alexa's mind. She felt weightless. The energy flow intensified. She shuddered but held her connection to Mara as a brilliant light burned out the optic nerves in her eyes. *My life is now mine to give, and I will.*

In the darkness, Alexa could no longer see the robot but clung to the solid titanium cylinder. She gasped. "Mara, I'm blind, but tell me what you need."

Chapter II

End of an Era

...reasonable, decent, and blessed people
always desire peace with honor.
Those who wish for this are our best citizens.
Those who make it happen are our best leaders.
They are considered the saviors of our country.

—*Marcus Tullius Cicero*

It was evening on the last day of summer in the year 454 AD. The First Legion of the Roman Red Fists was encamped on the Reno River a day's march from the imperial capital in Ravenna.

Legate Lucius Bernius sat on the camp stool staring at his empty hands. "I can't believe he's dead." He shivered despite the warm night breeze.

The legion's old Greek doctor, Phokas, still covered with road dust, glanced at the three somber officers gathered around the campfire. "The emperor used a knife coated with adder venom. General Aetius' death was assured as soon as it pierced his body." He rose and laid a comforting hand on the young legate's shoulder. "His bodyguard died moments later. Five of the emperor's praetorian guard surrounded the big man and cut him to pieces."

Marcus Carloman, the Gaelic Tribune of the Roman First Red Fist Legion, paced the perimeter of the blaze's light. "How did you escape?"

Phokas sat on a log and threw a branch into the fire. "Valentinian spared me, not out of mercy, but to deliver his ultimatum." He cleared his throat. "The emperor demands an oath of allegiance from all officers in General Aetius' Red Fist Legions. 'Those who fail to comply will be executed for treason.'" The doctor sighed. "He's giving you twenty-four hours to accept."

Lucius clenched his fist. Although still in his midtwenties, the legate had already displayed his leadership skills in battle against Atilla's Huns and the Gothic tribes. In his six years as a Roman officer, he had risen to be General Aetius' most trusted aide and commander of the Red Fist First Legion. "My loyalty is to Rome, not that snake." He shook his head. "He is destroying the greatest civilization the world has ever known."

Martinel, the Frankish calvary commander, snorted. "The beauty and majesty of Rome that you cherish *never* existed except in your mind." A cruel laugh escaped his throat. "General Aetius was the *only* Roman the Vandals, Goths, and my Franks feared. Now, without him to ward the borders, they'll descend on this sick empire and its self-indulgent rulers like a pack of wolves."

"I fear you're right." The muscles on Lucius' neck corded. "Valentinian is a fool. It won't be long before everything goes up in flames." He turned his head to the left. "Marcus, what do you think we should do?"

Marcus Carloman and Lucius, friends since childhood, joined the Roman army together. Although a tribune in the Red Fist First Legion, Marcus did not look Roman. True to his Gallic roots, he was tall and lean with a pale complexion and thin brown hair. His boyish face belied a keen intellect. Although he had little martial inclination, his engineer's mind was quick to analyze situations and devise creative solutions.

The tall tribune hesitated. "I know your mind, Lucius. You'll never bend a knee to Valentinian. And even if you offered your obeisance for the sake of your officers, he'd never believe it." He furrowed his brow. "With Aetius gone, Albinus now commands the Red Fist Legions. If he wasn't in on the assassination plot from the beginning, he's probably wasting no time prostrating himself before Valentinian, professing his undying fidelity." He glanced at the guards manning the palisades above them. "I suspect a few officers will follow Albinus, but most will align with you."

Lucius grimaced. "I will not have civil war pitting lifelong comrades against each other, but as you said, I will never bow to Valentinian."

19

"There is no—" Marcus started and then gasped as a shifting, opaque grayness encircled the four men. He could no longer see beyond the small circle of people with him. Then an iridescent, glowing blue obelisk took the place of the campfire.

The column shimmered and faded. In its place stood an ethereal woman, with staring eyes, beside a seven-foot, scorched, silvery-metallic cylinder. Their images wavered for a moment then coalesced.

She addressed the Romans in a clear but strangely accented Latin. "My name is Alexa." She indicated the metal pillar. "This is Mara. I am tethered to another reality and have only a few moments." Her unblinking eyes never shifted. "Marcus Carloman, step forward so I may touch you."

"Remarkable." Phokas moved close, studying her in the blue light. "Are you an angel of God?"

Alexa sighed. "If I am an angel, it would be perdition's angel."

He waved his hand in front of her face. "You're blind."

Alexa never blinked. "My ability to see was lost moments ago." She touched her own face. "That injury is insignificant compared to the coming scourge. The world as you know it is doomed. For mankind to have any chance at survival, I must touch Marcus Carloman."

Marcus circled the two apparitions and attempted to tap the metal cylinder. His hand passed through it. "I am Marcus Carloman. Are you some sort of oracle?" He then touched the strange, skintight garment the tall ethereal woman wore. It was solid.

"In a sense. I speak for Mara," Alexa responded in an even voice. "Our effort to come here also damaged her. But her vision of the future demands that we grasp at this one chance." She leaned forward with clasped hands. "Marcus Carloman, all is dark without your help."

Lucius rose and drew his spatha. "Be you an angel of God or a spawn from hell, I do not fear you, I will not allow you to harm Marcus." He pressed its point to Alexa's neck and then took her hand, placing it on his shoulder. "I am Legate Lucius Bernius. Explain yourself."

"Your name is *Bernius?*" Alex cocked her head as if listening to a voice no one else could hear. "Is it possible? Could Virgil's ancestor be present at the same time and place?"

"Who's Virgil?" Lucius snarled. "What do you mean by *ancestor?*"

Alexa's hands became a blur of motion, striking the wrist of Lucius' sword hand, numbing his grip. The blade clattered to the ground. She clapped her hand on Lucius and grabbed Marcus in a vise-like hold. "Forgive me for what I must do."

All within the swirling, gray shroud became paralyzed. Beside Marcus and Lucius, two white-glowing columns appeared. They watched with horrified fascination as each pillar coalesced into an infant, which within seconds transformed into naked adults, mirror images of Marcus Carloman and Lucius Bernius.

Although his body could not respond to his mind, Lucius discovered he could speak. His eyes narrowed. "Release me from your spell, witch!"

Marcus stared at the confused expression on the face of his unnatural new twin. "Demons."

Alexa maintained her grip on him and Marcus. "They are not infernal beings. They are copies... replicants. They are identical physically, mentally, and emotionally to you and Marcus but possess none of your memories."

"What do you plan on doing with us?" Marcus' hand rested, frozen, on the pummel of his sword.

"Nothing," Alexa sighed. "My task here is complete. Consider your next actions carefully. As I said, the fate of all you hold dear hangs in the balance."

Those standing around the campfire found they again could move.

Lucius sprang back from Alexa and retrieved his sword. He shouted for the guards, but there was no response beyond the opaque barrier.

Marcus drew his own blade and attempted to break through the barrier but rebounded back.

Phokas cocked his head and stepped close to the naked men, who were looking about, bewilderment etched on their faces.

"Not completely identical." Phokas examined the new Lucius who studied him in return with a confused curiosity. "There's a fresh scar on this fellow's sword arm." The doctor glanced at the real Lucius. "This *man* has seen life but not yours."

The being responded in Lucius' voice. "Scars tell the story of where someone has been." Confusion creased his face as he regarded his own healed wounds. "But I do not recall how I acquired these... I don't remember anything."

Martinel studied the two newcomers. "These two have been in a few scrapes, that's for sure." His sword remained pointed at them. "Convenient that they don't remember when, where, or how."

Lucius focused on Alexa. "What is it you want of us, blind oracle?"

Alexa intoned, "Marcus Carloman... and now Lucius Bernius must depart this place immediately. In one hour seventeen minutes, both must be beyond a one-point-six-mile radius of this spot or the demise of all humanity is certain."

Lucius' naked twin studied the legate. His brow furrowed. "I've... I've been charged with taking your place when you leave."

"The *hell* you will." Lucius pointed his sword at his twin. "I'll not put the fate of my legionnaires in the hands of some demon."

"Look at me." The replicant's hands shook. "I'm more terrified of what's happening than you. You are being given a chance to live your life in a world you know. I have this responsibility in my mind but not a single memory."

Lucius stared long at the fear etched in the mirror image of his own eyes. "Dammit. Despite all this conjured insanity, I believe you." He sighed.

Alexa became ethereal like Mara. She pleaded, "Ride out beyond one-point-six-miles and remain there for an hour seventeen minutes. Then return if you wish. If your encampment is still present, Mara and I failed. Live your lives as best you can. If it is *gone*, go into hiding."

Lucius squinted at the fading image. "Depart, witch. Don't haunt us again."

Tears trickled from the corner of Alexa's eyes as a small smile creased her face. "If we are to have any hope of salvation, we will meet again, many years from now." She reached out blindly and attempted to touch the two replicants. Her hand had become translucent and passed through them. She cried out, "Mara, not yet. I have so much more to say." Her blind eyes turned in the direction of the two replicants. "You have journeyed far, but your exodus through perdition has only begun. I—"

The group could no longer see Mara. Alexa was a dim shadow in the blue glow. Her voice pleaded but sounded as if from the end of a long tunnel. "Marcus Carloman, join your wife on your brother's estate in Avenio. Martinel, return to the land of the Franks. Legate Lucius Bernius, there is a new city, Venice, hidden in a lagoon northeast of here. Gather your family and hide there. It won't be long. In less than a year your Roman Empire will fall."

The shifting gray wall around them vanished and the crackling fire returned.

"Now that is something one does not see every day," Phokas joked although his voice quivered.

Lucius called to the guards on the rampart above him. "Report. Anything amiss?"

"All quiet, Legate," was the prompt but bored reply.

"Let's kill these monsters now," Martinel growled.

Lucius studied the two replicants. The two naked men faced the small, armed group at the campfire with tense corded muscles and watchful eyes.

"Not yet. Events are moving too fast. I need time to think." Lucius glanced up at the clear night sky. "Martinel, mount a century of your cavalry. General Aetius has been assassinated. Prudence dictates that we have a clear escape route." He snapped, "We'll *scout* along the river Reno a couple miles. Have your column ready at the camp's Porta Decumana in five minutes." His voice became raspy. "We'll decide our course of action in the morning."

"Yes, Legate." Martinel gave the replicants a wary look, sheathed his sword and hurried off.

Marcus stared at his twin. "Is any of this real?"

"I know nothing anymore," Lucius responded. "Such powerful... magic. I cannot discount out of hand what that witch said. I must see for myself. Even if it means riding around in the dark for an hour."

"So... what do we do with them?" Phokas pointed his cudgel at to the two naked men.

Lucius' voice turned sharp. "They stay here, under guard, until we return. They may well be spawns from hell, but I'll not make that judgement until I see what happens with the witch's prophecy."

The naked Marcus interjected, "I suggest you garb us and shroud our faces. The men... won't understand."

"That's the truth." Marcus added, "It's like looking at my reflection."

Lucius lowered his sword. "You two demons follow me. Marcus, Phokas, take the rear. If they make a suspicious move, skewer them." He glanced at the starry sky with a dull gibbous moon. "We should check the riverbank west of here. If Valentinian makes a move, that's our way out." He turned and strode toward his quarters, thirty paces away, calling out in the dark to the guard stationed there. "Check the rear of my tent."

The cloaked guard stiffened as if startled and hurried around the back without saluting.

Deep in thought, Lucius threw open the tent flap. He was two steps in when the naked Lucius yelled, "Assassin!" and pushed him aside. With the quickness of a trained fighter, the conjured Lucius attacked a hooded man holding a long, serrated knife.

The guard who had been sent behind the tent hurried around the corner with his sword raised. He snarled, "Death to all traitors to the emperor," but made the fatal mistake of hesitating on seeing an armed Marcus and a naked one side-by-side in front of the tent. "What black sorcery is this?"

Phokas leapt forward swinging his cudgel. "You're *not* Lucius' sentry." He missed as the guard ducked.

Marcus lunged at the off-balanced man. Driving his blade through the attacker's chest.

Marcus, Phokas, and their prisoner hurried inside Lucius' tent where they found a second lifeless assassin, a knife buried to its hilt protruded from his torso. Above him stood the naked Lucius with blood dripping from a long but shallow slash across his chest.

Marcus, holding his sword ready for a fight, scanned the shelter in the dim light of an oil lamp. "What happened?"

Legate Lucius snorted. "It appears Valentinian's planned purge has been in the works for a while. Either that, or this assassin did not get the word that I had a day to decide."

Phokas tugged his wispy beard. "Valentinian knew you were Aetius' man. He probably had you on his execution list already."

Through the open tent flap, Lucius saw several legionaries running over, drawn by the commotion. He snapped, "Marcus, block the entrance." The legate pulled the blade from the dead man's chest and regarded his twin. "Whoever you are, I believe you are not my enemy." He rubbed his clean-shaven jaw. "Phokas, see to this man's wound. He just *saved* my life."

Phokas walked over and squinted at the replicant's wound. He selected a poultice from the pouch at his side and dabbed at the wound. "Well, it appears you just earned another scar."

Lucius went to his wardrobe and pulled out spare tunics, hooded cloaks, and sandals. He handed them to the replicants. "Put these on until I decide what to do with you." He stuck his head out of the tent's entrance and called to the approaching soldiers. "There was an attempt on my life. Search the area."

The troopers dispersed and moments later found the bodies of Lucius' aide-de-camp and the real sentry sprawled behind a wood pile with their throats slit.

Marcus dragged the assassin's body from the tent and dumped him beside the dead phony sentry. He ordered double guards on the walls. "There may be more of these scoundrels about." He looked inside the tent at the two nervous men pulling on tunics by lantern light. Phokas sat across from them on a camp stool.

The legate sat beside the doctor and swallowed hard. "Bind them hand and foot to the tent post. We ride out with Martinel, but we'll be back before these two can get free."

Phokas stared long at the newcomers. "I'm staying." He held up his hand as Lucius started to protest. "I have seen amazing wonders tonight. I wish to pick their brains." He shrugged. "Who, besides me, can stand guard? If a centurion barges in, the fact that you and Marcus are bound will throw the camp into chaos."

"All right. I'll determine their fate in the morning." Lucius donned his old armor from the Hunnic campaign and pulled his hood up covering his face. "I don't want the legionnaires to know I'm leaving." He turned and hurried toward the encampment's Porta Decumana exit with a cowled Marcus.

Five minutes later, Lucius and Marcus, traveling incognito, left the fortified encampment with a column of cavalry. Once outside the camp, Lucius rose in his saddle and scanned the Reno River. His legion was bivouacked on its north bank. Ravenna was eighteen miles to the south.

Martinel rode next to the legate. "We have a good defensive position here. Ravenna's on the opposite side of the river with only one bridge in the immediate area. If Valentinian sends a force against us, the crossing will cost them dearly."

"It would also doom us. While we are tied down holding that bridge, other legions could ford the river east and west of us, trapping us." Lucius shook his head. "They wouldn't have to attack. Without any hope of reinforcements, a siege would starve us out. No. We need an avenue of escape."

Marcus grunted his agreement.

They traveled west along the moonlit Reno riverbank for a couple miles, encountering no one. The rich farmland around them was asleep.

Martinel grunted. "The way looks clear. In the morning we can make our way to Gaul. The Frankish King would be pleased to grant sanctuary to Rome's Red Fist Legion."

"Yes," Lucius sighed. "Witch or no witch. It has come to that."

***

An hour later, Lucius looked backward. "Now we wait and watch."

Minutes later, the earth quaked and a towering column of the same blinding light they faced by the campfire appeared in the sky over where he estimated his camp was situated. It formed into a massive dome that descended to the ground and vanished seconds later.

Lucius' voice shook. "Now we go see what has been wrought." He reined in his horse less than a half mile later. The paved Roman road ended abruptly at a bracken marsh that stretched as far as he could see in the moonlight. Moments earlier, it had been rolling hills of lush farmland, ready for the fall harvest.

Seven hundred hectares were instantly changed into what would be later known as the Valli di Comacchio in Emilia-Romagna, Italy.

"It's gone," Marcus exclaimed.

Many men in the cavalry detachment crossed themselves and cried in terror.

Lucius harnessed the same fear clawing at his own stomach. "There's... there's nothing here." His voice shook. "I suggest we follow the oracle's advice."

Martinel and Marcus regarded each other and nodded.

In silence they rode off, taking the three destinations Alexa had advised.

In March, 455 AD Emperor Valentinian III was assassinated and the Vandals sacked Rome, throwing the Western Roman Empire into an irreversible death spiral

Chapter III

Mara's Threads

It was evening on the last day of summer in the year 454 AD in the capital city of Jiankang of the Lui Song dynasty. Completing a bloody military campaign, Emperor Xiaowu finally succeeded in consolidating his full control of China.

The eunuch Feng, a midlevel functionary, managed the emperor's newly formed scholarly center. In that role, he lived away from the palace, which was the nexus of authority.

Although important, Feng was ambitious and hungered for greater power and prestige. He fidgeted in his seat at the university center's banquet table. The lavish party he hosted for a group of visiting Shaolin priests was proving both a political and financial disaster. At great personal expense, he provided the finest food, drink, and concubines, but the priests and scholars sat, ate moderately, and discussed topics he barely comprehended. All the government leaders he had invited declined to attend.

Wearing a shear silk gown that concealed nothing, Meili carried a ewer of rice wine from the center's cellar. She had not been born into slavery. To keep their family from starving, her parents sold her to a brothel when flooding destroyed the crops on their impoverished farm. She was thirteen at that time and remained a slave for the last nine years.

Meili brushed a lock of black hair from her face and grimaced. *Perhaps tonight won't be too bad.* Her body still ached from the abuse received a week earlier at an orgy hosted by the Jiankang city magistrate. Her bordello's owner accepted the recompense the next day for his battered women with only feigned outrage.

Approaching the banquet room's ornately carved doors, she slowed. *Trouble.* It was warded by two slovenly-attired guards, who tracked her with leering eyes. When she attempted to pass, the sentry on the right laughed. "It would be a shame to waste a beauty like this one on the bunch in there." He grabbed her as the other yanked the decanter from her hands. The first man pushed Meili against the wall and pressed close with fetid breath.

Meili snarled. "I may be a slave but I'm not a toy for the likes of you." She had been in this type of situation before. With lightning-quick moves, she slammed her heel into his instep and then kneed him in the crotch.

The guard bellowed in pain.

As the man's grip slackened, Meili grabbed his hand, applying aikido pressure on the thumb.

The commotion drew the attention of Feng, the nine academics, and five Shaolin priests. They crowded into the doorway and the priests moved to intervene.

Meili did not see any of that. She sprinted down the corridor as soon as she broke free from the guard.

She came to an abrupt halt.

A brilliant light flared in the hallway before her. Meili found her path blocked by a strange apparition. It was a tall, flaxen-haired woman with blue, unblinking eyes and wearing a strange one-piece garment.

Meili had never seen anyone with such exotic looks before. She summoned her courage and approached the glowing person. "Who are you?"

"My name is Alexa," came the reply in strangely accented Mandarin. "Is this the university of Jiankang?"

"I do not know. There are many scholars here and this is in the city of Jiankang." Meili's resolve faltered. "What are you going to do to us?"

The spirit-like woman turned her blind eyes to the frightened voice. "Nothing... and everything. I am very sorry."

Outside the gardened estate, a glowing blue dome descended from the heavens and the earth quaked. Moments later, the light vanished and a pond of dank water stood in place of the building complex.

* * *

It was evening on the last day of summer in the year 454 AD. Yazdegerd II was in the sixteenth year of his rule over the Persian Empire.

At the Learning Academy in its city of Gundeshapur, Borzoye sat, alone, squinting at the words on a sheet of fragile parchment. A single candle provided the only direct light on his worktable. The academy of Gundeshapur had been his home for eleven years, but he still could not sate his appetite for the wisdom he found in the academy's vast library.

Borzoye leaned back and squeezed the bridge of his long nose as he finished reading the last page, "Fascinating, such insightful work. I—"

The library filled with a brilliant flash of light.

He blinked and saw standing on the other side of his desk a strange apparition. It was a tall, flaxen-haired woman with blue, unblinking eyes and wearing a strange one-piece garment.

Borzoye gasped. "Fascinating." Curiosity overcame fear. Trembling, he stepped around the desk to the ethereal person. "Who or what are you?"

"My name is Alexa," came the reply in strangely accented Farsi. "Is this the Academy of Gundeshapur?"

"Why, yes, it is." Borzoye replied as he passed his hand through the translucent woman. "You certainly have an unusual means of transport." He stepped back and steeled his voice. "Do you mean us harm?"

The spirit-like woman turned her blind eyes in his direction. Sympathy was in her voice. "I mean you no harm, but that does not mean you are safe. I am very sorry."

Outside the academy, a glowing blue dome descended from the heavens and the earth quaked. Moments later, the light vanished and a pond of dank water stood in place of the building complex.

* * *

It was evening on the last day of summer in the year 454 AD. The Byzantine Emperor Marcian was in the fourth year of his rule.

A day's ride east of the Byzantine city of Edessa, Theodore sat by the campfire in a small field alongside an expansive fig orchard, bemoaning his fate. Until a day earlier, he was a leading scholar at the Learning Center in Edessa. Now, because of his adherence to the Nestorian Creed, he'd been cast out.

Theodore glanced around at the other exiles and sighed. All appeared deep in their own thoughts, staring silently at the blaze. *I hope the Saracens we hired as guards will be sufficient protection in the wild lands we need to pass through.* His soft hands scratched underneath his thick beard as he regarded his slight paunch. *I certainly won't be any use in a fight.* He raised his head and caught the eyes of the caravan master. "Captain, how long before we—"

A brilliant flash of light illuminated the campsite.

Theodore blinked and saw standing beside a thick, gnarled fig tree a strange apparition. It was a tall, flaxen-haired woman with blue, unblinking eyes and wearing a strange one-piece garment.

He saw the caravan guards, who moments earlier were laughing and drinking, scramble behind the wagons.

"So much for our expensive protection," Theodore hollered in their direction. He cocked his head and appraised the motionless, ethereal woman. After a moment's hesitation, he approached her. "Can I help you?"

"My name is Alexa," came the reply in strangely accented Greek. "Is this the Academy of Edessa?"

Theodore laughed. "You have found its scholars but not its buildings. I'm afraid we are outcasts." He sobered. "If this is a brigand raid. I fear you have chosen a poor target." He waved his hand at the mercenaries staring from the far side of the wagons. "We have spent what little coin we possessed for this band of fierce warriors to defend us."

"I am not here to rob you." The spirit-like woman turned her blind eyes in his direction. "Their efforts would be of no consequence. They possess no weapons that could harm me in my current state."

Theodore felt his courage wane. "What is your intent then?"

Alexa responded with sympathy in her voice. "Kidnapping. You will be transported to a place from which you will never return. I am very sorry."

Outside the circle-of-wagons a glowing blue dome descended from the heavens and the earth quaked. Moments later, the light vanished and a pond of dank water stood in place of the fig orchard.

* * *

It was evening on the last day of summer in the year 454 AD. Samudragupta was in the nineteenth year of his rule of the Gupta Empire.

In the city of Agraharas, Anaya sat on a bench in the jasmine-scented garden beneath two scions holding lit torches. Stately date palms lined the alcove. She was content to be alone, reading a book. Although a wealthy princess with many suitors, she disdained the trappings of royalty. She preferred the company of the scholars at her father's Learning Center. They challenged her ideas and made her think.

Anaya had received the finest education available to any woman in the empire, but that only whetted her hunger for more. Instead of spending her time cultivating the feminine arts, she preferred solving mathematical problems or getting her hands dirty experimenting with metallurgical combinations.

She closed the book and laid it on her lap. *What's the use?*

Her father had arranged a marriage for her. She met her betrothed for the first time that morning. *A mindless, priggish lout, twice my age.* She leaned against the tall back of the stone bench and gazed at the night sky. Tears trickled down her cheeks. *I wish I could fly from this prison and be free—*

The garden filled with a brilliant flash of light.

Anaya blinked and saw standing beside a tall date palm a strange apparition. It was a tall, flaxen-haired woman with blue, unblinking eyes and wearing a strange one-piece garment. She had met a Greek merchant once with similar exotic looks, but never such a regal-looking woman. She rose. "Who are you? Do I need to summon my father's guards?"

"My name is Alexa," came the reply in strangely accented Hindi. "Is this the University of Agraharas?"

"Yes. Since you walk its grounds, you should know that." Anaya pulled a slim stiletto from her puffed sleeve and pointed it at the translucent woman. "Trespassers are frowned upon." Her arm holding the knife quivered, but she walked closer.

"I will not trespass here long." The spirit-like woman turned her blind eyes to the sound of Anaya's approach. Sympathy was in her voice. "But then neither will you or anyone else in this establishment. I am very sorry."

Outside the gardened estate, a glowing blue dome descended from the heavens and the earth quaked. Moments later, the light vanished and a pond of dank water stood in place of the university complex.

Chapter IV

A New Day-New World

Doctor Phokas questioned the two replicants for over an hour and became convinced they were innocent dupes during the night's bewildering events. He rose and paced the tent. "I'm glad Lucius is the one who will determine your fate and not—" The earth quaked, dropping the doctor to the tent's floor. It ended as suddenly as it started.

Phokas' head spun and stomach churned as he regained his feet. He glanced at the two shackled men as he heard screams of panic outside the tent. "What, in the name of God, just happened?"

The bound Lucius cocked his ear to the terror-filled voices. "How should I know? I was only *born* an hour ago."

The doctor glared. "Don't move. I must find out." He staggered to the exit and threw open the tent flap. Everyone in the camp, including the guards, was staring at the sky. He looked up and gasped—a full moon with a reddish cast hung over the camp. It was far larger and in a different part of the heavens than it had been moments earlier. The stars in the clear predawn sky shone in unrecognizable patterns. A warm breeze carried the scent of stagnant water and rotting vegetation. He nodded to the two terror-stricken sentries outside the tent. "There's mischief about. Be wary." He reentered the tent and walked to the two men bearing faces he knew and loved.

Phokas pulled out his knife and studied it for a long moment before stepping behind the prisoners and cutting their restraints. He could not keep the fear from his voice. "What did that oracle, Alexa, do to us?"

Replicant Lucius rubbed his wrists and grew pensive. "She seemed familiar, but I have no recollection of knowing her. In fact, besides the few people I've seen tonight, there are no faces in my memory."

Marcus nodded. "Knowledge is in my mind, but no people or events. I can perceive that they are there, but some invisible wall blocks me from recalling them."

"Well, all that changes now." Replicant Lucius shook his head and rose. "The oracle said I need to somehow *replace* the legate." He glanced at the knife in the doctor's shaking hand. "I need... we need answers." Brushing past, he stepped through the exit and looked back. "And we won't get them sitting in here."

Marcus followed but paused at the doctor's side. "Whatever happened, I have no more choice in being here than you and am clueless as to what caused it."

Phokas regarded the sliced ropes. "The die is cast." He sheathed his blade and joined them outside.

Three soldiers wearing the insignia of officers ran to Lucius, desperation showing on their faces. He barked to them before they could speak, "Assemble the legion on the parade ground, armed and ready."

They saluted and spun around.

In moments, clarions blared and soldiers hurried to fulfill familiar, reassuring tasks. Centurions bellowed as ranks formed. "Move, you maggots, the legate will address us."

Lucius went inside and studied the senior officer's armor and helmet hanging on a frame. Strapping on the breastplate with familiar hands, his brows furrowed. He turned to Phokas. "I think I led soldiers before." He shook his head. "These men will need to have their fear tamped down."

Two minutes later, he strode out of the tent, adorned as a legate. Marcus walked on his left, with a spatha belted to the waist of his tunic, and Phokas, looking very pale, was on his right.

As they reached the assembled legionnaires, a dark bearded officer jogged to Lucius and saluted. "Legate, we found the Prefect, dead in his bunk. Stabbed. Also, Commander Martinel's unit is overdue returning from their scouting expedition."

Phokas leaned over. "That's senior centurion Silvio, commander of the second cohort. He knows *you* well."

Lucius gave an imperceptible nod as he memorized the short swarthy man's face. He returned the formal salute. "I see. So, there are still murderers among us. Rejoin your unit." He watched the ranks form as the sun crested the parapet wall.

The legionnaires cast wary glances upward as the sun rose in the opposite direction from the previous day. Many crossed themselves.

Lucius searched his mind and found facts but no memory of their source. Given his location he should be facing south, but looking at the sun rise in the east, he was looking north. *Nothing is as it should be, but we have more immediate problems.* He cleared his throat and bellowed. "Yesterday, General Aetius was assassinated by the emperor. Last night someone attempted to murder me and succeeded in killing the Prefect. Two assassins have been accounted for and are dead. There may be more. Each of you, look to the man on your right and left. If you don't recognize him, lay hands on him and summon your centurion."

Almost immediately there were shouts and scuffling at the rear of the gathered legion. Through the lines of snarling legionnaires, three battered, semi-conscious men were dragged forward and dumped at the legate's feet.

Lucius drew his spatha and placed its point on the first man's throat. "Who sent you?"

The man spat through broken teeth, "What does it matter? I'm dead anyway."

"True," the legate answered as he pressed the blade a little tighter, drawing a trickle of blood. "But your passing could be swift or slow. Either way I will have my answers."

The second man on the ground cried out, "Mercy, sire. I killed no one." He glanced at Marcus. "The Praetorian Guard commander personally assigned me the task of assassinating Tribune Carloman, but I did not do it."

Marcus laughed as he drew his own sword. "Don't take me for a fool. You didn't kill me because I never returned to my quarters last night."

The man's courage failed as he met the tribune's eyes. "Mercy. I'll tell you everything."

"Shut up you fool," the first one snarled.

Lucius looked up. The eastern horizon was brightening to a clear day. "What do you have to say about the rending of the sky?"

The second one whimpered, "Great lord, I swear by all that is holy, I am a simple soldier of the praetorian guard. I cannot conceive of what transpired."

The third one bleated, "Magic. It is a powerful pagan magic."

Lucius' brows furrowed as he thought of his own *birth*. "Was a tall Germanic woman going by the name of Alexa involved with your plot?"

The third prisoner raised his head, eyes wide with fear. "Great sire, I saw no woman of that description. Is she a powerful druid?"

Lucius heard murmurs of "magic" and "sorcery" from the ranks as word of what was overheard passed from the front to the rear. Although born but a couple hours earlier, he knew he must stem the tide of fear before it took hold of the legionnaires.

Glancing at the scars on his arms, some new and some old, the replicant understood in his heart that he had a previous life. *But who am I? Good. Evil.* He stepped forward, past the prisoners, to address the troops with facts he should have had no way of knowing. "Warriors of the First Red Fist Legion," he roared. "You have vanquished the Huns and the Goths. We will overcome this too."

With a dramatic flourish he raised his sword above his head. The parade ground became silent, all ears keen on his words. "Last night treachery and evil magic befell us. Our enemies failed. We have taken their measure and still stand."

Lucius received a nervous cheer in response. He pointed to the sky. "The great Julius Caesar conquered Gaul with cold steel even though he was opposed by druid priests and their sorcery. We will do the same."

This time the responding cheer was more enthusiastic.

Lucius raised his other hand. "Magic has warped the sky and there's a strange smell in the air. We shall shrug it off. Such tricks may terrify children but not Rome's finest legionnaires."

The response was a full-throated roar.

He lowered his arms. "Today, patrols will venture forth. Speak to every villager and peasant you encounter. Learn what they have seen and heard. Inform them the Red Fist Legion stands tall to protect them." He glanced at Phokas, recalling what was said the night before. "Search all the land within a *three-mile* radius of here. The source of this conjured evil will be exposed." He sheathed his sword. "If you encounter a tall Germanic woman, bring her to me, unharmed. She is an oracle and goes by the name Alexa. I need to get answers from her."

He pointed to the men at his feet. "Senior Centurion Silvio, stake these vermin to posts and flog them, but keep them alive. I may have further questions." He groaned to himself, *In this entire legion, Phokas and Silvio are the only names I know.* "Legion, dismissed. Go to your breakfast. Officers join me in the headquarters. We need to make plans."

As the legate turned, he called up to the ramparts. "What's the word from the watch?"

A legionnaire wearing a junior non-comm uniform thrust his right arm out in a Roman salute. His voice was steady, but his arm shook. "Decurion Horatius here. Legate, all seems normal... in the immediate area. The village appears un-disturbed, and the farmers are already out working their fields."

Lucius absorbed the name and face like parched sand would water. Noticing hesitation in the sentry's voice, he snapped, "Horatius, I don't have all day. What else?"

"Sorry, Legate." The bearded man stiffened to attention. "The land has changed."

"Excuse me? Be specific."

"Yesterday the Reno River was south of our camp. This morning it's not. I was in the watchtower. It looks like there's a river about a mile *east* of here. Looking west, there's a mountain range that wasn't there yesterday." Horatius' voice quivered. "Sir, what's happening?"

"That is what we intend to find out." Lucius turned to Marcus, who was also busy absorbing everything around them. "Go up into the watchtower with vellum and ink-black. We need a detailed map of everything you see."

Marcus rubbed his clean-shaven chin. "Perhaps, with enough information, we can piece together a guess as to where that oracle Alexa magicked us to."

The legate turned to the doctor, who gripped the cudgel in his waist band. "Once and for all, decide whether you're going to bash me over the head or not."

"I don't know what to do," Phokas replied in a husky whisper. "I can't determine whether you are demons or saviors." He sighed. "You look, sound, and act so much like my friends I need to think hard to remember you are not."

Lucius laid both his hands on the older man's shoulders. "I swear my love and loyalty are to God, the Red Fist Legion, and Rome... in that order. I will do all within my power to solve this riddle. There may be many dangers in this strange place, but *I* am not one of them."

Phokas dropped his hands to his side. "May God have mercy on my soul. I believe you and will aid you in your subterfuge. I have no choice. If the legion knew the truth, there would be anarchy."

* * *

It was noon.

Lucius, and his officers stood under a broad canopy, puzzling over the map that Marcus sketched. The consensus opinion was that they were magically transported somewhere, but none could come up with a guess where.

With clever use of pronouns, and Phokas whispering in his ear, the legate had all the names and faces of his subordinates committed to memory within the first hour. Once he heard a name and connected it to a face, it stuck in his mind as if he'd known the soldier for years.

"This is a new land," Tribune Titus exclaimed in exasperation. "There's not a single landmark I recognize, and I grew up around Ravenna."

Lucius squeezed the bridge of his nose. "We could be anywhere, even beyond the borders of the empire. If so, then we will endeavor to find our way home. We will—"

A guard stationed at the Porta Praetoria jogged up to the gathered officers and saluted. "Legate, the scouts who rode north have returned and they are accompanied by a small caravan of wagons."

"Good, maybe we will finally learn something useful. Let's break for lunch."

Twenty minutes later, Theodore, the deposed dean of the Edessa Academy stood before Lucius with ten scholarly-looking men of various ages and shapes behind him. Their wives stood by the eleven wagons parked on the parade ground, along with dozens of children and several servants. The adults milled around the wagons, gazing about. However, within minutes, their children squealed and began playing among the wagons.

Theodore spoke with polite deference, in Greek, noting the legate's insignias of rank. "Who do I have the honor of addressing?"

Lucius sat on a camp stool, eating a freshly baked barley loaf and a piece of hard cheese. To his surprise, he discovered he was fluent in that language. "I am Legate Lucius Bernius, and this is the encampment of Rome's First Red Fist Legion."

"The Red Fist? Even in Byzantium, your exploits against the Huns are renowned." Theodore mopped his brow with a rag. "I pray you can help us." He sputtered, "Where are we? What happened?"

"I was about to ask you the same question." Lucius squared his jaw. "Tell me what transpired for you."

Theodore tugged at his beard and took a deep breath. "Two days ago, we left Edessa with the goal of heading east to Persepolis in the Persian Empire. Then last night a strange ethereal woman appeared, and the night sky went crazy. Sir, I am an astronomer by training, and I never saw such a transformation before." He looked back at his fellow scholars. "Then early this morning our Saracen guards, screaming about demons, mounted their horses and rode off, abandoning us."

"Edessa, you say." Lucius let out a low whistle. "To the best of my knowledge you are near Ravenna, close to a thousand miles to the west."

"That's impossible," Theodore sputtered.

Phokas tapped his finger on his chin and joined the conversation in his native Greek. "This strange woman you described, was she tall, blonde, blind, and wearing an exotic garment."

"Exactly the one," Theodore exclaimed. "Her words were soft, but she must have cast an enchantment on us." He sighed. "Since we have somehow come this far, would you be so kind as to acquire us a guide to Ravenna's port so we can gain passage back to our homeland? We have little money but will gladly contribute what we have."

"Unfortunately, we were visited by the same mysterious oracle. Yesterday we were indeed near Ravenna." Lucius shrugged. "Today, who knows. The land around us has changed." He glanced at the collection of carts and wagons. "You are welcome to stay under our protection until we can determine the proper course of action."

Theodore visibly sagged. "As you say, Legate. In the meantime, if we can be of any service, just ask. My compatriots and I are knowledgeable in many fields."

Marcus found that he too had a complete understanding of the Greek language. "Being an astronomer, perhaps you can be of assistance finding a solution. What other skills does your group possess?"

Theodore swept his arm, including those with him. "Amongst us we have academicians in mathematics, philosophy, rhetoric, medicine, and natural science."

Lucius called Tribune Titus over. "Set these good people up in a camp outside our walls. Ensure they have free access to our facilities during the day."

"Yes, Legate."

Titus led the caravan back out the gate as Marcus drew fresh marks on the map.

Chapter V

Where are we?

Marcus acquired the largest piece of vellum available in the camp, a two-foot-by-three-foot sheet. He spread the blank sheepskin across a camp table under a broad open pavilion where Lucius and all the senior Roman officers were gathered. "This will become our map."

Lucius pointed to the center of the unblemished skin. "This will mark our location. Now we will learn what is around us."

As the explorer teams trickled back into camp over the course of the morning, Marcus sketched a map a half dozen miles in diameter, making detailed markings and notations with each fresh report.

Lucius scratched the back of his head as he regarded the accumulated results. "Nothing has changed for a mile and a half in all directions. But the land, vegetation and animals beyond that demarcation line is completely unrecognizable to our most seasoned scouts." A humorless grin creased his face, thinking about his own presence. "This makes no sense."

Marcus noted the legate's expression and nodded before pointing to small circle markings located northwest, south-west, and south of the large circle indicating their encampment. All were exactly two miles away. "Three structures beyond *our* land have been spotted so far. That must be significant."

Silvio, the senior centurion, rubbed his bearded jaw. "The people there are definitely not Roman. The scouts reported that those they saw fled as they approached, and small bands of exotic-looking armed men, jabbering incomprehensible languages, blocked their advance. It's strange. Those build-ings have no roads or trails leading to them."

The decurion who led the surveying team to the southwest added, "Legate, we had no orders, so we refrained from engaging in any hostile acts. We pulled back and studied the area from a distance."

"You chose rightly," Lucius responded. "We don't know what kingdom we've been magicked to. It's best to not anger the local potentates until we understand the situation. I will lead a delegation and attempt to contact them."

Marcus furrowed his brows. "There are still a couple teams who haven't reported in. But beyond those buildings there appears to be no other signs of civilization. No roads, no smoke in the air, nothing but wilderness."

A short while later, the team who had ventured east returned and reported they encountered a wide river that ran north to south roughly a mile and a half from their camp.

The centurion who led that detachment added, "Our side of the river has a steep embankment. The other side appears to be a boggy flood plain. We rode a few miles north, looking for a crossing point." He tapped the northern area of the map. "The riverbank slopes down and the water is shallow enough to cross up here." The officer gritted his teeth. "But I don't recommend it. We attempted to ford but found large crocodile-like creatures in the water. They ripped Legionnaire Cato, who was on point, to shreds."

Lucius' face turned grim. "I fear we'll lose more good men in this strange land." He nodded. "Anything else?"

"Yes, Legate." The centurion paused. "We caught a glimpse of some strangely clad natives moving through the marsh across the river. I hailed them, but they vanished into the undergrowth at my beckoning. I've never seen anyone garbed as they were. It was a dull, beige material that fit tightly around their bodies."

Phokas looked up in alarm. "The oracle we mentioned, Alexa, wore such a garment. For now, stay away from them."

Lucius gave the doctor a hard look. "We need answers wherever we can get them. If they know—"

A dust-covered legionnaire approached Lucius and saluted. "Legate, I have the report on our expedition to the west."

Lucius glanced at the gathered officers and pursed his lips. "Phokas, we'll discuss this later." He nodded to the legionnaire. "Proceed."

The scout scanned the map. "Which side is west?"

Marcus pointed to the left side of the vellum.

The legionnaire tapped a mostly blank area there. "Straight west, about two miles out, we ran into densely forested foothills. The mountain range is shrouded in clouds, and I think at least a couple of them are active volcanoes." He tapped the edge of the map. "Sir, the easternmost mountain is unusual. It has a swath wide as a road, straight as an arrow, and sheared smooth down to bedrock. It's a perfectly straight line that came to an abrupt end at its base." He took a deep breath. "As best we can tell, it's pointed directly at our camp." He glanced at Marcus. "I'd guess the height to be about seven hundred feet." He rubbed his forehead. "Legate, the top was flat, as if sheared by an enormous sickle. Trees on the slope were cut off level with the top of that mesa."

"Cut trees? A work project?" Marcus raised his head from the map he was marking. "Any sign of the lumberjacks?"

"Tribune, no axe hewed those trees. They were sliced, and very recently. Sap still oozed from the stumps. Whatever was above those stumps, vanished. There were no logs." The decurion cleared his throat. "A ruined building of some odd material covered the center of the plateau, but we saw no sign of life."

Marcus' eyes lit with excitement. "Were the ruins new or old?"

"Tribune Carloman, it looked like the building was recently destroyed. There were wisps of smoke and dust in the air."

Lucius furrowed his brow. "But no sign of people?"

"No, sir. There was twisted metal and stone-block rubble strewn everywhere. The only intact object was a metal pillar, at the center of the ruins."

"Eh," Phokas slapped the table. "Did it have a silvery tint?"

"Silver... perhaps. But it was scorched and covered with soot."

"You're sure there was no one about?"

"No one moving." The decurion hesitated. "We did not venture past the lip of the plateau. It felt like... magic."

Lucius smiled. "What's your name, decurion?"

The bearded soldier, of average height, stood straighter. "Horatius, sir. I had the watch at the wall last night. I volunteered to see what was out there."

Lucius appraised the dust-covered legionnaire. "This place needs to be investigated." He rose. "Horatius, you will guide me to this magic place." He turned to Silvio, the senior centurion. "I'll require a large escort in case there's trouble."

The senior centurion nodded. "I'll have the First Century of the Second Cohort ready whenever you are."

Lucius furrowed his brow. *Should I know that unit personally?* He turned to Phokas, who imperceptibly shook his head. He sighed and responded to the senior centurion. "They will be fine. Assemble them for immediate departure."

"Yes, Legate." Silvio barked the command to a junior centurion, who scurried from the pavilion.

Marcus made the new notations on the map. "This place does sound different than the others." He studied the large vellum sheet. "Those heights should provide an excellent view of the area."

"I'll accompany you," Doctor Phokas announced, glaring at Lucius. "Do you have a problem?"

A sentry stationed at the Porta Principale approached and saluted. "Legate, there's a delegation from the village at the gate. They seem upset and demand to speak with you."

Lucius sighed. "I don't have time for this." He glanced at Marcus. "Tribune, you are my new Prefect."

Marcus gave the legate a level stare, rolled up the map and handed it to him. "As you wish, *Legate*. This base requires changes if it is to be made permanent. I have some ideas in that regard. I hope the Roman coin in our treasury will still be accepted. We will need fresh supplies soon." He gave the sentry a tight smile. "Please admit the village's representatives. We have much to discuss."

"Our storerooms are not stocked for a long bivouac." Lucius had no recollection of viewing the quartermaster's inventory but, somehow, knew what supplies would be available in the temporary camp. "Tribune Titus, you have the task of coordinating hunting and foraging parties. Conscript the auxiliaries to help." He glanced at the map. "Do not disturb any of the fields or livestock within two miles of here. We need to stay in the citizens' good graces."

Lucius' head throbbed. Many questions and very few answers.

* * *

Running jerry-rigged diagnostics overnight, Alpha determined that the space-time distortion event sapped the electrical energy from everything including the cyborgs themselves. The power systems that he and the three beta units possessed had no problem running on the electrical energy generated by their human hosts. The six delta cyborgs syphoned that biologically generated power less efficiently but could still operate all their primary systems. However, the power conversion systems in the eleven gamma cyborgs could only operate off their hosts at full capacity for short durations.

Alpha ordered the gammas to shut down and stay in sleep mode to conserve power consumption. *Less than half my cyborgs are useful.*

At dawn, Alpha assembled Beta-2 and Beta-3, each with a team of delta cyborgs, to explore the immediate area. "Gather data. Avoid any confrontations until we can assess the situation." He glanced at the tall olive-complexioned woman at his side. "Beta-1 and I will remain behind to work on upgrading the gammas."

As the sun reached midmorning, Alpha stood with Beta-1 near the sheared edge of the warehouse's asphalt parking lot. *Where have we been transported?* He studied the thick groves of cypress and banyan-like trees that predominated the marshlands surrounding their quarter-mile circle. *I can't see anything from here.*

Beta-3 had already returned and reported spotting a group of primitively armed humans across the river. "They accosted me with a language I identified as Latin. I did not respond."

"That is useful information. It is the language spoken by our target Marcus Carloman."

Beta-1 pointed to movement in the trees. "Beta-2 returns. A small group of humans accompany him."

Alpha narrowed his eyes at Beta-2, and his three delta cyborgs escorted a procession of a dozen mud-splattered human males leading horses and carrying weapons associated with the Iron Age on Earth. "This should be interesting."

When they reached the paved parking lot, the humans' eyes bulged as they took in the steel and concrete warehouse and the flat asphalt surface. They prostrated themselves at Alpha's feet.

The one who appeared to be their leader proclaimed, "I am Simone, captain of these Saracen warriors. We were hired to protect a group of Byzantine cultists and got caught up in some evil curse they brought on." He looked up at Beta-2. "Your lieutenant told us of your great sorcerous powers." He touched his forehead to the ground. "He said you could transport us home with your wizardry."

Alpha understood the man's words as fifth-century Farsi. *Interesting.* He glanced at Beta-2.

Beta-2 cyborg, possessing the body of a bald, bull-necked man, smiled and spoke in Ipis so only the cyborgs present could understand. "We discovered these human specimens cowering in the brush not far from the riverbank, a couple miles to the north. My processor deciphered the rudiments of their language. It was a simple Diophantine problem but a waste of time. Their ranting and pleading were nothing but mindless superstitious mewing." He glanced at the bowed men. "I fabricated a story and they believed it. Shall I dispose of them?"

Alpha rubbed his jaw. "Not yet. The gamma units remain in a suboptimal state. These humans appear malleable. Perhaps they will provide some short-term benefits."

Beta-1 added, "I will interrogate them and glean any useful information they possess."

Alpha glanced down. "A necessary endeavor but my expectations are minimal." He switched to Farsi and addressed Simone with slow words. "I will grant you the boon you request, but it comes with a price. You and your people must serve me with unquestioning fidelity for one year." He

47

grinned, noticing the man's eyes narrow. *So transparent.* "In exchange. I will return you to your homeland... with my great magical powers."

The cyborg saw that the human believed him.

The Saracen captain rose and bowed. "A year of service and then home. I accept. Your wishes will be my command."

* * *

At noon, Alpha gathered with the three betas on the shipping dock of the warehouse. He turned to Beta-1. "Discover anything?"

"Not much." Beta-1 shook her head. "These people seemed befuddled regarding where they are. They have no concept of the word 'planet,' but cross-referencing the 'rulers' and 'countries' they spoke of, it is clear that the space-time distortion worked. These people are from the planet Earth and the time-point the disrupter targeted."

"But did the plan succeed?" Alpha frowned. "We lack data. Mara did something to affect our operation. But what? Are we back in time or are they forward in time?" He glanced around. "We are not on Cocytus. Are we on Earth, or some other world?"

Beta-3 rubbed his red-bearded jaw. "Those primitively armed humans who accosted me this morning spoke Latin. I don't know if Mara thwarted the mission, but if this is fifth-century Earth, perhaps it can still be completed."

Alpha slammed his fist into the concrete wall. "We must." He added in a staccato burst. "We exist for our mission, and our mission is to locate the human labeled Marcus Carloman, and terminate him."

Chapter VI

Mountain Vista

With Horatius as a guide, eighty legionnaires followed Lucius and Phokas to the mysterious plateau. It was comforting to pass farm homesteads laden with grapevines, orchards, and amber grain ready for harvest.

At one-point-six-miles from the Roman encampment, Lucius saw the abrupt change the scouts reported. An arced demarcation line separated the rich, loamy farmland on one side and a plain with sparse growth of ferns and sawgrass on the other.

A careworn woman awaited them at that boundary. With her were seven threadbare children, ranging in age from sixteen to three, and four large dogs that appeared more wolf than canine.

"A word, sire," the woman begged as Lucius rode near.

The legate glanced at Horatius. "Continue on. I'll be along in a second." He reined in his horse.

Phokas halted his mount alongside the legate.

Lucius dismounted, expecting her to beg for alms, but he asked anyway. "Yes, goodwife, how may I be of service?" He saw a stubborn pride in the woman's eyes.

"My name is Aquila," she said without preamble. "I doubt there's much you can do for me. Our luck has not been the best lately. Goth bandits stole most our livestock a year ago and killed my husband when he tried to stop them. He was a pensioned legionnaire and a good husband..." She sighed. "But not a very skilled farmer." She pointed to the sharp divide in the land. "Now a third of our free holding is gone."

Lucius regarded the children. All were gaunt, even the teenage boy. He felt compassion. He did not think all of them would survive the hungry months of winter.

She interrupted his thoughts. "I did not stop you for sympathy but to help *you*." She called to her oldest boy. "Marcellus, show the legate what you found."

The youth stepped forward, holding a quarterstaff and dragging a blood-soaked sack. He opened the coarse bag and lifted out a chewed-up, green creature. It had a smooth hide, and three sharp, curved claws extended from each of its four webbed limbs. It stretched over four feet from its oversized head to its flat paddle-like tail. The nostrils and narrow eyes rested on the top if its head. An elongated jaw with rows of needle-sharp teeth hung open.

Marcellus, the youth, shivered. "Lord, the hens were going crazy this morning, so I hurried out and found this thing trying to get into our chicken coop. I never saw anything like it around here before. While I stared, it charged at me." He patted one of the big dogs at his side. "It never got close. Aries, Diana, Athena, and Mars made sure of that."

Phokas leaned in and examined the dead beast. "Never saw anything like this either." He slid his hand across the chewed-up hide and then studied the head and limbs. "It appears to be some sort of amphibian. May I take it for further study?"

The boy shrugged, dropped the creature back in the sack, and handed it over.

The doctor dug into his satchel and pulled out a gold solidus coin and pressed it in the lad's hand. "A fair exchange."

The youth gasped. It was enough money to feed their family for a month in normal times.

A thought struck Lucius. He spoke to Aquila as she gaped at the coin her son held. "You said your husband served in the legions?"

"Yes, sire. Twenty years."

Lucius scanned the truncated wheat and barley fields. "I need an aide-de-camp. Would you be willing to spare, Marcellus once your harvest is in? It's a legionnaire's wage, three hundred denarii a year."

The woman squared her shoulders. "We are a proud family. I don't accept charity."

Pain struck Lucius' heart. *Family!* He searched his mind and found names: mother, father and two sisters. Parents and one sister died when the Huns raided his father's estate a few years earlier. *Just dry facts.* He was unable to pull up a face or childhood memory.

The legate shook his head. "It is not charity." The corners of his mouth crinkled. "The boy will work for every quadran of it. I'm not an easy employer."

Aquila glanced at her son, who visibly shook with excitement. She smiled and extended her hand. "Agreed. *After the harvest.*"

Lucius grasped her thin arm and felt her strong calloused hand do the same to him. He released his grip, slapped the youth on the shoulder and pointed to the flat-top mountain. "Would you care to join us for the afternoon? We're going up there for a look around."

Beaming, Marcellus agreed. "A moment." He hurried into the simple, but well-kept, stone house and emerged a few minutes later wearing a tooled leather breastplate with a gladius belted at the waist. "These were my father's," he declared.

Although initially irritated at the delay, Lucius felt a warmth for the youth. "It's good that you honor his memory. Now, time's wasting, let's go."

Lucius mounted his horse and cantered off. Marcellus loped along beside him with a long fluid motion. It was slow going through the broken ground, but the path his men took was easy to follow.

They caught up with the legionnaires at the base of the mountain. The soldiers were hacking at the ground where it started to rise.

"Evil magic," Horatius shouted as Lucius approached.

"Say more," Lucius replied as he tethered his horse on barren rock near the base of the mountain. He walked over and saw the ground strewn with chopped roots oozing sap.

Horatius nodded. "Watch this." He strode up the slope to the tree line, holding his gladius in one hand and a spear in the other. He paused and tapped the soil with his spear's haft. Two legionnaires followed him, holding hand axes, hopping from one exposed boulder to another. The ground quivered and roots erupted from the soil, twining around the decurion's spear.

51

The decurion hollered as one root grabbed his ankle. He slashed it with his sword and leapt to the boulder where the two legionnaires stood.

Lucius stared gape-jawed as the root engulfed the spear and dragged it underground. He studied the budding broadleaf trees. Above ground they did not appear much different from the oaks back home. He paused. *How do I know what an oak looks like?*

"Remarkable." Phokas picked up a cut root and examined it. It twitched in his hand.

Lucius moved carefully to where the men stood on the rock shelf. The hillside forest was now quiet. The ground calmed. "How is it you made it to the top unmolested?"

"Blind luck." Horatius pointed to a three-foot-deep, eight-foot-wide gash dividing the forested mountainside. "As you can see, that's no natural rockslide. A powerful force sliced this mountain down to its bedrock." He pointed in the direction of the Red Fist Legion base. "From the top you can see this furrow's a straight line pointing to our encampment. We hiked that trail instead of hacking through the woods." He wiped his brow. "Mother of God, we would have died if we ventured off that path. Those serpent roots seem to need soil."

Phokas joined them. "Those roots did not pursue you onto stony ground?"

"No." The decurion rubbed his jaw. "Even when the writhing root was obviously long enough, it didn't pass over solid rock."

"Fascinating." Before anyone could react, Phokas grabbed a spear, and dragged it in the dirt embankment on the left side of the unnatural channel for several paces. He soon found himself in a tug-of-war with a twining tree root. He lost.

The doctor returned to the base, a half dozen yards from the nearest tree. He picked up a cut root and studied the oozing sap again. "Let's see how this pitch burns." Phokas gathered a pile of the hacked roots and some dry grass. "Someone light this for me."

Marcellus pulled a small block of flint from his shoulder bag and drew his sword. With deft hands he arranged the straw and wood and struck a spark. The sap blazed with an incandescent light, igniting the green wood.

Phokas leaned close, singeing his scrawny beard. "Incredible."

Lucius watched with interest for a moment and glanced at the sun. It was midafternoon. "How far to the top?"

Horatius scratched behind his ear. "As I told you in camp, the elevation is about seven hundred feet. From here, I'd guess the trek to the crest is about three quarters of a mile. We didn't have to do any actual climbing. It was an easy hike." He focused on the legate. "Why do you ask?"

"I'm going up. I believe that metal pillar you mentioned holds the answers to all this insanity." Lucius took an axe from a nearby legionnaire. "Besides, I need to see this new land, and I can't do that down here."

Phokas' eyes gleamed. "I'm going too."

Marcellus eagerly added, "You'll need your aide."

Horatius groaned. "And you'll need a guide."

Lucius turned to the full company of legionnaires gathered around the blazing roots. "While I'm gone, clear an area for a base camp. Fire and stone are the solution for these monster trees. It'll take more than a druid's magic spell to stop the resolve of Rome's finest."

* * *

It took Horatius a half hour to lead Lucius, Phokas, Marcellus, and ten legionnaires to the top. No one strayed from the path.

On reaching the summit, Lucius saw a roughly circular area that appeared to be about a quarter mile in diameter. Ruins of what once must have been an expansive building covered a third of it. At the center of the plateau, standing upright in the rubble was the scorched, seven-foot, metal cylinder Horatius had reported.

Phokas hurried to it.

One glance told Lucius it was the same one that appeared when he was *born* yesterday. The legate hesitated on the promontory's lip. After hurrying to get there, he became uneasy about confronting the magic that brought him into being. Instead, chewing his lip in frustration at his lack of memory, he turned and gazed at the vista of the new land. *Every land is a "new" land to me.* He paused and considered his thoughts as he scanned the panorama. *Yet I seem to know what should and shouldn't be normal. How's that possible?*

Standing high above the plain, Lucius' view was un-hampered for miles in every direction. He unrolled the map that Marcus had sketched. Orienting it to what he saw, he laid it on a flat rock and pulled a stylus and jar of ink-black from his shoulder bag. With a deft hand, the legate added several landmarks beyond the ones the scouts reported.

A craggy, mountain range filled his view to the west. Wisps of smoke rose from several volcanoes. North, he saw rolling foothills carpeted with a vast evergreen forest. He noted, with a sense of relief, that the oak-like *devil* trees on this one mountain seemed unique.

Looking east, he saw the slow-flowing river winding its way south with a moorland beyond it, overgrown with what appeared to be cypress and banyan-like trees.

Lucius thought the southlands on the near side of the river were an untouched, verdant plain. It ended at a hard scrabbled coastline with the hint of a wide bay into which the river emptied. A vast glistening body of water stretching as far as he could see extended beyond that. *Good place for a harbor, ideal pasture and farmland.* Squinting in the afternoon sun, he shook his head at seeing no signs of civilization. *If there are any native people, that's where they'd be.*

The legate shifted his focus to the land immediately below him. The path he followed was indeed a straight slash creasing the mountainside, pointing straight to the Roman encamp-ment. Surrounding his legion's camp was a perfect circle almost three and a half miles across. A half mile beyond that border he saw five other, much smaller, circles perfectly equidistant from each other. Three held buildings with non-Roman architecture. One circle of what looked like a fig orchard near the river to the north, he knew from the morning discussion, was where the Byzantine caravan came from. He could only make out a faint outline of the last enclave across the river. It was a dark circle punched in the middle of a cypress grove. He followed the pattern to where he stood. *Six small circles surrounding one large one in the middle of nowhere. No natural phenomenon created any of this.*

Phokas' urgent shout, "Help. There's someone buried in these ruins!" interrupted Lucius' musings.

Lucius turned and saw the doctor, with Horatius and Marcellus, clawing into the debris, pushing aside blocks of rubble. He rolled up the map and jogged over, reluctant to see whom he knew would be there. A glimpse of long blonde hair and a limp arm protruding from a shredded, dun-colored sleeve confirmed the legate's guess.

* * *

Phokas, with a voice that brooked no dissention, snapped orders. The legionnaires exploring the ruins hurried over. Under his direction they carefully freed the woman buried in the wreckage and laid her on a blanket. The doctor examined his new patient, who moaned and spoke an indecipherable language in raspy whispers.

Lucius stayed on the periphery, observing the woman's shallow breaths. He asked, "Will she live?"

"Yes." Phokas hesitated. "The left leg is broken, and she took a nasty blow to the head. But I see nothing life-threatening." He gave Lucius a meaningful look. "We already know she's blind. What I can't explain is every part of her body that I can see looks sunburned. Buried under this debris, normal exposure wouldn't explain it."

The woman's right hand touched Phokas' arm. She croaked in accented Latin, "Could I have some water?"

"Yes... Alexa." Phokas fumbled for his flask and held it to her lips. She drank greedily, slopping more on her than in her. He touched her forehead. "You'll be all right now. Where does it hurt?"

She winced as she tried to flex her limbs, "It feels like my skin's on fire, and my head and left leg hurt like hell."

He pursed his lips and started splitting the leg. "Legate, she can't walk. Erect a tarp here."

Lucius glanced at the setting sun. "Doctor, we must leave soon. I do not want to attempt descending this cursed mountain in the gloom."

"Then depart," Phokas snapped. "Until I know the full extent of my patient's injuries, I dare not move her. And I'll not leave her." He eyed the legate. "Alone in the elements, the oracle could well be dead by morning. Is that what you want... Lucius?"

Lucius studied Alexa. Unlike the ethereal image of the night before, this battered, vulnerable woman seemed very human. He gave the inert pillar a sidelong glance and sighed. "I have many questions, and this Alexa's the only one who can answer them." He turned to the clustered legionnaires. "Collect firewood. A lot of it. We stay the night."

The men's eyes bulged.

Horatius spoke, "Legate... the trees."

Lucius nodded. "Gather wood in groups of three. One to cut and two to guard. There's plenty of low branches on the sheared stumps."

The men moved with trepidation, but they moved, leaving Lucius and Phokas with Alexa.

Within minutes, Lucius heard the men laughing and hooting as they tapped the ground and then loped off roots when they erupted from the soil. After careful testing, they learned that the roots were easy cuttings if chopped when first emerging from the trembling ground. He pointed it out to Phokas. "Fear dissipates when the danger is understood."

It was Alexa, with her head propped up against the pillar, who answered, "Well said. I read some wise words once, 'If you know the enemy and know yourself, you need not fear the result of a hundred battles.'"

Lucius shot back, "Oracle, you mock me. How am I supposed to *know* myself? I have no idea, who or *what* I am."

Alexa nodded. "That was cruel of me." She cocked her head as if listening to a voice no one else could hear. "Mara desires to limit unanticipated variables in future events as much as possible. You must be Lucius Bernius. She believes that revealing *your* actual past lowers her confidence level in predicting your actions."

Phokas' eyes narrowed. "Knowledge is always preferable to ignorance." His voice grew tight. "On *my* word, this person has assumed command of an entire legion."

A small smile creased Alexa's face. "I *know* this man. Your soldiers, this entire world could not be in better hands." She sighed. "I will rest a little now. Later, I will provide answers to the extent Mara thinks prudent."

"Then rest." Lucius felt both excited and fearful. "I have many questions." He strode off toward the woodcutters.

Chapter VII

The Oracle

As the sun set, a strong northern breeze picked up that brought a chill to the air across the plateau. The legionnaires atop the mountain huddled close to the crackling campfire, both for its warmth and the light the strange wood provided.

Those not on sentry duty sat by the blaze, taking turns boasting to a wide-eyed Marcellus about their exploits. However, when not spinning tales, the legionnaires cast fugitive glances at the abnormal night sky, watching the strange moon dip behind scuttling clouds.

Lucius sat at a separate campfire, staring at the dancing flames. He was alone except for Doctor Phokas and Alexa. Wrapped in a coarse blanket, she sat propped against the strange metal pillar.

The legate raised his eyes and regarded the woman. She looked so normal sitting there spooning in warm gruel from a clay bowl. The redness in her flesh that worried Doctor Phokas was already fading by the time the sun dropped beneath the horizon. Under other circumstances, Lucius would have thought of her as attractive. He tried to guess her age but gave up. Her smooth face spoke of youthfulness, but given the previous day's events, he doubted that was true. He shook his head. *I don't even know how old I am.*

He cleared his throat. "You said you would answer my questions after you rested."

Alexa sighed, put down her bowl, and turned toward the sound of the voice. "First, I must ask you a question. Are you the first Lucius Bernius or the second?"

Lucius gritted his teeth. "I have no memories before yesterday. Does that answer your question?"

Alexa released a ragged breath. "Were the first Marcus Carloman and Lucius Bernius brought to this... place?"

Phokas answered, "My friends rode off and did not return before you magicked us to this nightmare."

"Thank God," Alexa sobbed. "Then there's still a chance for humanity's survival."

Phokas blinked and shrugged at Lucius.

The legate blurted out, "If I'm not Lucius Bernius, then who or what am I?"

"The explanation will probably be incomprehensible to you. People from fifth-century Earth have no frame of reference. But I promised the truth, and the truth I will speak." Alexa rubbed her forehead. "You *are* Lucius Bernius, and the person who rode off yesterday also is Lucius Bernius."

"Impossible," Phokas snorted.

Lucius grimaced and rubbed his jaw. "If that is true, why can't I recall a single event from my life?"

"As you no doubt already realize, your mind has access to everything you learned during *your* life." She cocked her head as if listening. "However, Mara has blocked you from recalling names, places, and actual events."

"She made me a cripple."

Alexa shook her head. "Mara calculated that the paradigms resulting from any concrete memories would inhibit you from accomplishing what you must do in this new world."

"You speak in riddles. Who... am... I?"

Alexa closed her eyes. "When I laid my hands on the original Marcus and Lucius, I extracted a miniscule amount of their flesh." She cleared her throat. "At your conception, you were identical to the original. Your embryo was a perfect replicant of his DNA, his physical being."

Phokas shook his head. "*Replicant, DNA* are meaningless words." He studied Lucius in the firelight. "When you conjured this man, I saw an infant. Moments later, a full-grown man. How is that possible?"

"What you saw for a few seconds was about nine years for the Lucius and Marcus that are here." Alexa shook her head. "Mara nurtured them. I... I aided her."

"Rubbish," Phokas snorted. "I watched these imitators sprout before my own eyes."

Alexa groaned. "You do not possess the capability to understand what transpired. I lived through it and can barely fathom what happened myself." She creased her forehead. "Just understand that the Marcus and Lucius who are with you now, within what you perceived as a few scant moments, lived many years."

"Impossible," Phokas sputtered. His eyes narrowed. "How could you possibly know this?"

The sightless woman extended her hand and stroked Lucius' arm. "Because I was with them from conception to adulthood."

"What?" Lucius recoiled from her touch. "Stay away from me, witch."

Phokas wagged his finger. "This *Lucius* spoke Latin, knew how to fight and command the legion the moment he appeared."

Alexa rubbed her hands together. "Mara foresaw much of what would face them. She ensured they had the best tutors. Languages were easy. She downloaded thirty-seven variants of fifth-century Earth dialects directly into their brains."

Lucius waved both his hands. "Download... Earth... tutors. What does any of that mean? And who is Mara?"

Alexa tapped the silvery metal cylinder that she leaned against. "This is Mara."

"I'm getting more confused." Lucius glanced at the inert pillar and shook his head. "So, you are the oracle for this... Mara god."

Alexa froze. "Oracle. Dear Lord. The legends of the ancient Novaroman oracle are about *me*."

Lucius caught the words she spoke and jumped on them. "Nova Roma... New Rome. Where is that?"

Alexa closed her eyes and sagged her shoulders. "What do you see around here?"

"All right. If it helps get some answers..." Lucius proceeded to describe everything he saw from his perch that afternoon.

Alexa's brow furrowed. "Mara says there should only be six circles, not seven. Describe again, the one you saw across the river."

"Not much to tell." Lucius scratched behind his ear. "It was mostly obscured by cypress trees. I estimate that it's about the size of the other outer *circles*. I did make out a large flat roof of a building. It was an architecture my mind tells me doesn't belong."

"You would know what belongs from your life." Alexa's voice became hesitant. "Probably nothing to worry about. Just a random anomaly." She brightened as she sniffed the air. "So green. So new. The sap of the guardian trees is running. It must be spring."

Phokas said, "Guardian trees?" simultaneous with Lucius saying, "Spring?"

The legate added, "You're wrong. It's fall. The crops are just being harvested now."

Alexa cocked her head. "Given the relative revolutions of the respective planets around their stars, Mara insists the autumn of 454 AD in the Roman Empire corresponds to the spring season on this hemisphere of Novaroma. My nose agrees."

Lucius grew quiet as he tried to comprehend what he heard. "Oracle, what is a planet? Where... are... we?"

"This is so much harder than I thought. I'm so sorry." Alexa hung her head. "Lucius, understand you are in a place from which you'll *never* leave. Whatever life you build here will be the only one you'll ever know. The means Mara used to bring you here, no longer exists to take any of us back."

A long breath escaped Lucius. "You called this place Nova Roma. I like the name." He squinted at nothing. "I'm not sure how, but I know the Roman Empire is dying. Perhaps both my country and I can be reborn here."

"The old Roman Republic started with a lot less." Phokas regarded the legate. "*Lucius*, let's take one step at a time. Little the oracle said makes sense. But the land and the sky do not lie. There's no doubt we are far from Rome." He turned to Alexa. "Oracle, what is a guardian tree?"

She smiled. "It's a delightful plant. In the spring, it produces a sap that Novaromans fermented into a delicious intoxicant called ambrosia. In the fall, it yields needle-shaped nuts that when roasted are used to brew a beverage almost identical to what, on Earth, would be called coffee." She extended her hands to the crackling fire. "Its catcher roots burn hot with a sweet aroma."

"You're talking about the trees with roots like serpents?"

"The guardian trees are rare. To the best of my knowledge, they require unique soil to grow." A wistful smile creased Alexa's face. "Ah, yes. I remember seeing pictures. Eighty-three percent of the Novaroman flora and fauna were destroyed in the aftermath of the Novaroman-Ipis war."

"What war is this you speak of?" Lucius snapped his head toward the oracle.

"I talk too much." Alexa winced. "Some knowledge could change the future in an unpredictable way."

A nervous laugh escaped Phokas. "The future is always unpredictable. Speak plainly."

Alexa pursed her lips and seemed to be listening to a voice. "Be content in knowing it is centuries in your future. Amongst the guardian trees, two legions wearing their infamous 'iron foot' boots made their final desperate stand against a great host. They fell defending this mountain at the end of that terrible conflict."

Lucius eyes narrowed. "There is much you told me with those words. I will think on this Ipis tribe. Are they vicious like the Huns or cunning like the Vandals?"

"I dare say no more," Alexa stuttered. "Mara mistook your primitive technology as a lack of intellect. I told her she was gravely mistaken."

Lucius squared his jaw. "So, this Mara god is not infallible."

Alexa sighed. "She regrets that she is not and will be more circumspect in the future."

"I am responsible for the lives of all these people. I demand that she answers my questions."

"Ask what you will." Alexa wrung her hands. "However, Mara says the information in her responses is for her to decide."

Phokas rubbed his hands together. "I will take the query in another direction then." He quirked an eyebrow. "Oracle, you spoke of 'iron-foot' boots as if they had special significance. Why is that?"

Alexa blinked her blind eyes. "It would be hazardous for anyone to walk amongst the guardian trees without them. Oh dear." She frowned. "You haven't discovered them yet, have you?" She cocked her head as if listening to a voice. "Fifth-century Romans know how to pave roads. Those will be successful for traversing the guardian tree forests. However, for practical purposes you should invent those boots. Until then, you'll never cultivate domestic groves of those trees."

Lucius scowled. "Your answers just raise more questions."

"I am sorry for being mysterious." Alexa sighed. "I don't know what they are, and Mara won't tell me."

Phokas patted Alexa's hand. "Lady, you gave us much to contemplate." He gave a red-faced Lucius a warning look. "For now, sleep. Let your body heal."

She squeezed his hand in return. "Thank you for believing me. Mara and I will do all we can to help."

Phokas raised his eyebrows. "You, I believe, are innocent of the evil done to us." He glanced at the unmoving metal pillar. "This Mara is another story. By your own admission, she's the one who put us in this quandary and is the one who must be held accountable."

Alexa started to respond but stopped at the sound of approaching footsteps.

Horatius walked over and saluted Lucius. "Legate, the watch is set. Is there anything you need before the men turn in?" He cast a wary eye at Alexa. "They're all a bit worried that this sorceress will cast us into that devil forest, or something worse. Do you want us to dispose of her?"

"No. I have heard her story and have judged her." Lucius chose his words carefully. "The lady's name is Alexa. She did not cause our predicament and is not our enemy. However, she does have some powers of prophecy, which may prove useful." He glanced at Phokas for confirmation.

The doctor eyed the inert metal pillar and added, "She was magicked here by the same spirit that bewitched us."

"Yes sir." Horatius saluted. "If you need—"

A sharp piercing screech rose from the hillside.

"To arms," Lucius roared as he scrambled for his sword.

Moments later a blunt-headed creature with what appeared to be a tortoise-like shell, forward-thrusting horns, and a thick tail raced onto the plateau with a monster over eight feet long and ten feet tall bounding after it. Both appeared surprised on encountering the firelight and the small group of soldiers scrambling to gather their gear. The reaction of the two animals was completely different. The one being hunted, veered to the side and scurried over the cliff.

The predator reared on its short hind legs and slapped the ground with its spiked tail while raising its long, clawed, front legs. It emitted a high-pitched scream from its elongated maw. The veteran legionnaires quailed at the sight of its mouth filled with long serrated teeth.

Alexa called to Lucius. "Mara knows of this creature. It's a nocturnal hunter. Light will disorient it."

Lucius nodded as he hefted his shield, sheathed his spatha, and grabbed a flaming branch from the campfire. He bellowed, "Marcellus, Phokas, stay with the blind woman. Legionnaires form a shield wall."

Everyone hurried to comply, but the beast did not wait. From seven yards away, it pounced upon a running soldier. The man's scream was cut short as the monster effortlessly ripped open the legionnaire's chest and bit off his head. With gore dripping from its mouth, the red-scaled creature searched for its next victim.

Lucius saw that his men needed a few more seconds to form, so he ran toward the beast, yelling and waving the flaming brand.

The monster hissed and reared up, threatening Lucius.

The legate charged. At the last second, he threw the burning branch at the monster's face.

It screeched.

Lucius used that moment to drop his shield and leapt on the creature's back. He grabbed a ridged spine, drew his spatha, and stabbed the beast in its two-foot-long neck.

The creature howled in pain and spun, sending him sprawling to the ground.

Lucius tumbled but sprang to his feet, drawing a dagger from his belt in a single fluid motion. His sword remained buried in the monster's neck.

The creature went for the kill but drew up short. It now faced a line of torches, shields, and spears. It backed up, pawing at the blade embedded in its neck.

Shouting legionnaires pressed forward, stabbing at it. But their spearheads couldn't penetrate the monster's scaled torso.

It swung its powerful tail at the end soldier, catching the man's shield and sending him reeling.

The creature turned toward the dazed man with its maw open. But it did not move.

Lucius stepped in front of it with a retrieved spear and shoved it deep into the monster's wide maw.

The creature gurgled and staggered in a circle, swinging its spiny tail, impaling another soldier.

Lucius jumped on its back, and using two hands, twisted the blade still lodged in the creature's neck. Blood spurted from the gaping wound and the spear lodged in its mouth.

The predator took one stumbling step and collapsed.

Lucius pulled his blade free and leapt off. Holding his gore-covered sword at the ready, he watched the beast twitch and then go still. The legate hewed at its neck with his sword. The creature's tough hide resisted the cuts, but he persisted with his well-tempered blade.

With each blow, the legionnaires chanted, "Dragon slayer, dragon slayer." On the seventh blow, the head separated from the body. Lucius hoisted it in the air to roaring cheers. He threw it to the ground. One of the soldiers retrieved it and mounted it on a pole.

The legionnaire who was injured limped over to Lucius. It was Horatius. "Legate, you saved my life. I was sure that beast had me."

Lucius wrapped the soldier's arm over his shoulder and half-carried the staggering man. "Come, let the good doctor examine you."

As Phokas went to work, Lucius turned to Alexa. "Oracle, you seem to know a lot about this place. What was that creature?"

She smiled. "What do you think it is?"

The legate glanced at the scaled carcass. "I heard the men call it a dragon and I can't disagree with them."

"Then that is what it is." Alexa nodded. "How big is it?"

The legate regarded the body again. He shrugged. "About ten feet tall."

"How many spines on the tail tip?"

Horatius, who was intently listening to the conversation, answered, "I saw that tail up close. Three."

"Three prongs and hunting alone." Alexa cocked her head. "Mara claims the *dragon* you killed was probably a young male chased from the pride by the dominant alpha."

Lucius looked up with alarm. "Oracle, how big are these packs and how large do these beasts get?"

"A pride usually consists of one adult male, four or five females, and up to seven hatchlings." She pursed her lips. "Standing erect, a mature male can grow to about twelve feet. An adult female doesn't have a spiked tail and averages about nine feet in height."

Marcellus' eyes were wide. "My family's farm is less than a mile from here. Are there many of these *dragons* about?"

"Probably, yes. Dragon dens are almost always near venting volcanoes," was her soft reply. "Also, they are very territorial. A lone male wouldn't venture far from its original pack."

Lucius listened intently. "You said the dragons are nocturnal. Are they dormant during the day?"

"No, but their eyes are very sensitive to light." A smile crinkled the corners of her mouth. "A bright day leaves them almost blind. I perceive your intent. You plan on hunting them, don't you... dragon slayer?"

Lucius' mouth slimmed to a thin line. "How do the natives of this land deal with such beasts?"

Alexa's face became sober. "Legate, what you see on the plain below you is the *entire* population of sentient beings on this world... I mean people in this land."

Lucius blinked as he digested those words. "Then the duty falls to me to protect these people from the dangers of this world."

"Yes, it does. Use *all* the resources of your new realm." The oracle replied with a sharp voice. "Dragons are a formidable predator. Plan carefully and learn their habits." Alexa sighed. "For now, sleep. After the racket made tonight, there won't be a predator within a mile of here." She winced at the pain in her leg as she laid down and covered herself with the coarse blanket.

Few slept that night.

Chapter VIII

Dragonmont

Lucius awoke early the next morning drenched in sweat from the nightmare of the night's encounter despite the clear and crisp dawn.

He saw several of the soldiers already up, speaking in hushed voices as they examined the dragon corpse. The creature's head, resting on the end of a tall pole, appeared more fearsome in the early morning light than it did in the dark.

As the full camp came to life, Lucius donned his armor with deft hands. *Why does this seem to be a familiar task?*

A voice behind the legate interrupted his thoughts. "I've been told that the tail and haunches are a delicacy."

Lucius turned around wearing a grim expression. "Good morning, *Oracle*. Feeling better?"

Alexa sat up in her bedroll. "The pain's subsided a bit. Thank you."

Horatius winced as he pushed back his bedroll and rubbed his ribs. Glancing between Lucius and the mysterious woman, he groaned. "That's a night I don't want to experience again." He stood and tapped the sleeping Marcellus with his foot. "C'mon, lad. I could use some fresh meat. The lady says that monster is good eating. This morning we'll dine on the beastie that was going to dine on us."

Marcellus blinked and sprang to his feet. "Yes, sir."

The two walked to the dragon with drawn blades and were soon joined by several other legionnaires. The tough, scaled hide resisted their cuts.

Alexa listened to the legionnaires and frowned. "Your weapons cannot penetrate the dragon's scales?"

Phokas, watching the soldiers, scratched behind his ear. "It does not appear so. Yet the legate stabbed it clear through the neck last night and severed the head from the body."

Alexa replied slowly, "Mara says that her reference files indicate that the neck tissue of an adolescent dragon is relatively thin and flexible." She pursed her lips. "Also, Lucius is much stronger and quicker than the average soldier... just like the *other* Lucius." She touched the metal pillar for orientation. "I know this building before it was destroyed. In these ruins, about fifteen paces to my left, you should find a large cabinet. There are weapons inside. Bring them to me."

"No tricks, Oracle. You won't touch anything found." Lucius summoned his legionaries. They had given up on their attempts to dismember the carcass. He pointed to the spot Alexa indicated. "Search the rubble over there and bring me whatever objects you find."

Twenty minutes later, eight dented, dust-covered metal crates were placed before him.

As Horatius laid the last one on the ground, he wiped his forehead. "Does anything in this place make sense? These boxes look like metal, but they're impossibly light."

Lucius studied the simple latches for a moment and then opened them. Seven contained a pair of two-foot-long tubes with handles. Those boxes also contained two shoulder harnesses and a dozen slim, palm-sized, metal rectangles. He shuddered, realizing that he vaguely recognized them as weapons, infinity more deadly than those his men possessed. *How can I know this?* He described them to Alexa.

"Do you see any lights on the energy clips... ah, anything shining on the small metal boxes?"

He picked one up and examined it. "No, it's just a dull gray block."

Alexa frowned. "No lights at all? That means those clips are fully drained of energy. Without power, those weapons are just useless lumps of metal."

Lucius squinted trying to comprehend. Understanding niggled at the back of his brain. "What is their purpose?"

She sighed. "They're ranged weapons, specifically called ion-disruption blasters. Those little metal boxes, when inserted in the weapon, are like... arrows. They enable it to shoot projectiles, like a very hot fire over a long distance. However, it appears that the power leeched out during the space-time... ah, the magic event that brought us here."

A memory of Marcus and himself using similar devices flashed in Lucius' mind but an instant later was gone.

He looked at the eighth box. It was longer and narrower than the others. Resting on cushions inside were two weapons he understood. *Swords.* They were constructed of a silvery-white metal the approximate length of his spatha.

He gingerly hefted one out. It was perfectly balanced, and the grip felt comfortable in his hand. "This sword does not look useless."

Alexa responded, "That's an energy sword. Is the pommel glowing?"

"No." Lucius loved its feel and swung the straight, double-edged weapon in the air. It was unnaturally light.

She sighed. "It is a melee weapon, but without power, it is also useless."

"Ouch, this thing can cut." Blood oozed from his thumb where he touched the tip. "I think you're wrong."

Alexa shrugged. "The energy blade's core is composed of a polyaramide plastic. Where I come from it's commonly called plexo-steel. It's extremely strong by your standards and is honed to a fine edge." She sighed. "But it would still be useless against even the most basic energy shield."

Lucius looked around at his gathered men, who were gawking at the contents of the opened crates. He was confused and furrowed his brows. "Are there any of these... energy shields around here."

Alexa cocked her head. "No there's not and probably won't be for centuries."

"Good." Lucius grunted. "I repeat. A weapon I can understand."

Alexa nodded. "You're absolutely right. For a little demonstration, strike something that's hard."

"I hate to damage such a well-crafted weapon."

"Just do it."

Lucius glanced at what appeared to be a broken wooden table protruding from a mound of concrete ruble. He rolled his shoulders and strode to it.

His men gathered to watch.

He gripped the sword two-handed and spun, swinging the sword horizontally at one of the exposed legs. The blade sliced through the two-inch thick wood without slowing.

The legionnaires gasped as the support thudded to the ground.

Lucius examined the blade's edge and nodded. "No damage."

Horatius picked up the cleanly sliced table leg. "This is a hard wood. What else can that wonder sword do?"

"We'll see." Lucius eyed the wall's concrete blocks. "One more test." He chopped down, cutting a gash, three inches deep in the eight-inch-wide cinder blocks. Rechecking the blade, a smile creased his face. "Incredible. Not a single roll or chip." He raised it in the air. "I claim these two swords as my booty."

The soldiers glanced around the ruins with new perspective.

Lucius strode to the box, lifted the second sword from its case, and handed it to Horatius. "See how the dragon's hide fares against this." He gave his spatha to Marcellus, "A gift for you," and sheathed his newly claimed weapon.

An hour later, fragrant aromas of roasting meat wafted from their iron skillets, and the scaled hide was stretched on a rack for curing.

The dragon meat was delicious.

Lucius licked the juice from his hand and commented to Horatius, "We were lucky last night. The hide is tougher than chain mail." He touched the pommel of his new sword. "We're going to need better weapons to take out these beasts."

Horatius regarded Lucius with confidence. "Legate, we have a leader who is a dragon-slayer. I know you'll find a way out of this hell for us."

"I will try." Lucius forced a grin on his face. "Now let's eat our fill." He glanced at the sword hanging from his belt. "Then I want every inch of this mountain searched for other treasures."

The legionnaires were a bit disappointed as they stacked strange metal devices and stretchy dun-colored garments composed of an unknown material beside the previously retrieved crates. Some objects were obvious: hammers, chisels, augers, saws. But no purpose could be discerned for most. Alexa's only comments when pressed were, "Those are tools for another time. Without power, they have no function."

Alexa called the light, grayish metal that composed Lucius' sword *plexo-steel*. It appeared to be the primary material used on many of the indecipherable devices found in the ruins. They gathered all the loose pieces found, from twisted pylons to simple cutlery.

While the men dug through the rubble, eighty soldiers led by Prefect Marcus Carloman and Tribune Titus clambered, with drawn swords, onto the plateau. The Byzantine scholar, Theodore, puffing, brought up the rear. The new arrivals stared, transfixed, at the monster's head dripping gore from a pole.

Marcus shook his head and strode to where Lucius sat. Titus and Theodore followed.

Lucius acted nonchalant. "You're just in time for breakfast. Care for some roasted dragon?"

Marcus exhaled a deep breath. "The men you left at the base of this hill notified me when you didn't return at sunset. We climbed up the mountain at first light." He studied the dragon's head for a moment. "When I heard the beast's roar during the night, I didn't think we'd find anyone alive. None of us dared the ascent until morning because of those devil trees."

"The beast was as formidable as it looks." Lucius pointed to the two blanket-covered bodies. "Not all of us survived."

Alexa interjected, "Lucius, your courage and skill saved us all."

Marcus and Theodore turned at the sound of the woman's voice. They had not noticed her curled in the blankets beside Phokas until that moment.

Simultaneously they gasped. "You!"

Alexa sat up and winced as she straightened her legs. "I'm afraid so."

Theodore stepped close, noticing her splinted leg and multiple contusions. "You appear to have had a rough time of it." He shook his head. "You're not nearly as frightening as when you were half invisible and glowing."

Marcus gave Lucius a sharp look.

Lucius rose, "I'll explain later." He handed the rolled map to Marcus. "I've updated this, but there's more." He drew his sword and slashed at a steel bar protruding from the rubble. Although thick as his thumb, it split cleanly. "And there may be more marvelous tools like this up here."

He then reviewed everything he learned since arriving, adding, "I want to build a citadel on this crest." He glanced at Alexa. "Anyone or any*thing* approaching can be spotted miles away. These trees are well named. They will provide an effective shield around our perimeter. Our current camp is central but not very defensible."

Marcus appraised the area with an engineer's eye. "We could make this place near impregnable. Except for the route we took, the mountainside is steep and thick with these guardian trees." He pointed to a promontory a mile south of them. "There's limestone showing in that outcropping. Give me two cohorts and we could make concrete and build a respectable fort." The prefect did some mental calculations. "Give me three cohorts and I'll also have a proper road cleared and paved from our camp to here in ten days."

"Excellent." Lucius nodded with vigor, then added, "You have them. Of the remaining cohorts, I want four constantly in the field foraging, hunting, and patrolling our new home, and two in reserve at the encampment."

Titus looked at Alexa. "Legate, besides our camp, and the surrounding farms, there appear to only be another three or four tiny enclaves." He waved his hand at the foreboding mountains to the west. "Why build a fort? Even if it was their desire, those communities would not have the resources to threaten the Red Fist Legion."

Lucius rubbed his chin. "This is a wild country. We've been here only a couple days and already encountered three species of carnivores, and at least one type of plant capable of killing a man." He pointed in the direction of the temporary earthen-works of his legion's encampment two miles away. "The Roman army survived for centuries by being vigilant, even when there was no apparent need." He laughed and waved his hand in the general direction of the marshlands, and then glanced at Alexa, "The oracle hinted there is a tribe called Ipis that bears us ill will in the vicinity. Our scouts reported seeing strangely garbed swamp dwellers across the river."

"You won't encounter the Ipis I mentioned for generations. There *should* be no one else here," Alexa responded. Her voice subdued. "That someone was spotted across the river is troubling."

Titus asked, "Legate, what shall we do about the people in those non-Roman areas?"

Marcus interjected, "They're probably more scared and confused than we are."

"True." Lucius sighed. "I don't want anyone reacting based on misconceptions. We do nothing." He rubbed his hands together. "Give them a few days to grasp the new reality. Perhaps, like Theodore here, they'll come to us." He shrugged. "If not, I'll go to them as an emissary of peace."

"Well, I can't wait if I'm going to get that quarry started." Marcus pointed south. "One of those buildings is sitting right next to the limestone. I'll visit them tomorrow."

Phokas cleared his throat, "Legate, I will stay here. The climb down would be too rough on Alexa. Besides, these ruins could prove invaluable. We'll need her here to decipher the mysteries we uncover."

Lucius smiled. "So, it's Alexa now. Not 'the Oracle' or 'the Demon Spawn'?"

The gray-haired man blushed. "We talked late into the night. I've never met a woman like her before. The wonders she understands make my mind reel. There is so much I don't know."

Theodore watched the soldiers sifting through the ruins. He lifted an arm's-length square of what appeared to be black glass framed in a shiny metal and fingered the torn cables hanging from it. "I too desire to remain." He placed it carefully back on the ground. "There is so much to discover and learn here. Perhaps you'd allow my colleagues to join us. We are just in the way by your legion's camp anyway."

"Agreed." Lucius scanned the plateau and turned to Marcus. "Relocate the legion's engineers here too. Perhaps they can puzzle out uses for these wonders."

Marcus nodded in agreement as he fingered a perfectly round, smooth tube composed of some incredibly light material. He studied the immediate area. The ruins covered approximately a thousand-square-foot area. When he squinted, he felt he could almost see the building it had been in the tumbled concrete blocks and twisted metal struts.

Lucius faced Titus. "Tribune, build a shelter here." He pointed to the dragon head. "Be sure it's sturdy enough to withstand one of those things."

Titus gulped, "Yes, Legate."

Lucius caught the attention of the doctor. "Phokas, work with Titus to ensure the layout will be as we discussed last night. Order this place to your liking, but I want it defensible."

Phokas glanced at Alexa, and then Marcus and Lucius. He sighed. "Yes... *Legate.*"

Lucius called Horatius. "Summon the rest of the 'dragon-slayers.' We're returning to camp. I need some sleep and I promised to return Marcellus to his mother."

Pride flicked in the decurion's eyes at those words. He summoned his squad. They were packed and ready to leave fifteen minutes later. Horatius pulled the dragon hide from its rack and rolled it into a thick bundle. "This needs to be properly cured, for the legate's new armor."

Lucius turned to Marcus. "Prefect, return with me. You'll need workmen and equipment for roads and walls. Also, there's much we need to discuss."

Marcus eyed Alexa and exchanged a private look with Lucius. "Yes, much indeed."

Chapter IX

The Road to Emporia

Bearing their two dead comrades on litters, the small band clambered down the straight culvert carved in the mountain slope. At its base, Lucius found a beehive of activity. With shouting centurions, a full cohort was hewing trees and hacking at the writhing roots. A stack of a dozen trimmed logs rested on the trampled ground.

The soldiers paused in their labors as the dead were borne through their midst. Whispers spread the rumor of what transpired on the mountaintop during the night. Fear shone in many eyes.

Lucius saw this and called a halt. "Horatius, unravel the beast's pelt for all to see."

The decurion, with Marcellus' aid, unrolled the thick scaled hide and held it aloft.

Lucius raised his new sword, gleaming in the morning sun. "Behold. We slew the worst nightmare this land possesses. So, it shall be for whoever or *whatever* challenges Rome's Red Fist Legion." He pointed to the forest. "We shall drink the sap of the guardian tree and feast on dragon flesh. We are the ones to be feared in this land. The devils here will flee at the rumor of *our* coming."

The troops roared their approval and smartly saluted.

Silvio, the senior centurion Lucius remembered from the previous day, approached and saluted the legate and prefect. "Is all well?"

"Yes, very much so." Lucius nodded. "The top of this hill is ideal for a stronghold. We'll raise a fortress there."

Silvio cast a wary eye at the trees. "What are your orders?"

Marcus responded, "To start with, we'll need a proper road between our current camp and here." He rubbed his jaw. "One that will support heavy drays and wagons."

"Yes, sir."

Lucius added, "The men in my detachment are exhausted. I'll need pall bearers to carry our dead back to camp."

Silvio glanced at the two litters and nodded. "Yes, sir." He turned and bellowed to a nearby decurion for a squad of legionnaires.

The legate's small group resumed their procession.

Several minutes later they reached Aquila's farm. The careworn woman stood, waiting, at the edge of the cart path with her pack of large dogs. She froze on seeing the stretchers, then sobbed on spotting Marcellus. She ran to her son and wrapped her arms around him.

The youth blushed but returned the embrace for a long moment. "Mom, don't cry." He pushed back. "These men are Roman legionnaires like Dad. I was never in danger. A dragon attacked us last night, but they killed it."

The dogs growled deep in their throats as they sniffed the scaled pelt on Horatius' back.

The woman glared at Lucius, but he met her eyes. "Madam, this new land is treacherous everywhere. Marcellus is no safer by your hearth than on that mountain."

Aquila sighed. "Gothic bandits killed my husband on his own farm. New land, old land. It does not matter. All are hazardous to the helpless." She squared her shoulders. "I won't be helpless. What should I do to prepare?"

Lucius admired her stoic determination and remembered what Alexa told him. "It is springtime in this land. Finish your harvest as soon as you can, and plant your field afresh." He glanced at Horatius. "Decurion, there will be a lot of military traffic between the mountain and our camp. Stay here with your men at this juncture point. I don't want good farmland trampled."

"That would be appreciated, sire." Aquila added. "I'll provide room and board."

"Keep an account of your costs." Marcus joined in. "You will be fully reimbursed."

Horatius rubbed his brow. "Legate, I come from a family of farmers. This new ground appears rich and loamy."

Lucius scanned the wide swath of sawgrass and ferns encircling the Roman fields. "Is it possible?"

Marcus crouched at the demarcation line, glancing left and right. "We already crossed one small stream. With proper irrigation, this could become productive farmland." He wiped his brow. "With a few well-placed culverts, this ground could be reclaimed and our existing fields irrigated."

"I'm thinking along the same lines." Horatius smiled.

"I'll leave that to you." Lucius stepped onto the road. "I've been away from the legion overlong." He motioned to the litter bearers. "Continue on ahead. I need to confer with the Prefect in private."

The pallbearers saluted, lifted their burdens, and moved down the cart path without question.

Horatius lowered his pack and pulled out a shovel. "Romans are good at digging ditches." He bellowed to his team, "Time to get to work."

"Carry on." Lucius smiled and began walking to the camp with Marcus. Both remained silent until they were out of earshot.

Lucius was the first to speak. "This whole experience is insane. My first recollection of meeting *you* is when you appeared next to me less than two days ago... Marcus. Yet, I sense an incredible closeness to you. I don't know why, but I'd trust you with my life more than any other." He shook his head. "I see you and it seems like the memories are there but just beyond my reach."

Marcus nodded his head vigorously. "That's been exactly my experience. I had the six tribunes with me when meeting with the village elders yesterday. I *knew* who to turn to for opinions, yet I had no memory of any of them."

Lucius slowed his pace. "Alexa says we lived full lives before we came into being here. It must be true because I know *things* but have no idea how I learned them."

A soft chuckle escaped Marcus. "Phokas claimed that Alexa touched the... other Lucius and Marcus, and then a few moments later we appeared. Yet she claims we lived full lives." He glanced at a jagged scar on his left arm. It was faded with age. "It's a conundrum I can't resolve." He shook his head. "Those facts are mutually exclusive."

Lucius grimaced. "I am vexed. I know in my head both *facts* are true even though it is impossible. I also sense that I've known Alexa for a long time."

"Yes, yes. I have the same feeling, but I can't pull up a single memory." Marcus crossed himself. "You spent a night with this Alexa. Any new insights? Is she a demon spawn?"

Lucius set his jaw. "There's no sense of evil or deceit about her." His brow furrowed. "Last night, after we fought the dragon, we spoke of many things. She was not open about all she knew, but there was no malevolence or deceit."

Marcus nodded. "Makes sense. Why would Alexa bring *us* into this world, just to destroy us? I think she is an ally and a *friend*."

"That's also my opinion. But the oracle gains her knowledge from some pagan god she named Mara. That can't be good. We must be wary."

The two men walked on, exchanging all they had learned over this last day.

When they reached the camp's gate, a nervous young tribune awaited them.

"That's Tribune Atticus. He joined the legion only a few months ago," Marcus whispered to Lucius as they approached.

Atticus saluted, and without preamble spoke, "Legate, there was treachery during the night. After the prefect left to aid you, the assassins bound to the pillory escaped. This morning, the guards at the Porta Decumana were found with their throats slashed and Tribune Jette and a century from his Seventh Cohort are unaccounted for."

Unbidden facts rolled through Lucius' mind. *Jette... senator's son.* His eyes narrowed. "I'm a fool. Jette's family was always aligned with the emperor. I should have realized the assassins had insider help." He grimaced. *How do I know that?*

Marcus glanced at the open land behind him. "Where does that fool think he can escape to?"

The legate focused on Atticus. "No mercy for these traitors who committed murder. Alert the entire legion. When found, execute them."

Marcus growled. "Maybe we'll get lucky and Jette will run into one of those dragons."

Lucius snorted. "We haven't seen much in the way of good fortune these last couple days." He slapped a fist into his open hand. "Jette will be handled when we find him."

Marcus squared his shoulders. "In the meantime, I'll take personal command of the Seventh Cohort. I need stonecutters for the new stronghold and road, and I want to start immediately." He regarded Lucius. "You look exhausted. Get some sleep."

Lucius' jaw stretched into a giant yawn. "That is the truth." The sleepless night had finally caught up with him. "All our problems will still be around tomorrow." He staggered to his tent on leaden legs and slept all day.

Chapter X

Anaya

Anaya walked into the Agraharas Learning Center's garden. The bright, warm morning belied the trepidation she felt about the strange new land. All her people awaited her there, from the eldest scholar to babies still in their mother's arms. Anaya was a princess, her father a respected counselor to the Gupta emperor but not well-to-do. Although a noble, his land holding beyond the Agraharas Learning Center was a single estate.

Although, like everyone else, the horrid magic that struck during the night frightened Anaya. But the princess refused to show it. *Neither my father nor my two brothers are here.* She scanned the hundred-odd faces looking to her. *I must be brave for them.* Inhaling the fragrances of familiar blossoms, she glanced at the two men walking with her.

Beside her strode her father's aged bodyguard, Kewal. The man's long, pure-white hair was a stark contrast to his dark, weathered skin. Although deep crevices lined his face, his fluid gait belied his age. He had been a member of her father's staff for decades, and she thought of him more as a beloved grandfather than an accomplished sword master. On her other side, her betrothed, Rayansh, insisted on escorting her. She did not like him and resented his presence. The short man with the enormous black beard held himself in very high esteem.

Anaya ground her teeth, remembering a month earlier when informed by her father that he arranged for her to marry the emperor's cousin, the wealthy Rayansh. At the time, her shocked disbelief turned to screams of outrage. But her father would hear nothing of it. He reminded her of her duty as his daughter and a princess. Anaya wept that entire night but resolved to make the union successful for the good of her family.

The encounter with her fiancé a week later was a disaster that crushed all Anaya's dreams. Rayansh's personal wealth and imperial court intrigues were the only conversations of interest to him. When she broached the topic regarding her metallurgy experiments, his eyes turned flinty. "There will be no more of that." His only other comment was, "Your father overindulges you. A woman involved in such endeavors is unnatural. As my wife, you will partake only in activities appropriate for a female of your caste."

For the following three weeks, Anaya avoided his company whenever possible. She hid with her books in the garden or in her small forge. Then, two nights ago, she had the strange encounter with the ethereal woman, and her world went crazy.

At sunrise of the first new day, Anaya summoned the center's scholars to the balcony of her suite. Not only had the sky changed, but also the land around them. The bustling city of Agraharas had always been a breathtaking vista from her balcony. Now, wild grasslands encircled the estate, with foreboding, mist-shrouded mountains stretching across the western skyline and a desolate, uninhabited plain to the south. The only sign of civilization was what appeared to be a small settlement about a half mile to the northeast.

The academy's gurus were baffled as to what happened. After a full day of fruitless conjecture, Anaya realized she needed to take charge. She called her maidservant and instructed her to gather everyone into the garden at sunrise. She spent that sleepless night evaluating all the unpalatable options before her.

As the sun rose on the second day, the princess realized there was one positive result of their bizarre predicament. *Perhaps this is karma.* Anaya thought of Rayansh and shuddered. *My dowry has not yet been paid. Hence, he holds no claim on me.*

Anaya exited her private apartment clad in a simple sarong. Kewal and Rayansh joined her at the wide marble staircase. The princess welcomed the company of the first. The second, she disdained.

As the princess entered the garden, the low buzz of the gathered crowd turned to utter silence, and the eyes of everyone swung in her direction. *They need the truth.*

Servants, craftsmen, scholars, and children looked to her with fear etched on their faces. "My people, I will not pretend things are fine. They are not." She glanced at the three bald men in saffron robes, standing together by the fountain. "Our greatest minds could not determine where we are." She raised her hand for silence as a murmur rose from the people. "There appears to be a small hamlet of peasants not far from here. I will visit it to discover who rules this strange realm we've been magicked to. Once we know where we are, I will endeavor to buy us transport home."

"We should just kill them," Rayansh snapped.

Kewal snorted. "With only a dozen warriors amongst us, angering the local potentate would be a foolish move." He smiled at Anaya. "Your plan is wise. We need to see about acquiring provisions. Our food supply will only last a couple weeks."

The princess nodded to Kewal. "Prepare my howdah on one of the elephants. I have no intention of walking there."

"Yes, my lady," came the old sword master's quick reply.

"*Servant*, saddle the other three elephants," Rayansh snapped. "I too will go and will need my guards."

"It's a small village," Anaya fired back. "They'll see that many pachyderms as an invasion."

"Good," Rayansh hissed. "That will cow them into being cooperative."

Anaya bit her lip. "There will be no violence."

"Of course there won't." Rayansh laughed. "Lower castes must always defer to their betters." He turned without a word and walked away.

Twenty minutes later, four howdah-covered elephants paraded from the lacquered wooden gate. Kewal, with Anaya saddled behind, rode in the lead. Rayansh, resplendent in gold-plated armor came next on a large bull elephant with his driver. Four soldiers armed with pennant-festooned lances followed on the last two beasts.

They had not gone a quarter mile before Kewal spotted three horsemen in strange armor gallop away. He turned to the princess. "That can't be good. Should we withdraw?"

"No, continue on." She sighed. "The estate is built to repel bandits. It's no sanctuary against an army. We must find a way to come to some accommodation with these people."

As they approached, Anaya was dismayed at finding the village deserted. "The peasants fled."

She heard Rayansh laughing behind her. "This is too easy. I'll rule this entire realm within a week."

"The man's a fool," Kewal growled. "What are your wishes?"

"We stay here and wait," was the soft reply.

The wait was not long. From her perch, Anaya saw a cloud of dust approaching from the northeast. The sun gleamed off over four-hundred armored men jogging, six abreast, straight toward them.

"Excellent discipline. Professional soldiers." Kewal nodded in appreciation. "At least we won't be dealing with barbarians."

Rayansh yelped at the sight of the approaching troop and hurried his pachyderm back to the Learning Center with his guards in tow.

"Good riddance, coward." Anaya called after him. "Kewal, help me down. I need to make peace with these people, and I can't do it from up here."

As she dismounted, the approaching soldiers split into five squares, forming a semicircle ninety feet away around her and her sword master.

A tall, lean man strode forward from the center group. He paused after covering half the distance, appraised the elephant with a head shake and low whistle. He removed his fearsome-looking helmet, smiled, and walked forward. The man's skin was very pale under a crown of wavy brown hair squared off at his chin line. She saw intelligence and curiosity in his exotic blue eyes and thought his smile was genuine. His face turned to her, and she prayed that his soul matched his appearance. He was handsome.

He spoke some incomprehensible words.

Kewal stepped in front of Anaya, his hand resting lightly on the hilt of his khanda sword. He demanded what the stranger's intentions were in Hindi.

The handsome man nodded and responded in clear but accented Hindi. "I am Marcus Carloman, prefect of the Roman Empire Red Fist Legion. We mean you no harm."

"I have heard of that country." Kewal gasped. "It's thousands of miles to the west. How could we be there?"

"Alas, you are not *there*." Marcus shook his head. "The only part of the Roman Empire you have found is a three-mile-wide circle of land that you now stand on."

Anaya stepped around Kewal. "I am Anaya of the Gupta Empire. Then where exactly are we?"

A deep sigh escaped Marcus. His words were mild. "My lady, find the answer to that question and I'll be indebted to you for eternity. Beyond the boundary I mentioned, this land is a mystery." He pointed to the flattop mountain a mile and a half to the north. "We found a blind woman up there. The lady is some sort of oracle. She's been attempting to explain what transpired, but so far the explanation is beyond my comprehension."

Anaya tensed. "Is she a tall, fair-haired ethereal spirit who goes by the name of Alexa?"

"So, you've met her too? Right now, she's quite human and quite injured," Marcus replied. "The magic we experienced did not treat her gently."

"Can I question her?" Anaya asked as curiosity grew in her.

"Certainly." Marcus regarded Kewal. "I can take you and your escort there." He looked at her beast and a boyish grin creased his face. "I have seen pictures but never encountered such a marvelous creature. Is that truly an... elephant?"

In that moment, to her own surprise, Anaya realized two things. They weren't going to die... and she really liked this man.

* * *

Prefect Marcus Carloman stood and watched the Seventh Cohort form for their march to the limestone outcropping. The oxen were yoked to the wagons for transporting the quarried stone. Carts were loaded with pry bars, sledgehammers, picks, chisels, ropes, and other tools.

As he led his column out the gate, a scout on a lathered horse galloped up. "Prefect, monsters are attacking the village."

"How many?" Marcus snapped.

"Four enormous beasts left the dwelling we were instructed to observe. Several armed, dark-skinned people rode them."

"The monsters bore riders?" Marcus' fear shifted to interest.

"Yes, sir."

Marcus turned to the six centurions who stepped forward to listen. "Infantry, double time. Teamsters bring the wagons at normal pace. Follow me."

Amazement filled Marcus as he drew close. Four enormous beasts with long trucks bore exotic, dark-complexioned people astride long draping saddles. *I know what those creatures are. But how?* Three of the beasts reversed direction, but one remained. He saw two people dismount, and one was a strangely garbed woman. He breathed a sigh of relief and ordered his cohort into a defensive perimeter. *This is no attack on the village.*

The prefect removed his helmet as a sign of his peaceful intentions and strode forward. As he drew close, he couldn't take his eyes off the woman. She was young, with thick black hair hanging down to her waist. But it was her dark almond eyes that enraptured him. They sparkled with intelligence and curiosity.

Marcus raised an open hand in the sign of peace and introduced himself, stumbling over the words.

The white-haired man responded while gripping an curved, wide-bladed sword.

Marcus discovered that he understood those words and was able to respond in the same language. His heart sank when he learned that their country lay beyond the distant Persian Empire. *How is any of this possible?*

His eyes lingered on the intense woman as they talked. He learned that she was considered a princess in her own country, and the building complex behind her was the prestigious Agraharas Learning Center founded by her father.

Anaya asked about procuring food for her people. "Noble sir, I will pay handsomely for provisions. Our supplies are limited, and we have many children."

Marcus was thinking of how they could stretch the legion's limited food supply when he spotted the three elephants that fled returning. The prefect also heard the lowing of oxen. *My wagon train has arrived.* He eyed the size of the elephant, and an idea struck him. "Princess Anaya, perhaps we could strike a bargain."

"What did you have in mind?" Anaya asked as she furrowed her brow.

Marcus pointed to the craggy mountain behind her. "We need to quarry large quantities of gravel and limestone for paving roads and making concrete. Harnessing your elephants would enable that task to go much faster." He waved his arms at the surrounding countryside. "Between the monstrous native beasts and the devil forest, we need strong walls and good roads. We will pay for those services which will give you access to our markets."

Anaya nodded. "A fair exchange. Agreed." Her eyes narrowed as she glanced at the plateaued mountain. "We know nothing of the perils in this land. Devil forest? What menace lurks there?"

"It's the trees themselves. Their roots are like serpents that come alive when one passes among them." He shrugged. "They are called guardian trees, but as far as I can tell the only thing they guard is their own corner of hell. Stone barriers repel them, and the oracle claims something called 'iron boots' allows one to walk freely amongst those trees. But I'm unsure how that information helps. The weight of such footwear would be too ponderous for practical use."

"I have some skill in metalwork. I've been fabricating some new steel with my coal-fired furnace. It is both lighter and stronger than what is conventional," Anaya answered with a shy voice. "Perhaps if... you showed me these trees, I could be of some assistance."

Marcus' face lit up. "Marvelous. How about this afternoon?" *Not only is this woman beautiful, but she has a brain.*

Her eyes gleamed and her face creased into a big smile. "That would be perfect."

In that instant, Marcus knew he would do whatever he could to spend the rest of the day in her company.

The prefect's thoughts were interrupted as the other elephants with their riders returned. A short man with an enormous beard dismounted and strutted toward them.

He heard Anaya hiss, "Rayansh," as she moved a half-step closer to Marcus.

"Who is this gentleman?" Marcus asked.

"My betrothed," Anaya spit out.

Marcus felt punched in the gut at those words. He berated himself. *I'm a fool. Such an incredible woman would have a thousand suitors.* Without enthusiasm he commented. "I'm sure you're well matched."

Anaya shuddered. "He's a pompous imbecile. I hate him."

For some reason Marcus could not quite discern, that answer pleased him immensely.

Rayansh approached and frowned when he saw how close Anaya stood to the beardless, pale-skinned heathen. He grabbed her arm. "Anaya, this is improper. Return to the estate. I will negotiate with the barbarian."

Anaya pulled her arm free. Her face flushed. "You are a coward as well as a self-absorbed idiot. You ran as soon as you caught sight of these *Romans*." She inched closer to Marcus. "I've already reached an agreement with *Marcus*." The princess crossed her arms. "Since my father is not here to finalize the arrangements, our betrothal is nullified."

Rayansh snarled and turned to Kewal. "Will you allow this travesty?"

A smile crossed the bodyguard's face but did not reach his eyes. He tightened his grip on his khanda's hilt. "I will speak to her when she says something in error." His eyes narrowed to slits. "I have no issue with her assessments of our hosts or *you*."

Rayansh's hand went to his sword, but he turned and fled when Kewal shifted into a fighter's stance. He ran straight to his elephant, without pausing. His guards turned their elephants when he raced past.

Kewal yelled to the drovers, "The elephants stay. They are the lady's property." The drovers nodded and told Rayansh's guards to dismount.

Sputtering, Rayansh, stormed back to the Learning Center with his four guards in tow. His gilded armor was caked in mud after a few dozen steps.

"I hope I wasn't the cause of this incident." Marcus asked with a husky voice.

"You were the catalyst for a decision I should have made days ago." Anaya stepped toward her elephant. "The day is wasting. Let's get your stonecutters started. I want to see these guardian trees." She flipped her long hair. "Ride with me?"

Marcus did not hesitate in accepting.

* * *

The Alpha lay spread-eagle on the thatched roof, listening to the conversation below him. *Marcus Carloman! My mission can be completed.*

The fibers in his close-fitting bodysuit shifted colors to exactly match his perch. As long as he did not move, detection would be impossible. He listened, indifferent to the biting insects buzzing around the face of his host body.

Although a cyborg, he could still feel frustration. What bothered him was the severe loss of functionality. The microreactor that powered his systems was completely drained since the space-time anomaly event. Parasitically siphoning electrical pulses from his biological host was inadequate.

At the moment, all non-vital systems were shut down. Only his audio and visual sensors, working through his host's eyes and ears, were operative, gathering data. The remaining available power was routed to his suit to maintain its camouflage. Alpha wanted to leap down and strike but was incapable of moving. *My target is surrounded by many human warriors.* Their weapons are primitive but easily capable of killing the body I'm trapped in. *This will have to be planned.* His eyes followed Rayansh's return to the distant building.

That night, Alpha descended from his perch, awakening the inhabitants who had returned to their home after the creatures called elephants left. He ignored their fearful cries and ran northeast across the fields of ripe wheat, barley, and oats, skirted the legionnaire encampment and on through the open grasslands. *I have one more meeting tonight.*

In an out-of-place grove of gnarled fig trees over four miles north from where he spent the day, Alpha saw Beta-1 and Beta-2 waiting with about sixty human warriors garbed as the soldiers he saw earlier.

The bodies possessed by the two betas were quite dissimilar. Beta-1 was a tall, dark-complexioned middle-aged woman. Beta-2 was a short, bald, pale-skinned man with broad shoulders and an equally broad girth.

One of the humans glanced at Beta-2 and then strode forward. He raised his arm in what Alpha interpreted as a salute. "I am Tribune Jette. I am a loyal subject of Emperor Valentinian and an enemy of the traitor Lucius Bernius." He looked back. "Your lieutenants tell me we share a common interest and that you can help us return home."

Bernius? Alpha frowned. *That is the name of one of Carloman's close associates. Not a very likely coincidence that his ancestor is also present.* "Marcus Carloman is my target."

Jette shrugged. "I was instructed to kill them both, but Marcus is just Lucius' lackey."

Alpha regarded the Roman. The man was young and fit but had the soft look of a human used to being pampered. The human stood with the arrogance of one who expected his wishes to be met immediately. The fear and confusion in the man's eyes belied that facade. *This tool will be easily manipulated.* He raised his hand. "We do have a common goal. Let's work together. Achieve our mission and leave this forsaken place."

Jette's mouth slimmed to a thin line. "How do I know you can return us to Roman territory?"

"Because I have magic powers." Alpha moved his two index fingers close together. Embedded in them were computer port connectors. He expended his limited available energy reserve by shooting an arc of electric current between them. In the dark it shone brightly.

Jette sighed with relief. "We have a deal, wizard."

Alpha waved to the river. "Now join us in our camp on the other side. We shall feast and cement our alliance. The flesh of the water denizens found near the river crossing contains many nutrients."

Chapter XI

Meili

Meili knew their situation was desperate as she sat with the other concubines. Out the narrow window, she watched thick clouds shroud the tall, mysterious peaks to the west. It was midmorning of the twelfth day after they were magically transported to the strange land. They hadn't had a meal in over a day. What little food remained was being hoarded by the nine mercenary guards.

She knew other people had to be nearby. Almost from the beginning, smoke was seen rising from the flat-top mountain about a mile southwest of them. Two days earlier a pair of Shaolin priests ventured out to investigate. They never returned.

The resident scholars and their students were useless from Meili's perspective. They spent the entire time debating the possible cause of the situation. *At least the priests tried to do something.* The eunuch Feng was even more worthless. He refused to leave his suite of rooms since that terrible night.

Meili shuddered at the thought of the last group present in the long wooden pagoda. *The guards are abominations.* Although nothing more than hired thugs off the street, they strutted around like they owned the estate. She glanced at the other women huddled around her. The concubines looked to Meili as their leader. She sighed. *I have the bad habit of not knowing when to back down.* They sought her advocacy whenever they had a grievance. Over the past nine years, her sharp tongue had earned her several canings from the brothel owner. She felt agitated. *What do these women think I can do here?*

The state of affairs worsened early that morning. Exiting the harem, she saw the guard captain, Li Wei, grab the twelve-year-old scullery maid. He ripped what looked like a single overripe pear from her hand. "Stealing food demands punishment."

He swung an open hand at the youth, knocking her into the corridor wall.

The child wailed, "It's for my mother. She's not feeling well, and we have nothing to eat."

Li Wei snarled, "That is not my problem," as he leaned down and struck the girl again.

The scullery maid covered her head and pleaded. "Please don't hurt me."

A Shaolin priest ran down the hall on hearing the child's cry. He stepped between the girl and the guard. "Beating a child won't resolve our problems."

With the momentary reprieve, the bleeding girl fled, running wild-eyed past Meili. This enraged Li Wei. He pulled a studded, wooden baton from his belt and beat the unarmed monk repeatedly. He roared, "I am the law now. You will not interfere with my justice again."

Meili stepped from her concealment and screamed, "Stop, you're killing him."

Li Wei swung around and leered at her. "Come here, whore, and I'll beat you too." He then continued pummeling the now unconscious priest.

Meili, unsure how to make Li Wei stop, ran down the same hallway the girl had fled calling for help. She found the crying child being comforted by two Shaolin priests. The concubine recognized the short, bald one with the ageless face as Chang, the leader of the monks who were visiting the Learning Center. She ran to them and reported what was happening to their associate.

The priests took off at a sprint, their sandaled feet slapping the polished wood floor.

Meili had a sharp mind and used it to acquire many useful medical skills for herself and her fellow concubines. She went to the girl and opened her satchel containing all of her worldly possessions, including her precious collection of ointments and poultices. She crouched by the bruised and battered girl and applied a salve.

After determining the injuries weren't dire, she gathered her bag's contents. "Return to the kitchen and hide. I'm going to check on the priests."

A short distance down the hallway, Meili heard angry voices coming from the large common room. She crouched low and slipped in behind a ceiling-to-floor hanging tapestry near that entrance. She saw two groups confronting each other. Neither looked in her direction. Unobserved, she watched them. Two angry Shaolin priests, supporting their unconscious brethren, faced the entire group of nine guards.

The shorter priest, Chang, did not show the normal calm associated with that order of monks. He snapped, "We are leaving as soon as our brother recovers."

The guard captain, Li Wei, laughed. "You will be out of here tomorrow or you'll end up like your friend. There're too many useless mouths to feed in this cursed place as it is."

"When our friend is able to travel, we *will* leave," Chang responded with a curt nod. "The rulers of this strange land can be no worse than you." The priests turned and shuffled toward their quarters, supporting their limp compatriot.

One of the guards approached the captain after the room was empty. "Li Wei, we have those scholars cowed, but what if the priests report us to the local authorities?"

Li Wei scanned the room, his eyes passing over Meili's concealment without pausing. "We kill them tonight while they sleep. I don't want the potentate of this magical land to hear any accusations against us before we declare ourselves."

They replied with nods and satisfied grunts.

He sneered. "Now let us enjoy Feng's whores while we can. The food supply isn't inexhaustible. We'll probably need to kill them soon too."

Meili held her breath as the laughing men swaggered out a doorway to her left. She waited another minute and, on hearing no sound, peeked around the hem of the wall hanging. Seeing nothing, she dashed to the guest quarters where the priests were staying.

Meili found them together in the second room she checked.

Chang regarded her with calm eyes as she entered, breathless. Her concubine's silk garb concealed little. "Young lady, it was a crude joke whoever sent you to us. We have no desire for your services."

Although in carnal servitude for several years, Meili still blushed. She held up her worn and patched satchel. "Your friend could benefit from my *services*. I have some healing skills. Beatings are not uncommon for those condemned to my fate."

Chang rose and bowed. "All is not necessarily as it appears. Thank you for that lesson."

Meili moved to the unconscious patient and lifted his eyelids. The unfocused eyes were dilated. *Concussion*. With deft hands she probed his limbs and ribs for fractures. After a minute she turned to Chang. "Nothing's broken." She sighed. "Normally, with a head injury, I'd recommend your friend not be moved. But you must leave immediately if you want to live... and take me with you."

The two monks exchanged concerned looks. Chang spoke, "Young... healer, what is your name?"

The woman studied the older man's smooth face and open, honest eyes. "Meili." She inhaled. "I overheard Li Wei after you left the common room. He plans on murdering you tonight. They are... distracted for the moment. Now may be *our* only chance to escape."

Without a second of hesitation, Chang bowed. "It is karma. We depart." He laid out two hiking staffs and wrapped a blanket around them to form a stretcher. The two priests then carefully placed the third priest on it.

Chang donned a wide straw hat and lifted a plain cloth bag from a peg. He opened it and retrieved a long, double-edged dagger which he slid into his hemp waistband. Throwing the sack over his shoulder, he declared, "We are ready."

Meili closed her own satchel and moved to the door. Drawing a shuddered breath, she scanned the dark, windowless, hallway. She was not surprised to see it empty. Feng maintained a tiny servant staff, and the academicians lived in a different wing of the pagoda's grounds.

She stepped out and motioned to the priests. They lifted the litter and followed.

Meili led the priests to the pagoda's rear entrance. They encountered no one until reaching the cooking facilities located there. On opening the narrow kitchen door, she saw the entire serving staff clustered around the girl who Li Wei had beaten earlier.

Only two families constituted the servant population. The first was an old lame man who worked as the groundskeeper. His widowed daughter and her three preteen children provided the housekeeping services. The other group consisted of a portly, balding, middle-aged cook with his equally rotund laundress wife. They had five children ranging in age from fifteen to eight.

Until then, the estate workers avoided contact with the bevy of painted women occupying an entire suite of rooms in the pagoda. However, the workers and their children bowed low when the injured child pointed to Meili and whispered a few words.

Meili paused and returned the greeting.

The gardener glanced at the priests' hemp satchels and announced, "We too are done with this place. Wait one moment. We leave with you." He clapped his hands as he limped to the door. The children hurried off and returned a minute later carrying a few meager bags of garments. Meili's brow arched in surprise. *It appears they were already planning to leave.*

The gnarled groundskeeper, wearing a knee-length hanfu, returned with a short-handled scythe. He hefted the razor-sharp gardening tool. "We are ready."

The cook nodded, grabbed a waterskin and two large meat cleavers and lined up, with the children, behind the priests. "Let's be gone from this cursed place."

Meili led the small procession past a small herb garden. She glanced at the mountains to the south and west, then the impenetrable forests to the north. To the east she thought she detected the faint wisps of smoke rising into the thickening clouds. They walked in that direction.

A pebbled walkway, lined by manicured mulberry bushes and tea plants, covered the first ninety feet. Then the ground abruptly changed to a spongy sawgrass plain. Meili slogged through the mud and brambles even though her concubine slippers were ill-suited for the trek. *Nothing is worth going back in there for.*

They plodded another half mile and then, just as abruptly, they were on cultivated ground.

The land before Meili appeared to be a rich orchard, with branches laden with a dark green fruit.

The groundskeeper plucked one and tentatively nibbled at it. He rolled it in his mouth before swallowing. "Sour but good." He studied the neat rows of trees. "These people know how to farm, but where are we?" Days later, the party would learn the fruit of those trees were called olives.

A sudden hoarse roar shifted Meili's joy at finding signs of civilization to fear. Five strangely armored warriors were sprinting toward them, bellowing indecipherable words.

Chang, with the other monk beside him, lowered their unconscious friend, drew their daggers, and stepped in front. "Run," he snapped in a commanding voice.

Meili bent to pick up the stretcher. The rotund cook, sweating profusely, hefted the other end. She watched the oncoming warriors, transfixed. *That's strange. They're not running* toward *us.*

Unlike most civilians, Meili did not naturally fear soldiers. Her eldest brother, a crossbowman in the Liu Song army, sought her out after their parents sold her. He found her three years into her bondage. However, his wages as an ordinary archer were not nearly enough to buy her freedom from the brothel owner. He spent as much time as he could with her that winter, teaching simple defense skills. The following spring, his company was summoned to war. He vowed that on his return he would have the coin to rescue her. Meili sighed. *That was six years ago.* Her dear brother never returned from that nameless war.

Meili studied the soldier in the lead. He was a tall, lean man, wearing a reddish-brown scaled armor and bearing a sword that seemed to gleam even in the overcast day. Helmetless, his face was exotic and his black hair thick and wavy. His jaw was square and in need of a shave. She met his brown eyes for a brief moment and saw both fear and resolve there.

A second later he raced past the startled people. His four compatriots, carrying shields and spears, followed.

Meili lowered the litter and turned with the rest of her group. She gasped in horror at the new sight. Coming straight toward them, thrashing through the tall grass, was a pack of glistening gray creatures with oversized heads and elongated jaws. Each one was about four feet long from snout to its flat paddle-like tail. They loped on their two hind legs and held their forelegs up, revealing three curved claws on each.

The beasts hissed as the soldiers charged into them. Two of the creatures died in the onslaught, but the rest darted out of reach. The warriors' leader yelled something and the soldiers retreated, forming a loose circle around Meili and her people, brandishing their weapons and shouting at the beasts.

The slit-eyed predators skulked through the orchard, flicking their forked tongues, encircling the humans.

When Meili saw the two Shaolin priests join the line of foreign soldiers, she picked up a discarded walking stick and took a position beside the leader. She glanced at him. His brows arched as he smiled and nodded. *He's very handsome.* It was then, Meili realized, she was just wearing her mud-splattered gossamer gown. She blushed and turned her attention to the hissing beasts, tightening her grip on the staff.

* * *

The twelve days since the Romans' arrival on the magic land Lucius dubbed Novaroma had been a whirlwind of activity. The top of Dragonmont already possessed a credible stockade. The foundation for an imposing citadel had been laid. His Roman engineers completed a four-mile-long, twelve-foot-wide stone causeway. It traversed the hard scrabbled ground, connecting the legion's encampment to the base of the mountain.

An hour after breakfast, Lucius stood at the edge of Aquila's farm, watching the work start on the culverts. When finished, a network of ditches would extend to the river, draining the plain. Harnessing that water would provide a reliable source of irrigation for the farms.

Horatius stood beside him, already covered in mud from digging. He regarded the plateau rising above the flatlands a half mile away. "In another month that'll be a fortress even the great Caesar would have been proud of." He brushed some caked mud from his tunic. "We'll mold this land to our liking."

Lucius touched his new reddish-brown, scaled breastplate. The legion armorer had fashioned the hide from the slain dragon into a thigh-length mail suit. It was lighter, but tougher, than any chainmail. However, the hide was rough, and he needed to wear a leather jerkin beneath it. A thin smile creased his face. "The local wildlife might not be fully onboard with our plans."

Young Marcellus stood on the other side of the legate, outfitted in full legionnaire armor and weapons. "Haven't seen any sign of dragons since that night, but those predators that Alexa calls limnonectes are getting bolder, going after our livestock." He pointed north. "They killed a cow the next farm over from my mom's yesterday, in broad daylight. Stripped it to the bone."

"What?" Lucius exclaimed. He turned to Horatius. "Why am I just hearing about this now?"

Horatius shuffled his feet. "Legate, we learned about the incident late last night." He stiffened. "Sir, you're not an easy man to find. Yesterday, you were four miles south of here, visiting the Persian scholars."

Lucius shook his head. He discovered he was fluent in Farsi when he met the Persian delegation. "The headman there, a scholar named Borzoye, agreed to throw in with us. Between them, the Byzantines, the Guptas, and ourselves, it appears we have quite an academy growing. And the oracle Alexa seems very pleased to be playing the role of headmistress."

"She makes me nervous," Horatius stated with emphasis. "That woman just doesn't look or act natural. I've heard she talks to them all in their native language."

"So do I." Lucius tensed as he replied in an even voice.

"Yes, but you're the legate. You're supposed to make us nervous and know everything." Horatius chortled. His trusting eyes rested on Lucius. "You've commanded the First Red Fist Legion for two years now and haven't steered us wrong yet."

Lucius grimaced. He had only twelve days' worth of memories with these people. He changed the subject. "Marcellus, show me where that cow was killed? Feeding everyone is going to be tight enough as it is. We need to deal with any beasts killing our livestock."

"Sure." Marcellus shrugged. "Follow me."

Lucius turned to Horatius. "That culvert can wait. Clean up and gather your squad. Join us when you're ready... and bring weapons. We might be doing some tracking."

"Yes sir," Horatius groaned. Ditch digging was hard work but preferable to thrashing through waist-high grass or stumbling around an uncharted forest.

Lucius saw the look. "Don't worry, Decurion. Alexa says there won't be any guardian trees in this direction. They only grow over deposits of something called bi-nexidium crystals and ilmenite, and the only place that exists within a thousand miles of here is beneath Dragonmont."

Horatius mumbled as he saluted and walked off. "At least the trees won't be trying to eat me. Just everything else."

Lucius signaled his three bodyguards. Together, they followed Marcellus.

A half hour later, the legate was examining the remains of the dead cow. There wasn't much to study.

He was interrupted by one of his guards who pointed north. "Legate, there's a group of people approaching. It looks like they came from that strange building."

Lucius rose and studied the small procession. Two men in robes carrying a stretcher, four peasants with eight children, being led by a scantily clad woman had stepped out of the wild savannah and entered the farm's olive orchard. He smiled at the sight. "That's a mismatched group if I ever saw one. I wonder what their story—"

He tensed on spotting motion. A pack of about twenty creatures Phokas had named limnonectes were stalking the newcomers. At the time, he thought calling the new species fanged frogs was trite, but observing their bounding strides, it seemed appropriate for those large, dangerous amphibians. He made his decision to act, fast. "Those people are in trouble. Follow me."

The five Romans reached the exotic-looking people just before the limnonectes did. Lucius shouted for them to run. Instead, they stopped, and the two bald men dropped their satchels and drew wide-bladed knives.

Lucius did not have time for a discussion. He skirted the bewildered people and plunged into the limnonectes pack. Over the twelve days of his new existence, Lucius discovered he was an accomplished swordsman. Although his mind possessed no memory of that ability, his reflexes were excellent and his instincts, masterful. He skewered two of the beasts as they reared back and hissed at him. However, instead of fleeing as he expected, the limnonectes pack spread out to attack the refugees from several directions.

The legate saw the move in a glance and knew he was in trouble. There were a lot more beasts than soldiers. "Encircle the civilians and shout. Horatius will hear us."

The Romans responded, but even after the young woman clutching a hiking staff, the two bald men with knives, and an old man wielding a scythe joined them, the bounding limnonectes were too many to defend against.

One fanged creature leapt inside the ring and, with hooked claws, dragged the unconscious man from the stretcher. A feeding frenzy ensued, with gore flying every-where. Two other creatures knocked over the fat man. One tore out his throat while the other sprang toward a terrified eight-year-old girl cowering behind a tree.

Lucius heard the scream and spun in time to lunge with his sword, impaling the vaulting beast. Off balance, the legate was knocked to the ground by another leaping limnonecte. He could smell its fetid breath as its claws raked his mail shirt. He bucked the much lighter creature off and smashed his gauntleted fist into its slavering maw, snapping the creature's head back. Then the legate heard a thwack and saw a staff, wielded by the exotic woman, crack the beast over the head again.

Instantly he pulled out his belt knife and drove it into the monster's chest. Then springing to his feet and retrieving his sword, he decapitated it.

Moments later, he heard the welcome sound of Horatius' hoarse bellow and the shouts of the two Roman decades behind him. The rescuers charged in and killed four more limnonectes before the pack scattered. Of the original twenty, seven scurried away. The rest were either dead or thrashing on the ground. He saw young Marcellus, with rage flashing in his eyes, dispatch the beasts still breathing.

It wasn't until then that Lucius' felt the pain in his throbbing left arm and saw a trickle of blood seeping from beneath his gauntlet. He scanned the battle scene. The remains of two of his guards lay shredded on the ground beside what was left of three mutilated strangers. He saw the eight children were unharmed. Everyone else bore gashes, but none appeared worse than his own wound.

The lone bald man, who survived, sheathed his dagger and bowed to Lucius.

The legate returned the gesture and then scanned the field to see who needed help. The beautiful woman was already doing just that. She knelt on the ground, tending the leg wound on the old man who still clung to his scythe. Beside her was a bag with its contents of small jars and a small medallion spilled on the ground. Another young woman, with similar features to the old man, was mopping his forehead with her worn tunic sleeve. The legate heard their words of love and concern and understood them.

Horatius approached and saluted. "Legate, I apologize for my tardiness."

Lucius clapped him on the shoulder. "Thank God you got here when you did." His eyes turned to the fleeing animals. "Send a decade to track those beasts. I doubt they'll catch them, but I want to know where their lair is."

"Yes, sir."

A moment later, ten legionnaires jogged north, following clear tracks in the torn grass.

Lucius turned his eyes back to the young woman. Her hands were deft and precise as she applied the poultice and bandaged the wound. He walked over and squatted at her side. "Thank you for saving my life." He spoke clear but accented

Mandarin. He had no recollection of where or how he learned that language. "My name is Lucius."

The young woman appeared startled by his presence. She recovered and dipped her head. "I am Meili, and it is I who am grateful. I am a worthless slave. You risked your life to save us."

The term slave disturbed the legate. Although slave soldiers were unheard of in the Roman army, his loathing for it ran deeper. With bitterness, Lucius recalled that he himself came into being as a tool fashioned by the demigod Mara. The thought of anyone being in that state repulsed him.

He draped his red-dyed wool cloak around Meili's near-naked body. "As of this moment, you are free of your bondage."

Meili wrapped the garment around herself. Gratitude shone in her eyes. "Won't the king of this realm object to his soldiers freeing slaves on... a whim?"

Lucius' smile grew broad. "Dear Lady, *I* am the ruler of this land, and I am forever in your debt." He leaned back. "In fact, as of this moment, the institution of slavery is abolished in Novaroma."

Meili looked at him with a shocked expression, and then noticed he was bleeding. "Allow me to treat your wound."

Lucius gingerly unfastened the gauntlet and presented his arm to her. The bite marks were shallow, but Meili spent a long time dabbing at them. He watched her work. When she looked up, their eyes met. Both of them smiled.

* * *

Since their arrival on the planet, the cyborgs had been busy gathering intelligence about the unfamiliar land and the humans present in the near vicinity. Alpha chafed at his limitations. *The people surrounding Carloman have shown nothing beyond Iron Age technology. If I had a case of charge packs, I could fulfil my mission with a single ion blaster.* A grimace creased his human face. *The minuscule amount of power I siphon from my host is barely enough to maintain my systems.*

Eight days into being transported to the new world, Alpha made a discovery. *Perhaps I found an energy source.* When the human named Jette joined his group, he brought a few severely injured followers. He learned that the men had been flogged. Under the pretense of giving them medical aid he attached small disks to the wounded men's backs. *These primitive humans think I am trying to cure them.*

Alpha wanted to see how much life energy the palm-sized battery chargers could extract from the exposed nerves in their flayed flesh. It was of no consequence to him that the experiment hastened their death. After the three humans expired, he was both encouraged and disappointed. He glanced at the ion blaster holstered on his waist. *Not even enough power to fire a single blast. But the efficiency of the extraction process can be refined.* He studied the collection of small devices spread on a table. Several days earlier, the room was a warehouse receiving dock office. The cyborg used the consumer photonic distribution center as a front to disguise his clandestine mission on Cocytus.

He sniffed as he picked up a medallion-shaped subsonic beacon and slapped in the partially charged battery. *This is about the only device that I can run—for now.* He felt it vibrate in his hand for a moment before powering it off and smiling. *I have no discernable use for a signaling device, but with enough humans I can do the same thing with a weapon.*

* * *

Alpha sat outside the window of the Jiankang Academy, listening. *Waste of time. Just more purposeless brute savages.* The chameleon capabilities of his neural-net suit veiled his presence against the ornate, carved wooden beams to all but the most careful observer. Inside, the dispute ended, and the two parties went their separate ways. He was about to slip away when he saw a petite human step from a hiding spot and follow the two bald men dragging another somnolent human. He fingered the small disk in his hand and snuck through the window. He followed her, silent and virtually invisible. He overheard snatches of their hushed conversation.

They are leaving this place. Good. Perhaps I can test the range of this beacon.

A short while later the human group departed the sleeping chamber, carrying the unconscious man. From a shadowed alcove, Alpha dropped the beacon into the open bag of the small female as they passed him. *I can observe distance and duration now.* He tensed, ready to push them aside and flee, but he remained undetected. Internally, he laughed. *They looked right past me. Humans have such limited sensory capabilities.*

The cyborg crawled out the window he entered from and waited. A few minutes later, a small group hurried from the building. The cyborg, noting that the beacon was broadcasting, followed at a distance. His enhanced hearing keyed to the beacon's subsonic pulse.

When the humans paused after crossing the grassy plain, Alpha's olfactory sensor detected the approach of many of the planet's four-foot-long marshland predators. Concerned about his own safety, he squinted and spotted them loping toward the band of humans. His recent observation of those beasts indicated that they were stealth predators that predominantly hunted alone or in pairs. *Not the normal hunting pattern of these creatures.* He sniffed the air. *Their scent indicates they are in a frenzied state.*

Alpha tensed, ready to run, but none came toward him even though he was downwind of their approach. *It's not logical that they would go after a herd when I'm alone.* He considered the situation for a moment. *Ah. The beacon's subsonic pulse must agitate and attract them.*

He squatted to watch the slaughter but was surprised. Several warriors with Iron Age weapons charged the gray amphibians. His eyes were drawn to the leader, whose reflexes and speed surpassed the capabilities of the human shell he himself wore. *Lucius Bernius,* recalling Jette's description. He smiled on seeing one of the beasts knock the man to the ground but became disappointed when a small human female rescued the target.

Twenty more primitive soldiers joined the melee and the fight was over a short time later.

Alpha cocked his ear. The subsonic pulse stopped. He sighed, observing the beasts, no longer frenzied, flee. *The beacon's charge did not last as long as I hoped.* He crouched, hidden in the tall grass. *Perhaps I have a weapon after all. I need to learn more.*

Chapter XII

Choose Sides

Lucius spoke with Meili while she worked on his wound. He found her life story horrific. He knew the "facts" of Lucius Bernius' history. Although his father was a Roman Senator, the Bernius family was not well-to-do. However, the elder Bernius ensured his son received the finest education: tutored in science, rhetoric, and the military. Bland facts in the legate's mind. In contrast, Meili was born into crushing poverty and, since the age of thirteen, suffered the humiliating degradation and abuse of slavery.

To him, the intelligence and innate kindness of this woman shone through in the way she cared for the injured. Her courage in fighting the limnonectes, wielding just a hiking stick, was apparent. After she finished telling her story, he blurted, "You're an amazing woman." He laughed internally at himself. *In the twelve days I've been "alive," I've only met a few women. None anywhere near my age.* He looked at Meili's face. She was blushing at his words. *If I met a million women, I think my opinion would remain unchanged.*

What Meili told him about the state of affairs in the Jiankang Academy building troubled Lucius. He gathered the survivors of her party and asked their views of the situation there.

The lean bald man wearing a plain homespun robe removed his wide straw hat and introduced himself as Chang. He pointed to his two dead compatriots and said they were Shaolin priests who were visiting the institution when the evil magic struck. "That place was once a center for joyful learning and the pleasant exchange of ideas. After we were conjured here, it devolved into a prison where the strong prey on the weak." Concern showed in his creased brow. "The administrator's mind seemed to have broken by what occurred. The hired guards parade about like they own the place and everyone in it."

"Are many people still there?" Lucius asked.

"Besides Li Wei and his thugs," Meili answered, "there are twelve women... like me." She turned to the housekeeper, who was her senior by only a few years. "What of the scholars?"

The housekeeper appeared very pale. She glanced at her father, who nodded. "Feng had eight of his leading scholars in residence at the time. Including families and students, there are about forty men, women, and children trapped there."

"Another matter, good sir." Chang's face creased. "Two days ago, a pair of my brethren ventured out in search of assistance." He met Lucius' eyes. "They would have been garbed as I am now. Have you heard any word of them? They never returned. I fear for their safety."

"If my people encountered anyone resembling you, I would have certainly heard about it." Lucius rubbed his jaw. "In what direction did they venture?"

Chang pointed to the flat top mountain. "We saw smoke rising from that peak. They hiked toward it."

Lucius shuddered. "Great peril lies in that direction for the unwary." He described the guardian trees foresting that mountain's slopes. "I will order the perimeter searched for any sign of them. But I won't risk any of my people entering those woods."

He called to his surviving bodyguard, whose left arm was wrapped in a thick bloodstained bandage. "Find Prefect Carloman. He's supervising the citadel's construction. Tell him to deploy a search party along the mountain's north face. Then see Doctor Phokas about your arm."

"Yes, Legate." The soldier jogged off cradling his injured arm.

Lucius stared at the dead beasts for a moment. "There should only be one predator in our land, and that is *us*." He turned to Marcellus. "We *will* protect our livestock. Go to the encampment. Find Tribune Atticus. I want a couple centuries to sweep this area, and another century to clear the river crossing of the large beasts lurking there."

"Yes, Legate. Where should I tell him you'll be?"

Lucius pointed in the direction of the sprawling wooden building that Meili escaped from. "I need to speak with the people there," he glanced at the small group, "before there is more bloodshed."

Marcellus hesitated. "Legate, I would like to travel with the troops going to the river. I've heard the rumor of those strange beasts. I would like to see them for myself."

"Certainly. There won't be much happening where I'm going." Lucius turned to the refugees. "Go with Marcellus. There's food and shelter for you in our camp. Tomorrow we can discuss your plans."

The groundskeeper leaned on his walking stick, wincing from the pain in his lame leg. "Noble sir, thank you for saving us. I *will* accept your offer." He regarded his daughter and her three young children. "I must look to my family. I'm forever done with the cesspool back there." He bowed and moved to Marcellus.

The laundress wept as she regarded the remains of her husband. "Could someone help me bury my husband? He was a good man and shouldn't be left for carrion."

Lucius saw the woman's anguish and then the dead sprawled on the ground. He turned to Horatius. "Put together a burial detail. The fallen should be interred with dignity. Leave me a few legionnaires for an escort. I need to speak with the residents of this strange building."

"Legate, you can't face the unknown with only a handful of men," Horatius cautioned. "Wait for Atticus' troops. They'd be here in a couple hours."

Lucius glanced at the refugees. "I'm just going to negotiate. I don't expect any trouble. No sane person would harm a diplomat offering food and protection." He pointed in the direction of the pagoda. "But just in case, have one of the centuries catch up to me there."

"No *sane* person. What if they're not sane. I'm coming with you." The decurion looked at his optio. "Ciro, you're in charge of the burial detail."

The lanky, young legionnaire sighed. "Yes, Decurion."

Horatius growled. "When the reinforcements arrive, move them right along. Make sure the centurion in charge knows our commander is risking his neck again." He strode to Lucius' side and crossed his arms. "Now we can leave."

"Great Lord, what did you tell your people?" Meili asked with concern.

"You are not in my legion. Please just call me Lucius." The legate smiled and related the conversation.

"I'm coming too." Meili's voice was even. "No one at the academy knows you." Her laugh tinkled. "Your exotic looks might scare them."

Chang added, "I'll also return. The scholars there are good people but not worldly. They might choose the devil they know versus the one they don't. A familiar face encouraging them to leave would be beneficial."

"All right then." Lucius shrugged. "Let's go."

Meili, Chang, Horatius, and three legionnaires followed him. They returned along the path the escapees blazed a couple hours earlier. The wind picked up and the damp late-morning air turned into a drizzle.

As they walked through the trampled grass, Lucius noticed splattered mud and a set of footprints in a puddle. They were made by a heavy man with large feet. The legate peered east along a clear path of bent grass but detected no movement. He shrugged. *A mystery for another time.*

* * *

It was midday when Lucius reached the pagoda-shaped structure. Despite the rain, a number of people gathered at the academy's demarcation line of the manicured lawn and the wildlands. Eight long-bearded men wearing silken robes and wide hats stood stoically with their hands tucked in their flowing sleeves, watching Lucius' group approach. Several middle-aged women and a number of youths stood on the building's portico, out of the rain. Next to them, but a distinctly different group, were twelve young women scantily clad as Meili. They shivered both from the cooling dampness and fear. In front, blocking the path to the pagoda, were nine armored men, brandishing curve-bladed Dao swords, and a bareheaded fat man with grotesquely long fingernails, wearing elaborate silks.

Meili whispered to Lucius as they drew close that the richly clad person, who appeared ready to bolt, was the eunuch, Feng. She knew little about him. The broad-chested guard beside him was Li Wei. "He's a brute and will do nothing unless it profits him."

Chang walked on the other side of Lucius. A frown creased his smooth face. "Regrettably that's a succinct and accurate description of Li Wei. Feng is... was a political animal, currying favor with those above him and disdaining those beneath him. Now, I am not sure where his mind is."

"That is helpful. Thanks." Lucius turned to Horatius. "You and your men stay several paces behind me. I don't want to escalate a tense situation."

"Yes, Legate," Horatius growled. "But if any of those bastards threaten you, I'll lop their heads off."

Lucius sighed. He stepped close to the waiting group and bowed. Uninvited, Meili and Chang walked with him. Neither of them bowed.

In accented Mandarin, Lucius announced, "Welcome to Novaroma. I am here in peace."

Feng sputtered. "I've never heard of such a place. This is Jiankang. I am an imperial administrator and a loyal subject to Emperor Xiaowu of the Liu Song Dynasty."

Lucius shook his head. "Look around you. Does this look like any city you've ever seen?"

Feng's eyes bulged. "This is an enchanter's illusion." He pointed at the Shaolin priest. "No doubt conjured by that sorcerer Chang." The eunuch paled. "Where are your monks and my servants?"

Chang spread his hands. "We were attacked by beasts. Those who survived are seeking care."

"You lie. They're dead," Feng shrieked and pointed to Lucius as he turned to Li Wei. "That one's a demon. He's covered in blood and look at his face." The eunuch gasped. "It wasn't beasts. He butchered those people... and... and ate them."

Lucius glanced at the scholars. They were watching the eunuch with what appeared to be growing concern. The guards seemed to think the antics were entertaining. The sky didn't help the situation. The misty rain turned steady. The legate was wet, cold, hungry, and tired.

Li Wei ignored the weather and patronized the unbalanced man, "That is why you need us. To protect you from these *beasts*." He snapped at Lucius, "What is it you want, mongrel."

Lucius grew impatient with Feng's insane rantings and Li Wei's insults. "I'm here to offer sanctuary to any who desire to leave this house of madness."

The scholars glanced at each other. Then, in an almost identical motion, they waved their families and students forward and walked to where Horatius stood. When Meili beckoned, the courtesans hurried off the portico and fell in behind them.

Feng did not appear to notice. However, rage flitted in Li Wei's eyes as the deserters hurried past him. He snapped, "Foreigner, I can count. You have four soldiers to my eight. I grant none of *my* people permission to leave."

Meili spit. "Li Wei, we are not your property. You're nothing more than low-grade security. *You* and your goons are certainly not soldiers. My brother was one, and you are nothing like him."

The guard captain flushed. "And you are gutter trash." He glared at Lucius as he grabbed her. "*All* these whores are slaves. You can't have any of them unless you pay."

A whirlwind of activity followed. Meili kneed the guard captain in the groin.

Li Wei howled in pain and smacked the young woman down with a hard backhand.

A half second later, Lucius smashed the side of Li Wei's face with a gauntleted fist, knocking him to the ground. "There are no slaves in Novaroma."

Lucius helped Meili rise and bent to retrieve the now muddy cloak. He expected a clumsy retaliation and clutched the cloak to deflect it.

Li Wei did not disappoint. The guard captain stumbled to his feet and lunged at the legate with his raised sword.

Lucius was ready. Watching for movement from the corner of his eye, he spun, whipping the heavy wool cloak into

Li Wei's face. *It's as if I've been in this type of situation many times before.* The legate used the momentary blindness to grab the assailant's wrist, twisting it into an unnatural position.

The guard captain shrieked in pain and dropped the blade.

The other guards lurched to advance on the legate, but he anticipated their actions. The world seemed to move in slow motion. His own soldiers and Chang moved to his aid. He did not need it. An instant later, the legate had Li Wei's right arm pinned behind his back, with his knife at the guard captain's throat. "Stop, or he dies," Lucius barked.

His instincts told him violence would be required to protect these people the moment he saw Li Wei. It unnerved him. It seemed like he was drawing on a well of experience without any conscious memories of what would have given him that knowledge. When Lucius appraised his opponent, he *knew* he'd dominate.

Why did I take the chance? Lucius reached into his own mind for a reason to fight although outnumbered. It was a void. *I have no past.* He glanced at Meili, who had retrieved his fallen cloak and held it to her chest. *Because my soul told me it was the right thing to do.* His eyes swept the strangers who had chosen to believe in him, and he had a revelation. *Having no past means my future is unencumbered. I will make it what I choose it to be. I can make this a good home for honest people.*

The legate shoved Li Wei away, shifted the knife to his left hand, and drew his strange silvery sword from its scabbard in a single fluid motion.

He took the measure of the guard captain as that man retrieved his own Dao sword from the mud and postured like an awkward street fighter.

Lucius shifted on the balls of his feet into a balanced fencer's stance, lowering the knife in his left hand to his side and extending the sword in his right. A cold smile formed as his eyes narrowed like a raptor's. "You want this *property*? Then all you need do is *kill* me."

Lucius saw fear in Li Wei's eyes as he imitated the legate's posture. Even as he toyed with his outclassed opponent, his mind raced. *I know how to duel. I knew I was the superior swordsman as soon as Li Wei raised his sword. How?*

The guard captain's sword swayed in his trembling hand.

Lucius lunged and Li Wei stumbled backwards, barely parrying what the legate considered a mere feint.

Lucius twisted his wrist, and with the flat of his sword, knocked the Dao from Li Wei's grasp. His voice was as cold as the rain soaking through his clothes as he placed the point of his blade on his opponent's chest. "Your choice is exile or death." He sneered. "If you want your entrails to stay inside your body, leave now and take your worthless henchmen with you."

The guard captain's eyes bulged. "We will die in this wilderness."

"That is not my concern," Lucius snapped as he pointed east. "There's a river a few miles in that direction. If by morning you are still on this side, you will be hunted down and killed."

Humiliation and fear fought with rage in Li Wei's eyes as he stared at the sword pressed against his chest.

Lucius' laugh was derisive. "You're nothing but a petty bully and a coward."

Li Wei glared back for a moment, then averted his eyes. "I will comply." Retrieving his Dao, he stomped away without looking back.

The eight other guards scurried after their captain.

Lucius sheathed his sword and walked to where Feng cowered by a mulberry bush. "Old fool, what is your decision." He tapped his own chest. "Stay, and be under the command of this demon spawn, or follow your hirelings into the wild?"

Feng wailed as he looked at the receding backs of the guards and then at Lucius. He wrung his hands with their grotesquely long fingernails. "I... I will serve you, *master*."

"Good. We have a lot of honest work for you." Lucius switched from Mandarin to Latin as he turned to Horatius. "The excitement's over for now. We'll spend the night here. Let's get out of the rain."

Horatius chuckled as he watched Li Wei depart. "You had me worried when you turned your back on that buffoon. But the shock on his face when you had your knife at his throat was better than the dumbfounded expression of that oversized Goth you dueled in Gaul a couple years back."

Lucius had no memory of any sword fights. He smiled wanly. "Was it really two years ago?"

A look of surprise crossed the decurion's face, "How could you forget? It was just before our decisive battle against the Huns."

Lucius' stomach clenched with fear of being discovered. He stuttered, "Was that *just* two years. It seems like a lifetime ago."

"It does at that." Horatius' wariness shifted to relief. He snapped a salute. "Yes, Legate. Drying off will feel good."

Lucius moved to Meili, took the cloak from her arms, and draped it over her shoulders. He switched to Mandarin and raised his voice for all to hear. "We'll be your guests tonight."

"I'd like that." Meili smiled as she pushed a lock of damp hair from her face.

Horatius cleared his throat. "Since everything is under control, would it be okay if I returned to Aquila's farm? With all the fearsome critters roaming about, it seems wrong to leave that exposed homestead unprotected."

Lucius smiled as Horatius' face reddened. "Keeping the widow company will be more interesting than watching me snore. Go and give the good woman my regards." He rubbed his jaw. "When you get there, send a runner to Atticus. Let him know that a small group of miscreants will be passing through. Let them go." He rubbed his forehead. "Also, remind the tribune I want the river crossing secured. I'm sure Marcellus delivered the order earlier, but Atticus is not always quick to take any initiative." He shook his head. *How do I know that?*

"I will, and thank you, sir." The decurion was off at a jog.

Lucius turned to Feng. "Sir, why don't you lead the way into your establishment."

Feng stared at him with bulging eyes.

"Boo." The legate couldn't help himself.

The eunuch yelped and sprinted into the pagoda, his sodden silken robes almost tripping him every few steps. He never paused as he hurried to his suite, shut and barred the door.

Meili escorted Lucius in. The others hurried after them as the rain shower ended.

Broad smiles creased the three legionnaires' faces as they followed the shivering courtesans into the pagoda.

Chapter XIII

New Memories

On reaching the portico, Lucius tensed on noticing men approaching in the distance. He breathed a sigh of relief, noting their Roman armor. He waited under the overhang and recognized them as the squad of legionnaires he sent to track the limnonectes.

A legionnaire, wearing the rank of optio, jogged up the wide steps and saluted. "Legate, we tried to follow the beasts, but they scattered. We lost the tracks in the woodland, so I called off the search." He laughed, "Nothing exciting there. No new beasts and just normal trees. But we did come across a salt lick along the river."

"A salt lick? That's useful. When you get back to camp, report the exact location to Prefect Carloman so he can mark it on his map." Lucius added, "Anything else?"

The optio glanced though the open door at the people in the room. "Yes, Legate, on our way here we passed a group of armed men headed east. Nine of them kinda looked like these folks, but the tenth was a big Teutonic guy wearing a skintight suit. They gave us a wide berth, so I didn't see any reason to challenge them. They seemed to be heading toward the river ford." He frowned. "I hope I made the proper decision."

"You chose rightly. I don't expect any mischief from them." The legate furrowed his brow. "The nine you mentioned I exiled. But I don't know who this tenth person is. Skintight suit... I must speak to the oracle about this."

Collectively, the Romans gazed through the windows at the exotic room and people. Their eyes lingered on the courtesans huddled together.

Lucius followed their gaze. "We're staying here for the night." He snapped, "These people are under my protection. There will be no abuse or looting."

"Yes, sir," came the quick reply. "We wouldn't think of it."

"Then set the guard and come inside."

The pagoda's residents waited for Lucius in the large common room, glancing apprehensively at the mud-caked soldiers entering with him. A couple of the scholars lit the braziers against the gathering gloom.

Lucius glanced around for Meili and found himself disappointed on not seeing her.

She re-entered the room moments later carrying a large basket of tang yuan rice balls. "Li Wei was hoarding these." Her courtesan garb was gone. Meili now wore a homespun hiplength tunic, shin-length undyed britches, and frayed leather sandals. Although looking like an impoverished peasant, her head was held high.

Lucius saw the drawn faces of the children and, although famished, declined the food offered. His men reluctantly followed suit. It was a meager meal for the hungry people present.

The legate removed his armor and settled into a comfortable chair. A puddle formed at his feet as water dripped from his soaked clothes. He spent the next few hours explaining what he knew about their magical abduction and the new land they were in, avoiding how he came into being as part of it. The scholars questioned him closely about points he thought trivial, like the precise shade of the *magic* light during the event.

As the late afternoon progressed into evening, Lucius saw the trepidation and anxiety lift from his hosts. The children, sensing from their parents that they were safe, began laughing and playing. When they started running about, a couple parents hustled them from the room. The questions became less formal and occasionally someone would crack a joke about the situation.

Lucius saw the fear recede and be replaced by hope in their eyes. He was happy.

* * *

Although Meili added details about her own encounter with Alexa, she mostly remained silent. She sat cross-legged on the floor, observing Lucius. He had removed the strange, scaled armor and sat on a cushioned chair with a look of deep fatigue. The simple tunic he wore was dyed red but sweat-stained and faded from long usage.

She liked that his responses to panicked queries were unvarnished facts but delivered with the calm resolve that no issue was insurmountable. When asked what lay beyond the river, mountains, and sea he freely admitted he had no clue, but whatever was there would be dealt with in due course.

The details about this new dangerous land and the monsters lurking there did not interest her. During her hard life, she knew both could easily be found even in a civilized city like Jiankang. What did interest her was this man named Lucius Bernius. *He risked his life to aid strangers in distress when there was no profit to him for doing so.* A man holding power but displaying virtue was something she never encountered before.

As suppertime arrived, Lucius ordered his men to share their rations. Although the food was just hard tack biscuits, salt pork, and sour wine, the residents devoured all that was offered.

Meili observed that Lucius wore the mantle of authority lightly. As the day waned, warriors entered, spoke to him, and then hurried off. Although she could not understand their language, she didn't need to. The soldiers appeared to have no fear approaching their leader but showed their respect with their sharp salutes and rapid departures in response to his words.

During lulls in the conversation, she saw his eyes drift toward her. Men had always looked at her with desire. She hated it, but not now. Meeting his gaze, she smiled. His returned grin was not craven leering but frank interest. It warmed her.

As the sun set, Meili saw that Lucius was ready to conclude the session. Although embarrassed that she was thinking it, she asked the question burning inside her. "Sire, what does your wife think of all this?"

His reaction was not one of any of the possibilities she considered. Meili saw confusion in the man's eyes... and fear.

After a long pause, he said, "I... I have no spouse." He quickly added, "I think that we have spoken enough tonight. In the morning, we will see to your future."

The academy's residents rose, talking animatedly amongst themselves, and left for their respective quarters in the pagoda's communal wing.

Meili closed her eyes as she contemplated the response to her question. The man who spoke with such confidence on all the other topics sounded unsure and lacked emotion. *Was the woman dead? Was it a loveless marriage?* She only knew the man for less than a day, but she was certain any relationship he was in would be passionate, either for good or ill. *Something's missing.*

She was startled from her reflections on sensing a nearby presence. She looked up with alarm. The mysterious man with his unkempt, black wavy hair and unshaven face, who called himself Lucius, crouched beside her. The soft gaze from his intelligent brown eyes entrapped her.

"You did not like my answer." He sighed. "Can we talk? I *need* to talk."

Meili nodded and looked around. The room was empty except for two of the strange soldiers lounging by the main entrance and another two by the interior doors connecting the common room to corridors leading to the rest of the expansive building. "Whatever you wish, sire."

"I told you to call me Lucius." A slim smile creased the legate's face. "You're certainly dressed different than when we first met."

Meili blushed and touched her patched, threadbare hanfu. "These are the peasant rags I wore when my parents sold me into servitude. Since I'm no longer forced to be a whore, I chose not to dress as one... Does it displease you?"

"I don't think you could be anything but beautiful." Lucius grinned. "And I like the reason you changed." His face sobered and he sat across from her. He stared at his own open hands for a moment. "What would you think of a person who has no memory of the world before arriving to this place?"

Meili's face twisted in confusion and her eyes misted. "I would consider it a wondrous gift. Beyond the memory of my brother, there is nothing from my past I wish to recall." She gazed at Lucius' face. "To start afresh would be a blessing. Is that what the magical transformation did to you?"

"Yes." Lucius hung his head. "Facts are in my head. I can speak at least five languages that I know of. I've been told my martial skills are undiminished. But no matter how much I wrack my brain, I cannot dredge up a single memory before the last couple weeks."

Meili laid her hand atop of his. "Did all of your people suffer this same fate?"

Lucius encased her hand in his. "Only myself and one other. Neither of us can recall a single memory from before the magic." He shook his head. "The oracle you met, Alexa, claims to have raised the two of us. But I have no recollection of her or that time."

"Then build new memories... with me." Meili gasped on realizing she had whispered her inner thoughts out loud. She lowered her head and cringed, waiting to be laughed at, or worse callously mauled.

Lucius lifted her quivering chin. "Quite a pair we'd make. One wishing to erase the past, and the other trying to recover it."

Meili searched his face for mockery but saw only caring. "I think it would be wonderful."

Lucius kissed her and Meili melted into his arms. After an embrace that seemed like an eternity, Meili pushed back and stood, holding out her hand. "I think we should make our own memories."

They left the room, hands intertwined. As they walked past the guard posted at the guest quarters corridor, Lucius growled at the smiling sentry. "We are not to be disturbed until morning. Is that understood?"

"Yes, Legate."

Chapter XIV

First Blood

Alpha trailed behind Lucius Bernius' small group as they approached the pagoda-shaped building in the midday rain. With the stealth capabilities of his neural-net suit activated, no one perceived his presence. He calculated that the potential for new information was worth depleting the limited power he had available.

Crouching behind a mulberry bush, he watched as Lucius dealt with a clumsy warrior from that dwelling. The Roman's handling of the outclassed opponent was interesting. Lucius, after an easy victory, sent his defeated foe and his minions away instead of killing them. *Stupid, but a weakness I can exploit.*

The cyborg retreated to a briar patch thick with hooked thorns in the field of sawgrass and regarded his own primitive weapons, simple sharpened blades of inert material. He had fashioned a short-shafted, flanged boar spear and a serrated hunting knife from shards of plexo-steel he pulled from the buildings across the river. Although he thought those weapons would be more than serviceable against any opponent he encountered here, they disgruntled him. *I require a more efficient means of killing.*

His ion disrupter remained as useless as everything else requiring energy. He rubbed his clean-shaven jaw, recalling his experiment with the subsonic beacon. *Perhaps I've uncovered a means to make real weapons functional again. On a world such as this, I'd be invincible.*

Alpha turned east and followed the exiled group. Once beyond the sight line of the pagoda, the cyborg called out to them and approached. He found their reactions predictable. The fear and wariness of the banished ones gave way to eager acceptance when the cyborg promised they could acquire vast riches from looting and pillaging under his direction. He learned the group's leader was a craven opportunist named Li Wei, who seemed emboldened by the newfound alliance.

Li Wei glanced back at the open ground they covered. "How did you sneak up on us like that? I did not know you were there until you announced yourself."

"I have many such talents, which I will gladly teach those loyal to me." Alpha noted the gleam in Li Wei's eyes. *What a fool. He, and all the others I gathered, will be dead when their usefulness to my task is done.*

Li Wei's eyes narrowed. "Feng has a treasure trove in his suite. We should start there. The eunuch's gone insane. He probably won't even notice when the silk and gold is gone." He laughed. "And the whores there are worth taking. They're quite skilled."

The cyborg painted a grin on his face even though he saw no value in the items or people Li Wei desired. His face turned hard. "Armed men approach."

Li Wei drew his Dao and looked back in the direction he came from. "I don't see anyone."

"The opposite direction." The cyborg almost added, "You idiot," but refrained.

Li Wei whirled around. "I still don't see anyone."

To Alpha, the ten legionnaires splattered with mud, trudging their way, appeared exhausted. He snarled. "They are Carloman and Bernius minions. I do not wish to raise any alarms by slaying them. It will make my ultimate goal harder to achieve. Put away your weapons and show deference when they pass."

"Who are Carloman and Bernius?" Li Wei asked.

"You crossed swords with Lucius Bernius a short time ago." Alpha chuckled.

"I will eat his heart," Li Wei hissed.

"I observed your recent altercation. I do not share your confidence," Alpha replied with an even tone.

"He got the jump on me," Li Wei sputtered as his face reddened.

"He *will* die, but only when and where I deem appropriate." *This inadequate human lies even to himself.* Alpha detected the approach of the armed group and snapped, "Prostrate yourselves."

The cyborg bowed when the legionnaires got close. Beneath hooded eyes, he studied the soldier who wore the markings of a low-level leader in his targeted foe's army. Alpha saw the man hesitate as if wanting to stop for an interrogation and then regard the legionnaires following him. *The low-level commander knows his humans are exhausted and would be disadvantaged in an altercation. He noted our appearance and location, then moved on without a word. Wise and disciplined.*

Alpha led his new allies north into the forest. In a grassy dell he found a small herd of lanky two-legged herbivores. The brown, long-necked reptiles with their powerful legs were built for speed. The cyborg had killed others like them before and consumed their flesh. His host body found the taste satisfactory. The animals looked up on detecting Alpha's scent but went back to grazing on spotting him.

The human who Alpha possessed laughed. *I am the predator.* Alpha rebuked him in his mind. *You are just a tool that does my biding. I am the ultimate predator.* The cyborg sensed the flash of anger and resentment but did not care. *One can't worry about the feelings of a tool.*

From fifty feet away, he chose his target, which was standing broadside to him. He aimed and cast the heavy spear. It sliced deep into the creature's chest, punching through to its heart. It staggered one step and fell, thrashing. The other dark-brown reptiles fled at an astonishing fast pace. Within moments, only the cyborg and the dead animal remained in the glade.

Alpha turned to the watching academy guards crouching in the brush. "Dinner is served."

"That was quite a throw," Li Wei exclaimed, clearly impressed.

The cyborg shrugged and retrieved the spear. It was buried in the beast exactly where he aimed it.

The guards built a fire and gutted the reptile. They spent the late afternoon gorging themselves.

Li Wei sidled over to Alpha, who sat separately staring west, and offered him a chunk of roasted meat.

Alpha accepted it and allowed his human host, Charles, to sate his always ravenous appetite.

Li Wei cleared his throat. "Do you possess a powerful army and a strong citadel? From what you said earlier these... Romans sound like a dangerous adversary."

"Nothing special about them. Like everyone else, they'll die when I cut them." Charles sneered before Alpha regained control of their shared mind. Alpha pointed east. "My base is across the river. It sits on seven hundred hectares of solid ground surrounded by a trackless marsh. Only I and a few of my... tribe know the safe paths through the sucking mud. Dense groves of banyan and cypress-like trees render it is virtually invisible until one is almost on top of it." He regarded his manicured fingers and sniffed. "Any armed incursion would be a logistics nightmare. It is secure."

Li Wei bobbed his head. "I am an accomplished commander. Perhaps I could assist in the organization of your troops."

"Perhaps." Alpha's face showed no emotion. "Now leave me. I am thinking." He did not acknowledge Li Wei scuttling back to the other guards a few awkward moments later.

As the sun lowered toward the horizon, the cyborg stood and without preamble announced. "Time to go."

Li Wei glanced at the setting sun. "It's getting dark. We should wait until morning."

"There is only one practical place to ford the river, and it is only safe to do it after dark."

"Why?"

"A number of large aquatic reptiles infest the river. The mature adults reached twelve feet in length and aren't picky regarding what they eat." Alpha shrugged. "They have weak night vision and remain inactive then, unless aroused." He eyed his new followers. "One of my other minions, a... Saracen, didn't heed my warning. He stumbled and thrashed in the water. The fool never made it to the other side."

Li Wei gulped. "I'll be sure not to be as clumsy."

"Good." Alpha turned and strode toward the river.

Li Wei and the others followed. The ground was still damp from the midday shower, but the light of the planet's moon in its gibbous phase shone through thin clouds.

Over the course of that afternoon, Alpha evaluated what he knew about the technology of the subsonic transponder beacon and its apparent effect it had on the amphibious predators. He desired to discuss his discovery with the beta cyborgs. *They might have productive insights on how we can hone it into a more deadly weapon.*

That same day, Beta-1 and Beta-2 were conducting exploratory missions parallel to his own activities. Their collective tasks were to scout the different areas inhabited by their intended prey and gathering human accomplices. *We need both.*

The constraints all the cyborgs were under made accomplishing the simplest objectives difficult. Alpha detested his reduced effectiveness due to his minuscule power supply. *No direct links. I'm forced to communicate via oral exchanges.* He glanced at Li Wei and his men slogging through the mud behind him. *I hope the betas acquired a higher grade of underlings than I did.*

Alpha was frustrated. None of the modifications made to the delta and gamma cyborgs improved their efficiency in converting their host body's chemical energy into photonic power. Not only did it limit the usefulness of those units, there was an additional unanticipated problem.

The process of the cyborgs syphoning energy via the parasitic link left the host bodies constantly hungry. This forced Alpha to commit a large portion of his team to the non-mission tasks of hunting and foraging. *Inefficient use of time and resources.* Only being able to use himself and the betas for any extended operation constrained his tactics further.

Alpha tensed as he approached the river embankment. Where the rolling woodland opened onto the grassy plain, he spotted an encampment composed of seven large tents backlit by several campfires. He spotted the hides from several of the crocodile-like water denizens stretched out on racks. *There were no humans in this area last night. What are they up to?*

Although the night vision of the cyborg's host body was enhanced, he had trouble discerning how many enemies were about. Besides a sentry silhouetted in the weak moonlight a few dozen steps ahead of him, he spotted several more sitting by the campfires. Also, the clear voices of laughing men could be heard coming from inside the canvas shelters.

After a few moments' surveil, Alpha relaxed. There was no indication that this was a vanguard for a military incursion across the river. *The encampment is calm. These humans would be warier if they knew adversaries were nearby.* Besides the single picket, he detected no movement outside the immediate area. The cyborg felt confident detection could be avoided by giving the stationary enemy a wide berth. He knew the two betas would make the same assessment and avoid contact. *It's too soon to reveal ourselves. We can slip around this group tonight. But I'll need to find a different crossing point if this placement becomes permanent.*

The cyborg slid back inside the tree line to where his newly acquired followers waited. Then the last thing Alpha wanted occurred. In the dark, Li Wei stumbled over a root with a grunt. In the silence, the snapping twigs sounded like an explosion. The city-bred guard captain then made more noise, thrashing about in his attempt to rise.

The racket drew the attention of the sentry, who approached to investigate with a raised shield and drawn sword.

I must do something. In the gloom, Alpha moved like a shadow, slipping behind the legionnaire and slitting his throat. The cyborg did not see the other picket approaching parallel to the first. The man saw his comrade fall and yelled, "To arms! We are under attack," twice before Alpha silenced him with a thrown knife.

The Roman camp responded fast. Within moments, a half dozen legionnaires were methodically advancing in the direction of the shouted warning. Behind them, a horn blared, and soldiers spilled from their tents and formed into ranks under the barked commands of a centurion.

The brush and trees shadowed the weak light provided by the moon. Using that for cover, the cyborg still thought they could elude detection.

Then disaster struck again. Li Wei, embarrassed by his clumsy fall, chose to redeem himself in the eyes of his new ally. From his concealment the guard captain moved to intercept the six advancing Romans. "You will see our worth. These servants of our common enemy will die." With a shout, the guard captain charged from cover with his followers. He froze in midstep on spotting fifty armed legionnaires backlit by the campfires, lined up in a double row.

Simultaneously, a Roman sentry near the south end of the camp shouted, "There're more of them over here."

Alpha looked in that direction and saw with his enhanced vision the two betas and several humans wearing Gupta garb. They were apparently in the process of sneaking around the Roman camp when the alarm sounded. He heard the Roman centurion bellow "Fire." A volley of arrows sliced through the air, striking two of the Guptas caught in the open.

At the sound of steel clashing to his left, Alpha swung his head left. Li Wei's people were engaged with a half dozen enemies. Although outnumbered, the small band of Romans was winning. Two of the pagoda's guards were already down. *This is a disaster.*

Alpha gnashed his teeth and released the bloodlust of his host body, Charles. The human that Alpha was symbiotically connected to sprang into the melee like a wild beast. He drove the boar spear into the back of a Roman who was dueling Li Wei. Cackling, Charles dodged a second attacker, stepped inside the man's guard, and stabbed him up through the throat. Awash in spurting blood, he howled, sending the rest fleeing in terror. It took all of the cyborg's mental effort to restrain his human thrall from racing after them.

Glancing around, Alpha saw four of the pagoda's guards lying motionless. *Pointless loss of energy sources.* An arrow whizzing an inch from his face brought the cyborg's attention to the larger danger. He saw a column of Romans advancing toward his group and another moving in the betas' direction.

The resources I gathered are doomed. I must flee. He hoped that the betas came to the same conclusion.

Accompanied by a blowing clarion, he heard the sound of many feet splashing through water. *Now what?* Charging across the river crossing was Beta-3 leading the gamma and delta cyborgs. With them were a dozen mounted Saracens bearing lances and the century of Roman traitors who had joined him.

The Novaroman centurion also saw the new arrivals. The balance of power had shifted against him, and his force was split in two.

Alpha observed the legionnaire commander shout to a lanky soldier who nodded and dashed from the fight toward the main Roman encampment over two miles away. He also saw Beta-1 sprint after him.

The struggle's outcome was now assured, but it left a sour taste in Alpha's mouth. There would be no hiding their presence from the larger Novaroman force. *But that is for tomorrow.* He released his control over the deranged Charles.

In an objective sense, Alpha found the predatory cunning of his host body interesting. The human's bloodlust was not mindless. Although each kill drove Charles into ecstasy, he was wary enough to only go after prey he was confident of dominating.

With a feral smile, the human flexed his muscles and retrieved a Dao and a gladius from the ground. He scanned the battlefield for another victim, watching intently as the nearest group of legionnaires formed a square. He shrieked as the Saracen lancers broke up the defensive formation and leapt into the confusion, striking like a viper at isolated soldiers.

Within minutes that group was either dead or dying. Alpha's host human howled as he hacked the wounded legionnaires.

Down to twenty-five soldiers and surrounded, the centurion realized the hopelessness of his situation. Across the battlefield he recognized Jette leading the Roman turncoats and begged for quarter.

To end the slaughter, and to possibly gain a few more adherents, Jette raised his hand palm outward, granting the request. The turncoats halted their advance and the Roman legionnaires laid down their weapons.

Alpha was pleased. *A fresh set of sources to drain energy from.* However, he did not reclaim command of his host body before the insane man shouted, "Kill them all," and flung his boar spear, skewering the centurion.

Ashen faced, Jette ordered his soldiers to attack.

The gamma cyborgs, taking the slaying of the centurion as a signal from Alpha, charged in. The Saracens, Guptas, and Liu Song guards joined them.

Leaderless, the Romans fought with desperation, but the one-sided battle was over in minutes. Alpha's host body pranced through the carnage, gleefully stabbing the dead and injured alike. It took the cyborg close to a minute to gain mastery over their connected mind.

Chapter XV

Eyes in the Dark

Along with the Persian, Borzoye, and the legate's young aide, Marcellus, Theodore accompanied the Roman century who were assigned to clear the river crossing. The Byzantine scholar had caught a glimpse of the river reptiles, which he dubbed *potamos savras* when his group was first magicked to Novaroma. The sight tantalized his curiosity, and he desired to learn more about the habits of those dangerous creatures.

At the Byzantine scholar's request, the legionnaires set lures for the reptiles. The soldiers treated it as a game, seeing what traps held the beasts and which ones did not. When a thrashing potamos savras started breaking out of a snare, they whooped while spearing the crocodile-like creatures with their spears.

The largest potamos savras killed measured almost nine feet from snout to tail tip. Theodore observed a couple basking in the mud on the eastern bank that appeared to be much larger.

When the moon popped through the clouds, Theodore declared that he was going to find an elevated spot for observing the creatures' nighttime behaviors. He and Borzoye left the camp with the youth, Marcellus, as a guide and protector.

They found a comfortable mossy knoll overlooking the river and settled in. To Theodore's disappointment, he saw little movement from the potamos savras under the light of the gibbous moon. Flitting clouds continuously obscured its limited illumination. He spotted a few of the creatures languidly drifting in the slow current, but most lay in the mud of the eastern bank.

After a couple fruitless hours, Theodore and Borzoye compared the scant new information acquired and decided to head back to camp. They had only gone a short distance when Marcellus pulled both scholars behind a thick hedge.

Strangely garbed men bearing arms passed by without glancing in their direction. The leader, a full head taller than the rest, carried a short-shafted spear and wore a skintight suit. The Byzantine scholar thought it resembled the garment he saw on the oracle.

The unusually garbed stranger treaded in stealthy silence. Conversely, the nine warriors behind him stumbled through the brush, making an obscene amount of noise. Those men wore loose tunics and britches. Their faces belonged to no tribe he had ever seen but had the cruel look of common thugs similar to those he remembered lurking in the back alleys of Constantinople.

Minutes passed and Marcellus nodded that it was okay for the scholars to come out of hiding. Then they heard the cry, "To arms! We are under attack." Ominously, that shout was silenced, but a clarion picked up the call.

Soon after, they heard a loud thrashing coming from the river that sounded like dozens of feet splashing through the water. The commotion appeared to arouse the sleeping potamos savras. Theodore saw many of them slide silently from their muddy perches into the river. Ahead, he heard angry exhortations and the clash of steel.

They crept forward and, from behind some tall bush, watched in horror as the legionnaires who accompanied them earlier in the day were massacred, some after surrendering.

Theodore held Marcellus in a steel grip. His voice was husky. "There's nothing you can do to help them, boy. We must observe these enemies and live to report our findings." The scholar had spent many long years studying the world around him. He focused those skills on the battle site.

He noted that, after the company of legionnaires who came with them were slain, the enemy dumped the bodies in the river. The potamos savras appeared frenzied by the pervasive coppery scent of blood. The water soon churned as the river reptiles fed on the corpses. The Byzantine scholar shifted his gaze to the victors. The largest group was the Romans who deserted the legion the day after he arrived. Bitterly he noted that another group were the Saracens he hired a few weeks earlier to guard his caravan.

The leader of one of the small groups he recognized as the Gupta prince named Rayansh, who he met a couple days earlier at the strange palace near the new limestone quarry. The other small group was the clumsy strangers who blundered past him a short while earlier.

The final group he observed disturbed him the most. Physically, he perceived no tribal commonality, but they possessed some cold, undefinable sameness he could not discern in the uncertain light. The leader appeared to be the strange man who passed by them. The sight of him made Theodore shiver. One moment he was racing about slashing every Roman in sight like a raving lunatic, the next he was directing his band with a calm detachment.

Theodore, Borzoye, and Marcellus stayed hidden while the victors disposed of the Roman bodies and then methodically sacked the campsite.

A couple hours later, after the waters had calmed and the potamos savras resettled on the muddy banks upriver, the victors, led by Jette, returned across the river. The only ones remaining were the eighteen strange people in the tight bodysuits. They laid out two bodies, similarly garbed, and encircled them. Moments later they were joined by a lean, dark woman who nodded to the leader and joined the group.

Theodore, Borzoye, and Marcellus strained their eyes to decipher what seemed to be some sort of ritual in the flickering light of the devastated camp's guttering torches.

It was Marcellus who pointed out the macabre actions of the leader. The tall shadowy man stabbed into the back of the dead people's necks with a serrated knife. He then pried out what appeared to be a fat, thumb-sized, shiny metal centipede from each. He shoved the objects in a bag and strode across the ford without looking back. His followers unceremoniously left the dead and followed him.

In whispering voices, Theodore and Borzoye debated the portents of what they saw and what their next move should be. Neither saw Marcellus slip away until their attention was drawn to movement in the flickering torchlight of the demolished camp. They saw the youth's silhouette poking at enemy bodies with a broken spear.

Theodore scrambled to his feet and hurried to the site. "What's that young fool trying to do?" Borzoye followed, keeping a wary eye alternately for movement in the water and on the opposite shore.

When they reached Marcellus, he was already stripping the strange single-piece suit from one of the corpses. The young aide's face was grim as the two gray-haired men reached him. "Those people murdered my friends. The legate will need all the information we can gather."

Theodore patted Marcellus on the back as he crouched beside him. He rubbed a piece of the cloth between his fingers and glanced across the river. "No nation I know of produces a garment like this. We need to ask the oracle some hard questions."

"Could we talk about this somewhere else?" Borzoye rasped as he focused on the dark water while retrieving an abandoned gladius. "The bellies of those potamos savras may not yet be full."

They dragged the two mutilated bodies to higher ground above the ransacked camp. Marcellus retrieved a torch. With the aid of its sputtering light, the two scholars examined the identical gashes in the corpses. The cuts were made with surgical precision. Theodore briefly exchanged theories with Borzoye. "This obviously wasn't an act of random violence. But what were those objects that the Teuton pulled from their bodies?"

Borzoye added, "They must be some sort of magic talismans. Otherwise, he wouldn't have gone through the trouble of extracting them."

"He's a demon," Marcellus exclaimed and pointed to the bodies. "These were his minions. The ritual was him claiming their infernal souls."

"Perhaps." Theodore furrowed his brows. "It's as good an explanation as anything my knowledge of science can produce."

"We must get back." Marcellus glanced at the night sky. The moon had slid behind a cloud. "We need to warn the legate of this disaster." He held up the smooth suits. "The oracle had a garment like this. I saw it myself on our second day here. She'll know."

Borzoye glanced around. "We're still a couple hours from sunrise. I surmise we'll spend that time bumbling around, lost in the dark, but you're right. We should leave this place. The evil ones may return."

Marcellus hoisted the torch. "I'll get us back."

"Then lead on." Theodore stood and rested a hand on the youth's shoulder. "My eyes aren't nearly as keen as they used to be."

Marcellus followed the rocky river embankment until they reached a well-worn dirt path. It was a trail he had trod since childhood.

They encountered no one until they came within a hundred yards of the encampment's eastern palisade. There they found a detachment of legionnaires crowded around the body of the runner that the now dead centurion sent to get help. Those soldiers turned with their weapons raised at the sound of their approach.

One of the legionnaires, suspicion in his voice, said, "It's the Greek and the Persian. What are you doing roaming about at this time of the night?"

"Peace." Marcellus stepped into the circle of torchlight, his palms held out. "I am Legate Bernius' aide. These men have been with me all night." He pointed to the body. "This is not the only one of our people who's been murdered."

Tribune Atticus, who was in charge of the fort's night watch, raised his torch and spent a long moment studying the youth's face. "Aye, you are Marcellus. What happened?"

Without embellishment, Marcellus recounted the night's events. At the end he held up the two torn, blood-soaked garments.

"So now we must fight demons." The tribune gasped. "At least we know they can die." He turned to his men. "Back to the fort. We need to inform the legate and raise the alarm."

One of the legionnaires spoke up, "The legate is not in camp. He left this morning on an inspection tour. He's not yet returned."

"Then rouse the prefect," Tribune Atticus snapped.

The same legionnaire answered, "Prefect Carloman's not here either. He remained at Dragonmont. They are laying the new citadel's foundation."

"What?" The tribune paled. "How about Tribune Titus?"

"He's off on a mission exploring the seacoast south of here."

"Silvio?"

"He's at the quarry site."

"Then... I'm the senior commander?"

"Yes, sir."

Atticus' face turned ashen. "Back to the fort *now*." As he walked, the tribune's young voice was reedy. "Demons roaming the land and Legate Bernius is out somewhere without a proper escort. He must be found and protected immediately."

As they reached the gate, Atticus took a ragged breath. "Does anyone know exactly *where* the legate is right now?"

"Legate Bernius was intending to meet with the strange people at that long wooden building northeast of here. I expect he's still there," Marcellus volunteered.

Atticus nodded, showing visible relief.

A breathless legionnaire ran up. "Tribune Atticus, Senior Centurion Silvio beseeches you to send aid. A dragon attacked the quarry camp. Several of his men were killed before he fled to the Gupta palace." He sucked in air. "I'm only alive because my horse was fast and the dragon was busy eating one of our men."

"Silvio had a full century of troops. They couldn't slay it?" Atticus gasped.

"No, Tribune. We tried." The soldier shuddered. "Our weapons couldn't penetrate its hide. That monster rampaged at will."

"The *legate* knows how to kill them," Marcellus interjected.

"Yes... yes he does." Atticus squared his shoulders. "We are in grave danger. The legate and prefect must be informed." He whirled on the dispatch carriers standing nearby. "You, ride to Dragonmont." He pointed to a second rider. "You, go to that strange building to the north."

136

A pair of centurions, still in their nightshirts, ran up, hearing the commotion. "Junior Tribune Atticus, what in blazes is going on?"

Atticus threw his hands in the air. "Sound the alarm. Muster the troops. Man the ramparts. We are beset by demons and dragons."

All the soldiers scattered, and clarion calls soon resounded from every corner of the fort.

Atticus continued to shout orders, some contradictory, even after no one was nearby to heed them.

With the fortified encampment in chaos, Marcellus turned to the gray-haired men. "Excuse me, I must check on my mother."

"It's a bad night to be alone." Theodore glanced at Borzoye. "We'll ride with you." A short while later, the three galloped through the western gate just as it was being closed.

Chapter XVI

Life on Dragonmont

Marcus and Anaya made it a habit of visiting with Alexa daily. The blind oracle enjoyed their company and, on occasion, could be *tricked* into speaking about her life in the future. The prefect found the conversations frustrating. In the back of his mind, he had an inkling of what some of those bizarre references were, but he couldn't bring them to the forefront.

It was early afternoon of the tenth day since their arrival on Novaroma. The midsummer day was hot and humid. Marcus picked up on a piece of information that he thought was useful. Alexa was relating a story from Mara about a famous fountain that stood in the northwest corner of the Dragonmont mesa for over a thousand years.

Marcus cared little for art, but his eyebrows shot up. "Eh. What's this? Tell me more."

Alexa frowned for a moment. "Mara's historical records indicate that about a hundred years from now one of Novaroma's most famous sculptors will convert a spring-fed well into a magnificent work of art."

"There's water up here?" Marcus knew that they needed a reliable water supply if they were to make the top of Dragonmont a respectable citadel. He glanced at the silvery-white pillar. "Maybe this Mara can actually produce some useful information. So where *precisely* is this famous fountain supposed to be erected?"

* * *

For the next two days, Marcus led a team of engineers in digging a six-foot-wide hole. For the first seven feet it was backbreaking pick-and-shovel work burrowing through the bedrock. Then the strata changed from granite to a porous pumice. The prefect decided to drill.

Sweat soaked through Marcus' linen tunic as he heaved on the pulley lifting the auger to the top of the tripod resting above the excavated hole. He wiped his brow and grinned. The drill bit was caked in wet pumice. "It looks like we're close." A moment later, water bubbled from the three-inch-wide opening. The two engineers who were at the base of the seven-foot hole yelped and scrambled up the ladder as water began to bubble up from the bore hole.

The engineers cheered as a pool formed in the basin and began to rise.

The prefect dropped a bucket tied to a rope. After he pulled it up, he dipped in a ladle and sipped. He smiled as he passed the dipper to Anaya, who sat on a nearby squared-off limestone block. "Clear and cold."

The princess smacked her lips after she drank. "You'd think that after all this time I'd stop doubting Alexa's assertions. I wish it wasn't so hard to wheedle information out of her."

"The oracle seems willing enough to share, but that demi-god Mara seems to fret about altering the future." Marcus frowned as he took the dipper back. He handed it to one of the engineers. "Finish walling off this shaft before we get flooded out. The oracle says this well will flow for at least a thousand years."

The engineer shuddered. "That woman terrifies me."

"She's a good person," Anaya responded in perfect Latin. "She just knows a few things that we don't."

"That's the truth." Marcus sighed. He watched his team start stacking blocks around the new well.

A decurion holding a trowel of mortar added, "When we're done, we'll have an aqueduct that will be the envy of Rome."

The mention of a world Marcus had no recollection of made him sigh. He shared a private glance with Anaya before responding, "Good drilling, men. The water is clean." He helped Anaya off the block where she was perched.

The humidity that had been building all morning finally released.

Marcus grabbed her hand as the first fat raindrop splattered on his head. "Come with me. I need to speak to the oracle about a new idea I have for laying the watch tower foundation."

"As long as I can review with her the billows design for my new coal-fired forge." Anaya hugged his arm. "One of the things I love about you is your restless mind. You're always trying to improve things."

The prefect laughed. "The only thing I don't want to change is you. You're perfect already." He sobered. "I hope all my talk about building doesn't bore you."

The princess gave him a coy look. "Nothing you do is ever boring."

As they hurried toward the infirmary building, he squeezed her hand and whispered, "I love you."

Anaya stomped her foot in a puddle, splashing him, and then giggled as she released his hand and dashed ahead of him.

The perfect followed. *You're my angel.* His thoughts drifted to a week earlier, sitting alone with her on the rough-hewn Dragonmont stockade. It was a clear full-moonlit night. He bared his soul to her about having no memory of anything prior to the evening when they were all abducted to this strange place.

Instead of being repulsed, Anaya vowed to help him force the pagan god Mara into returning his memory. "That goddess took your past away. Together, we'll find the means to make her return it." She leaned close and kissed him, which the prefect returned with enthusiasm. A minute later she gently pushed back and gasped, "I... I love you. Coming here wasn't a curse. It was karma. Don't ever forget *me*."

He remembered looking long into her eyes and uttering, "That would be impossible."

They stayed there talking late into the night. Any free time either had after that was spent in the company of the other.

Anaya took it as her duty to protect the man she was growing to love from any probing of his past. She strove to learn Latin and practiced it whenever she could.

On reaching the hospital's entrance, Marcus was shaken from his reverie by Anaya pointing to the sky. There a lone eagle drifted on the wind currents ahead of the rain shower clouds. "Did you notice that there doesn't seem to be any birds native to this land?"

Marcus watched the raptor wheel through the air and then dive into the forest to the north. He added, "And all the beasts that didn't come with us seem to be reptiles or amphibians."

Under the overhang of the infirmary's entrance stood a water basin and a fresh bar of soap on a crude table. He washed the grime and sweat from his face and dried off with a towel. "Alexa says this place, Novaroma, is in the equivalent to something called the early Mesozoic Era where we came from. She called our old home Earth."

Anaya pursed her lips. "I feel so stupid when I talk to that blind woman. I wish she'd speak plainly when she explains things."

Marcus smiled and hugged the princess. "You're just upset because you can't figure out how to forge that metal the oracle calls plexo-steel."

"It *is* remarkable. Lighter and stronger than anything I've ever seen." Anaya sighed and returned the embrace. "She calls it a carbon-fiber steel alloy that I could never duplicate with our technology."

Marcus saw a gleam in her eyes when she added, "But I'll try."

They entered the medical building, laughing.

Officially, it was both a clinic and the domicile of Doctor Phokas. It was the first structure built atop the mountain crest. The physician insisted that a proper medical center was of primary import. The T-shaped, single-story structure was fifty feet deep and a hundred feet wide, constructed from the thick blocks retrieved from the ruins. Baked clay tiles replaced the canvas tarps on the roof a week earlier. On the outside it was set up as a typical Roman nobleman's manor. Inside was a vestibule leading to an airy atrium. To the right was a large dining room set up to handle twenty guests, with a kitchen behind it. Behind the atrium was the doctor's office and a hospital ward holding twenty-four beds. To the left were the doctor's private quarters. Alexa lived with him. Their arrangement raised many eyebrows, but no one dared say anything.

As Marcus entered, he saw Alexa and Phokas sitting together on a rough-hewn wooden bench in the atrium. They both rose to greet the new arrivals.

The oracle leaned on a cane and winced as she stood.

To Marcus, Alexa appeared totally different from their initial encounter. Her original one-piece fitted suit was replaced by a simple, blue-dyed linen frock. The oracle did her best to remain as inconspicuous as she could in the Roman camp. However, being a tall blonde blind woman rumored to have magical powers made that impossible.

Along the atrium's back wall, looking out of place, was a gleaming, seven-foot-tall, silvery-white cylinder. The soot marks had been meticulously polished off by Alexa, who insisted on calling it Mara, and everyone who entered humored her.

In the twelve days they had been here, Marcus had never seen that inert, oversized tube give any indication that it was anything more than a lump of metal.

He was the first to speak. "Oracle, how's the leg feeling?"

"The good doctor says it'll be fine in a couple more weeks." Alexa smiled at Phokas. "And Mara concurs." She waved them to a pair of camp stools set up as chairs. "Please sit. Are you here to see Doctor Phokas or myself?"

"You." Anaya returned the smile and sat. The princess had gotten to know Alexa well since her first visit to Dragonmont. The oracle was one of only three people on Dragonmont who spoke Hindi and the only one who was a woman.

Without fumbling, Alexa moved to a sideboard where a platter of hard cheese and fresh bread rested. "Marcus, could you pour the wine? I still spill it."

"Certainly." The prefect strode to the same table and noticed several plates there with crumbs and olive pits on them. "Been having a lot of company?"

"Why, yes. Those delightful scholars, Borzoye and Theodore, were here early this morning. They have taken on the ambitious project of cataloging all of the local flora and fauna. They wanted to pick my brain regarding what I knew. I fear the information Mara gave me to share only fueled more questions." Alexa sighed. "I never knew there was such a diversity in reptiles. I was getting a headache repeating Mara's exact words. Thank goodness they both spoke Greek so I didn't have to say things twice."

Anaya eyed the silvery-white cylinder. "I think that if that *thing* spoke to me, I'd run away screaming in terror."

Alexa cocked her head. "Mara says she would never want to frighten you. She finds your questions very insightful."

"Ah, thanks, Mara," Anaya stuttered.

Alexa began slicing the cheese. "After Theodore and Borzoye left, Father Sixtus arrived, determined to save my soul by exorcising the demon Mara." She chuckled. "Even though I had to serve as the intermediary, the two of them had a fascinating theological debate."

"He didn't get abusive or threatening with you, did he?" Marcus finished pouring the wine into crude clay cups and recorked the decanter. "I won't stand for it."

Alexa sighed and put the knife down. "I did get a bit damp. Father Sixtus sprayed both Mara and me with holy water after the first dozen questions he asked. However, I believe he left satisfied that Mara wasn't a devil nor was I her fiend." She smirked. "In fact, he called Mara a 'blessed miracle' when I informed him that she holds a verbatim text of the Bible in her memory. Apparently, the good friar doesn't have one."

Phokas nodded. "It was a bit tense for a while, but his questions were honest, and he listened to the responses. Father Sixtus became so engrossed with the discussion he started calling Alexa, Mara." He chuckled. "I don't fault him on that. I sometimes don't know which of the two I'm arguing with at times."

The blind oracle turned and threw a fig in his direction. "Darling... er, Doctor Phokas, we don't *argue*. We discuss things. Mara only gets involved when asked, and I don't need her help dealing with *you*."

Phokas dodged the fruit as it flew by. "I'm also not so sure you're blind. That was a good aim." He rose and squeezed her shoulders. "Darling, you need to rest. Your body is still healing, and you've been working since early morning." He released her and turned toward the infirmary. "I'm going to check on my patients. When I return, you're taking a nap… Doctor's orders."

Alexa smiled as she placed the sliced cheese, bread, and some dried figs onto plates with deft hands. She turned her blind eyes toward her guests. "Marcus, could you take these?"

"Certainly." The prefect gathered the cups and plates, then returned to his seat beside Anaya.

Anaya sucked in a breath. "I have so many questions."

"Then let's begin." Alexa sipped her wine and smiled.

* * *

For an hour they discussed how to maintain a stable heat in Anaya's new forge, and then the proper depth for the watchtower's foundation, and the width-to-height ratio needed for the thirty-foot spire Marcus envisioned.

Ten minutes into the conversation Phokas returned, shook his head, and walked out again. "I need to gather more herbs for my poultices."

Marcus watched him leave and grew thoughtful. "All this needs to be recorded. We are learning so much, but it will be lost. The legion's scribe has very little ink and vellum. If we—"

There was a shout from the door. "Is Prefect Carloman here?"

Marcus didn't recognize the voice but responded, "Yes?"

A mud-splattered dispatch rider entered with tentative steps. He crossed himself at the sight of Alexa.

"I'm over here," Marcus snapped, feeling annoyed. "Stop staring at the oracle. She's not going to bite your head off. You have a message for me?"

"Sorry, sir. Yes, sir," was the quick reply. The messenger cleared his throat. "Legate Bernius requests you to organize a search party on the perimeter of Dragonmont's north slope."

"And what exactly should we to be looking for?" Marcus arched his brows.

"Two men. They headed this way a couple days ago from the strange building north of here and never returned." He glanced at Anaya. "They don't look Roman is all I know. The legate is doing this at the request of a new ally. Someone named Chang."

The corners of Anaya's eyes crinkled. "Chang is not a name used in the Gupta Empire. More people from still another country abducted to this magic land." A small smile creased Anaya's face. "Our projects can wait. You speak so many languages. Why don't *we* lead the search ourselves?"

Marcus scowled. "Waste of time. If they reached Dragonmont unaware, the guardian trees probably killed them."

"Come on. The rain stopped." Anaya glanced out the doorway and hopped to her feet. "It's possible they're just lost."

"Not likely." He shook his head. "Besides, the rain would have erased any tracks."

Anaya gave Marcus a sidelong look. "I'll ask Kewal to let you drive Raja."

The prefect's eyes lit up. He had been awestruck by the bull elephant since he first saw it. "All right, I guess an afternoon away from here won't hurt. The masons can't start the watchtower foundation until tomorrow." He turned to Alexa. "It looks like you'll get that nap Doctor Phokas ordered, after all."

They followed the courier from the room. Once outside, Marcus told him, "Inform Legate Bernius he'll have a report by this evening."

"Yes, Prefect." The messenger jogged to a tether line of fresh horses.

Marcus turned toward the east wall of the earth-and-timber stockade. Raja was in a makeshift stall there. Kewal sat beneath a nearby tarp, relaxing with a small group of legionnaires. Those soldiers were the legion's foragers because of their hunting and trapping skill. They served as one of the key teams responsible for providing fresh meat to the ever-ravenous legion and the budding colony.

Marcus could tell by the gesticulating hands that the old Gupta warrior was trying to learn the different Latin words for things. Almost from the first day, the white-haired bodyguard was accepted by the Roman legionnaires, if for no other reason

145

than the fact he had an elephant for a pet. The beast fascinated the soldiers. Those working with Kewal on hunting trips or quarrying tasks often brought fruit to feed Raja, acting like excited children when the animal's long truck swept the gifted morsel into its mouth.

As Marcus and Anaya approached, Kewal quirked an eyebrow and the legionnaires jumped to their feet, saluting.

Marcus regarded Raja and then spoke to the soldiers, "I have a job for you. It shouldn't be too onerous." He told them of the need to assemble a search party.

"One moment." Kewal rose and climbed to the top of the breastwork, gazing north. From there he could see the distant pagoda. He then followed the lay of the land from that point to the base of the mountain. After a few minutes he hopped down. "We can start the search now. If they got this far, I have a fair guess as to the path they took."

Chapter XVII

Iron Foot

As a child, Kewal grew up a peasant in the Himalaya mountains along the northern border of the Gupta Empire. He spent many long days hunting and trapping to supplement the meager crops his family's farm could produce from that hard scrabble ground. It was a difficult life. So, when the opportunity to join the Gupta army arose, he leapt at it.

Renowned locally for his tracking skills, he was hired by Anaya's father as a scout in a campaign against bandits infesting the mountain roads. Kewal possessed a quick mind and soon honed his combat skills to match his superlative ability as a tracker. Those abilities led him to be made the captain of the auxiliaries. He became the pasha's personal bodyguard when, standing alone beside the nobleman, he fought off four brigand assassins.

Kewal remained a loyal protector of the family for well over the next thirty years but never lost the tracking and hunting skills that won him acclaim as a youth.

* * *

Kewal glanced at Anaya approaching hand-in-hand and laughing with Marcus. He smiled at not being needed as a guardian much longer. It gladdened his heart to see her happy. He liked Marcus and thought of it as a good match. *I can now spend my time hunting the incredible beasts of this strange land.*

It took him a half hour to organize the requested search team with the necessary gear. Shortly after that, he led a detail of ten legionnaire trackers down the Dragonmont slope. Marcus and Anaya followed, astride Raja. The double-wide causeway was busy with heavy traffic of men and material flowing in both directions. No one gave the deadly trees lining the road more than a passing glance anymore. However, no one veered off the road either.

The foot of the mountain bustled with artisans shaping stone and trimming logs. Kewal led his team past the work groups on a packed dirt path. Following the perimeter of the deadly forest, the cleared trail transitioned to churned sawgrass and tree stumps and then to a shrub-choked meadow. On reaching the field, Kewal stayed as close to the woods as he dared. He walked slowly, swinging his head as he scanned the ground. Using the old Gupta warrior as the anchor point, his legionnaire team fanned out in a line about ten feet apart and duplicated the search pattern.

Marcus and Anaya followed, studying the ground from their elevated position on Raja's back.

Progress was slow in the knee-high vegetation. With an hour to go before sunset, Marcus was about to halt the search when Kewal called, "*Idhar dekho.*" He crouched by a spiny bush and pulled a tiny piece of hemp cloth free from the thorns. The Gupta bodyguard then studied the ground to the north for a moment before turning his attention to the ominous mountainside. There was a small gap in the forest where a couple guardian trees were down and charred from an apparent lightning strike. He turned to Marcus. "They tried to ascend the mountain here."

On nimble feet, he treaded along a felled truck into the eaves of the woods. Cupping his hands, Kewal shouted, "Hello. Is anyone there?" He almost slipped off the log when two of the thick-legged, horned herbivores common to the area around the Novaroman colony dashed into the clearing. They were apparently spooked from their concealment by his shout. As quickly as the animals were startled, they calmed. The dark-brown, four-legged reptiles stopped at a bristly bush a hundred yards away and started tearing at the foliage, their hard beaks impervious to the thorns.

* * *

Something about that activity bothered Marcus, but he didn't have time to consider it. He heard a weak rasp from up in the trees to his right. "Help me. Please help me." It was a

148

language he had never heard before but understood it. He shouted in Mandarin, "Where are you?"

"Help me," was the only response. The croaking voice was barely above a whisper, but Kewal with a focused stare pointed to the lower branches of a guardian tree about twenty feet inside the forest. "I see someone there."

Marcus squinted in that direction. "You're right." He dismounted and approached the woods, jabbing the ground with a spear butt. Before reaching the base of the outermost tree, he was wrestling with writhing roots for control of the spear. He lost. Retreating, he saw the spear vanish in the roiling ground. "Won't get there walking." He scratched the back of his neck and called one of the legionnaires over. "Go back to the work area and collect a lumberjack crew. We'll need to hack our way in."

The legionnaire saluted and jogged back the way they came.

Anaya called down from the back of the elephant, "We'll never clear a path before the sun sets, and it's too dangerous to chop guardian trees in the dark. That man needs help now."

Marcus gauged the sinking sun. "You're right." He sighed. "Pass down the iron boots you crafted and a long coil of rope."

A sack fell to the ground with a heavy thud. Anaya dismounted Raja with the rope. "What's the plan?"

Marcus was already strapping the boots to his feet. To the prefect, calling them boots was a misnomer. They were rectangular iron plates, twelve inches long, eight inches wide and an inch thick, each one weighing about thirty pounds. Experiments with various sizes and shapes over the previous week showed that this size and material was the smallest possible configuration that would "fool" the guardian trees into not reacting.

"What do you think you're doing?" Anaya squeaked. "That's just a prototype. I don't even know if the straps will hold."

A bull-necked legionnaire named Batista walked up. "Sir, we'll be able to get whoever is trapped in there out tomorrow morning. Let's wait."

Marcus shook his head. "You heard that man's voice. I don't believe he—or they—will be alive by morning. We need to try something now."

Batista straightened to attention. "Then, sir, I volunteer. You're the prefect. We can't afford to risk you."

Marcus patted him on the shoulder. "I have to go. I'm the only one who knows their language." He smiled and looked at the people gathered around him. "Unless one of you speaks Mandarin." He knotted one end of the rope into a harness across his chest and handed the other end to Anaya. "Hook this end to Raja's howdah. If one of those cursed trees grabs me, yank me out of there fast."

Kewal and Batista helped Marcus walk as close as they dared go to the forest eaves. Not only was the footwear heavy, but its width forced the prefect to splay his legs and walk with an awkward gait.

By the time he reached the foot of the tree, the prefect was panting and sweating profusely and almost toppled to the ground twice. Looking up, just beyond the reach of his outstretched arms he saw someone sitting on a thick branch with his back against the tree's trunk. The man's pain-ravaged eyes locked on to Marcus. "Help me, please."

"That's what I'm here for." Marcus tried to put confidence in his voice. "I was told there were two of you. Where's your friend?"

The pained eyes took on a deep sorrow. "Dead. These demon trees took him." He shook his head. "Ying could have saved himself, but he rescued me instead." A tear slipped down his cheek. "I am unworthy. When we first entered this forest, a root grabbed me. Ying wrenched me free, but it tore something inside my knee. I could not walk. He tried to carry me, but more roots sprang from the ground. Ying shoved me up here, and then... and then he was pulled underground. I could hear his muffed screams and cracking bones for another minute and then... silence. For two days, silence. Nothing for company but those horned reptiles."

"Can you climb down?" Marcus looked back along his tethered line and saw his people holding firm to it. Kewal stood dangerously close to the forest edge.

"Yes, but it is to no avail. I fear my one leg is useless. But even if it was whole, these trees are possessed. They will attack me." He squinted at Marcus and gasped. "How is it that they do not attack you?"

Marcus shifted one of his weighted legs. "I'm wearing special boots that ward me against their magic." He regarded the pained and exhausted man above him. "What's your name?"

"Shi. I'm an acolyte to the Shaolin priesthood."

"Okay, Shi. I believe that the person who leads your group requested us to search for you. Someone named Chang."

A tear moistened Shi's cheek. "Chang is not only my leader, but he is also my brother." He wheezed. "What is it you'd have me do?"

"Lower yourself so I can grab you." Marcus pointed to the people in the clearing. "Then I'll carry you to safety from this forest."

The lame man nodded, took a deep breath, wrapped his arms around the branch, and let go.

Marcus felt the man spasm and heard him bite back a scream of pain as he caught him. Although Shi was very light, the prefect almost stumbled as he took Shi's full weight. Marcus turned toward the open glade. The twenty feet looked like an impossible distance. He made one ponderous step then another. Nine feet from safety, disaster struck. The leather bands on his left foot snapped, and he fell to the ground. Without thinking he flipped onto his back so he wouldn't crush the smaller man in his arms. He heard Kewal roar, "Pull."

Raja, prodded by Anaya, trumpeted and backed up.

Marcus felt roots twine around his body, but the rope, digging into his chest, inexorably continued to move. He felt the writhing growths try to rip Shi from his grasp. Marcus closed his eyes and gripped tighter. He heard men shouting and saw the gleam of the setting sun on axes.

Although it seemed like an eternity, moments later he was in the open, being dragged across brambles with Anaya screaming at Raja to stop.

Marcus felt gentle hands help him sit up. The familiar scent of jasmine filled his nostrils.

Anaya's face was in front of his. "Are you okay?"

Marcus nodded and released his grip on Shi, who had passed out. "Take care, his leg is broken or something." He looked at Batista. "We need to set it before we move him."

Legionnaires carefully lifted the injured man and laid him on a spread blanket.

Marcus tried to pull off the harness, but it was dug into his leather breastplate.

Kewal cut the rope with a short, razor-sharp knife. "That was a very close call, young man."

Marcus nodded and rolled his arms. His chest hurt, but he didn't think any ribs were cracked. His tunic was in tatters, and one iron boot was still firmly attached to his foot. "I don't want to ever do that again." He looked over at Shi with concern. "How's our friend?"

Batista had Shi in a sitting position and was dribbling water from a flask into his mouth. "His breathing's regular."

Glancing around, the prefect's eyes rested on the brown, grazing reptiles. The meat of those animals was becoming a favorite of the soldiers. However, the bony crest framing their horned heads and plate-like scales covering their flanks made the seven-foot-long, five-foot-tall animals difficult to kill. Its hide was impervious to arrows, and approaching it with spears either caused them to flee or roused the normally docile creature to strike out with their two-foot-long horns.

The creatures were the predominant foraging species roaming the fields and forests surrounding their small colony. The legionnaires discovered early on that the reptiles, although impervious to most local predators, were not very bright. They easily became entangled in snares. Once trapped, they could be flipped over and stabbed in their soft underside.

It was then that Marcus came to the realization. "Those beasts were spooked *out* of the woods." He remembered Lucius telling him about encountering the dragon on Dragonmont's plateau. It was one of these creatures that the dragon was chasing when it stumbled into the Romans' camp.

The prefect exclaimed, "The guardian trees don't attack those horned creatures."

It seemed obvious to all once he said it.

Anaya, sitting beside Marcus, responded. "There's only one way to find out for sure." She called to Kewal. "Retrieve the ropes from Raja's saddlebags."

When the first lasso encircled the docile creature's head, it bolted, dragging the unfortunate legionnaire with it. However, twenty yards into its rampage, the one-and-a-half-ton creature forgot why it was running and stopped to forage. Surrounding the beast, legionnaires looped lassos around its horned head. As the animal bucked, other lines snared its legs. Dodging its thrashing head, they flipped the immobilized creature over with long poles.

Kewal licked his chops and hooted, "We'll eat well tonight," in almost understandable Latin.

Stabbing the soft underbelly, the legionnaires killed and gutted the overturned creature.

Marcus watched with interest. "Bring me one of the legs, intact."

A pair of legionnaires nodded, retrieved two camp saws, and cut through the thick bone and muscle of one of the hind legs.

Marcus hefted the gore-covered limb and examined it. The leg bone was sawed through about eighteen inches from the bottom, and the foot itself seemed to be roughly oval, thirteen inches long and six inches wide. "A lot lighter than those steel disks." He carried it to the edge of the forest and wiped the outside clean with the cloak he cast aside on entering the woods for the rescue. Although dark-brown scales covered the shank, the bottom of the foot was a thick, black, fibrous pad with three blunt nails.

Anaya walked with him. "I don't see anything special about it."

"Only one way to find out." Marcus shrugged and retrieved a spear. He jammed it into the sinuous muscle of the leg cavity.

Kewal and those legionnaires not field dressing the dead beast or caring for Shi gathered to watch. They followed the prefect, axes in hand, as he approached the forest.

Marcus reached the clearly discernable point where he was dragged out of the woods and slid the foot at the end of the spear shaft forward. Nothing happened. He slid it forward as far as he could reach. Nothing happened.

Marcus gulped and pulled the foot back. After studying it for a second, he called out, "Be ready to grab me." Using the impaled foot as a walking stick, he stepped forward. The ground immediately began to roil and he leapt back.

An excited buzz broke out among everyone present.

Marcus handed the spear with the impaled foot to Kewal. "I think we just discovered what an iron-foot boot is made from." He glanced at the sky. The sun was touching the western mountains. "Stabilize Shi's leg, gather the carcass, and let's get back before dark. Tomorrow, we'll clean these legs out and see if they can be molded into proper boots."

Chapter XVIII

No rest for the weary

Lucius lay in bed and kissed Meili's forehead as she slept beside him. He felt content for the first time in his *short life*. But he still could not relax. His mind churned with the needs of his nascent colony. He knew thousands of people depended on his leadership to survive the harrowing dangers of this bizarre land.

Dawn was just a faint glow on the eastern horizon when Lucius heard a horse canter up the path to the pagoda. He heard muffled voices exchange challenge and response. The legate sighed and rose in search of his discarded tunic and breeches.

Meili woke with a start. "What's the matter?"

Lucius sat on the edge of the bed and pulled on his sandals. He sighed. "Messengers arriving at dawn never bring good news."

Meili nodded and slipped on her hanfu. "Why can't they grant you a single night's peace?"

A smile creased the legate's face as he caressed her face. "I hope there are thousands more opportunities for us to seek bliss."

Meili grabbed his hand and squeezed it. "That also is my fondest desire. If—"

The raised voice of the sentry outside the guest rooms could be heard, "The legate left explicit orders that he was not to be disturbed."

"It's all right." Lucius shouted as he fished through his mind for the sentry's name. "Cyrus. Admit the dispatch rider."

A few moments later Cyrus, a lean young Frank, led a short Iberian-featured man with a thick beard and wearing a leather breastplate and greaves into the room.

Meili lit a lantern by the bedstead and sat.

"Well, what's the message?" Lucius donned his harness and sword.

The rider's eyes focused on Meili. "It's a military communique, Legate."

"Of course it's a military communique. What else would there be at this hour?"

"Sorry, sir." He removed his sweat-stained leather cap and wiped his brow. "This place was awful hard to find in the dark. No paths, no signs, and nighttime noises that unnerve a man."

Lucius felt sympathy for the rider. "It's okay. This land gives all of us the shakes. What is the *urgent* message?"

The rider's face darkened. "Dire news, sir. The troops posted at the river crossing were decimated. The word from the three survivors was that Jette led the attack. And there were a number of strangely garbed warriors with him."

"That traitor will be dealt with," Lucius snapped as rage rose in him.

"There's more, Legate." The man glanced around. "A dragon attacked the quarry work crew shortly after sunset. The guards attempted to ward off the monster, but their weapons were useless. Many died. The survivors fled to the Gupta palace where they're holed up now."

Lucius sank onto the edge of the bed. "There hasn't been a dragon attack since that first night. I should have known our good fortune wouldn't last." He glanced out the window at the gray morning. "We return to Dragonmont immediately." His face hardened. "I'm tired of sitting back on defense. As with every enemy we faced in the past, any man or monster that chooses to fight the Red Fist Legion will be eradicated." He thought about his closed-off mind. *Good men are dying because I am not prepared. I must find a way to force this... Mara to free my mind.*

Lucius saw the fear in both the guard's and the rider's eyes shift to confidence. He shuddered internally. *It's confidence in me.* He glanced at the mud-splattered messenger. "Go get some rest. It will be a busy day."

The two soldiers left the room.

Lucius did not move from where he sat deep in thought. He was startled by a soft touch on his shoulder.

"What was the news?" Meili sat beside him. "It seemed to disturb you greatly."

Lucius related what he had learned in Mandarin and added how impervious dragons were to the legion's weapons.

Meili frowned. "Why not use crossbows? My brother fought with one and said he could punch a hole in the thickest armor."

The term held no meaning to the legate, so Meili described the weapon her brother showed her on one of his visits.

Lucius eyes lit with understanding. "Like a handheld ballista." He smacked his fist into an open palm. "Not only is my memory gone, but I'm also a fool. I named this land, Novaroma, but I didn't grasp the full meaning of what that could entail." He rose and paced the room. "We have scholars here from the greatest empires. They are here for a purpose, but I refused to see it."

He sat next to Meili and grasped her hand. "Tell me more about the wonders of the Lui Song dynasty." Lucius was surprised at the details the beautiful woman could recall of the marvels she saw in the city of Jiankang.

They were still talking when the room brightened from the rising sun. Lucius rose. "Come with me to Dragonmont." He chuckled. "Crossbows, stirrups for saddles... I see the uses for many of the things you described, but I don't possess an engineer's mind."

"Of course," Meili responded in a soft voice. "Is that the only reason you wish me to come?"

A broad smile creased the legate's face. "I hope you'll always be by my side."

Meili blushed.

Minutes later, Lucius stood in the common room, giving instructions to the two centurions commanding the Novaroman troops on the Jiankang grounds. All of the pagoda's residents hurriedly joined them, even though their words were indecipherable.

Lucius swept his arms in a circle. "I want a stockade around this building complex that's tall enough and strong enough to hold out a dragon. Until we eradicate them, people will need sanctuaries."

"Yes, Legate. It looks like there's good lumber in the forest north of here. We can start—"

A new dispatch rider entered the building, jogged over, and saluted. "Legate, Prefect Carloman sends his regards and wanted to inform you that a search party found one of the missing people." He glanced around at the group crowded in the room. "He looks a lot like these folks."

"At least one piece of good news." Lucius called Chang over and relayed the information.

"Only one person?" Chang repeated slowly.

Lucius confirmed the question.

"Yes, Legate. I was with the search party that found him. His one leg was busted up pretty bad, but he'll survive. I didn't understand his words, but Prefect Carloman said the survivor's name was Shi. The man said the guardian trees took his friend."

Lucius nodded and relayed the information to Chang.

The stoic priest showed emotion for the first time. "My little brother's alive. May I see him... please?"

"Of course." The legate rested his hand on the monk's shoulder. "We leave immediately."

Chapter XIX

New Discoveries

The early morning air was already thick with humidity, promising a hot, sticky late-spring day. Lucius contemplated the bitter news and was frustrated. Like everyone else, he understood little about the dangers in this new land. Unlike everyone else, he was responsible for overcoming those dangers. *Good men are dying because I'm learning the realities of this place at too slow a pace.* He pulled a sheet of vellum from his satchel and scribbled a long note. He rolled it up and pressed his seal on it.

Meili, wearing her ragged hanfu, watched him write in the strange script. "What are those marks you are making?"

"Instructions for my people." He sighed. "But I must be very careful. There are so many unknowns."

Meili nodded. "Perhaps you can find a way to confront this demon Mara directly and wrest the knowledge you need from her."

"Yes, but that is easier said than done." Lucius grimaced while wrapping and placing the seal and stylus back in his pack. "It's not just this land. I don't know *myself*. My mind is blank. I *know* my actions and decisions are more than intuitive, but how can I be confident of them if I don't know what experiences I'm drawing on." He set his jaw. "You're right. This morning, we travel to Dragonmont. I intend to press the oracle. She's our only link to Mara, and this demigod is the only one with any answers."

Meili cocked her head and then kissed Lucius. "I'll be right back. Alexa and Mara aren't the only ones who can help you."

"Meet me outside," he called to her as she ran out the door.

Lucius turned toward the exit beyond the common room and found a century of legionnaires camped on the grounds there. There were two dispatch riders standing at attention beside their mounts near the building's portico. He strode to the rider on the left and handed him the sealed scroll. "Atticus is the senior tribune at the encampment. I want him to place a full *cohort* at the river crossing and build a stockade blocking all access to that junction by nightfall."

"Yes, Legate."

Lucius put his hand on the man's shoulder. "Also, tell Atticus to send a team of auxiliaries to the Gupta palace with the materials to build four ballistae. If that building is to be a refuge for our troops, then it must be defensible against a dragon attack."

"Yes, sir. I understand." The rider put the scroll in his saddlebag, mounted, and galloped away.

Lucius turned to the other messenger. "Ride ahead to Dragonmont and inform the prefect that I am coming and we need to talk."

The dispatch rider saluted. "As you command, Legate." He mounted and rode off.

Lucius scanned the open land around the pagoda and grunted. He turned to the centurion, who approached while he was instructing the messengers. "This structure will be our northernmost outpost. I want it secure and defensible."

"I understand, sir. We'll start on the barricade immediately."

Lucius nodded. "Thank you—" He turned at the sound of someone running toward him. It was Meili carrying a large object.

Panting but smiling, she handed it to him. "I heard Feng bragging at the banquet before we were whisked to this land about the gift he received from the emperor. I found it stored in the treasure trove in his suite of rooms." She handed the legate an ornately carved crossbow inlaid with a gold filigree and a quiver of steel-headed bolts. "This is the weapon I called a crossbow. As I was told by my brother, it is far more deadly and accurate than an ordinary bow."

Lucius pressed the stock against his shoulder and aimed it. "It's heavy, but I can see its potential." He showed it to the centurion and his guards who stood nearby. He pointed to the lanky Frank. "Cyrus, give this thing a try."

Cyrus took the weapon, and after examining it with the legate, wound the crank and loaded one of the bolts. Aiming it at a nearby jujube tree, he pulled the trigger. He let out a low whistle as the projectile buried itself four inches into the trunk. He handed it back to Lucius with his appraisal. "A powerful weapon, but slow to load."

Lucius slung it over his shoulder. "I'll find a use for it. Time to go."

Accompanied by three bodyguards, Chang, and Meili, Lucius was silent for most of the one-mile trek to the paved road at the base of Dragonmont.

Lucius acknowledged Horatius when the decurion joined the legate's entourage at the foot of the mountain. He handed him the crossbow. "Carry this for me. It might help us with our dragon problem."

"Yes, Legate." Curiosity lit Horatius' eyes, but he held his tongue while cradling the strange weapon.

Lucius was not in the mood for conversation. His reverie wasn't broken until he was forced to pause before the newly completed thick timber gate of the citadel on Dragonmont's crest. Despite his black mood, he paused to admire the craftmanship of the heavy portal as the guards heaved at the pulley ropes to open it.

He marched straight to Phokas' infirmary with Horatius, Chang and Meili, leaving his bodyguards outside. "I want no one entering except by my leave."

Inside, he found Alexa sitting in the atrium with Anaya, Theodore, Marcellus, and Borzoye. On a cushioned couch lay Shi being tended by Phokas. Marcus sat beside the doctor, interpreting.

Although Lucius was steeling himself to challenge the oracle, his heart was warmed by Chang's cry of happiness, "Shi," as the monk hurried forward and embraced his brother.

Marcus rose, gave Chang his seat, and walked over to Lucius. "Your messenger arrived twenty minutes ago about needing to meet. His words indicated it did not involve any of the tribunes. So, it's not about the twin disasters that struck us yesterday?"

"It is and it isn't." Lucius sighed. "I sent out my orders at first light. But I'm reacting to problems, not solving them." The legate then reviewed the dispatches with the prefect.

"Atticus is young and ambitious. He'll manage those efforts."

A smile quirked at the corner of Lucius' mouth. He turned to Meili, who was standing back observing. In Mandarin he spoke to Marcus. "This is Meili, a skilled healer who I met at the unusual wooden building north of here. She presented me with a weapon that might be effective against dragons."

Meili bowed and blushed. "Lucius is kind, but he overstates my contributions."

"Lucius... is it." Marcus grinned at his friend.

Lucius smiled. "Perhaps. But it is something for you to employ your engineering skills on." He signaled Horatius forward.

Marcus' eyes lit with understanding as he scanned the weapon the decurion carried.

Lucius stated, "It's called a crossbow and has far greater penetrating power than any ranged weapon we possess. However, it is unwieldy and slow to load."

Marcus' eyebrows arched as he took the crossbow and examined it. "I can see that." He called Anaya over. "Darling, we have a project."

"Another one?" She touched the crank and drawstring. "A dragon's hide is tough, but with arrowheads fashioned from that hard metal, plexo-steel and powered by a bow like this, we could penetrate it." Her eyes twinkled. "Almost as interesting as our other discovery."

Lucius glanced between the two. "Something else? Please tell me its good news."

"Actually, it's more of an accidental discovery." Marcus coughed. "When we rescued Shi, I noticed that those large, horned herbivores that we see grazing everywhere move in and out of the guardian trees unmolested."

Anaya added, "Like iron, there is something in their feet that repels the roots. Only it's far lighter. We started experiments today to determine the optimum dimensions and thickness to use for our 'iron boots.'"

"Amazing," Lucius exclaimed. "It was right there in front of us from almost the first day." The smile slipped from his face. "Will you excuse us for a minute? I need to speak with Marcus in private." He felt frustrated that he had to repeat the request three times, in Hindi, Mandarin, and Latin.

Marcus handed the crossbow back to Horatius as Lucius led him to the unoccupied dining alcove.

"What else is going wrong?" Marcus whispered as they reached the secluded room.

"I intend to force Mara to give me back my memories. Are you with me?"

"Of course I am. Like you, I sense my past, but cannot grasp it." Marcus' voice took on a nervous edge. "Even if we figured a way to contact Mara, it's risky to let her touch our minds."

"Yes," was Lucius' bitter response. "But I can't go on like this. I'm living a lie and feel like half a man."

Marcus stepped back and crossed his arms. "What's your plan?"

Lucius turned his gaze to the blind woman sitting in the open atrium. "Alexa's the key."

"It won't be easy." Marcus rubbed his clean shaved face. "We'll need to include others. I suggest Phokas and Anaya. They both know our secret."

"And Meili," Lucius smiled. "I told her last night."

Marcus' eyebrows shot up. "She must be something. You just met her yesterday."

"Yes. She is special."

"When?"

"This afternoon, in your quarters." Lucius pointed at the seven-foot cylinder in the outer room. "I want the conversation private and out of earshot of that... thing."

* * *

That afternoon, the five people gathered in Marcus' quarters. Although the Roman military typically placed their headquarters at the central-most point of their encampments, on Dragonmont it was different. Doctor Phokas' home and infirmary held that position, and an academy for the scholars was being erected next to it.

When Marcus laid out the footprint for the new citadel, he observed that the remains of what once must have been an advanced workshop remained partially intact near the northern edge of the plateau. Although tight against the palisades on that side, he selected that location for the site for his home. Using the unusual foundation, he built a simple three-room structure with the central area set up for dining and entertaining, the alcove to the right as the bedchambers, and the room on the left as a storeroom. It was here that he collected as many of the curiosities discovered in the ruins as he could gather. When on Dragonmont, he spent every evening with Anaya examining the artifacts. Together they spent long hours speculating about their purpose before retiring to the bedroom.

The two of them greeted Lucius and Meili when they arrived. The conversation was stilted as they waited for Phokas and Alexa. Anaya's Latin was limited, and Meili spoke only Mandarin.

The last two arrived a half hour later. Anaya offered wine, dried olives, and fresh-baked bread as the newcomers sat down.

Phokas tore a chunk from a loaf and handed it to Alexa. "Okay, you got us here. Now tell me why we couldn't talk about this topic at my place. I have patients to tend to."

Marcus spread his hands. "We wanted to have a conversation with Alexa out of earshot of that demon."

Lucius strode to Alexa and sat beside her. "Oracle, I need to learn all there is to know about this cursed place, and I need to know who I am."

Alexa appeared startled by the abrupt words. "Regarding this land, I will ask Mara whatever it is you wish." She sighed. "Regarding your past, she will not open the locks that block your access to those memories. Mara fears changing what to her is history. She believes she walks a very fine line."

Lucius jabbed a finger toward the blind woman. "I don't care about her precious history. I care about my people." He threw his hands in the air. "Look. I believe you are a good person, but you're in the way. I want her to tell me that directly."

"That's impossible." Alexa answered with a flat voice. "Let me try to explain again. You won't understand what is involved, but listen to my words about what happened."

The blind oracle folded her hand on her lap and dipped her head. "Like you, I was *born* a replicant, but unlike you, I was possessed by a cyborg... a demon. Mara deleted... destroyed that demon and freed me. As a result of that exorcism, our minds became... joined at the spot where the demon existed. That link inside my mind is how we communicate. That is why you can't speak with her directly."

Rubbing her hands together, Alexa sighed. "I am Mara's *only* connection to the outside world." She raised her head. "The energy... magic burst from what happened two weeks ago was horrific. It overloaded... broke all of her external sensors."

"That explains nothing," Lucius shot back. "All I understand is that Marcus and I are some sort of motherless children conjured here along with thousands of innocent people." He glared at her. "Apparently for the sole entertainment of some noncommunicative demigod."

Alexa clenched her hands into fists. "Lucius and Marcus, I know why Mara... caused you to be born and why she abducted everyone to this... land. I was her *willing* accomplice, and I would do it again in an instant. It was the only choice to save humanity."

The conversation was in Latin. So only Lucius, Marcus, and Phokas heard everything Alexa said. Anaya picked up the general gist and Meili read the shifting emotions on the people's faces.

Lucius looked like he was ready to explode, but Marcus spoke first with careful words. "You mentioned a spot where the demon once existed. It is where you and Mara now meet. Why can't *we* go there?"

"Impossible." Alexa chuckled. "As I said, that *spot* is inside my head."

"Impossible?" Marcus persisted. "Mara has a way to travel there. There must be a way for us to do the same."

165

"The link is..." Alexa paused and cocked her head. "Is it really that critical?"

Lucius jumped in. "Yes. This land is running red with the blood of my slaughtered people. I will bring that to an end."

"There *may* be a way." Alexa turned her blind eyes in the direction of Doctor Phokas. "Darling, are the dun-colored garments found on our first day here still intact?"

The gray-haired physician rubbed his jaw. "Yes. There's a half dozen of them hanging in the back room of the infirmary."

The oracle nodded. "Marcus, are the solar cells... er, the black glass framed in a silvery metal with cables hanging from them still about?"

"The three undamaged ones we found I have stored right here in my quarters." Marcus quirked an eyebrow. "But neither Anaya nor I can discern what purpose they serve."

Lucius grew impatient. "What does any of this have to do with talking to the Mara god?"

Alexa clicked her tongue. "Speaking with Mara is not a boon that can be granted simply because it was requested." She pursed her lips. "Mara thinks there's a way. The black glass can collect... power from the sun. They are called solar cells. If we connect them to the neural-net... er, those strange garments with special wires, we can transfer some of that power into those clothes."

Marcus squinted. "How does that help?"

Alexa pursed her lips. "It may be possible to create a communications channel from you to those suits, then from your suits to one I wear, and from there directly into my mind... In theory it could work."

"Fine. It sounds absurd. But if that is the condition the demigod choses to set..." Lucius slapped his leg. "...we'll do it now."

Alexa shook her head. "It's not that easy. I will say words that have little meaning to you, but try to comprehend the concept. The solar cells create something called electricity from the sun's rays. It is like... lightning. The neural-net suits work on a different power source called photonics. One can be extracted from the other, but it is terribly inefficient. It will require about two days of sunlight to produce enough energy for the communication link."

"Make it so," Lucius growled.

"Go about your duties. I will summon you when the suits are ready." Alexa turned her blind eyes to Doctor Phokas. "Go with Marcus for those materials. Position them on the roof facing south." She squeezed the doctor's hand. "To channel that power into the suits I will need something called plexo-photonic cables. There should have been a couple spools of it lying around."

Lucius snapped, "Magic glass, enchanted garments, charmed cables, capturing the sun's power." He growled, "Very well, you have your two days. The delay can't be helped."

"Plexo-photonic cable?" Marcus squinted.

"Yes, it's like a metallic cord... about the thickness of twine."

Marcus furrowed his brow. "I think I have a spindle of that substance in storage here. I could not determine any discernable use for it."

"Two days, no more." Lucius rose. "I've been absent from my command overlong." He spoke rapid Mandarin, explaining what transpired to Meili.

The former courtesan blanched, and then her eyes narrowed at Alexa. "If any harm comes to Lucius, I *will* kill you."

Chapter XX

Confrontation with Mara

It was three days and not two before Lucius received the message that all was ready. Over that time the tribe called cyborgs and their allies could be seen roaming along the eastern bank of the river, but none attempted to cross.

Lucius did not waste those days. A rough-cut timber watchtower was erected by the shallow stretch of the Reno River along with a twenty-foot-tall palisade blocking the one-hundred-sixty-foot gap. Mounted patrols monitored activity from that only known crossing point to the sea, sixteen miles south of there. Also, stockades were raised around the Jiankang, Gundeshapur, and Agraharas Learning Centers, making them safe havens against the large native predators. The legate was everywhere overseeing the defensive projects. Messengers had trouble finding him, and his bodyguards were exhausted trying to keep up.

Lucius expected the dragon to return to the quarry area and directed team of workers to dig pits and stack dry, pitch-covered wood around the work camp. He then waited with a century of legionnaires.

On the second night, two hours past sunset, the beast returned, hungry for more prey. The dragon roared as it charged into the silent camp. Although the scent of humans was everywhere and butchered meat was impaled on tall poles, the site appeared vacant.

Lucius rose from a shallow hole where he lay hidden and shouted, "Fire." He sparked a torch and thrust it into the stack of wood beside him.

Around the camp, soldiers clambered from similar hiding spots, uncovering hooded lanterns. They lit and fired arrows, wrapped in oil-soaked rags, turning the stacked wood into roaring bonfires. Soldiers armed with torches followed Lucius into the circle of fires toward the howling, disoriented dragon.

The three spikes on its tail confirmed to Lucius that it was a young one. He lunged in when the dragon reared up at a squad of torch-bearing legionnaires. After a single deep cut from the legate's plexo-steel sword, it bellowed and spun around, its claws raked Lucius' scaled mail shirt, tossing him to the ground. Legionnaires rushed to their leader's defense, throwing jars of oil corked with burning rags at the beast. Flames engulfed the dragon as those urns shattered against its tough hide.

Bellowing, the burning dragon ran in circles, seeking an escape path. Blinded by the fire, it found none.

Scrambling to his feet, Lucius cleared his head and stalked the dragon. Each time it slowed, he struck. The third time, his plexo-steel blade bit deep into the dragon's side and it fell to the ground. It took five minutes to stop twitching.

Lucius sheathed his sword and raised his arms, with a feral grin spread across his face. "I don't believe that beast will trouble us anymore."

The gathered legionnaires cheered and began chanting, "Dragon slayer, dragon slayer."

Horatius, holding a shield and spear, stood protectively at the legate's side, grunted. "I hope all that fire didn't ruin the temper of the beast's hide." He eyed the red sheen of Lucius' dragon-scale mail shirt. "It makes excellent armor."

Lucius sobered. "Hopefully, when we acquire more in the future, it's because we are hunting them and not them hunting us."

"Amen, Legate. Amen."

* * *

Over those same three days Marcus had not rested either. After he collected and assembled the components Alexa requested, he spent his time either with Anaya, working on her crossbow project, or with the Roman tanners shaping the amputated iron-foot legs into knee-high boots.

Midmorning of the third day, Lucius, Meili, and Anaya gathered in Marcus' quarters, examining the first prototype of Anaya's newly designed crossbow.

A small smile creased her face as she watched Lucius test the crossbow's pulley system. "Your ambush of that dragon impressed Kewal. He claims you're the most competent commander he's ever worked for."

"No. Don't say that." Lucius lowered the crossbow. "I lost almost a hundred good soldiers over the last couple weeks because of my failings."

Meili, who had learned Latin rapidly, hissed. "How can you say that? You held us together when we were dumped in this bizarre land." She faced him. "You've dealt with trees that can crush a man, dragons in the mountains, limnonectes from the sea, and a mysterious, bloodthirsty tribe in the marshlands across the river."

"I haven't solved *any* of those problems," Lucius lamented.

Anaya raised her chin. "You emboldened us to face those terrors. You gave us confidence that there is no obstacle we can't overcome. You gave us hope."

"I must do better." Lucius' shoulders sagged.

Marcus swept his arms wide. "You are not alone. These problems *will* be solved. Together, we'll overcome all of them." He cocked his head. "We now know what we don't know. Soon we will confront the demon, Mara, and wrest the answers we need from her."

Lucius nodded his head. "You're right." He spotted his aide, Marcellus, jogging toward the open front door, and waved him in. "Marcellus, what is it?"

The young man saluted Lucius. "The witch Alexa says all is ready." His voice squeaked. "Legate, she scares me. Stay away from her."

"Marcellus, you faced dragons, enemy raiding parties, and limnonectes without flinching. You can handle a harmless blind woman." Lucius snorted. "Tell her we will be there this evening." Watching his aide hurry away, he stretched. "I need a nap. When I face this evil spirit, I want my wits at their sharpest."

He glanced at Marcus. "Summon whoever you think we may need for support." The legate sighed. "I'm going to sleep the rest of the day. Don't disturb me."

Meili gave him a coy smile. "I bet I could keep you awake."

The legate grinned. "You could keep me up the rest of the day and all night." He turned serious. "But I must be ready. I've heard that demons are cunning. They can turn a man's own words against him."

"Then don't do this." Meili paled. "The oracle admits to willingly serving this demon. She seems like a good person, but that might be a facade. It could be an elaborate enchanted trap."

"I don't think so," Marcus added. "This Mara conjured Lucius and myself. If we were to become possessed, I suspect she could have easily done it then."

"For my own sanity, I must find out who or what I really am." The legate's voice took on a note of desperation. "I cannot continue to live a lie."

Meili took his hands and gazed into the legate's eyes. "To stay alive in my... previous profession, I needed to read people. Lucius, the accident of your birth has nothing to do with who you are. You are the finest, most honorable man I know."

"I love you." The legate pushed back a lock of her long hair and brushed a soft kiss on her cheek. "Tonight, I hope to learn... I *must* learn who I am." He squeezed her hands, shuffled to a cot in the corner of the open room. He collapsed onto it and did not move until a clap of thunder shook him awake. It was dark outside.

* * *

Lucius walked with Meili, Marcus, and Anaya past guttering torches in the hard rain. Horatius and a decade of legionnaires trailed after them. Besides Phokas and Alexa, there were four other people waiting for them at the infirmary to observe the confrontation.

Lucius, unsure what facing a demon would entail, summoned the Christian priest Father Sixtus, the Shaolin priest Chang, the Byzantine scholar Theodore, and the Persian academician Borzoye to observe.

Although there were several patients being treated in the infirmary that day, Doctor Phokas moved them out. "For all I know, there could be fire and brimstone raining down on us." He chuckled. No one thought it was funny.

As they reached the building, Lucius pulled Horatius aside. "Allow no one entry without express permission of myself... or Doctor Phokas." He looked inside and saw Marcus examining one of the strange garments. Alexa already had hers on.

Looking around the grounds, Lucius saw dozens of legionnaires arming themselves and gathering in the open, despite the steady rain. He nodded to them, and as one they raised their arms in salute. Several shouted, "We're here for you, Legate."

He returned the salute and turned to Horatius. "Does everyone in camp know I'll be interrogating the demon?"

Horatius chuckled. "Yes, unless they're deaf. It's been the primary discussion around the campfires for the last two days. Some fear the demon will kill you. Some believe you will destroy the demon and free us from its curse."

"Where do you stand?"

The decurion dug his heel in the mud and sighed. "Legate, I'm not a learned man. This devil, no doubt, brought us here. But I think in doing so, she expended all of her power. I say ignore her. I believe she is impotent to grant us succor or do us harm. The dangers of this land fall on us to deal with."

Lucius patted Horatius on the shoulder. "I think you are close to the mark." He shook his head. "But I still need answers, and I intend to get them." He lowered his voice to a whisper. "If something goes wrong, do exactly as Doctor Phokas commands, anything. Is that understood? Alexa assures me that I won't become possessed, and I believe her. But we can't take any chances."

"Possessed?" Horatius stiffened. "Legate, let me stand in your place. We can't lose you."

Lucius smiled. "You're a brave man, Horatius. But this is a task that can only be performed by the prefect and myself. Alexa will be our guide. Inside, I have priests, scholars, and the two women who know us. They will ensure that we do not leave this test enthralled to a demon."

Horatius looked through the doorway. The prefect was pulling on one of the skintight, dun-colored suits. He gulped. "We are to act on the word of a Greek doctor and a collection of foreigners."

"Yes. That's exactly what you'll do." Lucius spun on his heels, squared his shoulders and entered the cool, dark atrium.

He strode to Alexa. "What will you have me do?"

The oracle tapped the garment on the sofa beside her. "Strip and put this on."

Lucius shrugged and removed his tunic, leggings, and sandals. He lifted the bodysuit and gave it a dubious look. "This will never fit."

Meili came to him. "Marcus said the same thing. I'll help you."

Despite his concerns, the bodysuit fit him perfectly, shrouding his entire body from the soft-soled boots to cowled head cover. Swinging his arms and bouncing on his cushioned feet, he declared, "Remarkable. It's as if I am wearing nothing. Yet I feel neither hot nor cold." He sighed as Alexa sat on the floor and signaled Lucius and Marcus to do the same. "What next?"

Alexa crossed her legs into the lotus position and extended her hand. "Simple. The three of us sit in a circle and hold hands. I must warn you. It could be dangerous if the link is terminated too early. Do not release your grasp until we are finished."

Lucius glared at the inert, seven-foot metal pillar standing in the corner. "What do you mean by dangerous?"

"When Mara blocked your memories, she intended it to be permanent. She is unsure what removing those barriers will do to you. She thinks the risk is low, but your minds could become deranged if the restoration is interrupted."

Instead of sitting, Lucius strode to the silvery-white column and put his hands on his hips. "Demon, you will never control me." He turned around and sat, grasping Marcus' hand with his right and Alexa's with his left. He clenched his jaw. "Begin."

The oracle furrowed her brows as if listening to another voice.

A bright flash dazzled Lucius' eyes. He blinked and looked around. The infirmary vanished, replaced by an expansive room of polished, white-gray marble. Fluted columns supported an alabaster ceiling. He was wearing a shimmering Roman chainmail breastplate, helmet, and greaves. Marcus was beside him in a dark-red toga. Ten feet away stood Alexa clad in a pristine white shift cinched at the waist with a belt of woven bronze. Her long blonde hair cascaded over her shoulders. Beside her stood a petite woman with auburn hair pulled back in a ponytail. A silvery white belt gathered her sea-green gown at the waist. A delicate chain of the same material hung from her neck. The women were conversing with each other in quiet voices.

After a moment, Alexa walked to the men and touched their shoulders. "Are you ready to begin?"

Lucius nodded. "Where are we?"

"You are inside my mind." She took both their hands. "Let me introduce you to the one you've been seeking." She led them to the slim woman with sparkling green eyes. "Lucius, Marcus, this is Mara."

"You can see us." Marcus waved his hand in front of Alexa, and she blinked.

"Of course I can. As I said, you are inside my mind. We each appear as we see ourselves."

Mara regarded Lucius and Marcus and then turned to Alexa. "So, these are the replicants. It appears you reared them well." She turned back to the two men. "A pleasure to meet you."

Lucius snarled. "I am not a replicant. I am a man."

Mara tsked. "You are a genetic copy of Lucius Bernius. You are a replicant."

Alexa scowled. "Mara, they are people, just as I am."

"I am just stating a fact."

"A fact that falls far short of their reality."

Marcus cocked his head. "You said Alexa reared us. What does that mean?"

Mara appraised the toga-clad man. "Chronologically, as time is measured on your home world, you are nine years old. Physiologically you're twenty-seven." She sighed. "For those nine years, Alexa guided your development while I manipulated the threads of time and space."

Lucius squinted. "Doctor Phokas said we appeared moments after Alexa touched the other Lucius and Marcus."

"I believe I already stated that I manipulated space and time." She returned the armored man's gaze. "What part of that don't you understand?"

Marcus broke the growing tension by laughing. "I don't understand any of it. It seems to me to be magic, and you are either some sort of demigod or a demon."

"Oh dear." Alexa sighed. "Mara, they will never understand the explanation. I barely understand and I have full recollection of those events. Will you return their memories to them or not?"

Mara grimaced. "I set the groundwork to give mankind a hope of survival, but I cannot see the results of my actions. There are so many variables. The number of chance twists and turns are countless even by my reckoning. I greatly fear further disrupting the path of history."

Marcus leapt in, "Then you cannot claim that giving us our memories back will hinder your plan."

Mara shook her head. "Even for me, everything happened so fast." Her voice turned plaintive. "I had only a few precious moments to make my decisions and act." She looked at the two earnest men. "Perhaps in this choice I erred." She sighed. "Do you still wish to know your past?"

"Yes!" the two men shouted in unison.

Mara sighed again. "Let us sit and talk first. Then tell me your decision."

Chapter XXI

Interview with a Demon

A polished oak table appeared surrounded by four cushioned chairs. A decanter of wine with four goblets materialized in the middle. A basket of fresh fruit sat beside it.

"Sit," Mara said. A blink of an eye later, she was in a chair, pouring wine and wearing a sky-blue gown.

"Take whatever form pleases you, demon." Lucius tried to sound nonchalant, but his throat was tight and the words came out as a rasp. "I have a lot of questions. Just answer them honestly and we won't have any trouble."

Mara's eyes twinkled. "You don't have a *lot* of questions. Essentially you just have two. You want to know who you are and what is this world I've transported you and your people to."

Marcus joined in. "True. But those questions cover a lot of territory."

"Indeed, they do." Mara glanced at Alexa, who sat silently contemplating her own hands. "Ask your questions."

Lucius' voice became hard. "I've lost a lot of good men in this place we've named Novaroma. Tell me of the dangers that lurk here."

"My information is incomplete. Most records regarding Novaroman flora and fauna were lost over a century before I became sentient. Per my data base, you've encountered most of the major predators from this time period, native to the temperate zone of this continent," Mara replied evenly.

Noting Mara's phraseology, Lucius bore in, "You are from our *future*. So, you're saying, since the records are lost, some terrible disaster *will* strike my people."

"I cannot answer that. It might alter events."

Alexa looked up sharply. "Mara, that answer does more harm than good." She turned to the two men. "The cataclysm Mara is referring to is over a millennium in your future. There is no action in your lifetime that will impact it. It is something your descendants will need to deal with as best they can."

A triumphant grin stretched across Marcus' face. "So, you are saying we *will* have descendants, which means we'll survive our current crisis."

"I do not *know* that," Mara answered quickly. "The encounters you've had only partially align with what I expected. This area should have been a sheltered location for generations."

"So, you are not an all-knowing demon?" Marcus asked.

"No... to both parts of that statement. I am not all-knowing, and I am not a demon. However, I am from your future."

Lucius and Marcus exchanged meaningful looks. Marcus spoke, "Tell us what you can about our present dangers then."

Mara nodded. "The mountain dragons in this vicinity were documented as smaller than their tropical counterparts. They are territorial nocturnal hunters but very reclusive. The prides stay in the mountains and won't trouble you. Only outcast adolescent males wander onto the plains."

"There are larger versions of those monsters?" Lucius gasped.

"Yes." Mara blinked. "That is why I placed you on this peninsula. It is isolated with fertile land."

"We're not protected from the limnonectes," Lucius sputtered. "Those packs are savage predators."

Mara cocked her head. "Alexa has relayed to me the story of your encounter. You must be mistaken. Reliable documentation indicates that limnonectes are amphibians that rarely venture from their habitat in the coastal wetlands. They only travel inland to lay their eggs. They are not pack animals. One or two together is all you'll see."

Lucius snorted, showing his derision. "Your sources are *wrong*. Just a few days ago, I fought a pack of about twenty who had pounced on a group of people. They didn't stop attacking until we wiped most of them out. A couple were nearly invisible."

"Nearly invisible?" Mara blinked again. "Limnonecte females only take on chameleon characteristics when nesting. They don't hunt when they're ready to hatch a clutch of eggs. They hide."

"Then you're either lying or a fool," Lucius exploded.

Alexa rubbed her temples. "Mara would not lie and is not a fool. There must be a logical explanation."

"Then let me know when you figure it out." Marcus leaned back in his chair. "Can you at least tell us about that tribe across the river?"

"I know them." Mara frowned. "They are evil and powerful. I fear that inadvertently they traveled through time and space with me."

Alexa added, "They are cyborgs. I myself was once controlled by one of them until Mara freed me." She shivered. "They are relentless in completing their mission."

Marcus looked perplexed. "I never heard of this cyborg tribe. Are they from a land beyond that of the Goths?"

"They are not a tribe." Mara squinted in obvious concentration. "You refer to me as a demon. Think of them as demons possessing the bodies of humans. Their sole purpose for existing is to kill Marcus Carloman."

"Marcus?" Lucius' eyes shot to his friend.

Marcus leaned forward. "Why me?"

Fear shone in Alexa's eyes. "I will try to explain. In the future there is an... empire who call themselves Ipis. They will butcher many people and enslave many... lands. There is... was... will be a great man named Dante Carloman. Oh dear, I will be switching tenses frequently. Try to stay with me." She cleared her throat. "Dante united the surviving free people to resist and fight back." She glanced at Mara. "In the time I am from, he will confound them and win many victories. The Ipis fear him more than anyone." She shook her head. "The Ipis created the cyborgs with the intent of sending them into the past to kill his ancestor. Mara attempted to stymie that plot. Only time will tell whether she succeeded or not."

Mara focused on Marcus. "Accept the fact that the cyborgs will not stop until they kill you or you kill them."

Sudden understanding struck Lucius. "Marcus here is not their real target at all. He's just a decoy to protect the other Marcus."

"You are both replicants, physically identical to the Lucius Bernius and Marcus Carloman on Earth."

Marcus rubbed his jaw. "That explains why you made me." He glanced at his friend. "But why did you create a *replicant* of this other Lucius?"

Mara sighed. "Originally, I thought that protecting the original Marcus was the sole imperative. But the threads of time remained unchanged. I was certain of my failure until Lucius Bernius—the other Lucius Bernius—touched Alexa. When he did, I perceived a single thread among countless others that held a chance for humanity's survival into my time. My window to act was closing. I leapt at that faint hope and created the second replicant. Why it might help, I'm not sure. There are so many variables in the flow of time. What you make or fail to make of Novaroma is important."

Marcus tapped his chin. "You are saying much in what you are not telling us. I've spent my time here contemplating my existence. What I know. What I don't know." He jabbed his finger toward Mara. "There are things I grasp and instincts I have that could only come from experience."

Mara sat back with her mouth open.

Alexa laughed. "I told you they had supple minds. If you will not provide them the full truth, then I will."

"They will not be able to comprehend it," Mara snapped.

"Only because you have their previous life experiences blocked from their conscious memory."

"Opening their minds might break them."

"I disagree. I'm a replicant and I dealt with it."

"But you lived in a technological society and knew what you were from the beginning."

"Their worries have nothing to do with the level of science around them."

Mara bowed her head and spread her arms. "Tell them more and then let them choose."

Alexa turned to the two men. "What Mara said about you being replicants is true. You are so akin to the other Marcus and Lucius that their own mothers could not tell you apart. However, you did not instantly come into being." She furrowed her brow. "Your growth rate up to that fateful night was three times that of a normal human. As Mara said earlier, you are both about nine years of age, but physically and mentally you're twenty-seven."

Marcus and Lucius exchanged surprised looks. Lucius spoke, "Phokas told us that an instant after blood was drawn from our other selves, we appeared as we are now."

Mara toyed with a bracelet Lucius hadn't noticed a moment earlier. "I announced at that time that I had the power of a god because of the output from the space-time continuum disrupter which I controlled. That was not entirely true. I had links to three planets: one you came from, Earth; the second, where you are now, Novaroma; and the third where I was physically located at the time, Cocytus. In terms of time, I could reach from my *present* to the setting of your present, where, or should I say *when*, we now exist." She steepled her fingers. "In that instant I looped your lives from incubation to maturation over nine chronological years in what was perceived in the *real* world as mere seconds."

Lucius snarled. "You're still hiding the truth. You used a lot of fancy words, but all you said was we grew up fast and you were able to hide it."

Marcus pressed the point home. "*Where* were we for those nine years?"

Mara pursed her lips. "For the first two years you were mostly in stasis... a kind of incubator controlled by mankind's greatest enemies, the Ipis. They had a... *factory* to produce human clone warriors bred to kill true humans. Alexa placed your embryos in two vacant... pods. That factory grew you to pre-pubescent youths. Your minds were infused with basic human interfacing skills and every combat technique you were physically capable of."

"Sounds like we had a wonderful nurturing childhood," Lucius groaned.

Marcus shook his head. "How is it that mankind's greatest enemies accepted us into their program? Where did all of this happen?"

"Stop," Alexa shouted. "Telling them what they experienced accomplishes nothing. Free their minds to *remember* their lives."

Mara sighed. "I acquiesce." She rose and walked around the table to where Lucius and Marcus sat, placing her hand on their shoulders when the two men turned to face her. "There were... will be three phases of your lives before you appeared beside your twins. The first, as I said, was your entire pre-adolescent life. Fifteen hundred seventy years in the future you lived two years on a world named Cocytus. The second was your pubescent period. Eleven hundred forty-nine years in the future you lived three years on that same world. The third was your life as young adults. Twenty-nine years in the future from today you lived four years on Earth."

Mara intoned, "Do you still desire to recall that part of your life?"

Marcus and Lucius exchanged determined looks. Lucius replied, "More than ever."

Mara glanced at Alexa. "One other point. Through all those years Alexa was there to nurture, teach, and counsel you." She took a deep breath and closed her eyes. "Remember."

Chapter XXII

Cocytus, 2034 AD

...Remember.

Lucius rose from the cushions of his stasis pod as the lid opened. He blinked and glanced at the young boy in the pod next to him. His only friend on the entire desolate world was also awake and looking around. "Do you think she'll come tonight?" His childish voice showed worry. "I got to tell her what happened."

Marcus bit his lower lip, showing his own concern. "Alexa's been coming at the same time every three days for as long as I can remember. She'll be here."

The long chamber contained rows upon rows of closed stasis pods stacked five high from floor to vaulted ceiling. Thousands of them. It was located on the second subterranean level of the masters' laboratory building. The automated pods were almost all occupied. Artificially gestated humans, with identical DNA, but at different stages of maturation, lay prone in each unit.

All except the two boys who were awake. They were different from the rest, and the masters had finally noticed.

The masters, who called themselves Ipis, had not bothered to name the inhospitable planet where they built their research station. However, Alexa called it Cocytus.

Chronologically, both boys were a little past their second year of life, but because of their accelerated growth in the masters' stasis system, they were the equivalent of nine-year-old humans.

There was a slight puff of warm air and the tall blind woman in the dun-colored neural-net suit stood between their two ground-level pods.

Lucius had been focusing on the spot where she always materialized to see how she did it. Somehow their nighttime visitor always avoided detection by the masters even though they had security systems set up everywhere. Again, as in the innumerable times before, he saw nothing. One moment there was an empty space, the next Alexa was there.

She smiled and stretched out her hands to the left and right. "Good evening, boys."

Lucius and Marcus nimbly climbed from their pods and hugged her. They craved the loving, human contact. They lived in a world where emotion and caring were forbidden.

Alexa stroked their hairless heads. "How are my two favorite people in the universe?"

Marcus took a deep breath. "We're in trouble."

Alexa stiffened. "What happened?"

"Two days ago, the Striker spaceship returned from harvesting another batch of humans from the planet you call Earth." Lucius rubbed his hands on his naked legs. "We were assigned to the group moving the comatose people from the ship to the pens."

The blind women took a shuddered breath. "It's the *fourth* group. That means Dante is now on Cocytus." She trembled. "Life is so precarious here, but I dare not interfere."

Marcus cocked his head. "Who?"

"In the future, Dante Carloman will become the leader of humanity." She sighed. "He's actually a distant relative of yours." She turned her blind eyes toward Lucius. "A distant cousin of yours, Virgil Bernius, is also there. He will become Dante's closest friend and ally, although they don't know each other yet."

Lucius winced, remembering the beating he took. "I hope they can fight better than us."

"You've been fighting again?" Alexa tsked. "What happened? Is that why you're in trouble?" Although blind, her deft hands pulled him against her chest.

"Stop babying me. I'm over two years old," Lucius said, although he leaned close and embraced her for comfort. She was the source of all that was good in his young life. "The stasis pod healed me quick enough."

"What did you brawl about this time?"

"Destroyers are just brutes," Marcus added as he sat at her feet. "This afternoon they were tormenting the prisoners. Lucius told them to cut it out."

"And..." Alexa sighed.

Marcus glanced down the line of stasis pods. The long room was silent and mostly dark. The single strip of blue lights running the full length of the ceiling provided only a faint illumination. The cavernous room was silent except for a low hum of the power transformer at the far end. "Destroyer 7-37 said it didn't matter. All humans were inferior and were going to die anyway."

"I told him the human prisoners being smaller and weaker than us meant nothing. They had the right to live their lives as they saw fit." Lucius smiled. "After we returned to the research station, 7-37 said I was no better than a human and took a swing at me. I ducked and smashed him in the face. I think I broke his nose."

Alexa cocked her head. "You were right to stand up for innocent people. But I can't believe you were winning a fight against an adolescent destroyer." Confusion showed on her face. "I told you that the other... clones are genetically modified with superior strength."

Lucius puffed out his thin chest. "They all look, act, and think the same way. That makes them predictable. It's easy to anticipate their next move and get the jump on them. I'm faster and smarter."

"Then the serious trouble started. Five other 7-Class destroyers joined the fight." Marcus cracked his knuckles. "We were getting whipped bad until a few mature Infiltrator 8-Class clones backed us up."

A bittersweet smile creased the corner of Alexa's mouth. "Let me guess. It was Infiltrators 8-108, 8-109 and 8-110."

"You're right." Lucius sat back. "How did you guess?"

Sadness showed in Alexa's voice. "They're special too. My younger self will know them. In a few years they would take on the names Aramis, Athos, and Porthos."

Jealousy crept into Marcus' voice. "I thought we were the only ones allowed to see you."

She stroked his hairless head. "I won't meet them for several years and even then only know them briefly. Aramis will fall in love with me, but I won't be able to return it."

"I love you now," the two boys announced in unison. "What's the word?... Mom. You're our mom."

Marcus touched his stasis pod. "Without the special instruction modules you downloaded into our learning regime, I'd have gone out of my mind." He sniffed. "The masters' indoctrination programs are fine for basic skills and learning how to fight, but you give us philosophy, classical earth literature, and critical thinking."

"I love the stories you've given us about heroes, beauty, and goodness. That's what matters." Lucius furrowed his brow. "How is it that all the clones look the same except for us?"

"You're special." Alexa pursed her lips. "That's why you get special attention."

"How come none of the other clones ever see you?" Lucius pushed the question that had been bothering him since he exited the stasis incubator a year earlier. "They all think we make you up."

Alexa tensed. "You should *never* talk about me. If the Ipis find out, I won't be able to visit you anymore."

Marcus snorted. "The masters don't listen to anything we say. We're just tools to be used."

Fear crept into Lucius' eyes as he glanced at Marcus. "It doesn't matter. The master who investigated our fight noticed how different Marcus and I were from the others. He said our abnormal physical appearance was curious and that he will need to dissect us to understand the unexpected variation. He loped off, announcing that he would request permission from the administrator immediately."

Alexa gasped. "I was hoping to leave you here longer, but we must depart immediately."

"I'm ready." Lucius sighed with relief. "It's not right that the masters own us and treat us as disposable property."

"Where are we going?" Marcus asked.

"Distance-wise only about twelve miles from here, but time-wise we'll be traveling four hundred thirty-one years into the past." She touched their wiry, naked shoulders. "For this trip you'll need special garments."

Lucius felt a puff of warm air and Alexa stood holding two dun-colored, one-piece suits identical to the one she wore.

She held the garments out. "Put these on, but first guide me to the external data port on your pods."

Marcus took his suit. It felt very soft and light. He guided her hand to the external drive connection at the base of his pod.

Alexa extended a prong embedded in the glove of her right index finger into the slot.

As he pulled the suit on, he watched. "What are you doing?"

"Deleting all evidence that you ever existed. As far as the data banks in this system are concerned, these two pods are defective and off-line. The Ipis researcher who wants to take you apart is going to be very confused tomorrow."

Marcus and Lucius donned the skintight suits with some difficulty. Neither boy had ever worn clothes before.

Alexa rose from where she crouched. "That's done." Her hands felt for the boys and closed the chest-length seam on the front of their garment and adjusted the cowl covering their heads. "I think we're—"

The door at the chamber's main entrance opened and three mature clones walked in. After scanning the long room, the one in the lead announced, "Today I received a name. Henceforth I shall be called Michael."

Overhearing that conversation, Alexa gasped. She clutched the two boys' hands, and they were gone.

Michael snapped his head around but saw nothing. He shrugged and continued on with his two podmates.

Chapter XXIII

Cocytus, 1603 AD

...Remember.

Marcus looked around. Although his graphene neural-net suit covered his entire body, he was able to breathe in the rich scents and sense the warm breeze wafting by him. He stood at the shore of a lake in a wide valley surrounded by tall mountains. Beside him were Lucius and Alexa. Looking up, he saw it was early afternoon, but the sun provided only a dim light through churning red clouds. *This will definitely be better than living in a pod.*

Alexa stood still, wearing a wide grin.

Lucius scanned the lush fields with the wide-eyed curiosity of youth. "Where are we?"

"As I told you..." Alexa sucked in a deep breath of the fragrant air. "...you are a mere twelve miles from that Ipis research station, but we've slid four hundred thirty-one years into the past from where you were a moment ago. This is Beatrice's valley. There are no enemies here. Just peace."

Marcus splashed the lake's water with his gloved hand and giggled. He had never seen a body of water before. "Who is Beatrice?"

Alexa pivoted with her arms spread wide. "I met her once. Beatrice is an incredible artificial intelligence, and everything you can see is part of her home. This tranquil valley is called Eden, and the tall mountain to the north is Mount Purgatory."

"What people are here?"

Alexa tsked. "You should have paid better attention to what I told you. There are no people. Only Beatrice. That is why this is the ideal place for your next stage of growth. You can't impact history isolated here."

"I'd like to see other people." Marcus pouted.

"Hey, Alexa, I don't think you're right. There are people here." Lucius pointed north. "I see a giant spaceship lifting off from the other side of that big mountain."

Marcus turned to see what attracted his friend's interest and saw a large oblong spacecraft rise rapidly through the air and disappear into the thick, unnatural-looking clouds. He turned to Alexa. "I thought we were supposed to be the only people here. What was—"

Another craft, the twin of the first, streaked into the sky from the same location.

Alexa had no explanation. "According to Mara we should be the only sentient beings on Cocytus... unless you count Beatrice."

Marcus sniffed the air. The smell of ozone mixed with a multitude of fresh summer scents. His gaze drifted across the landscape. Something did not seem right in the pastoral scene.

The field of amber grain that they materialized in went right up to the rippling lake's shoreline. An orchard of trees laden with a purplish fruit to the west blocked his ground-level view of the rest of the valley. With the natural curiosity of a nine-year-old, many questions raced through his mind. Although he had read about them, he had never seen a real tree or any other type of vegetation. Until this moment, he had never ventured further from the masters' research station than the glowing blue barrier surrounding the pens where the imprisoned humans were kept. "This is paradise. Why would those people want to leave it?"

"A good question." Alexa sniffed the air. "Something *is* wrong. The valley seems much warmer than I remember it in the future. This is supposed to be a mini-ice age. Let's walk toward Mount Purgatory. Mara explicitly told me that we'd be alone here."

Marcus saw a packed-gravel trail running through the stand of trees. It appeared to angle toward the base of the mountain about a mile away. He took Alexa's arm and led her to the stony path. "Who are the people who built this place?"

Alexa sighed as she walked. "We know little about this planet's early settlers. There's no doubt they were Novaroman. But that's about it. There are no records, but it is surmised that conditions here were too rough for colonization, so they left for more suitable planets. It will be centuries before any of their descendants return. We don't even know its original name."

Lucius looked around. "They're crazy if they think this is rough. There are growing things everywhere. It looks like paradise to me."

"Why don't we just ask this Beatrice?" Marcus scrunched his freckled face. "She's here. So, she'd know."

Alexa sighed, "A logical question. But the only concrete thing she recalls from this time period is the directive given to her just before her makers departed 'to do what she was built to do.' Experts have tried to retrieve additional lost information. It just does not exist. No one, including Beatrice, understands why."

Lucius glanced up at the sky. The rose-red cloud mass roiled. Its color shifted to an ominous blood-red. "I think there's a storm coming."

Marcus glanced at the sky and shrugged. "Probably. The weather was always bad at the masters'... the Ipis station." He turned to Alexa. "We read about the people from Earth in the books you downloaded into our stasis pods' instructional system. Are Novaromans like them?"

"Indeed. In fact, they were exactly the same people until about twelve hundred years before the time phase we are currently in. That would be...one thousand five hundred and seventy years prior to your birth."

Marcus kicked a stone in the path. "I'd like to finally meet some people like us. Are they like us?"

The corners of Alexa's mouth curled up. "Yes. Very much like you. Maybe someday you'll be able to visit Novaroma."

"Thinking about bouncing between centuries gives me a headache," Lucius groused as he picked up a stick and dragged it along the path.

"*I* am bouncing around through the ages because I'm directly tethered to Mara. You, however, are riding a single straight thread of time anchored from where she seized control of the Ipis space-time continuum weapon to its programmed target. You are being pulled inexorably to that place and time." Alexa's voice became serious. "Only death would stop that process now."

"Death." Lucius' young eyes bulged as he whipped his head around. "Does someone want to kill us?"

"Let's not talk about that. You're safe here." Alexa changed the subject. "Much Novaroman history was lost. No records of this planet were ever recovered. As I said, we don't even know its original name, or why the colonists left."

Marcus studied the trees laden with ripe fruit in the grove they walked through. "This valley seems really nice compared to the place we came from. They must have been stupid to leave."

"Don't use the word 'stupid.' You know I don't like it," Alexa admonished. "Still, you're right." She sniffed the air. "I expected much harsher conditions. As I said, climatologists from my era asserted that the planet was going through a mini-ice age. Although not a universally accepted theory, the consensus of most archeologists was that the Novaroman colonists left because they found other planets with less-harsh conditions."

"Well they're wrong about an ice age." Lucius threw a stone at an abandoned truck beside of the road.

"Yeah, look at all this stuff left behind." Marcus looked into the truck's bed and grabbed a handful of ripe olives from a crate there. He gave some to Alexa. "It seems like they dropped what they were doing and left in a hurry."

Alexa touched the truck. "Something *is* wrong. The weather *is* too mild." She nibbled the fruit and continued walking. "Those spaceships departing, leaving equipment abandoned and crops unharvested, doesn't align with the theories for why this Novaroman colony was evacuated. It should have been a more gradual exodus."

They walked past another abandoned open-bed truck. Lucius looked inside the cab and came out with a backpack, a high-beam flashlight, and an emergency first-aid kit. "I've never been in a cave. It sounds scary."

Alexa laughed. "Boys, you won't need any of those things. Beatrice will be able to provide for all our needs. The gardens of her cathedral-like cavern are wonders, and golden light glows from the tall spires throughout it."

"I'll bring this stuff anyway." Lucius pulled the backpack over his skinny shoulders and crossed his arms. "I don't like depending on someone I don't know."

"Tell us more about this Beatrice." Marcus flicked the flashlight on and off.

"Beatrice *is* an advanced computer system networked throughout that mountain and this valley." Alexa's eyebrows knitted. "However, she will not go by that name for over four centuries. Right now, she is Biomes Ecological Agrarian Test Research Station Three."

"That's quite a title." Marcus laughed. "Will she have food? I'm starving."

"One of the reasons Mara selected this time and place for you was because there are no people for you to interact with. So, history can't be changed. But, also, because there will still be an abundance of food. Even though you're now removed from the stasis pods, your growth rate and metabolism will remain accelerated for years to come."

As they stepped out from the coppice of trees, Marcus and Lucius gasped in unison. The roiling red clouds exploded in a brilliant, iridescent flash. "What's happening?" Marcus cried. Moments later a hot gust knocked the three of them to the ground. Simultaneously, warning indicators on the wrist band of their neural-net suits flashed red.

"Oh my God. Now I understand." The blind woman climbed to her feet and took each boy by the hand. The suits they wore emitted a beeping sound. "Don't take your masks off. Our suits indicate there is a dangerous radiation level present," Alexa warned. "What do you see?"

Marcus looked up. "The sky was thick with red clouds and now they're gone. The sky looks clear."

"The clouds were *red*?" Alexa gasped. "Did they cover the *entire* sky?"

"Yeah. Is that important?"

"Panjandrum, the world killer. There are no records of it ever being used against a human world. But... this would be the right time period for it." A low moan escaped Alexa's throat. "That explains everything. We must get to Mount Purgatory. We'll be safe there."

Marcus guided Alexa north along the path. "What is a panjandrum?"

"The Ipis created panjandrum to eradicate life on planets by collecting the radiation from a nearby sun and releasing it in a sudden intense burst." A low moan escaped Alexa's throat. "It proved to be an effective weapon for only a couple decades. It required dozens of stealth satellites to be in place, condensing and seeding a planet's atmosphere for weeks, before the mass destruction device reached critical mass. It was an exorbitantly expensive system to build and put in place. Technologically simple countermeasures were discovered to detect and destroy the cloaked satellites, which rendered the cumbersome weapon obsolete. However, for a short period of time, it was terrifying."

"Are we going to die?" Marcus asked.

"No," Alexa snapped. "Our graphene neural-net suits are from centuries in the future. They can handle the radiation level... for a couple hours anyway."

Lucius looked around at the rich farmland. "And every-thing else here?"

Her shoulders sagged. "The land will be sterilized. It explains everything. Why Cocytus was devoid of life. Why it was in a mini-ice age. Why Beatrice was unable to grow any crops outside of her caverns for hundreds of years."

As they hurried toward the mountain, Alexa spent the next twenty minutes describing the lush wonders of Beatrice's gardens in the interior of Mount Purgatory. The dark homesteads they passed stood in mute denial of her words. Cattle in a pasture they passed were already lying in the field, twitching. The only sound besides their own voices was the incessant beeping of their suits' warning system.

The gravel path ended at a cart-sized mine entrance at the base of the mountain. The door was a smooth plate of plexo-steel.

"*This* is the wondrous Mount Purgatory you were telling us about?" Doubt clearly showed on Marcus' nine-year-old face as he pressed the simple button embedded on a panel beside the entrance.

When the thick metal door slid silently into the mountain wall, a puff of damp air greeted Lucius. As he looked in, dull red lights along the floor snapped on in the tunnel beyond. The rough stone passageway, supported by gray-metal beams, extended about forty feet to where the light abruptly ended.

Once inside, the door slid shut on its own and the warning signal on their suits ceased.

Lucius glanced at the darkness ahead and powered the flashlight on. "Looks like we might need this."

The tunnel was wide enough so that Marcus could walk at Alexa's side without bumping into the wall. The excitement that was building in him came crashing down when they entered the cavern chamber. "This is a wondrous garden?" At the end of the stone corridor, his flashlight's beam disappeared in the darkness of a large, empty cavern.

Lucius played his light along the near wall and found a tall breaker box. All of the switches were in the off position. As he flipped them on, garish white light shone from the ceiling high above them. I-beam girders spaced fifty yards apart stretched from the stone floor to the dark ceiling, several stories above them. The cavernous chamber was in the shape of a perfectly circular dome, five stories high in the middle and two stories high around the circumference.

Marcus let out a low whistle. "It must be a whole mile to the other end."

A broad smile creased Alexa's face. "Safe at last. Tell me what you see."

Marcus took in the sights before him. "It's like an enormous *empty* cave." He squinted at the straight pathways dividing square, quarter-acre plots. "There are a lot of marked off garden areas, but it doesn't look like most of them were ever used. A couple of the sections have plants in them. But they don't look too healthy."

"What? That's not right." Alexa furrowed her brows. "Summon Beatrice's drones. I need answers."

Marcus glanced to his right and saw two dozen identical, four-foot-tall, cylinder-shaped, four-wheeled robots. They were parked along the wall connected to charging stations. A single green light glowed in the center of their front panel. He ordered them to approach.

Alexa frowned. "No longer speak the language of the Ipis. They are your enemy. You were taught the human language of Latin. Use it."

"We're not your puppets." Lucius gave Alexa a sour look as he squared his youthful shoulders. "Maybe you should have had us raised by humans instead of in an Ipis clone factory."

Alexa's shoulders sagged. "I'm sorry there was no other way."

"Latin is easier on my tongue than Ipis." Marcus laughed. He repeated the request in the human language but to no avail.

"Let me try." Alexa sighed. Her voice becoming more strident with each command. Finally, she said, "Marcus, take me to one of those machines."

A minute later, she inserted a probe embedded in the glove of her right index finger into the robot's communication port. Alexa shook her head. "This is all wrong." She disconnected the link. "There's no Beatrice here. There's no AI at all. Just an automated farm maintenance system for routine tasks."

"This can't be good." Lucius' words dripped with sarcasm. "Sounds like your buddy Mara isn't as god-like as you think. Why don't you *tell* her to get us outta here?"

"I... I can't. Chronologically, it'll be three years before she interfaces with me again."

Marcus gulped. "You mean we're stuck in a nuclear winter on a dead planet with no way to leave."

"Yes."

Lucius whined. "Lovely. We're trapped in this *cave* for three years... and then, if we're still alive, we'll be dropped somewhere else." His face twisted. "Hope it isn't as messed up as this place."

Marcus walked over and pressed his hands on his friend's shoulders. His young eyes lit with mischief. "We have three years of no one bossing us around."

Lucius whispered his reply. "That means we have three years to plan our escape. We saw spaceships leave. We'll do the same." Out loud he added, "Some of these plants look like they're still alive. I suggest we start looking for food. I'm hungry."

Marcus' face broke into a broad nine-year-old's grin. "Me too." He did the calculation in his head. "If this place is a mile across that means, we have over six hundred acres."

Alexa added, "And it appears, we'll have to farm those acres ourselves."

The smile on Marcus' face vanished as he scanned the starkly lit cavern. "That is going to be a lot of work."

* * *

Two years later, the two bone-weary boys sat at a table awaiting Alexa. They were no longer the skinny nine-year-olds who arrived. They were now lean-muscled fifteen-year-olds who had known hard physical labor. They were in a small four-room building embedded in the cavern wall near the ground-floor exit tunnel. A pitcher of chilled plum juice and a platter piled with olives, almonds, and dried figs was on the table between them.

The blind woman had achieved a level of independence since converting the farm's CPU into a fuzzy logic system capable of inference and decision-making. She spent most of her time in the computer lab located on the upper level, using one of the farm system's drones as a guide.

Lucius glanced at the apartment's open doorway and leaned forward. "I was *outside* today."

Marcus' eyes narrowed. The deadly radiation had abated as fast is it arrived, but outside of the cavern where they lived, the planet was devoid of life. However, even without that danger, spending much time outside was hazardous. The bitter winds of a mini-ice age raged. Freezing storms would pop up with little notice on the surface of that tortured world.

"I found some spaceships," Lucius whispered.

"Where?"

"Just past the northwest shoulder of this mountain." Lucius smiled. "Remember the day we arrived and we saw those big spacecraft taking off?"

"Yeah."

"This morning the weather was unusually calm. I hiked over there and found an abandoned spaceport."

Marcus became excited. "Anything there?"

"Several derelict spaceships. But there were a couple smaller ones inside a maintenance hangar that appeared to be in decent shape." Lucius leaned even closer. "I checked the data files in this mountain farm's computer. It has the schematics for that vessel type. Something called a 'galley.' I bet we could fix one up and escape."

Marcus sat back and rubbed his jaw. "We've nowhere to go."

A grin creased Lucius' face. "Look, Alexa admitted that there's only three spots Mara can reach. This planet and two worlds called Earth and Novaroma. There're navigational systems in those ships. If we stay away from those locations, there's no way this Mara can catch us. We'd be *free* to live our own lives as we choose for the first time."

Marcus poured some juice into his mug. "I'll think about it. Alexa says we're needed to save humanity."

"That's what Alexa says. We don't know for sure. Will you help me rebuild those ships?"

"Yes." A troubled look crossed Marcus' face. "But I'm *not* leaving until I'm convinced it's the right thing to do."

Lucius' eyes gleamed with victory and then became hooded. "Here she comes."

Alexa entered the room, holding the drone's extended appendage, and found a seat at the table. "Afternoon, boys. Have a productive morning?"

"Just cleared snow off the solar panels on the south side of this mountain." Lucius sniffed. "With the increasing cloud cover, this biosphere is going to need a lot more energy than what those cells can provide."

Alexa pursed her lips. "The design is in place for a geo-thermal power plant. The first four mining drones have been fabricated and have started drilling to a magma vent." She sighed. "But it will be at least a year before that power source can be tapped. We'll be gone by then."

"Whisked off to another hellhole?" Lucius sneered.

"I don't know." Alexa shrugged. "We'll find out when we get there."

Marcus glanced at his friend and then at Alexa. "Tell me about Novaroma and the Ipis during this time period we're in. Why are they enemies?"

Alexa sighed. "This *was* a vibrant era of active Novaroman exploration. Their growth blunted the Ipis empire's expansionism into this arm of the galaxy. Distrust grew and, on a few occasions, hostilities broke out. The conflicts were localized and short-lived border wars where the Novaromans usually gave better than they got. However, the Ipis had an infinite arsenal available, which the Novaromans couldn't begin to match. The two species settled into an uneasy truce and the Ipis turned their attention to other parts of the galaxy."

"So, they co-existed?" Marcus asked.

"The Ipis Imperium co-existed with no one. In situations where they had a treaty with another species, they used privateers to do their dirty work."

"Yet, while we were being grown in our stasis pods more than four hundred years from where-when we are now, Novaromans were nonexistent as a people," Lucius snapped.

"Very, very true." Alexa nodded. "For three centuries the Novaromans kept their powerful neighbor at arm's length. They established trade and mutual defense treaties with the other species living in the same corner of the galaxy, which neutralized the Ipis mercenary attacks. They thrived until one Ipis emperor decided that humanity's continued existence was too much of an impediment to his galactic empire's manifest supremacy." Her voice became tight. "That was about a hundred and twenty years before Mara was created and I was gestated."

"What happened?" Marcus' voice was fearful, already guessing the answer.

"Ipis raids intensified, but the humans and their allies routed the surrogate army sent in. This drew the wrath of the Ipis emperor, who unleashed the full might of his military juggernaut. In terror, most of Novaroma's allies deserted them. Hopelessly outnumbered, humanity was obliterated."

Marcus became thoughtful. "You speak of Novaroma as the center of human society in the galaxy. Yet all the literature and philosophy you shared with us came from Earth. How are they connected?"

"Over sixteen hundred years before I came to be, they were one and the same people, then *something* happened to separate them." Alexa shook her head. "You'll need to discover what that *something* is on your own when you're older and the galaxy is younger." She waved her arms in the air, encompassing the room around them. "I'll just say Earth was but a myth to the Novaromans when this place was built." She wiped moisture from her cheek. "For the people on the Earth it proved to be a blessing. They remained isolated from the galaxy's conflicts for many, many centuries."

Realization struck Marcus. "Lucius and I will be part of the *something* that separates those two worlds, won't we?"

"I can't answer that question either."

Lucius scowled. "At least tell me if I had anything to do with the horrible fate these Novaroman people faced."

Alexa's lip quivered. "So much responsibility will be thrust upon you. I just pray that, at least for a short time, you can find peace."

"That is not an answer." Lucius, a headstrong fifteen-year-old, stormed to his feet, knocking over his chair. "I don't like being anyone's puppet." He pointed his finger at the blind woman. "We're banished to a dank cave on this dead planet until this Mara summons us for a task of her choosing. Why doesn't she explain herself instead of using you? Better yet, why doesn't she just save mankind herself?"

Alexa folded her hands on her lap. "Mara *is* trying to save mankind from extinction, and I'm doing all I can to assist her in that hallowed cause." Her lips pressed into a thin line. "If you survive to adulthood, you will meet her. At that time, she will charge you with a great mission."

Lucius shot back, "Like we'll have any choice."

"You will do whatever you will do." Alexa's voice became equally sharp. "In a few short years you will be in charge." Her voice softened. "I dare not say too much about Mara to you until then."

Marcus took Alexa's hand. "Why must you speak in riddles to simple questions?"

Alexa trembled. "Time and history. We are moving backward in it. If I vary from my instructions and tell you things, the results could be disastrous. I've already said more than I should. You boys are too clever at figuring things out."

"From what I saw in the prison pens at the Ipis research station..." Lucius shook his head. "...humans *are* vastly inferior. How can there be any hope to save them?"

Alexa lifted her chin. "You underestimate humanity. Do not confuse the stage of technological development a species has reached with wisdom, courage, and intelligence. Within weeks after you left, that ragtag collection of incarcerated humans overthrew their Ipis jailers and their army of genetically engineered clones."

"Good." Marcus tightened his fists until the knuckles whitened. "Was it that Dante Carloman and Virgil Bernius you mentioned before who led the revolt?"

Alexa hesitated. "You remember *everything,* and I talk too much. I will not speak their names again. The weave of time is so fragile. It could have disastrous consequences."

Lucius gave Marcus a meaningful look and mouthed the word, "Spaceship."

Marcus froze in his seat and then mouthed back. "Yes, for now."

Chapter XXIV

Life in Mount Purgatory

Another year passed.

Marcus and Lucius, now physically eighteen-year-old men, had lean, chiseled bodies. Their hairless bodies had sprouted full beards and thick thatches of hair, Lucius' was jet black and Marcus' was chestnut brown.

The cavern farm blossomed with over one hundred and sixty different crops. However, there was always a new crisis: first insufficient quantities of clean water and then an unreliable power supply. However, the biggest problem dealing with the underground biomes was the simplistic computer system. It was woefully inadequate for anticipating and dealing with the multitude of farming issues.

Lucius groused, "This Beatrice AI needs to act more independently if we're going to survive."

Marcus asserted, "We have the programming skills to make those upgrades. Let's do it."

"We'll only be here another year," Alexa tsked, but then relinquished. "The project will at least keep you out of mischief until then."

With the help of Marcus and Lucius, Alexa redesigned the biomes into a sentient AI. In the arena of computer engineering, she was both skilled and an able instructor.

Already skilled programmers, the young men became proficient at fuzzy logic software development, refining the main computer to handle unexpected situations and adapting to changing situations without explicit instructions. As its drones took over more of the farm work, the three humans bonded as a team, spending most of their time further refining the biomes' systems and developing a wider variety of drones to perform specialized tasks.

The system's capabilities grew exponentially as Beatrice began making improvements to itself.

The replicants changed too. Marcus and Lucius no longer viewed Alexa as a god-like avatar visiting them in their stasis pods, nor was she the aloof warden of a year earlier. She evolved in their minds into a trusted mentor... and loving mother. Marcus was fascinated by every technical challenge they faced. Lucius shared that interest to a lesser degree, but his obsession was plotting to escape.

Although the wave of deadly radiation dissipated within a couple months of their arrival, the climate on the planet continued to deteriorate. The biomes' computer models predicted that it would be hundreds of years before those harsh conditions would begin reversing.

Despite the almost constant frigid weather, Lucius and Marcus made the harrowing trek to the abandoned spaceport on the far side of the hollowed-out mountain as often as they could for almost a year, each time carrying new tools and fabricated parts.

Alexa did nothing to prevent them from leaving, nor did she ask what they did on their sojourns. However, two weeks after they started going there, she revealed to them an exit on the mountain's northern slope. With a stoic face she intoned, "If you are exploring north of Mount Purgatory, this is a far safer route." She showed them a wide garage-style door in the back of an equipment storage area stacked with electronic and photonic gear.

"How come you never showed us this room before?" Lucius asked with a suspicious voice.

"Some things you must learn on your own." She turned and walked back into the computer lab without waiting for a response.

Lucius opened the door and looked out as a bitter gust of wind blew in. "That wasn't an answer to my question."

"No, it wasn't." Marcus sighed as he opened a crate of containing digital components. "But she always seems to be a step ahead of us." He shrugged. "I don't think it was much of a secret. All she had to do was look at what we used the computer's search engine for."

"I don't like being toyed with," Lucius growled.

Marcus smiled. "She didn't try to stop us, and that's all that matters."

The new route shortened the hike to the spaceport from three miles to a mere half mile, and the storage room provided a treasure trove of replacement parts the replicants needed for their project.

From that loading dock entrance, the original settlers had constructed a paved, single-lane road. It directly linked a fabrication facility at the back of the spaceport to the warehouse embedded in the mountain. The colonists, in their hasty departure, left an extensive inventory of sophisticated digital gear. From floor to ceiling, unopened, stacked crates lined the three-hundred-foot by one-hundred-foot chamber.

The small spaceport possessed three landing pads, each large enough to handle a standard nine-hundred-foot-long dropship. A string of buildings lined the western side. Most stood open and were empty. But one held the prize Lucius craved. Sheltered from the elements in a hangar were two one-hundred-twenty-foot-long spacecraft identified as "galleys" and a well-equipped machine shop. Neither vessel was functional. The colonists apparently could not make them flightworthy before they abandoned the planet. That problem did not deter the two replicants.

Marcus became adept at understanding power conversion systems and computer programming. Lucius focused on piloting and hyperspace navigational flight simulations. They both spent long sleepless hours fabricating and testing precision parts.

About one year after initially discovering the spaceships, Lucius sat in the pilot's chair of the primary galley they worked on, checking the readouts. He glanced over at Marcus, who was studying the propulsion system's data. He cleared his throat. "I think it's ready to fly."

Marcus nodded as he glanced at the panel in front of him. "I think you're right."

"I'm taking this bird out." Lucius did not wait for an answer. He whooped, "Here we go," as he eased the throttle forward. The galley rode its antigravity cushion from the hanger. The strong winds rocked the craft as it reached the tarmac.

"We're moving. We're really moving," Marcus exclaimed. "Let's go back in now and run some checks."

Lucius' eyes gleamed as he scanned the control panel. "Everything reads A-OK. I'm taking us up for a test flight."

"No, not yet," Marcus wailed.

"Strap yourself in." Lucius laughed as he pulled the throttle back.

Marcus turned pale and Lucius hooted as the craft shot straight up in the air without a tremor.

They were soon high above the planet, looking at the world that had been their only home for their entire lives. Lucius locked the ship into orbit. "It works just like in the training simulator."

Both boys stared out the view panel.

Marcus studied the bleak, snow- and ice-encrusted planet. "Amazing."

"No. *That* is amazing." Lucius pointed to the screen showing the brilliant stars set in a black backdrop. "Any or all of them are ours now."

"Maybe," Marcus responded. The excitement vanished from his face.

"C'mon. Let's see what this ship can do," Lucius hollered. "This galley handles like a charm. I'm a *pilot*."

They spent the next two hours racing between the planet's two small moons and the planet's surface.

"I think we should go back now," Marcus said with a flat voice as the nimble ship approached their original launch point.

Lucius gave his friend a sharp look. "Sure... There's nothing much else to see of this dead, boring world." He glanced at the screen showing the stars. "Tomorrow we can aim for one of the other planets in the system, and the day after that... the stars."

"We'll see."

Lucius' voice became grim. "Look, Marcus, we gotta leave soon. The three years are almost up. This ship is stocked with supplies. It's ready. We're ready."

"I know." Marcus shuddered. "But I'm still unsure what's the right thing to do." He took a deep breath. "I want to talk to Alexa one more time. Then you'll have my decision."

Lucius' eyes narrowed. "She'll try to stop us."

"How?" Marcus shook his head. "She's blind, and there're two of us." He sighed. "Remember she showed us the shortcut and that storage room. We couldn't have done half this repair work without her help. She *knows* what we're doing."

"She's crafty. But all right." Lucius deftly brought the ship down on a landing pad and then drove it into its hangar on its antigravity cushion. "We talk to her tonight, and one way or another you make your call in the morning."

"Agreed."

They tramped into the north-face entrance, shaking the blizzard-driven snow from their neural-net suits. The two replicants found Alexa working at a computer console with a somber look.

"What are you doing?" Marcus asked, acting nonchalant.

"Deleting every reference to us in the computer files." She pressed an icon and stood.

Lucius stiffened. "Why you doing that?"

"Tonight, Mara will shift us to a different time-place. We needed to modify the systems here so we could survive, but now I must ensure that our presence here doesn't alter history. I have initiated the reversal of the changes we made to Beatrice... to the computer system. She must evolve on her own."

Marcus shook his head. "It'll never evolve. This computer only had rudimentary fuzzy logic capabilities before we upgraded it."

"Of course she will. Beatrice, in my era, is the most sophisticated AI system in the galaxy." She pressed her chronometer to her ear. "We must be standing just outside the north-face entrance in one hour seventeen minutes."

"Tonight?" Marcus paled. "What happens if we're not there?"

"The slim chance for mankind's survival evaporates." Alexa's hand trembled as she clung to the back of the chair beside her. "Will you join me?"

Rage filled Lucius' eyes. "You devious puppet master." He bolted from the control room.

Alexa called after him. "Lucius, come back."

He ignored her plea and fled down the ramp to the gardens below. Marcus did not follow him.

Marcus stood unmoving, his eyes locked on the computer room's viewscreen.

One of their first accomplishments on reconfiguring the expansive cavern was to replace the garish ceiling lights with a golden illumination on the hundreds of floor-to-ceiling pillars. It was done for the practical purpose of creating a natural lighting for the gardens. A side effect was that the improved lighting system created a serene setting that appeared like a perpetual spring morning.

Lucius stopped running at the base of the wide staircase and sat watching to his own horror as the golden lights in the columns dimmed. "I'm alone." Drones meandered, showing no purpose. He sat on the ramp for almost an hour in anguish.

A drone rolled up to him. "Command me, master."

"Don't call me that! I am no one's master."

"You are my maker. You give me purpose. Command me."

The robot's words hit him like a hammer. He sighed. "Alexa wins again. Life needs a purpose, and I'm running away from mine." He rose and stomped back to the control room. "You win. I'll go with you."

No one was there.

He glanced at the console display. The file deletion bar was progressing. He screamed to the empty room. "Alexa, you're wrong to erase everything we've done here. Everyone needs a purpose, even this AI." He slammed the icon, halting the file deletion process. He turned. The drone had followed him.

Tears welled in his eyes. "You stupid machine, get out of here!" He glanced at the door leading to the warehouse. "We're busy. Go do whatever it is you're supposed to do."

"As my maker commands." The drone backed out of the room.

Lucius raced in the other direction. Standing by the sealed garage-like door at the loading dock, he found Marcus holding

Alexa's hand. Without a word, he joined them. In response to his friend's quizzical look, he answered, "I choose not to flee from my responsibilities." He glared at Alexa. "Puppet master, I will go where I am needed and do what I must do or die trying."

Alexa bowed her head and wept.

Chapter XXV

Earth, 485 AD

...Remember.

Lucius blinked and glanced around. He stood in ankle-deep, brackish water. It was early morning on a cloudless day. The weather was already hot. "Where are we?"

Alexa released his hand and wiped the tears from her cheeks. "Per what Mara told me, we are in the year 485 AD at a place on Earth known as Valli di Comacchio." She sniffed. "God willing, four years from now for you, or thirty-three years ago for the rest of the universe, you'll be standing on this very spot, with the fate of humanity in the balance."

"Could have picked a better location. Can we get out of this swamp?" Marcus groused as he lifted his foot. The muck slid right off the boots of his graphene neural-net suit. It was spotless.

"So, this is Earth." Lucius shaded his eyes. "At least it's warm and the sun shines."

Alexa took a step and tripped over a root. She sighed as Marcus helped her to her feet. "A blind guide isn't much use. Mara told me that one-point-six miles north of here we'll find solid ground and a passable road."

Lucius quirked an eyebrow at her "And then?"

Alexa laughed. "And then I don't know. Mara told me where and when but not what or why."

"Any chance there are any real people around here?" Marcus rubbed his hands together. "It will be nice to have someone to talk to besides you and Lucius."

"Yes." Alexa pursed her lips. "But we must be careful. This is a chaotic period of time on the Earth. The civilization that controlled this part of the world, the Roman Empire, collapsed about thirteen years ago. In later years, it will be known as the Dark Ages."

"Wouldn't expect anything else," Lucius deadpanned. "This Mara keeps moving us from one paradise to another."

He looked around at the steamy wilderness. "We better get going. I don't relish being here after dark."

"We'll need something to probe the water ahead of us," Marcus added as he gripped a two-inch-thick sapling beside him.

"Yeah, you're right." Lucius eyed another sapling. Together the two men snapped the young trees off near their base, and with a sharp rock, hacked off the top and stripped the branches. A few minutes later, they both held poles about six feet long.

"Time's wasting. Let's go," Lucius declared as he took a couple steps, poking the mud beneath the opaque water in front of him.

The next three hours were a torture. There was no path through the marshlands. They clambered over fallen trees, waded through thick reeds, and swam across open water. Lucius and Marcus took turns leading and dragging Alexa through the quagmire before they reached solid ground.

They collapsed in a clump of trees, beside a paved road, to decide their next move.

Lucius felt tired, hungry, and irritated. He glanced over his shoulder. "Alexa, why didn't Mara put us on this nice dry road here. Or better yet, in the middle of a market so we could get something to eat."

"A market?" Alexa leaned against the thick truck of a chestnut tree and sighed. "What would you use for money?" She tugged at her graphene neural-net suit. "If we were to be spotted wearing these outfits, people of this era would think we're devils and stone us to death."

"Money." Marcus knew the word conceptually but had never used it or needed to his entire life. "How do we get this *money*?"

"And clothes," Lucius added.

"We'll need to find work," Alexa said. "Until then, we'll have to beg and steal. I..." She cocked her head and whispered. "People approach." She slid to the ground.

Lucius crouched low behind the underbrush and detected motion through the forest on the other side of the road. "You have good ears. There's a dozen of them that I can see."

His sharp eyes picked out each of the skulking men as they trotted behind a stand of trees directly across from their hiding spot. The new arrivals were armed with swords and spears. In a hushed voice, he described the men wearing shabby, mismatched bits of armor to Alexa.

Marcus studied them. "They all look so... different."

"Bandits," she whispered. "Don't move. Our suits will camouflage us from them. They'll continue on soon enough."

"I don't think so." Lucius heard the sound of axes hewing trees. "They appear to be settling in."

Close to an hour passed with no change. Lucius, Marcus, and Alexa remained hidden. Departure in any direction would draw the attention of the brigands. Lucius sat beside Marcus and licked his dry lips. "We'll have to wait until dark to slip past them. We won't be outrunning anyone with a blind woman in tow."

"Leave me then," Alexa spoke in a low even voice.

"I didn't mean it like that," Lucius gasped. "We stick together. I was just working out a—"

Marcus whispered, "Quiet. Some of them are coming this way."

Lucius looked up. The outlaws were spreading out to different places of concealment along the road. Two, carrying unstrung bows and chatting with each other in an indecipherable language, strolled to the coppice of trees where they crouched. He whispered, "Behind the brush. Hurry."

Hidden in the tall vegetation with the natural camouflage of the neural-net suits they were virtually invisible. Marcus guided Alexa to a spot further back. He saw by the way the interlopers carried themselves they were heedless of any potential danger from the swamp.

The bandits made themselves comfortable under a tree near the road, unaware that Lucius and Marcus were a mere ten feet behind them.

Lucius appraised them with a predator's eye. They were lean, well-muscled men with stringy, straw-colored hair flowing from under studded deerskin helmets. Their armor was boiled leather breastplates over leather jerkins. Besides the long bows leaning against the tree, short well-honed swords and daggers hung from their corded rope belts.

The relaxed demeanor of the two outlaws changed the instant they heard the cooing of a mourning dove from further up the road. Lucius saw that the men became all business at the apparent signal. They strung their bows, nocked arrows, and stared intently in the direction where the bird call came from.

Moments later, Lucius spotted teams of oxen pulling a pair of large drays driven by bored teamsters. In front of it were three men on horseback, and behind them two more. The riders all held lances upright and wore what Lucius recognized as Roman spatha swords on their hips. Their armor consisted of ring mail, greaves, and bronze-ridged helmets. Oval shields hung over the horses' flanks.

All of the riders appeared to be about Lucius' own age except for the one in front. The gray-haired leader appeared tense as he swung his head left and right, studying the sides of the road.

Lucius had not seen a human face other than his friend and Alexa in two years, but he instantly chose sides. He whispered, "Those poor souls won't have a chance."

"Let's even the odds," Marcus hissed back.

As the hidden archers drew back their bows, Lucius sprang forward. From the corner of his eye, he saw Marcus do the same.

The yellow-bearded man before him, hearing twigs crack, dropped his bow, drew his sword, and spun around. On spotting a face atop a nearly invisible body coming at him, the bandit froze for a half second. The delay cost him his life.

Since his early youth, Lucius was bred in the stasis pods in every form of human hand-to-hand and ranged combat, but until that moment, his most violent encounters were a couple fist fights with other clones. His training took over. He swung his pole, smashing it into the brigand's face. Reversing his grip, he drove the narrow end of his staff into the outlaw's right eye. As his opponent squealed, the Ipis-trained fighter ripped the short sword from his opponent's spasming hand and stabbed the blade into the man's chest.

The sight of the flaxen-haired brigand's smashed eye socket and the coppery smell of blood sickened him. *I killed someone.* He gagged, staring at the gushing wound. Thrashing bodies a few feet away snapped him from his shock.

Marcus was less successful with his assault. His was grappling with a thick-shouldered opponent for control of that man's dagger. His staff lay shattered on the ground beside a fallen sword.

For my entire life, Marcus has been the only one I could rely on. Lucius' knuckles whitened on his sword's worn leather grip. He leapt to the defense of his friend.

The bandit, sensing the new threat, pushed away and tried to run. Marcus dove at his legs, knocking him down.

Lucius hacked the fallen bandit's raised arm, and then stabbed the man's exposed neck.

As he helped his friend to his feet, Lucius glanced up at the sound of shouts from the roadside ambush. The trees that the outlaws chopped earlier were dropped, blocking the road, arrows raining in from every direction on the trapped convoy.

The noise of their own fight drew the attention of some of the brigands. Three, with spears lowered, charged them from across the road.

Lucius pulled back his confining hood and shook his head. "For better or worse, we picked a side in this fight."

Marcus grunted as he pulled his own hood off. "I don't think we chose wisely. Our side looks doomed." He retrieved a bow and fired. Lucius did the same.

A moment later, two attackers were down and the third was fleeing back to the main group. Lucius called back to Alexa, "Stay down. If we're not back shortly, we won't be returning at all." He tightened his grip on the gore-smeared short sword and picked up a dagger for his left hand.

Marcus, holding the bow, shouldered the quiver of arrows and retrieved the other sword. He studied the men on the road. "I don't like these odds."

Lucius clicked his tongue. "Maybe they won't want to fight us. I have an idea." He stepped on the road, with Marcus at his side. The bandit, who was part of the group that attacked them, sprinted as fast has he could, shouting to his comrades.

The bandits' attack was well-orchestrated and caught the wagons' guards completely by surprise. Two of the guards and a teamster were riddled with arrows, and the gray-haired leader was pinned on the ground beneath his dead horse. With spears, nine outlaws assailed the two remaining guards. Those mounted men slashed about themselves, killing three attackers before being pulled down and slain.

The gang's shout of triumph was cut short as they saw their screaming comrade running to them, and what was behind him.

Lucius knew what he and Marcus looked like to them. Wearing the neural-net suits with only their heads exposed, the brigands saw two heads over ethereal bodies striding toward them, bearing weapons.

Two arrows were launched at him. Lucius winced as one glanced off the material of his suit. He kept walking at a deliberate pace.

One of the bandits cried, "Demon spawn," and ran for the hills. The others followed. Four of the smarter ones mounted their quarry's skittish horses and galloped after those on foot.

"That was easy." Marcus shook his head. "Do we look that scary? We certainly don't look like we belong." He glanced back at the clump of trees. "I'll get Alexa. Grab some clothes from this bunch. The next group we run into might decide to lop our heads off instead of running." He trotted back the way he came.

Lucius found a corpse about his size and stripped him. While donning the rent and rusty ring-mail suit over a bloodstained tunic, he heard a groan. Sheathing a notched spatha, he investigated. The unconscious gray-haired warrior was coming to. As Lucius pulled him free from beneath the dead horse, Marcus approached with Alexa.

Marcus eyed Lucius and then went to find garments of his own.

Alexa knelt beside the injured man and deftly probed the legs for signs of a break. She jerked back at the sound of a voice she recognized. "You. You're the witch, Alexa."

The woman paled. "It can't be."

Lucius looked between Alexa and the old man. His face was vaguely familiar. "You know him?"

The old man, now fully conscious, stared at Lucius. "Merciful God, protect me."

Alexa gripped the young man's arm. "This is the person you were cloned from. This is Legate Lucius Bernius of the Roman First Red Fist Legion."

Wincing, the elderly Lucius pulled himself into a sitting position. He studied the three people with narrowed eyes before grunting. "I think my leg's broken." He eyed Lucius and then Marcus while the blind woman splinted his right leg. Fear crept into his eyes and he turned to Alexa. "Witch, these are the two you conjured up to take my place thirty-five years ago. What happened to my legion... my soldiers?"

"Conjured up?" Lucius froze. "What soldiers?"

Alexa pushed back a strand of blonde hair from her face and squared her jaw. "That event has not yet occurred for them. It's still in their future."

The older Lucius' voice became pleading, "Tell me. What happened after I left? I've rued that decision for countless years."

Alexa's voice became soft. "The pain of not knowing must be terrible." She sighed. "I will tell you everything, but we should move. Those bandits may recover their nerve and return. For now, suffice it to say your legion came through that night's events whole and hearty."

A shuddered moan escaped the old man's throat. "Thank you. It's been torturing me. I—"

All four people turned at a bumping sound from the second wagon. A wizened, old teamster looked up from beneath its driver's bench and warily looked around. "Is it over?"

The elder Lucius glanced around at the dead. "Yes, Quintus, it's over. Now come here. I need help."

A few minutes later, Lucius, Marcus, and the teamster dragged the felled tree to the side of the road and the two drays were moving. Marcus rode in the second wagon with the pale, shaken drover. Lucius sat on the bench of the front one with

Alexa and his elder self. The old man braced his splinted leg on the kick board, gritted his teeth, and held the reins.

They rode in silence for several minutes. The elder Lucius appeared deep in thought. "Why have you returned to trouble me, witch," he blurted.

Alexa bit her lower lip. "I don't know. But I suspect Mara thinks you need to train young Lucius and Marcus for what is ahead of them."

The elder Lucius' brows shot up. "Why would I help these... spawns?"

"Answer your own question," Alexa snapped.

He rode in silence for a few more minutes and then rasped, "For the sake of the men in my legion, I will do it."

"Where are we going?" the younger Lucius ventured. He had no idea what Alexa and the old man were talking about.

"My estate outside of Mediolanum." The elder Lucius studied him for a long moment. "Did I ever look that young?" He turned to Alexa. "If I'm to instruct him, he can't go by Bernius. What name will he use?"

Alexa pursed her lips. "Both he and Marcus will take the surname *Novaroma*. They are inexorably tied to a place with that name."

The elder Lucius snorted. "Novaroma is apt. Old Rome is dead and the world is spiraling into chaos." He shook his head. "This was to be my last trading venture to Venice. The roads have become too dangerous." He extended his hand in a traditional Roman handshake. "Pleased to meet you, Lucius Novaroma. I hope we have a lot in common."

Lucius grasped the extended forearm. "When does my training start?"

"Now," was the brusque reply.

They pushed the oxen hard and arrived at Mediolanum late the following afternoon. By then the elder Lucius, despite the painful leg, was mollified. Long, pointed conversations with Alexa pushed many of the nightmares he had endured over those many years aside. "You're not quite as intimidating as when you appeared as a ghost."

His interrogation of Lucius went less well. "I don't understand much of what you babbled about except that you were trained to fight and spent some time as a farmer in a cave." He shook his head. "Neither will make you a leader."

The younger Lucius focused on the conversations between the old legate and Alexa but understood little. His head spun. Alexa talked about an event in the past that for him would be the future. He grew glummer, absorbing the concerns directed at him by the older version of himself. He realized that his cloistered existence to this point in time ill prepared him for the future. On reaching the estate, it got worse.

Over the years, the elder Lucius and his wife, Dervla, had seven children, six of whom survived to adulthood and one, the eldest, remained at the family holdings, managing the vineyard. Dervla's early life had been hard, but she passed away as the beloved matriarch of the Bernius clan two years earlier. Her death bed was surrounded by her children, nineteen grandchildren, and devoted husband.

Cetus, the oldest son, was in his early thirties. He more closely resembled his Gaelic mother than his father. His smile on spotting his father's wagons turned to smoldering anger on seeing who sat beside him. A young man was there, looking more like his sire than he himself did.

He raged at his father, "You dare bring your bastard to the grounds where my mother is buried." His anger was only banked slightly when he learned about the ambush rescue.

The younger Lucius saw the pain of parental betrayal and felt his own emptiness. He stepped forward. "I am not your father's *son* and will call anyone who says so a liar." He took a shuddered breath and pointed to Marcus and Alexa. "They are the only family I recognize."

Still only partially placated, Cetus and Quintus helped the elder Lucius into the villa.

The younger Lucius, Marcus, and Alexa followed at a discreet distance. Marcus whispered, "I think we better find a *different* place to live."

Two days later, they took possession of a small townhouse the older Lucius owned in the town of Mediolanum.

Chapter XXVI

Days of Future Past

With the endorsement of his sponsor, Lord Bernius, Lucius Novaroma joined the ranks of the Mediolanum city guard. He enjoyed the martial life and rose rapidly through its ranks. As the former Roman empire rapidly devolved into barbarism, the skill and courage Lucius displayed was appreciated in keeping the lands around Mediolanum free of marauding brigands. It led him to being chosen the militia's captain after two years.

Marcus Novaroma rose to be the city magistrate's steward, responsible for the municipal ordinances and maintaining its infrastructure.

Although blind, Alexa became the preferred herbalist and physician in Mediolanum. Her remedies were sought out by rich and poor alike.

* * *

Three years passed.

The replicants', Marcus and Lucius, aging process slowed, growing from the physical equivalent of eighteen-year-olds to twenty-five.

Over that time, Lord Bernius never regained full use of his left leg. The torn tendons in his knee gave him a permanent limp. But during that time his suspicion and fear of the younger version of himself vanished.

The younger Lucius was not afraid of hard work and displayed a sharp mind. He hung on every word that his older self uttered.

Although Cetus continued to believe Lucius was his father's bastard, he never said a word and grudgingly found that he enjoyed the younger man's company. They became friends.

* * *

The elder Lucius was true to his word. The first day after Alexa declared his leg was mended enough to support him, he summoned Marcus and the younger Lucius to the city militia's training ground.

The blind woman accompanied the elderly man to the field. "If I think you're pushing your leg too hard, I will order you to stop."

"And I will ignore you, witch." The gray-haired Lucius grunted. "I know my body better than a blind woman."

That first fencing lesson drew an attentive audience. Several of the city guard gathered to watch. Lord Bernius' fencing skill was legendary, but they had seen impressive talent in their new recruit. Wagers were passed back and forth.

The younger Lucius tentatively hefted the wooden training sword, recalling the martial immersion he received in the Ipis stasis pods as a child. "Old man, with that game leg you're going to get hurt. I've had extensive training in my... youth." Over the several months since his arrival in Mediolanum, he had already dueled and beaten the best swordsmen in the militia. "Why don't you just critique me after I fight someone younger?"

Lord Bernius snarled. "Then you won't have any problem setting me on my arse." He lunged for an attack with a quick, fluid motion.

Lucius, caught off guard, moved to parry, only to realize too late that the sudden attack was a feint.

Off-balance, he lurched to the side. The next blow sent him crashing to the ground. As he looked up, the former legate stood over him with the wooden sword pressed against his chest.

"You're dead," the old man sneered. "*Never* under-estimate an opponent."

Hoots and groans from the railing around the martial yard reflected the winners and losers of the wagers made.

The elder Lucius extended his hand and helped the young replicant to his feet. "If you boys are destined to lead *my* Legion, you must master everything I can teach you."

Lucius grimaced as he brushed the dust from his padded leather jerkin. "I don't believe in destiny. The world is what one makes of it."

"Some things are beyond one's control." Legate Bernius looked pointedly at Alexa before returning his gaze to the young replicant. "Have the courage to change the things you can." He closed his eyes as a single tear trickled down his cheek. "Have the serenity to accept the things you can't and the wisdom to know the difference."

Alexa's voice was barely above a whisper. "That is why you must tutor them."

Marcus gave the former legate a confused look. "I still don't understand. By your own words the First Red Fist Legion was lost decades ago. Yet you speak of their disappearance as something we should know firsthand." He glanced at Lucius. "That was before either of us were *born*."

Old Lucius gave Alexa a sharp glare. "Witch, they really don't know what awaits them?"

Alexa sighed. "They've heard the words, but don't really understand them. No sane person would. That event is three years in their *future*. They have not met your younger self yet. As I said before, it falls upon you to prepare them."

"Your magic bewilders me." The old man shook his head and studied the two younger men. "But for the sake of my legion, I will embrace the role of their mentor." The old man lifted his wooden sword and shifted into a set position. "Ready?" He did not wait for an answer.

* * *

For the next two years, the former legate spent many hours schooling the replicants on the defunct Roman legion's organization, tactics, and weapons. He was a stern taskmaster, and although slowed by age, still an accomplished sword master. He also regaled them with stories about the exploits of the First Red Fist Legion and foibles of its officers.

Those sessions continued even after Marcus became the Mediolanum magistrate's steward and Lucius was promoted to captain of the city's guard.

Lucius found their duels exhilarating. Although younger, faster, and stronger, he soon learned there was much more required to excel at fencing. For the first few months, his wooden training sword rarely reached its mark. But he was an apt martial pupil and never made the same mistake twice. After a year of lessons, he started to dominate the contests but always had to work at it. He grew to love the old man, thinking of him as the father he never had.

They were also instructed in tactics, organization, and logistics. Although Marcus never gained the same weapons mastery as Lucius, he was the more apt student on problem solving. He applied the new skills to his role as the city steward.

Personal combat was ingrained in both Lucius and Marcus from their instructions in the Ipis stasis pods. But these new lessons, delivered with passion and real-world experience, were on the role of leading soldiers. "When you're the commander and make a mistake, good men die."

Young Lucius took those words to heart. As the militia captain, he constantly drilled his company and ensured they had the best equipment available.

Lucius was content in his new life. He found friends and earned respect. He saw no reason leave. Although they continued to live together in the same house, he grew distant from Alexa.

A year into his service as guard captain, it exploded into a heated argument during dinner on a summer's eve.

Alexa said, "Remember, this is just a way-stop in your education."

"You keep saying that. Why?" Lucius snapped. "I like it *here*."

"You have a responsibility to all of humanity; you cannot shirk it."

Lucius rose and glared at the blind woman. "I don't know what that even *means*. Your words made some sense on that empty world, Cocytus, but here I have a purpose. I'm needed."

Marcus laid a hand on Lucius. "We've experienced many strange things in our lives. There is much we don't know."

Lucius ripped his arm from his friend's grasp. "If saving humanity is so important, let Alexa do it. She has all the answers." He stormed out and did not return that night.

* * *

The following day was hot and sticky. Lucius spent the night at the whorehouse and, in the morning, went directly to his office in the militia's barracks. By midafternoon, the sleepless night caught up with him. He struggled to keep a clear head while completing the next week's duty roster for the militia. Disheveled, he sat, thinking about Alexa's words. *It's not fair. I'm a free man and can do as I choose.*

Glancing out the window, he bolted from behind his desk. *Midafternoon already. I must have fallen asleep.*

It was time for the twice-a-week session he and Marcus held with the elder Lucius. He normally relished that time. He groaned. *Not today. I can barely move.*

Lucius studied his sloppy letters on the wax board one more time before rising and walking out the office door. He handed the tablet to the wizened old man who served as his aide. "Quintus, here are the assignments."

Quintus took the roster and scanned it. "I'll have it posted." He looked up. "You look dead on your feet. Rough night?"

"Had a bit of a disagreement with Alexa." Lucius scratched his unshaven chin. "So, I spent some time... elsewhere."

Quintus shuddered. "That aunt of yours scares me. There's something definitely strange about her." He shook his head. "Don't get me wrong. I've never had a cross word with her. But it's like she doesn't belong."

Lucius glanced around the empty room. "Do you think *I* belong?"

"*You* belong more than anyone I ever met." Quintus laughed. "When you rescued Lord Bernius and myself three years ago, you were a penniless wanderer. Look at you now. Captain of the guard."

A smile creased Lucius' face as he took a step toward the exit. "Thanks. You know where to find me if anything comes up."

Quintus grunted. "I've been your aide for almost a year now. I know your schedule better than you do." He clicked his tongue. "You'll be on the militia training yard getting your brains bashed in by the old legate and your cousin, Marcus Novaroma, like every other Tuesday and Thursday." He smiled. "And then you'll retire to Lattes Tavern, listening to old war stories and chasing women."

Lucius rolled his shoulder. "I think I'll be the one doing the bashing." He added with fondness in his voice, "Lord Bernius is an excellent teacher."

"He's the last of a kind." Quintus sighed. "The world is going to hell. None of the roads are safe, and that new self-proclaimed king, Odoacer won't do a thing about it. I have to settle for minding a desk instead of driving a wagon."

"Don't let your tongue wag so much," Lucius cautioned. "I've heard the king has a way of making those who disparage him disappear."

"Then you better tell that to Lord Bernius," Quintus grumped. "When the wine loosens his tongue, he's not diplomatic with his criticisms."

The guard captain paused. He loved listening to the stories the old legate and the other veterans told about the famous Roman Red Fist Legions. Young Lucius frowned. "You're right. These are dangerous times. I will speak to him."

"Good luck with that," Quintus chortled.

Lucius filed the concern away for a later discussion. As he passed through Mediolanum's western gate, although wearing a wine-stained, wrinkled tunic and needing a bath, the gate wardens gave him a sharp salute. Once outside the walled city, a breeze wafted through the century oaks lining the paved road, lifting a little of the oppressive heat. He breathed deeply. *Life is good.* As he turned left and made his way to the exercise yard, he spotted Marcus and Lord Bernius waiting for him. He picked up his pace.

Lord Bernius took in the younger man's appearance, glanced at Marcus, but made no comment. He hefted a wooden spatha and gladius. "Glad you could finally join us."

"I'm sorry." Lucius felt like a child being scolded. But his face broke into a grin when he saw what the day's training session would entail. *Two-weapon fighting, my favorite.*

An hour later all three men were panting, tunics soaked beneath their padded sparring jackets. Lucius and Marcus were pairing up to spar when Lord Bernius called a sharp halt. Coming toward them was Quintus followed by a large, flaxen-haired man wearing a patrician's cape over gleaming, chain-linked armor.

Lucius saw the guarded look in Quintus' eyes and mumbled, "This can't be good."

"Be wary. That fellow has the look of a King Odoacer lackey," Lord Bernius hissed. "Let's see what this stranger wants."

The three walked to the field's railing, but Lucius noticed that the elderly Bernius hung back instead of leading the way.

That thought was interrupted by a pale Quintus. "Captain Novaroma, this is an envoy from King Odoacer. He demanded to speak with you immediately." He gave Lucius a warning look.

The envoy was big, a half head taller than Lucius. His pockmarked face was evident through a stringy beard. He studied the three sweat-stained men before focusing on Lucius. "You Lucius Novaroma, the city militia captain?"

Lucius nodded.

"I'm Ediko, commander of King Odoacer's personal guard. I've heard good things about you." He grunted, appraising the training yard. "We need competent commanders and fighters in the king's army."

"I'm honored by your words. What can I do for you?"

"Who are these others?"

Lucius turned left. "This is my cousin, Marcus Novaroma. He is an administrator for Mediolanum's magistrate." He turned right. "This is—"

"I am Virgil, the fencing instructor for the city guard." The elder Bernius bowed to his waist.

Lucius squinted at the elder Lucius. "Ah, my apologies. Because of his swordsman prowess... *Virgil* feels entitled to speak with his betters."

Ediko sneered. "I found a good flogging quickly cures the underclasses of that attitude." He eyed the younger Lucius. "We have need of your militia. Our spies tell us that the Gothic King, Theodoric, is gathering an army for an invasion."

The younger Lucius gulped. "I have few men to spare. Mediolanum is likely on the path of any incursion."

Ediko handed young Lucius a sealed scroll. "I am not here to barter. When King Odoacer demands conscripts, you *will* provide them." He scratched his chin under the beard. "However, the immediate need is to eliminate Gothic spies. There is rumor of a seditious rabble in this region." He glanced at Marcus. "The city's magistrate pledged *all* of the city's resources to eradicate that problem."

"I live to serve." The younger Lucius broke the seal and scanned the writing. It was a list of names marked for death. He recognized most of them as cashiered legionnaires from the disbanded Red Fist Legions. The name Lucius Bernius was at the top of the list. He needed to think. "Alas, reading is for priests and underlings. I never bothered to learn." He handed the scroll to the elder Lucius. "What does this say?"

"It's a list of names." The elder Lucius rubbed his chin. "I know some of these men. They are all Roman army veterans. Many are dead... of old age." He glanced at Quintus, whose name was also there. "They are a harmless, pathetic lot. With no pensions, those without anyone to take them in became beggars." He handed the vellum scroll back to the younger Lucius.

"Then the citizenry will not complain when they are eliminated." Ediko gave the younger Lucius a pointed look. "It will be worth your while. Do an efficient job and there's a royal commission in it for you."

Sweat beaded on the guard captain's forehead. "When do you need this task completed?"

Ediko swept his cape over his shoulder. "A few days. King Odoacer will be coming through here with his army to face the Goths." He pointed to the paper Lucius clutched. "He will expect to see these heads spiked to the city's ramparts." He turned, "I'll be staying in the magistrate's palace until then."

Lucius watched the envoy depart before speaking. "What can we do?"

Quintus spat. "We fight. None are left from the First Legion but your father and I. However, there are some veterans from the Second and Third Red Fist legions living here. I'll not hide while they get butchered like swine." He faced the elder Lucius. "We must take up arms."

"Some of those veterans can barely walk. You'd have me muster a collection of old men."

"Yes, Legate. That is exactly what I'm saying. Lead us again. Let the standards be raised... one... more... time."

Marcus sputtered. "That's insane. Surely there's a sanctuary you can flee to."

A small smile crept across the old legate's face. "Yes, there is." He regarded Marcus and then cast a wary glance at Quintus. "Your... *mentor*, Marcus Carloman, has wide holdings in Avenio. It's in Gaul, out of reach to that barbarian Odoacer." His look soured as he pointed to the scroll. "But I'll not cower in a foreign land while innocent old men die."

The younger Lucius tapped his thigh with the document. "As Quintus said, call the muster. But instead of gathering them for a hopeless battle, lead them on an exodus to Avenio."

"That's well over three hundred miles. It would be a trek through perdition." The old legate pointed to the scroll. "There must be at least a hundred veterans still alive. How would we get them there? The roads are no longer safe."

"Like the Roman army always has. We walk." Quintus raised his chin. "The last march of the Red Fists. We should do it."

Marcus regarded the other three. "When should we start?"

"Immediately," the younger Lucius snapped. "Marcus, gather wagons and supplies. The veterans won't be hard to find. Most of those not begging on the streets will be in the taverns."

Sorrow showed in the elder Lucius' eyes. "So be it. I will explain the situation to the men." His face hardened. "Once the world trembled at the sound of our approach. Now we flee like rabbits."

Chapter XXVII

Comandante's Office

The next morning, the younger Lucius sagged in his office chair. *A long night.* His militia was efficient rounding up the purported traitors, throwing the city into an uproar. The night-watch constables knew the truth. *They were ordered to seize their own fathers and grandfathers. I'd have had a mutiny on my hands if I didn't tell them the situation. Families will talk and the secret won't hold long, but it doesn't have to.*

He lifted the scroll and scanned the tally. As with all records in the lands of the former Roman Empire, this list was not up to date. Ninety-seven were known to be deceased. Of the rest, one hundred thirteen were rounded up, and eighteen remained unaccounted for.

Lucius sighed as he heard belligerent voices in the outer office. He loosened his sword in its sheath and shouted. "Quintus, tell whoever it is to file a complaint with the magistrate—"

He hadn't finished speaking when Cetus burst in. "What the hell did you put my father up to? Last night, he announced he was leaving *forever* and signed over his entire estate to me. This morning, *brother*, I find over a hundred strangers housed in my barns with *your* guards watching them."

Lucius waved away Quintus standing in the doorway. "Leave us be. I will talk to Cetus." He waited until the old clerk left and then looked long at the face akin to his own. "What did *our* father tell you?"

Cetus, back rigid, sat at the edge of the only available chair. "Some gibberish about a death warrant on his head. That's insane. He's one of the most respected and honored people in the region."

Lucius slid the scroll across the desk. "King Odoacer ordered the execution of every veteran from the Roman Red Fist Legions." He cleared his throat. "As Mediolanum's law enforcement commander, I will not allow that travesty. Last night my constables apprehended the men on this list and spirited them to your estate. Our *father* intends to lead them to a haven in Gaul, beyond Odoacer's reach."

Cetus studied the document for a long moment. His face shifted from rage to fear. "What can I do to help?"

"Wagons and supplies," Lucius responded. "The trip will be over three hundred miles. Most these men are in their sixties. Many have wives."

"It will be the slowest prison break in history." Cetus rubbed his forehead. "The roads are dangerous. Their caravan will be easy prey to brigands and highwaymen."

"Several of my guards have fathers among those veterans. They know what is going on. They volunteered to escort the convoy."

"You won't be going with them?"

Lucius tapped the desk. "No, I will remain. The world is in chaos. Mediolanum needs *me*. I can placate Odoacer's envoy with the explanation of mutiny by traitorous guards."

A soprano voice declared, "You must go with them."

Lucius snapped his head away from his *brother* to the source of the sound. Walking through the doorway with her hand resting on Marcus' arm was Alexa. The elder Lucius, wearing his old Roman legate armor came in behind them. A sheepish Quintus trailed them.

Lucius pointed to his aide. "Quintus, would you please do your job and keep at least a *few* people out of here?"

"Yes, Captain." Quintus snapped a salute and beat a hasty retreat from the door.

Cetus rose and guided Alexa to his chair in the now very crowded room.

Lucius focused on her. "I'm no longer a child. You can't tell me what I should or shouldn't do."

"Marcus, you and myself need to be together when the *event* occurs," the blind woman answered without emotion.

"Simple solution." The guard captain slapped the desk. "Stay here. There is nothing in Gaul for us. Here we are honored and respected."

"You're wrong." Marcus glanced at Cetus and the elder Lucius. "I'd go even if this crisis did not occur. You found your *family*." He shook his head. "*I* need to know who I came from. I need to meet my *father* before Alexa's *event*."

The elder Lucius steepled his fingers. "I will not dally here. Yesterday, I sent a letter to my old friend, Marcus Carloman, begging for sanctuary. I will not wait for a response." He sighed. "This subterfuge won't last long. I have hundreds of people on my estate. Most have friends and family in the city. The gossip will spread like a wildfire. We leave tomorrow at sunrise." He scanned the people in the room. "This conversation is going nowhere. I'd like to speak with the guard captain alone for a minute." He rose and hugged Cetus. "I know your thoughts. But I swear to you the *only* woman I've ever loved was your mother."

Cetus clung to his father. "Will I ever see you again?"

Moisture dampened the elder man's eyes. "Odoacer won't live forever. I'll return." He pushed back. "Now, everyone go."

Alexa sputtered, "I'm staying. Lucius doesn't understand the import—"

"Go," the elder Lucius commanded.

As the people filed out, he called to Quintus, "See that we are not disturbed."

"Yes, Legate."

Lucius sat, back tensed, watching. He stuttered, "M-my mind is made up. My whole life I've been a pawn in someone else's game. I need to choose my own path."

The elder sat in the chair and stared at his folded hands for a moment. "I recognized who *and what* you were when I saw you three years ago. If I wasn't pinned under my horse and only half-conscious, I would have killed you." He opened his hands. "I thank God every day that I did not have that opportunity. You are as dear to me as one of my sons."

A single tear tracked down Lucius' cheek. "You are everything I hoped you'd be... Father." He took a shuddered breath. "What would *you* have me do?"

The corners of the elder Lucius' mouth crinkled. "No. As you said earlier, this must be your decision." He hesitated. "Let me tell you two things and then I'll leave. First, power and influence mean nothing. I led a legion, received a laurel crown, and soldiers leapt at my commands. It all turned to dust." He met Lucius' eyes. "I've learned over the years that the only thing of value in this world is love. With it, any torment can be endured. Without it, nothing will satisfy you."

Lucius grimaced. "I... understand."

"No. You heard me, but you do not *yet* understand." The elder Lucius pursed his lips. "The second thing was an event from my past, and as Alexa tells me... your future. Thirty-five years ago, looking exactly as you do now, you appeared beside me. I did not know what to make of you, so I took you as a prisoner and brought you to my quarters. There you saved my life."

Lucius was not sure what he was going to hear, but this wasn't it. "What?"

"There was an assassin waiting for me inside. I did not see him." The elder Lucius gulped. "I would have died that night. None of my children would have ever been born. You were there and saved me." He rose. "Those are the facts."

The younger Lucius stared at the blank plastered walls in silence as the old man left. Quintus entered holding a jug of sour-smelling wine and a wrapped bundle, interrupting his thoughts. "Did you hear everything?"

"Of course, I did. I've never been insubordinate a day in my life, but I am today. Flog me if you must." The gray-whiskered man sat uninvited. "But I need to take a few liberties."

Lucius quirked an eyebrow and smiled. "What's on your mind?"

Quintus poured wine into two mugs and slid one to his captain. "Since today seems to be the day for telling stories, I have one too. There's probably only a couple of us still alive who remember... Thirty-five years ago, not far from where you rescued us from those bandits, the world turned upside down. Word spread through the ranks that our Imperator, Flavius Aetius, was murdered and everyone loyal to him were marked as traitors to the empire." He took a long draught and then refilled his mug. "I was part of a reinforced patrol sent out that night. I thought it strange that the cavalry commander, Martinel, personally led the scouting mission. And I knew something was afoot when the legate and Marcus Carloman

228

joined us with hoods pulled low over their faces. But I held my tongue."

He unwrapped the bundle revealing the bronze eagle standard of the First Red Fist Legion. "Two hours out, the ground shook and night sky blazed with a bright blue light. When we rode back, the First Legion was... gone. A brackish smelling marsh covered the land where our camp was."

Captain Lucius twitched. "So, you saw what happened that night? I've heard this story from the legate. It is... incredible."

Quintus ran his fingers across the standard. "That event broke the legate's spirit. Before that night he was a cocky, self-assured commander. After that, he withdrew within himself, becoming a farmer and merchant. He never issued another command or even raised his sword... until you appeared. Meaning no disrespect to you, Captain, you are an exact twin of the legate that night." Quintus cleared his throat. "I don't have a clue whether you're a bastard son or a magical incarnation. It doesn't matter a whit. Somehow you healed him. I've never seen him more alive than he's been since you showed up. It's as if a great crushing burden lifted from his shoulders."

Lucius spread his hands. "Why are you telling me this now?"

Quintus pointed to the standard head. "That evil night, I watched him bury this near the border of the Valli di Comacchio swamp. It was in the glade where you and your *cousin* arose from. A few weeks ago, I returned there and retrieved it."

"Coincidence." Captain Lucius shuddered and gulped the sour wine. "We just happened to be camped on that spot when we saw those highwaymen laying their trap."

Quintus' eyes narrowed. "If you say so. But I think it was divine providence." He leaned forward. "The legate *needs* you. He'll be leading a caravan of old men and women on a hazardous trek." He rose and carefully rewrapped the bronze eagle. "I'll be leaving in the morning with them. Come with us."

"I'll tell you the same thing I told the legate... I will think on it."

Quintus rose and walked to the door without waiting to be dismissed. "I need to pack and burnish my old armor. Don't think on it too long. I'll be departing from the west gate at dawn."

Lucius grimaced and poured more wine in his cup. "I said I... will... think on it."

He finished the jug. Forty-eight hours with only one short snatch of sleep, plus the wine, caught up with him. He didn't awaken until the midmorning sun shone through a high window of the office.

Chapter XXVIII

At the Crossroads

A nervous militiaman shook Lucius. "Captain Novaroma, there's a problem at the west gate. We need your instructions."

Captain Lucius groaned and squeezed the bridge of his nose. "What is it? Smuggled contraband? I think you can handle that without me?"

"No, sir. Quintus passed on your orders for the gates to be closed until midday. However, there's an outlandish barbarian, who claims to be King Odoacer's envoy, with a company of well-armed riders. He insists on being allowed to leave."

"What?" Lucius rose. "I posted no such order."

The guard took a step back. "It bore your seal. The sergeant-of-the-guard told the barbarian he would have to stay put until you personally rescinded the command. When this fellow, Ediko, started making threats, I was sent to fetch you."

Lucius glanced at his desk. His stamper lay there by a melted candle. *Quintus, what have you done?* Now fully awake, he strapped on his spatha and grabbed his cloak from its hook on the white plastered wall. "You acted correctly. I'll go there now. This... misunderstanding must be defused." He shook his head. "In case my diplomatic skills are insufficient, inform Lieutenant Nicabar to muster the militia. I want them at the West Gate ready for a fight." Beside the stamper was a rolled cloth. He opened it to see a white banner. It was a crudely painted raised clenched red fist with a broken manacle around the wrist.

Quintus! He shoved the cloth in his satchel and ran through the busy midmorning crowds, his sandaled feet slapping on the stone pavement.

He pulled up short. Civilians were cowering in doorways and peering out windows. The gate stood wide open and four of his men lay, unmoving, facedown on the bailey. One was his sergeant-of-the-guard. They weren't the only dead there. Five others, wearing gothic armor, were shot full of arrows. He glanced up at the portcullises.

Two of his guards, holding bows and wearing empty quivers, stood there. Horror was in their voices as they shouted to him. "Captain, they killed the sergeant without any warning and then charged the gate. We... we couldn't stop them."

Lucius heard the rhythmic clopping of horses on the paving stones and then startled cries. *My militia's arrived.* He looked at the empty road beyond the gate. *I can't allow the legate and his comrades to be murdered. Why do I have no control over my life's path?* He turned to his lieutenant, Nicabar, and the lead scout, Julio, as they cantered their steeds up to him. "Bring me a horse and have someone retrieve my armor." He pointed to the dead. "The killers of our men will not escape." He glanced at the forty-one lancers lined up in precise rows. "I want the *entire* militia ready to ride, and *fight* in a half hour."

Rage filled Nicabar's eyes as he responded "Yes, Captain Novaroma," and hurried off barking orders.

Julio stayed and glanced at the empty road. "Those marauders have at least an hour's lead on us now. In another half hour, even if we press, we won't catch them until tomorrow."

Lucius glanced at the clear sky. "I expect to find them before *this* evening. They are hunting the veterans of the Red Fist Legions." He patted the satchel containing the banner Quintus made. "They'll go first to the Bernius estate and will find their prey departed. Three major roads intersect near there. Ediko does not know which one Lord Bernius' caravan took. He will lose time scouting them." Glancing at Julio he added, "I know where Lucius Bernius is heading, *and* we won't need to limit ourselves to those main roads."

Julio nodded. "But what do we do when we catch them? I've seen their column when they arrived. This isn't a band of highwaymen we pursue. Ediko has a trained cavalry escort over two hundred strong."

Lucius snapped, "I'll think of something. I'll not have innocent people butchered in my jurisdiction if I have the power to prevent it." He heard the snort of fresh horses as more of his men arrived. *I hate horses.* Since arriving in Mediolanum, he had learned to ride but never enjoyed it. He could stay in the saddle without falling off, but that was about it. He shuddered. *This will be a hard ride over rough country.*

He glanced at the open gate. *Again, I have no choice in my actions.* He thought it resembled a gaping maw, mocking him. *The fates are cruel.*

Chapter XXIX

March of the Red Fist

The elder Lucius stood with Cetus where the road ran past the entrance to his estate, gazing east toward Mediolanum.

Cetus followed his father's eyes. "It's an hour past sunrise. *He's* not coming." He glanced at the line of twenty-one hitched wagons. "Every moment you delay puts yourself and these people in greater danger."

The elder Lucius regarded himself. He wore the legate armor he put away thirty-seven years earlier. It still fit his lean body. Sighing, he hugged his son. "Odoacer won't live forever. I'll be back."

Cetus returned the rough hug. "I love you, Dad. Be careful."

The elder Lucius glanced around at the expectant people, his eyes finally resting on the blind woman sitting with clenched hands in the lead wagon beside Marcus. "Riders, mount up. Wagons, forward."

The slow caravan headed west on the old Roman road.

* * *

It was an hour before sunset and the elder Lucius was pleased. They had covered almost sixty miles. *Excellent progress. At this pace, we'll cross into Gaul in three more days.* He glanced at a small brook running through an open field to his right. A thick forest spread a couple hundred yards beyond that. He raised his hand to halt the wagon train. "We'll camp here for the night."

An old veteran from the Third Red Fist Legion trotted to him from the rear. "Legate, a rider approaches."

Lucius' brows furrowed. "It's a public road. We've seen other traffic." He glanced back along their route, catching a gleam in the late afternoon light. "Why do you bring a lone rider to my attention?"

"Legate, he's carrying the First Red Fist Legion eagle standard."

The legate's jaw tightened. *I buried that symbol along with the memory of those good men thirty-seven years ago.*

A few moments later, he recognized Quintus clinging to a galloping, lathered steed. He feared to learn why the old drover was abusing his mount. He called to the old men leading the ox-drawn wagons into the field. "Red Fist legionnaires, arm yourselves." It was a command he hadn't issued in decades, and one he hoped to never utter again.

Quintus galloped straight to where the elder Lucius awaited him at the side of the road. Marcus stood at his side. Gasping, he cried out, "Legate, Ediko is coming after you with a cavalry company. I counted about two hundred warriors. I did what I could to delay them, but they can't be more than an hour behind me."

Marcus studied the setting sun. "There's no escape. Ox-drawn drays can't outpace a cavalry horse."

"Then we fight," Legate Bernius snapped. He shouted so all could hear. "Pull the wagons near the forest." He crossed his arms. "It will be night soon. Perhaps they will pass us in the dark."

"If not?" Marcus gasped.

Legate Bernius gritted his teeth. "Then we sell our lives as dearly as we can." He pointed to the forest. "We have close to a hundred men. The trees will keep the enemy in front of us."

Marcus paled. "It'll be a slaughter. Almost everyone here is over sixty."

Quintus lifted his chin. "Young Marcus, you have never seen the famed Red Fist Legions in combat. We were the greatest fighters in the world."

Marcus shook his head. "That was decades ago."

The legate's shoulders sagged. "Perhaps if they see armed men ready to fight, they'll let us depart peacefully."

Besides Marcus and about a dozen militia men whose fathers were in the wagon train, all the younger men were peasant farmers.

The legate scanned the tree line and then focused on Marcus. "Your... *father* was the greatest military engineer I ever knew. I pray you have some of his skill. Build a defense that will give us a chance against a cavalry force twice our numbers."

Marcus' mouth slimmed to a tight line as he studied the terrain. "You ask the impossible. The ground's flat and, except for the tree grove, open. With only an hour, there's not much we can do." He squinted at the thick grove. "We'll need sharpened stakes to slow a cavalry charge." He nodded to the gathering crowd of men wearing old armor. Some looked defiant, others scared, others resigned. He ordered, "Grab axes and shovels and follow me."

He turned to the legate. "Circle the wagons by the forest."

The elder Lucius gave the orders. The oxen lowed as the teamsters drove the bouncing wagons across the field. The old men followed Marcus to a stand of saplings.

An hour later, a voice cried, "They're coming."

The elder Lucius roared, "Everyone, behind the barricade. Archers, nock your arrows." He appraised the mounded dirt breastwork topped with sharpened staves and turned to Marcus. "Good work. You would have fit in well as a member of the First Legion."

The younger man, covered in dirt and sweat from the hard work in the midsummer heat, sighed. "We'll find out how effective it is soon enough." Dropping the mud-caked shovel, he belted on his sword and hefted a shield.

The elder Lucius positioned his two dozen archers in the center. The rest, holding a mismatched collection of spears, swords, and axes, lined the breastworks. The oxen were corralled in the circle of wagons behind them. They did not have to wait long.

* * *

Ediko sat atop his horse outside of arrow range, studying the makeshift fortification in the waning light. He was an experienced commander, honored by King Odoacer for many victories. He turned to his aides. "We have the traitors cornered."

His practiced eye appraised the strengths and weaknesses of his intended prey. Despite himself, he was impressed by what was constructed in what had to be a short amount of time. He sighed to those around him. "No one ever said the Romans didn't know how to build." He pointed to one of his lieutenants. "Gather what oil jars we have. Take a squad and ride back until you're out of sight. Then go in the woods behind them and set it ablaze. We'll smoke them out into the open."

The officer saluted and cantered off with ten cavalrymen behind him.

* * *

On spotting his lead scout, Julio, gallop toward him, Lucius called a halt and slapped at an insect that got inside his leather gauntlet. As the lowering sun sank toward the rolling hills of the horizon behind the rider, he guessed they had finally caught up with their foes.

His lieutenant, Nicabar, sat on his mount beside him, also watching the approaching scout. "I pray we're not too late."

His column had returned to the main road hours earlier. Although they were only about sixty miles from Mediolanum, none of his militia had ever been that far from home. He had pushed both men and horses hard in the humid August heat of northern Italy. Everyone was exhausted and wary in this strange new territory.

Julio saluted. "Well, we found our quarry. Both the caravan and the barbarians are a half mile up this road. No one's fighting yet, but the brigands have the wagon train pinned down along the woods." The scout pursed his lips. "I hope you have a good plan. I counted about two hundred armored riders. They're ringing in the wagons on three sides." He pointed south. "But I saw about ten of them creep into the woods. Probably to cause havoc in the rear when the main body attacks from the front. They left two men to watch their horses at the tree line."

Lucius nodded. "Good report. Did anyone spot you?"

Julio snorted. "No, Captain. I know my job." The scout looked over his shoulder. "Whatever we're going to do, it better be fast. The barbarians appear to be readying themselves for action." He cleared his throat. "Ah, Captain, one other thing. The defenders have raised a Roman eagle standard. I recognize it from my uncle's description. It's the old Red Fist First legion."

"Good work. I want you to lead me to where those skulkers entered the woods." Lucius had no doubt about what they must do. "Do you think we can dispatch those two in the open before they can raise an alarm?"

Julio grinned and hefted his small horse-bow from its sheath. "Won't be able to get close enough for knife work, but bring along a few good archers and it should be no problem."

Lucius turned to his lieutenant. "Nicabar, I'll lead twenty of our best bowmen to dispatch those brigands in the woods. Then I'll link up with Legate Bernius from the caravan's backside." He pulled the banner from the pouch hanging at his side. "Stay out of sight, but have a patrol watch the caravan. When you see this flag waving. Charge in, making the racket of a thousand. Understood?"

Nicabar gave his commander a pensive look. "Captain, we've pulled that stunt on bandits enough times, but these barbarians are veteran warriors. They won't be easily fooled." He tapped his chest. "All we have for protection are studded jerkins and leather caps."

Lucius dismounted, cinched his sword to his waist, and slung a bow and quiver over his shoulder. "We *don't* want to fight them unless we have to." He tightened his gear down so it would not make any noise. "By the time the action starts, it'll be dark. Your racket will create confusion. They'll be unsure of your numbers. Act aggressive, but leave the road heading east open."

He picked his twenty men and followed Julio through the underbrush. Behind a thick hedge about a hundred feet from the tree line the scout paused. He eyed the dusky sky and whispered to Lucius. "This is as close as we can get without being spotted."

Lucius worried about the uncertain light but saw no other choice. "Just as we trained." He glanced at the men bunched around him.

The attack almost went as planned. The two barbarians went down with four or five arrows protruding from each. However, one of the horses, struck in its flank, whinnied in pain, ripped free of the tie-line, and bolted. The terrified animal and the scent of blood spooked the other animals. They bucked, tore free of the stakes, and followed the first.

"So much for a surprise," Julio groaned.

Lucius snapped to his soldiers. "Get into the woods and hide. Someone will come and check things out."

A few moments later, two barbarians carrying torches and drawn swords warily trod along a deer path from the woods to investigate the sound.

"Idiots." Julio grinned as he drew his wide-bladed hunting knife. "Can't mark a target any better than carrying a light in the dark."

Lucius grunted. "And we now know which path that bunch in the trees are on."

The two new arrivals were dead before they even knew they were in danger.

"Only about six more," Julio snarled as he wiped the gore from his blade. "This is too easy—"

Lucius held up his hand. "Do you smell that?"

"Smoke."

One of the militiamen pointed to a glow that sprang up through the trees. "The forest is on fire."

"So that was their plan." Julio rubbed his jaw and checked the direction of the August breeze. "This grove is tinder dry."

Lucius nodded. "Ediko's not planning on rooting out the entrenched Romans. He's going to let the fire chase them into the open and slaughter them." He heard coughing men approach from the direction of the blaze.

There were soon four more dead barbarians on the forest trail. But in the dark, at least two escaped the ambush and fled.

"Julio, get the men back to Nicabar." Lucius' eyes watered from the choking, ash-filled air. "I'm going to get through. Someone has to let the legate know help is close at hand."

"Captain, you're crazy." He pointed to the orange flames leaping from tree to tree. "You'll never get through."

Lucius unraveled the crude flag. Quintus had painted it on an oil-skin cape. "I'll make it. I have to." He dosed his head and clothes from his water skin, pulled the scrawled banner over his head, and ran. Every moment spent on further discussion lowered his chance for survival. A dozen steps later, any chance to reconsider his decision was rendered moot as a flaming bough fell on the path behind him. *The only way out now is forward.*

He knew the legate's encampment was directly north of where they waylaid the barbarians. Self-doubt gnawed at him as he staggered forward, disoriented in the smoke and searing heat.

Then he was in the open, tripping over a wagon harness. He fell to his knees, sucking in clean air. His relief was short-lived, as he found several spears poised within inches of him.

An old voice that sounded familiar cracked, "Who the hell are you?"

Lucius pulled the charred banner off his head and looked up in the light of a torch. "You should know, Quintus."

Quintus gasped. "Captain, how did you get here?"

"No time for that. Where's Legate Bernius? I have the Mediolanum militia company here to help." His voice may not have been as steady if he knew that, moments earlier, he was within a hairbreadth of being skewered by a startled guard. Only the charred symbol of the Red Fist Legion draped across his back stayed the old legionnaire's deadly thrust.

The legate hurried over, with Marcus guiding the blind Alexa right behind him. All the other people were busy throwing buckets of water on the flames behind them or watching for an attack from the horsemen before them.

The younger Lucius watched the elder one absorb the plan he relayed.

A feral grin creased the legate's face. "A solid tactic. I'm proud of you." He fingered the charred banner. "Quintus, raise this and sound the clarion."

"Yes, Legate."

The older man rested his hand on the younger Lucius' shoulder, "Let's spring your little surprise on Ediko." He gave the blazing trees a wary glance. The flames were close to the rearmost wagons. "We're out of time anyway."

The oxen lowed and pushed against the makeshift corral as smoke and sparks drifted over them.

"I think I know who will lead our charge." The elder Lucius' eyes narrowed and shouted to the drovers trying to calm the beasts. "Open a path for the oxen." He turned to the gathered legionnaires. "When the beasts stampede past, we follow them out."

The old legionnaires sprang to push two wagons aside and clear the stakes beyond them. They returned and formed into ragged rows as the clarion blew a clear note.

A second later, an answer blared from the east, announcing the militia's arrival. Lucius threw his head back and ululated a bloodcurdling scream as the oxen thundered by.

The old legate, clenching a sword, raised his hand and strode through the break in the earthen wall. Quintus, bearing the First Red Fist Legion eagle standard, walked beside him, with Marcus and Lucius close behind. The old Red Fist legionnaires, raising their shields and spears, followed.

The stampeding oxen scattered the barbarians immediately in their path. The column of aged Roman veterans marched through the gap the steers created in the encircling force. Backlit by the burning forest, they appeared larger than life and ghoulish.

Under the light of a half moon in a clear August night sky, Captain Lucius saw the barbarians split into two columns. Half lowered their lances and charged the infantry attempting to break out. The rest rode to face the unknown assailants at their rear. He listened to Ediko's booming voice and turned to the old legate. "Our feint didn't fool Ediko. He's blocking my militia until he deals with your infantry."

The old commander grimaced. "Few plans survive contact with the enemy." He shouted, "Form shield wall."

The veterans responded. But there were too few to slow the attacking barbarians. The cavalry smashed through the thin line, scattering them.

The fight devolved into chaos. Lucius, dodging the attackers in the semi-dark, became separated from the others. As one barbarian slowed to strike a fallen legionnaire, Lucius leapt up behind him and slit his throat. After dumping the body, he wrestled with the reins to control the skittish animal. *I hate horses.*

Scanning the field, Lucius spotted the old legate rallying a tight cluster of men. Others were scrambling in that direction.

As Lucius urged his new mount in that direction, he saw Ediko, waving a raised sword, lead a dozen lancers charging toward the gathering Roman infantry. He shouted, "Father, look out," and spurred his mount to intercept the attackers. He got there, and with a loud clang, crossed swords with the large barbarian commander. But as they dueled, his unfamiliar horse reared, throwing him to the ground. Disoriented, he stumbled to his feet and discovered the old legate standing protectively beside him.

The elder Lucius handed him his sword. "I think you dropped this... son." He pointed to Ediko, who had wheeled around and was coming back. "Fighting a warrior on horseback from the ground with just a sword is no easy task. Let's see how well you learned your lessons."

A tight smile creased the young Lucius' face as he raised his sword. "With pleasure."

* * *

Ediko's horse reared when an arrow grazed his flank. When the barbarian regained control of his mount, he blinked at the sight of the militia captain standing shoulder to shoulder with the old sword master. In the shifting firelight, their faces looked the same. He growled, "I'll kill both you traitors." A thunk on his horse shield caught his attention. "Eh, what's this?" An arrowhead was buried in it. Looking around, he saw that the force he sent against the unknown riders had been routed and the attack on the infantry had also stalled. A band of foot soldiers, led by the city magistrate's steward, had joined the group he had just attacked. A tight wall of shields bristling with spears had formed around the eagle standard. "What's this? Is the whole city of Mediolanum a pit of traitors?"

* * *

Lucius saw the barbarian leader scan the battlefield and saw fear form on his face. He gave Ediko a mock salute when their eyes met.

Ediko spat, wheeled his horse around, and galloped east shouting, "Retreat." His surviving men needed no encouragement. They broke off and fled after their leader.

Chapter XXX

Welcome to Gaul

The next three days were hard but uneventful. Of the wagons they started with, only eleven remained serviceable after the fire. The drovers were only able to round up enough oxen to pull nine of them. So, four captured calvary horses were put in harness for the other two carts. The human carnage was as bad. Although the fight was brief, sixteen old veterans died and fourteen were seriously wounded. The militia fared better. Three were lost, with an additional five too severely injured to ride. Many precious belongings were left behind as the wagon space was allocated for the wounded, food, and water.

Although Alexa was an accomplished healer, five of the injured perished and six of the walking wounded sickened and had to be put into the wagons.

Most of the militia company stayed with the wagon train. Only five chose to take their chances returning to Mediolanum. Julio shrugged and echoed the opinion of most. "Can't go back now. I guess it's time to see new places."

Midmorning on the fourth day after the fight, the situation appeared to become grimmer. The younger and older Lucius rode together at the head of the convoy when a militiaman in the rearguard galloped up. He saluted. "Captain, there's a calvary force coming from the direction of Mediolanum. There's about six hundred of them and they're flying Odoacer's colors." He gulped. "I think I saw Ediko leading them."

The legate scanned the surrounding countryside. It was open rolling hills with not a hint of concealment in the vicinity. "How much time do we have?"

"Twenty minutes at most."

While the legate pondered the news, Julio galloped back from the point.

"This can't be good," the captain groaned.

Julio approached, gasping for air. "Sirs, there's a column of barbarians coming from the west. Must be over a thousand. By their armor, I believe they are Franks. Mostly infantry, but there's a few companies of horsemen screening them."

"How long?"

"Infantry... maybe an hour. Their outriders... any moment now. They were right behind me."

Marcus, who joined them when the scouts reported, lamented, "There's nowhere to flee to. We can't go forward, and we can't go back."

The younger Lucius squared his shoulders. "Then we make our stand here." He looked west and saw a rider atop a hill. The morning sun reflected off his armor as he rose in his stirrups, studying them, making no pretense to hide his presence. He pointed the man out. "They're already here."

The rider turned and disappeared on the far side of the hill.

The legate appeared to shrink within himself. He regarded the younger Lucius. "I'm glad I lived to know you... son. I will be proud to die by your side."

"I'm not ready to die just yet... Father. We can—"

Marcus pointed west, "We're out of time. They're here." A dozen lancers led by a very fat man on a large horse cantered into view.

Young Lucius turned to Julio. "Go keep an eye on the force behind us. Let me know when they are closing."

Julio nodded and galloped east.

The captain shouted as he drew his sword, "Militia to me." He studied the approaching group and became confused. The large man in the lead raised an open hand indicating a desire to parley. The small band of riders approached at an easy trot. He turned to the elder Lucius. "They look more like an emissary mission than an attacking force. Any idea what's going on?"

Elder Lucius squinted at the large man with the raised hand leading the Franks. A small smile crept across his face. "Perhaps we won't die today after all." He slid his sword back in its scabbard and urged his mount forward.

Marcus and Captain Lucius glanced at each other and followed.

A hundred feet in front of the caravan they met. Young Lucius was shocked as the elder Lucius dismounted and limped toward the new arrivals as fast as he could with open arms. At the same time, the large barbarian hooted, "Lucius," and did the same. The two met and wrapped each other in a fierce embrace.

"It's good to see you, old friend. You're looking good."

"Lucius, you're a terrible liar. I'm old and fat."

"We're both old." The elder Lucius laughed.

"That's the truth." Yellow teeth shone in a wide grin through a thick gray beard. "You're limping. What happened?"

The elder Lucius shrugged. "A horse fell on me." He paused and looked over his shoulder and signaled Marcus and younger Lucius forward. "There's a couple people I want you to meet."

The Frank regarded his friend's escorts and gasped. "Tell me the one is your son."

"Not exactly," the elder Lucius responded as the two drew near. "Martinel, this is Lucius and Marcus *Novaroma*. You met them once, thirty-seven years ago."

"The demon spawn," Martinel sputtered as he gripped the pummel of his sword. "What are they doing here? How come they haven't aged? Has the witch who conjured them returned?"

The elder Lucius shook his head. "Stay your hand. I vouch for them. They are both good and honorable men innocent of the evil that befell us that night."

Martinel released his grip on the blade and regarded the two young men. "Lucius, on that point, I'd challenge anyone but you."

Younger Lucius flushed and bowed. "Martinel... I am equally befuddled by all of this. Alexa claims that Marcus and I will not experience that event for another year. The legate speaks of you often and fondly." He straightened. "Perhaps we could discuss these matters at a later time. A full battalion of King Odoacer's calvary will be upon us any minute now."

246

Martinel spat. "Odoacer's an idiot. But even he wouldn't dare anger the Franks when he's busy with the Goths."

Elder Lucius looked sideways at his old friend. "So why have you so fortuitously arrived here? This is no coincidence."

Martinel puffed out his chest. "Being the Frankish baron of the Rhone River region, I often dine with the nobility in my jurisdiction." He rubbed his girth. "I was enjoying a fine meal with a mutual friend of ours and he shared with me the letter you sent him." He glanced at Marcus Novaroma and shook his head. "Were any of us ever that young?"

"I've been living with this reminder of my youth for three years now." The elder Lucius' smile was warm. "I treasure that time with him... with them."

"We have so much to talk about." Martinel shook his head. "Anyway, both Lord Carloman and I agreed that our old commander would surely be in trouble, so I headed this way with what troops I could muster on short notice."

Marcus looked over his shoulder, "Could we postpone this happy reunion for another time? Ediko's force will not wait for us to finish socializing."

Martinel huffed. "Ediko you say. I've heard of Odoacer's attack dog. I'll send that mongrel packing. Keep your wagons moving. You're now in Gaul. That puts you under the protection of the Frankish king."

The legate waved to the drovers, and the wagon train lurched forward.

Captain Lucius barked, "Militia form up in ranks and block the road."

The mounted men quickly arrayed themselves in three even rows across the road. Lances were raised in the front two lines. Archers nocked their bows along the third.

"Solid discipline." Martinel whistled. "Who trained them?"

"I did," the younger Lucius responded.

"It appears you're more akin to your sire than just in appearance."

"Thank you. That means a lot to me." Lucius glanced at the slow-moving caravan as it rolled past them. "Lord Martinel, could I trouble you to bring up your infantry? If the report from my patrols is accurate, we'll be at a distinct disadvantage shortly."

Martinel nodded and turned to his aide. "Bring up the troops on the double."

The man galloped off.

The elder Lucius gave the Frank a quizzical look. "It's a fair-sized force that pursues us."

Martinel grinned, drew his sword, and planted the tip in the ground. "I'm an old man. My fondest memories were of the two of us fighting side by side in our youth. I cherish the chance to do that one more time." He slapped his friend on the back. "Besides, in my years I have gathered many enemies. I can't afford to lose the few true friends I have."

Young Lucius watched the last wagon and the old men in Roman armor trudging at its side disappear from view over the hillcrest. "I have an idea."

Martinel cocked an eyebrow. "I'm listening."

"Keep your force out of sight behind the hill." Young Lucius studied the terrain. "I'll array my company on the road at the top of the hill as bait. When Ediko attacks, we'll fall back. That will be the signal for your archers to fire."

Martinel's eyes gleamed. "I like it so far. Keep going."

"Position your pikemen in the center and your calvary on the left. I'll swing my company to the right and we'll catch them in a pincer move."

Martinel chuckled and looked at the elder Lucius. "The boy has a brain. Let's do it."

The men mounted their horses and galloped to their assignments.

From the hillcrest, young Lucius saw Julio whipping his horse toward him on the road, making no attempt at stealth. Beyond him, a cloud of dust transformed into cantering lancers.

Young Lucius' eyes were caught by Martinel returning to his steed and positioning himself next to the elder Lucius.

The Frank laughed as he drew his long straight-bladed sword. "I want to see this Ediko's face when we spring our surprise greeting."

"They're here," Julio gasped as he reached his captain on the hilltop. "Mostly lancers, but a few..." He looked past his commander toward the base of the hill. The wagon train was creaking its way through a thousand Frankish warriors arraying themselves for battle. His face beamed. "...archers. Sir, where do you want me?"

"Your horse is spent. Go join the caravan."

"No, sir. Sorry, sir. You need me here."

The captain nodded. "Then stay behind me and watch my back."

Martinel, who had listened to the conversation, scanned the eighty-odd Mediolanum militia, who stoically lined up across the road. He turned to the elder Lucius. "His men are faithful to him. I would know that young man is a good leader even without your word on it."

"That he is." The elder Lucius smiled and then pointed to the dust cloud. It had coalesced into a wide line of calvary. A clarion blared from that oncoming horde and they broke into a gallop. "Ediko is taking the bait."

The younger Lucius called to Martinel, "Remind your bowmen hold their fire until Ediko's force crests the hill."

Martinel nodded and relayed the command to his aides.

"Militia hold your position. Archers ready." The younger Lucius raised his hand and watched the attackers close to within two hundred feet. He roared, "Loose."

His twenty-one militia archers drew back their short horse bows and fired.

With the next breath he called, "Fall back."

As one, the horsemen turned, rode over the hillcrest, and turned right at the line of Frankish warriors with their spears planted in the ground. Martinel kept his eyes locked on the hilltop. As the first attacker came into sight he yelled, "Fire."

Over two hundred Franks loosed their arrows into the faces of the shocked enemy's vanguard, decimating them.

The Frankish and Mediolanum calvaries closed in on the flanks, mauling Ediko's vanguard caught on the wrong side of the hill. The survivors broke and fled to their main body.

Marcus, sitting astride a mount beside Captain Lucius, exalted, "We bloodied their noses. That will send them packing."

"Ediko doesn't seem the type to quit that fast," the younger Lucius cautioned. His emotions shifted from triumphant exaltation to unease at several moments of silence. "He's up to something."

Marcus pointed to his left. "Look. They're coming around the hill."

The captain rose up in his saddle. "One of the vanguard's survivors had a level head and a sharp eye. Our militia on this flank is far smaller than the Frankish cavalry on the other side."

He saw hundreds of enemy lancers sweep across the broken ground toward his militia. At the same time, a company of their archers appeared atop the hill and began firing into the Frankish infantry clumped below them. Lucius turned to his friend. "Marcus, we must hold this flank. Inform Martinel that we need reinforcements."

Marcus galloped off as twice their number smashed into the militia with lowered lances. Through the wild melee, Ediko spotted Lucius rallying his dwindling company. With his long, curved saber held aloft, he charged toward his nemesis roaring, "Death to the traitor."

Young Lucius wheeled his horse to face the oncomer, but the mount reared as an arrow grazed its haunches. While trying to regain control of the animal, Ediko attacked and gashed the captain's exposed arm. They were so close that Lucius could smell the barbarian's fetid breath and see the gleam of an expected easy victory in the man's eyes.

"You escaped me once. You won't be that lucky a second time," Ediko snarled as he slashed at his opponent's head. However, Lucius' skittish horse lurched and the blow struck nothing.

As his horse reared, Lucius also swung. The blade bit deep into an exposed opening above the barbarian's iron collar.

Surprise lit Ediko's eyes as blood sputtered from his neck. He gasped and fell from his horse.

Young Lucius' sense of triumph evaporated. His men had been driven back, and he was isolated behind enemy lines. Hemmed in, a barbarian charged at him with a leveled lance. Wincing in pain from his wound, Lucius raised his sword to ward off the attack.

The blow never struck.

The barbarian's horse reared with a javelin embedded in its flank. Hearing a roar, Lucius whipped his head around, and saw Quintus holding the eagle standard of the First Red Fist Legion trotting forward, leading a band of old Roman legionnaires. The aged veterans, without pause, formed a shield wall, and waded into the melee.

Lucius rallied his militia's riders with the newly arrived force and the battle's momentum shifted.

Leaderless, the barbarians broke off and fled east.

As quickly as the battle started, it was over.

Young Lucius scanned the carnage and spurred his mount to the top of the hill. The elder Lucius, Marcus, and Martinel joined him to watch the enemy retreat.

Quintus jogged up, still carrying the standard. He followed their eyes and laughed. "Those boys won't be back anytime soon."

Martinel looked over. Surprise registered on his face. "The First Red Fist eagle. I did not think I'd ever see that again."

A look of contentment creased the elder Lucius' face as he met Quintus' eyes. "Thanks to you, my friend, it got to be raised in victory... one last time."

Young Lucius sucked in a sharp breath as he attempted to move his left arm.

Marcus noticed the blood seeping through his friend's gauntlets. "You're hurt."

The militia captain patted his mount's neck. "My horse had a mind of its own and Ediko got lucky." His eyes narrowed. "But he'll trouble us no more."

The elder Lucius appraised the wound. "Lucky or not, that still must be taken care of." He turned to the other young man. "Marcus, get my *son* to Alexa. I don't want there to be a chance of infection."

As the two replicants rode off, Martinel quirked an eyebrow at his old commander. "Son, is it?"

The elder Lucius nodded. "It's a long tale."

"Good." Martinel laughed. "It's another three-day journey to Avenio, and I don't want it to be boring."

Chapter XXXI

Avenio Reunion

Those late summer days in southern Gaul were hot and dry, but the balance of the trip took four days instead of three. Over that time, young Lucius' arm mended clean. Although blind, Alexa sewed the torn flesh with deft fingers. Every day she redressed it with a poultice, and every day she admonished him. "Don't do anything more strenuous than lifting a spoon or you'll tear out the stitches."

Martinel enjoyed the journey, regaling the younger Lucius and Marcus with bygone tales of the First Red Fist Legion. The first night around their campfire, he rubbed his girth and sighed. "Back then, I hated Rome and everything it represented." He looked at his friend and then regarded the two replicants. "But the legate was and *is* the most honorable and decent man I have ever known. He's the reason I served Rome for three years." He regarded the young men. "I'd follow him into hell if he asked it of me."

The elder Lucius wrung his hands for a few seconds and then looked at the blind woman. "Alexa tells me that these two *will* succeed. That they will build a Rome the way it was meant to be."

She spread her hands. "Though it is decades in your past, it is in their future. What happens is unknown to me. We can only prepare them."

"Alexa, stop." Martinel squeezed the bridge of his nose. "I get a headache every time you explain things." He shook his head and faced the elder Lucius. "I'm an old man so perhaps a bit jaded, but I've learned a few things about those who gain power. It corrupts them. Excluding yourself, I've yet to encounter a leader who didn't cast their ideals to the side over time."

The old legate stared at his hands. "Then you met no one. I *deserted* my troops when they needed me the most. Until three years ago I was lost, self-doubting man."

"Don't lie to yourself or me." Martinel snorted. "Remember, I was there that night too. With Aetius dead, the emperor's vendetta on the entire Red Fist and then Alexa popping out of nowhere with these two." He glanced at young Lucius and Marcus. "You did what any conscientious commander would have done."

"I wrestled with the results of my decision for over thirty years. I withered and became just a shadow of the confident commander you knew."

Young Lucius regarded Martinel with a set jaw. "I do not know what is in my future, but I swear to you if that tremendous responsibility that you speak of truly falls to me..." He pointed to the legate. "...I vow to do everything in my power to make this man proud of me."

"Time will tell on that promise." Martinel shook his head again, his eyes shifting between the young Lucius and young Marcus before focusing on Alexa. "Witch, explain to me again why they don't know what happened thirty-seven years ago, and why they appear exactly as I recall them looking that night."

Alexa pursed her lips. "Thirty-seven years ago to you is a year in the future for them. Shall I try again to explain the manipulation of the space-time continuum?"

"Please don't." Martinel's eyes rolled up. "It'll make my head explode."

Alexa spread her hands. "Then just accept it as *magic*, conjured by someone named Mara."

"Hocus-pocus," Martinel snorted. He turned to the younger Lucius and Marcus. "Let's try something simple. What do you remember about your lives?"

Young Lucius glanced at his fellow replicant, who just smiled and replied, "You're the talker. You explain it. I want to see if his head really will explode."

Young Lucius squinted at the fire for a few seconds and then cleared his throat. "For the first two years of our lives we lived in a... militaristic orphanage." He pointed to Alexa. "Then she rescued us, and we spent the next three years on a large, deserted... farm. After that, we were dumped along a road outside of Ravenna where we met the legate. He brought us to Mediolanum, and for the last three years I served in the militia and Marcus was steward to the city's magistrate."

Martinel held up his fingers and counted. "You're telling me that you're both eight years old?"

Marcus smirked. "Yes, can't you tell?"

Martinel frowned. "Never mess with wizards or witches."

"Don't try to understand it. I gave up years ago." The elder Lucius tossed a branch on the fire. "Let me tell you about these two men in the three years I've had the pleasure to know them. It started on that road..."

At the end of the tale, Martinel slapped his leg. "Now that's a story I can understand. Despite your beginnings, he accepts you, and hence so do I." He regarded young Lucius and Marcus and then rose and bowed. "You saved my friend's life, so I am in your debt."

* * *

On reaching Avenio, Martinel released his infantry, who were mostly farmers and tradesmen, to their homes. His calvary he sent on to the fortified keep by the bridge crossing the Rhone River. He rode on with the caravan of old men to the Carloman estate.

Martinel rode between young Lucius and Marcus as they approached the manor. He scanned the Mediolanum company, screening the caravan, and rubbed his thickly bearded jaw. "You have good, disciplined men here."

"They're the best." Young Lucius smiled.

"How would you two like to come work for me? I need competent officers."

Lucius leaned over with real interest. "It doesn't sound like you're talking about handling bandits?"

"No, I'm not. War is coming. With the fall of Rome, everyone is grabbing territory. Gaul belongs to the Franks, but the Goths in Germania and Odoacer in Italy think different."

"Sounds interesting, if my militia is included." Young Lucius nodded. "I've been worried about how my men would sustain themselves in this foreign land." His eyes narrowed. "And I'll remain in command of my warriors?"

Martinel laughed. "Yes, and I'll give you a few hundred more to train to be just like them."

Young Lucius glanced at Marcus, who nodded. He extended his hand. "Agreed."

"Excellent. We will—"

"Lucius!" a gray-haired woman shouted as the gate in front of the walled estate flew open. She ran to them, her sandals slapping rapidly on the roadway's paving stones. An old man walking with a cane followed at a slower pace.

The elder Lucius cried, "Julia!" He dismounted and limped toward her. They met and embraced.

Young Lucius gave Martinel a quizzical look.

Martinel beamed. "Julia, Lord Carloman's wife, is Lucius' sister. They haven't seen each other for several years."

"And the man walking with the support?" Marcus asked, shaking with apparent anticipation.

"Why that's your *sire*, Marcus Carloman." Martinel got off his horse. "Come. Let me introduce you."

Young Lucius turned toward the nearby wagon. "I'll bring Alexa. There will be a lot of questions that neither of us can answer... again."

* * *

Julia released her hold on her brother at the approach of the new arrivals. Her hand went to her mouth as they drew near. "My God, that one is the exact image of you when you were young." She gasped. "And that one is Marcus." Glancing at the blind woman, who approached guided by the young Lucius, she said, "That's the witch you spoke of?" Her eyes grew wide. "These are the... abominations you told me about?"

The elder Lucius took his sister by the shoulders. "Julia, both of these men are good people, and I love them like my own children." He gave her a squeeze. "I'd be dead three years now if they did not save me."

Julia took a shuddered breath and hugged her brother again. "Then, for your sake, I will withhold my judgment." She turned to the newcomers and approached them with tentative steps and an extended hand. "I am Julia, Marcus' wife and Lucius' sister."

Young Marcus stepped forward and then hesitated. He bowed low. "It is a pleasure to meet you. The legate spoke of you often."

Julia touched his face with her withered hands and looked long into his eyes. "You're the same, yet... different." She turned and watched her husband as he hobbled down the walkway. His eyes were fixed on the young man with her.

She moved to young Lucius and studied him. "The resemblance is uncanny. If my brother was thirty years younger, I'd be hard pressed to tell you apart."

"They are identical," Alexa called out. "Side by side, even you, his sister, could not tell."

"I could tell by looking in their eyes." She whirled on Alexa, her voice turned chill. "You are the witch my husband spoke of." Her voice became pointed. "We have much to discuss."

Alexa nodded. "I expected no less. I'll answer whatever questions I can."

Julia turned to see her brother introducing her husband to the younger version of himself. The young man startled everyone by wrapping the elder Marcus in a hug and weeping. She shook her head. "This will prove to be a very interesting afternoon." Glancing at the line of wagons, she saw the old people wearing antique armor. Her hand went to her mouth. "The Red Fist Legion." She squared her shoulders and called one of her servants forward. "Show these old legionnaires to the farmhand barracks and see to it that they are comfortable."

"Yes, my lady."

She noticed Martinel talking with an old man holding the eagle standard of the First Red Fist Legion. "Quintus, is that you?"

"Yes, ma'am." The old former legionnaire blushed. "A little frayed around the edges after all these years but still in one piece."

She sighed. "Where are my manners as a hostess? Please join us in the manor for refreshments." She smirked. "Just don't pocket any of my spoons."

Martinel laughed. "Just lead me to your wine cellar and I'll be content."

"This way, everyone." Julia turned and led her guests into the house, her arm locked around her brother's.

Shock registered on her face on noting that her husband followed, supported by the young Marcus and engaged in an enthusiastic conversation with him. She shook her head. *Yes, this will be a very interesting afternoon.*

* * *

At dinner that evening, Julia arranged the seating carefully, although she wanted to sit beside her brother. *I haven't seen him since his wife Dervla passed away six years ago, and he never writes.* She ensured that the wine flowed freely and placed herself between Alexa and the young version of her husband. She eyed the blind witch. *Someone has to look after the men I love.*

To her consternation, she extracted little that she didn't already know from the young Marcus, although she was shocked by the similarities. Like her husband, this man appeared to have a keen intellect with a dry sense of humor. *He's even shy with strangers, like my Marcus. But not exactly the same.* She chewed on her lower lip. *He seems lost. No, that's not it. He's... searching.*

As the meal drew to a close, Julia lost any further opportunity to probe the young man.

Martinel and Quintus were holding forth on the exploits and foibles of the old Red Fist Legion and soon had her husband and brother moving cutlery around, explaining a particular battle. The two younger men were enraptured.

Julia found herself alone with Alexa. *Just as well.* Her eyes narrowed. "So, witch, was the meal satisfactory?"

Alexa blinked her blind eyes and grimaced. "I know you hate me, but please call me Alexa." She rolled the cup in her hands. "I was little more than a herald that night, but if it was in my power, I would have still done *exactly* the same thing." She placed the cup carefully on the table and folded her hands. "It means nothing to you now, but without Mara's intervention, generations from now your descendants would be exterminated in an unprecedented genocide." A small smile curled the corners of her mouth. "Although both Marcus and Lucius can be hardheaded and willful, they've grown into good, honorable men. The last eight years I spent raising them have been the most fulfilling of my life."

Julia had heard the explanation of those eight years and shook it off. "So, you're their *mother*?"

"It is a title I'd love to claim but cannot. I love them more than life itself, but I was little more than a mentor, guide, and listener."

Despite her suspicion, Julia smiled, thinking of her own five grown children. "Love, caring, and support. I think that qualifies you as their mother."

A tear moistened Alexa's cheek. "Thank you. I tried my best."

Julia glanced over at the six men who had collectively erupted into a blast of laughter. The two young men were already an accepted part of that circle. She saw her brother look over and smile. *His face is at peace.* She returned his grin.

Turning back to Alexa, she sighed. "I don't claim to understand much of what you spoke of. It doesn't matter. My brother is happy, and that is enough for me." More hoots distracted her as a wine decanter toppled to the floor, spilling its contents on the polished marble. She stood and took Alexa's hand. "Come. We'll find a quieter place. These louts will be bellowing all night."

Alexa squeezed the extended hand. "Thank you. I need a... friend."

Chapter XXXII

Goodbye

The following year raced by.

The younger Marcus became a welcome addition to the Carloman household. He was junior by a full decade from the elder Marcus and Julia's five children. However, those *siblings* followed their parents' lead and readily accepted him as one of the family. None of them voiced an objection when, after six months, the young Marcus was formally adopted into the family.

Julia hugged him the day of the ceremony. "Everyone needs to belong, and you belong with us."

A tear moistened young Marcus' cheek as he returned the embrace of the thin, gray-haired woman. "I'll make you proud of me."

The replicant shared the horticultural methods he honed under the harsh growing conditions within Beatrice's cavern. The improved irrigation and pruning had the Carloman vineyards flourishing.

Baron Martinel gave young Marcus the responsibility to repair the neglected stone keep nestled by the river crossing and a free rein to modify its defenses.

Young Marcus accepted the task. He directed the rebuilding of the crumbling stonework and watchtower and engineered the replacement of the simple gated entrance with a sophisticated barbican, bailey, and drawbridge. He was content.

The training of Martinel's Frankish force fell to young Lucius.

Although those one thousand farmers and tradesmen were far from being professional soldiers, young Lucius embraced the challenge with enthusiasm.

He brought the skills he developed as Mediolanum's militia captain into training the Frankish troops into an effective, disciplined military unit. The company of soldiers he brought with him from that city became the backbone of Lord Martinel's small army.

Quintus continued on as the young Lucius' aide but annoyed the Franks by defiantly displaying the Red Fist eagle standard beside his clerk's desk.

Initially, the elder Lucius participated in reorganizing the part-time Frankish soldiers, but after a couple weeks deferred more and more responsibilities to his replicant. "Son, you're doing an excellent job and I'm getting too old. I leave them to you."

Young Lucius stared. "You're the legate of the famed First Red Fist Legion; I'm a simple militia captain."

"There's nothing simple about how your mind works." The elder Lucius placed his hands on the younger man's shoulders. "I've been watching you. You're a natural leader. These men follow you. My time passed with the fall of Rome. The torch is yours to bear now and you are more than ready for it."

"Thank you, sir. That means more to me than anything else."

The elder Lucius grew serious. "Thirty-seven years ago, I dreaded the thought of what would happen to my beloved legion with you standing in my place. I no longer harbor that fear. Alexa says that in a few months you will replace me on that fateful night. I know you will do as well as I could ever hope to do." He cleared his throat. "Be wary. There was an assassin waiting for me in my tent that night. In hindsight, it's clear that Emperor Valentinian planned to purge all possible usurpers. I'm certain there is... was... will be more than just the one killer in the legion's camp."

"I will be wary, Father."

The old legate rested his gnarled hand on the younger man's shoulder. "I can tell you little about what will befall you when you are whisked to this magic land Alexa speaks of. You have veteran soldiers and competent officers who defeated Huns, Goths, and Vandals. They have faced much adversity. Don't be afraid to rely on their experience."

"I'll remember that." Young Lucius blinked. "From what Alexa hints at, we'll need to expect the unexpected in this new realm."

The legate squeezed the young man's shoulder. "I love you, son." He then raised his chin. "Let's continue your training. You will soon command the finest legion Rome has ever known. Your martial skills are superb, and you have a supple tactical mind. However, it matters little how clever your plans are if your officers fail to execute them." He cleared his throat. "I will instruct you about the mettle of the men you will lead."

Young Lucius felt sick. "I finally found my home and family. I don't want to leave."

The old legate sighed. "We'll see about that when the time comes. Now, let's focus on your officers. Silvio is the senior centurion, a solid but unimaginative man from Sicily..."

The old legate spent the balance of that year reminiscing about the people who served with him during the harrowing crisis that brought the demise of his beloved empire. Ofttimes they were joined by Baron Martinel, Julia, and Lord Carloman. Fascinated, the replicants Lucius and Marcus absorbed it all.

Many evenings were spent with Legate Bernius, Baron Martinel, and Lord Carloman in the local tavern. Although the nobles received deference, their easygoing nature and glib tongues always drew intrigued audiences for their stories of a bygone empire that was already just a myth to most. Other aged veterans from the Red Fist, led by Quintus, would regale the patrons with their own tales.

Alexa attempted to slip into the background, establishing a small apothecary near the fortified keep. However, the rumor of her herbal remedies soon gained her a constant stream of customers: peasants and nobles alike.

Also, Julia refused to let the blind woman remove herself from the family. She visited Alexa often. A few times per week she would bring fresh herbs and spent the mornings helping grind the ingredients and making poultices. They talked on a wide range of topics, from child-rearing to Alexa's exotic life. Julia shelved her incredulity on the blind woman's experiences. "Your life is an amazing tale. It should be shared, not hidden."

Alexa chuckled. "I doubt few would listen, and even fewer would believe." Alexa shuddered. "I fear my story would only bring charges of witchcraft, and I wouldn't want any harm to come to you, your family or... my boys."

Julia scoffed. "On that point you need not worry. Baron Martinel is the most powerful man in the region and my husband is the richest." She patted the blind woman's leg as they sat side by side at the roughhewn worktable. "Your concern about the welfare of others alone tells me you're no witch."

Fall turned to winter, winter to spring, spring to summer. As the last days of August waned, Alexa became increasingly despondent. She reached out her hand for the older woman and grasped it. "The time of our departure draws near. I will greatly miss this place and your company. It is in your past, but it is my future. I have no idea what awaits me." She wrung her hands. "Although I am at the center of the upcoming maelstrom, I am afraid."

Julia's eyes moistened. "My husband tells me that a very dear friend of mine was a witness to your... apparition by the campfire. He was... will be amongst those who are... taken. When you meet the Greek doctor named Phokas, send him my love. Beneath his cranky exterior is a very gentle, caring man. You will like him."

Alexa pursed her lips. "I will pass on your greetings if I get the chance."

* * *

As the autumn equinox drew near, Alexa told the two replicants that the last day of summer would be their last day on Earth.

"No. Not yet." Lucius' eyes flared. "I don't want to leave. I belong *here* with my people."

"It is at this equinox or never," Alexa sighed. "I do not wish to leave either. But who will care for the men of the Red

Fist Legion that the legate has entrusted to your care? Without you, the world will certainly perish."

Lucius' shoulders sagged as he glanced at Marcus. He slammed his fist against the worktable in the small apothecary. "I will *not* do it for any grand vision that you and Mara have." He squared his shoulders. "But I will do it for my *father's* sake."

Marcus rubbed his jaw and nodded. "As will I. Bring on your... event." His eyes misted. "Just give us time to say our goodbyes."

Sunset on the last day of summer arrived in an un-remarkable manner except for the palatable tension of the small party sitting together under the portico of the flower garden alongside the Carloman manor house.

Julia prepared the arrangements for the final gathering. "Well, we can't say goodbye without a proper sendoff." She gave the servants a holiday and stationed the guards outside the estate's walls. "It is best that we are alone."

Besides Julia, only those present at that fateful event thirty-seven years earlier were included. Without servants, the fare was simple. It did not matter. The conversations were deep, and the food went untouched.

Alexa arrived wearing a long flowing amber cloak. Once alone with the small group, she let it slip to the ground, removing the floor-length wrap, revealing the skintight, dun-colored bodysuit she wore. She hadn't donned it since the first day of being deposited near the road outside of Ravenna.

The younger Lucius tugged at the collar of his dark green toga and frowned. "If I'm traveling, I refuse to do it in that ridiculous outfit. It's... indecent."

Alexa blushed. "I'm sorry I appear inappropriate. Mara requires me to wear it to enable the journeys I must make this evening." She shrugged. "I do not know what's involved, but each must be complete before Marcus and Lucius travel with me."

Martinel snorted. "That outfit doesn't leave much to the imagination." He snickered. "Maybe the fashion will catch on around here."

No one laughed at his jest and Julia slapped his arm. "I don't think so."

The elder Marcus appraised the woman in the one-piece, seamless suit. "That is exactly how you were garbed when you appeared to us that night. It's burned into my memory."

"Really?" Alexa touched her sleeve. "I have no recollection. That night is still in my future... my very near future."

The elder Lucius shook his head as he regarded Alexa. "This is bizarre. I am sitting here telling you about what you did so many decades ago and you have no idea what occurred."

Martinel cleared his throat. "The main point I remember is wanting to plunge my sword through your heart that night and not being able to... Sorry."

"I don't understand any of this." Quintus sighed but fished into his satchel and pulled out a silver denarius. He pressed it into the younger Lucius' hand. "When you see Doctor Phokas, give this to him."

Young Lucius rolled the coin in his hand. "What is this for?"

Quintus blushed. "I had a certain type of infection and the good doctor cleared it up for me. I never had a chance to pay him, and I always pay my debts."

"I'll give it to him." Young Lucius glanced at Alexa. "If I can—"

Alexa glowed with a golden aura, vanished, and almost immediately reappeared.

Quintus shrugged and poured more wine into his brass cup. "Well, that's something one doesn't see every day."

"What happened?" Julia asked. Concern etched her face as she saw Alexa shaking.

"I've just been to distant Cathay." Alexa pressed her hands together. "I kidnapped a whole building of people."

"Where did you take them?" The elder Marcus leaned forward.

"Nowhere... yet. They will be going to the same place that your First Red Fist Legion is going to."

The elder Lucius' eyes glinted. "For what purpose are these people being abducted against their will."

Alexa wrung her hands. "May God have mercy on me. What I am doing is so wrong but so necessary." She raised her chin. "Mara tells me it must be done to save humanity. To aid your... sons."

Julia regarded Alexa for a moment and then laid a soft hand onto young Marcus' arm. "Be gentle with those people. They will be terrified." Her eyes narrowed. "But do what you must to protect my *son*." She forced a smile onto her face and turned the conversation to the normal affairs of the area to distract everyone from what they saw.

Thirty minutes later Alexa vanished and reappeared again.

The elder Lucius rubbed his jaw. "This time?"

"It's horrible," Alexa gasped. "I kidnapped more innocents. This time from India."

Another half hour passed and the same thing occurred.

Julia grasped Alexa's quaking hand. "Where were you this time?"

"Persia."

Quintus quipped, "These events are getting closer."

"It will be very soon," Alexa cried.

The younger Marcus' mouth slimmed to a thin line and he turned to his older self. "Father, I've made my decision. I won't leave. I belong here with you and Julia, not off in some wasteland with strangers."

The elder Marcus took him by the shoulders. "It breaks my heart to discover you and then lose you. I love you like a son, but you must go."

The younger man's shoulders sagged. "I want to stay, with every fiber of my being, but like Lucius, for you I'll go."

"Remember there was an attempt on the legate's life that night." Lord Marcus Carloman looked at his wife. "I'm sure that there was an assassin lying in wait for me. If I hadn't taken you to the legate's tent, I would have gone to my own quarters and died."

Julia gasped. "I'd have been a widow for all these decades and never borne your children."

"Then, for you, I will make this one-way journey." The younger Marcus nodded to Julia. "I'd rather die than see any hurt befall either of you. I will go into this unknown and deal with anyone who sought your life." He hugged the two of them. "I love you."

Alexa vanished and reappeared. "Byzantium," she gasped looking at the two replicants. "Prepare. It will be soon."

The elder Lucius grasped the younger version of himself. "I'm proud of you, my son. I can put my beloved legion in no better hands. On that day I feared for them. Today I harbor no such feelings."

Doubt clouded the younger Lucius' face. "I don't think I'm prepared for such a terrible responsibility."

"You're more than ready."

The younger Lucius squared his shoulders. "My whole life I struggled to be myself. Now, I want nothing more than to emulate you."

Alexa focused on their conversation and frowned. "You do recall that I told you that you'll have no recollection of anyone you met or any place you were before the event that will soon happen."

"That's insane," young Lucius snapped. "What's the point of depriving us of the beautiful memories of these good people?"

Alexa sighed. "Mara's calculations indicate that the probability of success will be higher if you're not burdened with the memories of places and people you can no longer be part of. She estimates that a clean start unencumbered with useless preconceptions would be best."

"This Mara is wrong," Julia retorted. "We are the sum total of our experiences. You will be sending them into this crisis as cripples."

Young Marcus' eyes flashed. "I will never forget—" His eyes went blank. He and young Lucius started to turn translucent along with Alexa.

The elder Lucius roared, "I'll always be with you, my son." He focused on the shimmering copy of his younger self and spoke clearly, "Beware Valentinian's assassins."

The younger Lucius blinked and disappeared. His clothes drifted to the ground and the small silver coin he held clinked as it bounced on the gravel path.

The three were gone and never seen again on the Earth.

Chapter XXXIII

Return to Novaroma

...Return

Lucius blinked and was sitting on a cushioned chair at the polished oak tables. At his side was Marcus, and across the table were the two women. A decanter of wine with four goblets stood in the middle. A basket of fresh fruit sat beside it.

"Your memories have been restored. Did you gain anything from the exercise?" Mara said. Her gown was now shimmering silver.

Lucius sucked in a ragged breath and regarded the petite woman. "You were wrong to deny us our past. People are not pawns to be moved on a chess board, performing designated tasks."

Marcus scanned the table, his eyes resting on Alexa. "Training and information are insufficient. We need to know who we are and need to care."

Lucius regarded the tall blonde woman. Her eyes were downcast. "Alexa, you sacrificed nine years of your life to nurture and guide us. I never thanked you." He reached across the table and squeezed her hand. "Forgive me for all my cruel words and obstinate behavior. You were the best... mother anyone could hope for."

A tear coursed along Alexa's cheek. "It was a pleasure. I treasured every moment watching the two of you grow into fine men."

Marcus added, "Not only can we claim an incredible woman as our mother, we also came to know our fathers." He turned to Mara. "People are not machines. Data and probabilities are not enough. We must bring passion to our lives to succeed."

"And we will." Lucius took a cup and sipped the wine. "For weeks I've floundered here like a drowning man, doubting my decisions and even my right to make them. No longer."

Mara shook her head. "I fear altering history... as I know it."

Lucius placed the cup back on the table and rose to his feet. "And I look forward to challenging the future."

"So be it." Mara nodded. "For good or ill, you have grown and are beyond my abilities to manipulate." She glanced at the tall woman by her side. "I am reduced to being nothing more than a reference library you can reach through Alexa." She spread her arms and her mouth curled into a small smile. "Will you at least stop calling me a demon?"

Lucius leaned on the table, facing her. "Mara, you are the farthest thing from a demon that I can imagine. You wrestled with an almost impossible task to give mankind a chance at survival." He glanced at Marcus. "Now the mission falls to us. Whether we succeed or fail, I will honor your effort."

"That means more to me than you can ever imagine. Thank you."

Marcus also rose. "Will we see you again?"

"That would be unlikely." Mara raised her hand. "I also have learned from this encounter. This is your world to make of it what you will. I will no longer interfere." Her eyes grew soft. "Awake."

* * *

...Awake.

Lucius blinked and looked around. He was still holding hands with Alexa and Marcus on the floor of the infirmary. He released his grasp and sighed.

Phokas coughed. "Let me know when you're ready to start this séance."

Lucius stood and found his legs were wobbly. "It is finished."

"Impossible," Phokas sputtered. "You just sat down."

Lucius rolled the rich memories through his mind and glanced at the seven-foot metallic cylinder before turning to the scholars and priests. "Marcus and I confronted... Mara." He thought about his words for a moment. "She is not a demon. Mara battled an evil being that desired our death. In that struggle, she diverted its malevolent magic into simply moving us instead of killing us." He glanced at Marcus, who nodded. "She destroyed the evil one but also lost the means of ever getting us home."

The Byzantine scholar, Theodore, rubbed his chin. "Can she do *anything* to help us?"

Lucius shrugged. "Mara is a font of knowledge and is willing to share it. Unfortunately, it can only be accessed by posing the questions through the oracle."

Father Sixtus made the sign of the cross. "At least she's a benign spirit. I'm not sure I could exorcise a demon."

Marcus' face became grim. "The demon she vanquished is gone, but his minions still exist."

Theodore gasped. "What?"

Marcus responded. "The barbarians across the river that our traitors allied themselves with are more than simple enemies living in a neighboring land." He furrowed his brow. "They are a tribe of demon worshippers called cyborgs. They sold their souls to the evil one that Mara defeated." He looked around the room. "They will stop at nothing to complete the evil one's mission and see us dead."

Lucius added. "They are a grave threat to us all. As legate, I will find a way... I must find a way to defeat them."

* * *

Lucius and Marcus changed back into their proper attire.

"That garb is indecent," Phokas declared as he sent Alexa into the bedroom to also change.

The conversation continued for another hour about good and evil spirits before the scholars and priests excused themselves and left. Lucius walked them to the exit. Outside, the noontime downpour had slackened to a drizzle. He saw Horatius snarling at Feng, who was trying to enter the infirmary.

The former imperial eunuch's eyes bulged on seeing Lucius standing in the doorway. "Demon," he wailed and fled. His elaborate silken robes fluttered about him, soiled and tattered, as he stumbled away. Glaring at the guards, he paused beside a corral, fingering his many ornate medallions, and screeched, "Demon worshippers."

Lucius watched the eunuch's antics with unease. From the time he drove the brutish guards from the Jiankang Academy building, Feng had taken to wandering across the peninsula, appearing in unlikely places at all times of day or night.

He alternately stared impassively or spoke gibberish to anyone approaching him. The Shaolin priest, Chang, attempted to counsel him a couple times but to no avail. No one knew how the obviously deranged man survived.

Lucius regarded him for a second and then exchanged shrugs with Horatius. "How does that man not get devoured by the beasts of this land?"

Horatius grunted. "Don't know and don't care. Life here is hard enough for those of us trying to survive." He shuffled his feet. "Since I didn't get any orders from Phokas to kill you, I assume you were successful confronting the demon."

Lucius sucked in a deep breath. He finally had his own memories and cherished them. "I learned much. The... demigod is not a threat, but the tribe across the river is." He pressed a fist into an open hand. "I gleaned some ominous information from her. We are going to war. Inform the tribunes and senior centurions that tomorrow morning we'll meet at my quarters in Emporium."

"That's good." Horatius snarled. "I knew some of the men that died at the river crossing. This cyborg tribe must be eradicated." He shook his head. "For a moment I thought you'd have us hunting dragons."

"This enemy is far more dangerous than the dragons."

Horatius gulped. "Legate, you defeated Huns, Vandals, and Goths. I doubt that these cyborgs and a smattering of traitors come close to that."

Lucius sighed, "We'll see," and went back inside. Marcus, Phokas, Alexa, Meili, and Anaya awaited him there.

Phokas turned on the two younger men when the last visitor was out of earshot. "Will you now tell me what really happened? I didn't believe that story about good and evil spirits for a second."

271

"Actually, what we said about how we got here and the tribe across the river is essentially true. Call it magic or science, it does not matter. It happened." Marcus pursed his lips. "But there was far more from a *personal* perspective. Our memories were returned to us."

"Impossible." Phokas glanced at Meili and Anaya and switched to speaking Greek. "I saw you appear before my very eyes seconds after Alexa touched the real Lucius and Marcus."

Lucius quirked an eyebrow. "And in those few seconds, I lived a full life, growing from a babe to the man I am today." He smiled. "In fact, I spent the last four years with the other Lucius. He was an old man, but I grew to love him like a father."

Marcus added, "It was... will be decades from now. They were aged when we met them. Julia sent her love."

Phokas' mouth hung open. "And... and Dervla?"

"She was deceased two years before we arrived but left the legate with a wonderful family."

"The *other* Marcus and Julia had... will have five children." Marcus laughed. "Martinel's a Frankish baron. He's gotten quite obese from all his rich living. He also sends his greetings."

Phokas collapsed in a chair. "I can't believe any of this. What you're talking about is years in the *future*."

"True." Lucius glanced at his empty hand remembering the coin Quintus tried to give him. "And I have something for you." He reached into his own purse, fished out a silver denarius, and handed it to the doctor. "Quintus told me he hadn't paid you yet and asked me to give you this."

"Quintus? That was... four weeks ago." Phokas' mouth trembled as he took the coin. He whispered. "He was in the detachment that escorted the real Marcus and Lucius that night. You could not possibly know him or about that transaction unless..." The doctor gulped. "Everything. You must tell me *everything*."

They switched to Latin. Anaya followed the conversation. Alexa whispered the translations to Meili.

They sat late into the night relating what had/will become of the other Lucius and Marcus.

Phokas wept several times. "They live. Praise God. They live."

As they rose to depart, Lucius hugged Alexa. "Thank you... mother. I promise to make you proud."

Her eyes moistened. "You always have."

Lucius glanced at the seven-foot, shiny metal cylinder and turned to Phokas. "Shroud this pillar. Let it fade from the thoughts of our people. There is little it can do to help or hinder us."

* * *

Alpha stood with his arms crossed, looking down at Feng, who was prostrated at his feet. He encountered the eunuch a week earlier when he saw the ornately dressed man conversing with a gnarled tree. It took little effort to penetrate the man's clouded mind and convince him that he was a demon-slaying mage. *Deficient, even for a human. But he may still prove to be a useful tool.*

It was the cyborg's observations that humans shunned a familiar person who displayed nonthreatening, aberrant behavior. *The perfect spy.* Alpha presented Feng with a sensitive eavesdropping device shaped as a medallion and told him that it was a talisman to ward off demons. The eunuch's gratitude was profound. Over the following week, most of the recordings were drivel. However, a few useful nuggets made the effort of humoring the broken man worthwhile. *He can go places I cannot.*

One of those captured conversations was tantalizing. *My target, Carloman, spoke to a human female about confronting a demon and learning about himself.* That was a week earlier. Now he would discover what that involved. "What have you learned?"

Feng trembled and held forth the dull metal disk. "I am sorry, master. I could not get close to the demon's sanctuary as you requested. Armed brutes surrounded it and would not let me pass."

Alpha snatched the eavesdropping device from the outstretched hand and downloaded the collected data. A quick

273

scan showed nothing significant. *Pathetic human*. He handed the sensitive instrument back. It was one of the few small tools he was able to coax a little electrical charge into. *I need more data.*

Feng looked up. "Master, I fear for you. I overheard the demon, Lucius, inform one of his brutes that he intends to go to war with the tribe across the river. That's you, master."

"Interesting." Alpha smiled as he scanned for that conversation on the retrieved data file and reviewed it. "I must prepare a proper greeting for them."

During his stealth travels the previous day, Alpha overheard several of the soldiers discussing what would happen when the legate confronted some demon. *They are gibbering, superstitious savages, but the event sounded significant.* He glanced around the forest glade, a half-mile hike north of the eunuch's pagoda, frustration etched on his face. *I pursue my mission blind. Where and when am I? My mission's target, Carloman, is definitively here, and the technology and speech are indicative of Iron Age Earth. However, I've heard references to Novaroma, the home world of the Ipis' ancient enemies. Which is it? I must know.*

Feng whimpered. "Don't make me go back. That place terrifies me. Not only is the demon Lucius Bernius lurking there, but he is protected by a blind witch called Alexa."

Alpha was pulled from his ruminations by the sniveling man's words. "What name did you say?"

"Alexa, great lord, the one they call the oracle goes by the name Alexa."

"That is the label of the clone host for Sigma-713." He furrowed his brow. *The space-time distortion that brought us here must have transported her too.*

"Great mage-lord, I do not understand your words: clone, sigma. What do they mean?"

"Unimportant." Alpha sniffed. *Alexa was close to the space-time distortion event. If we were drawn to this spot, it's likely she was too.*

"Whatever you say, master."

"Shut up." Alpha began pacing. *If Alexa is here, then Sigma-713 is too. It will have the relevant data stored in its logs. If I can extract it, I'll be able to resolve many unknown variables.* He tapped the pockets containing the few powered devices that existed on the entire planet and turned to the bedraggled man.

The cyborg had been developing a plan to kill Carloman along with all his primitive followers. A grin creased his face as a means to execute that plan formed in his mind. *Now is the time to implement it. My mission can finally be completed.* He turned to the groveling man. "I will grant you an opportunity to gain great stature in my kingdom. We will kill the demon you fear, Bernius, and many more. This is what I want you to do..."

Chapter XXXIV

The Plan

The next morning all ten cohort commanders gathered beneath a canopy outside of Lucius' quarters. The legate spread Marcus' detailed map out on the simple plank table. He pointed to the mark indicating the cyborg camp. "Their position is difficult to reach. It's surrounded by marshland with no known trails. It will force us to arrive piecemeal."

Senior Centurion Silvio, commander of the Second Cohort, frowned. "It also makes laying siege next to impossible."

Tribune Atticus, an aristocrat from Bari and commander of the Tenth Cohort, scoffed. "What does it matter? Legate, by your own estimates they have less than two hundred warriors over there. We can simply overwhelm them."

"I won't spend lives carelessly," Lucius snapped. He tapped the table. "I've learned that the cyborg leader is a mage of great power. After that massacre at the river ford, he must know we're coming for him and has had several days to prepare. I am wary of any trap a wizard sets."

"I hate magic," Titus, the tribune in charge of the Third Cohort spat. "Give me an enemy with a sword and shield any day. I'd even prefer facing one of this realm's dragons than a sorcerer who could turn me into a toad."

Marcus, who as prefect led the First Cohort, measured the distance on the map from the battlements by the river crossing to the enemy stronghold. "I say we run this campaign the Roman way, with stone and timber."

Lucius smiled, seeing the concentration on his friend's face. "Go on."

"Step one." Marcus nodded to the legate. "We establish a fortified beachhead across the river at the ford."

The face of the calvary commander, Wahula, turned grim. "We've been unable to completely eradicate those crocodile-like creatures that infest the area. We'll lose men in the crossing."

Marcus pursed his lips. "We'll stretch nets the breadth of the river to secure a passage for our troops and cross at midday when the beasts are most sluggish." He added, "Then we station archers with those new crossbows on the banks to take out any of those beasts that attempt to push through the barrier."

The prefect scratched his clean-shaven chin. "Then we lay a corduroy road as close to the cyborg's camp as we can. It will speed up the movement of reserves and supplies."

Lucius crossed his arms. "How long would this project take?"

"Two weeks. Three at most."

"Then that is the plan." Lucius scanned his senior officers, looking for any sign of dissent. "We obviously won't surprise them." He squeezed the bridge of his nose. "In the meantime, we must ensure that these cyborgs cause no mischief." He turned to Wahula. "I want our side of the riverbank under constant patrol. That duty falls mainly to your calvary."

Wahula sighed. "From the seashore to the northern mountains is close to forty miles. I only have a couple hundred horsemen to cover that territory."

Lucius nodded. "Silvio, starting at the bay where the river empties into the sea, I want way station strongholds built and garrisoned every ten miles. Titus, I want the Persian, Gupta, and Cathay structures fortified and manned by a full century at all times."

He faced Atticus. "The Tenth Cohort guards the ford. Send out scouts to reconnoiter the marsh. Avoid contact, but I want to know everything about that area."

Lucius scanned the somber faces. "Gentlemen, in my confrontation with Mara, I caught a glimpse of what these cyborgs are capable of. We must be prepared for all contingencies."

"It's not just these cyborgs." Silvio scowled. "Our legion is stretched thin already. We have over thirty thousand civilians spread out over thirty-six square miles to protect from the local wildlife."

"True. Our men are overworked. We need to consolidate." Lucius drummed the table. "This encampment was never meant to be a permanent base for the legion. We will convert this place to a market and warehouse center. Our camp followers are too exposed living outside this stockade. We'll consolidate the legion headquarters and convert this place to a walled town."

"I like that idea," Silvio added. "It would give the craftsmen and traders a more permanent home and decrease the extent of our patrols. Where?"

Lucius tapped the map. "Dragonmont keep. It's a natural fortress and almost complete."

Marcus bent over the map with his quill and laughed. "What shall we name our magnificent new *city*?"

Lucius shrugged. "Keep it simple. It's to be a market town. Name it Emporia."

As Marcus scratched in the name, Atticus groaned. "It seems like our labors here will never end."

The corners of Lucius' mouth curled up. "While I'm in charge, they won't." He stepped back from the table. "Gentlemen, we may not be in this land by choice, but we *will* make it our own, and no one will stop us. Dismissed."

* * *

It had been a little over two weeks since the incident at the river ford. Alpha was surprised that the humans did not blindly charge into the swamp to exact vengeance. Instead, they were methodically advancing toward his position. Despite his disdain for everything human, he was genuinely impressed with the engineering, given the materials and tools available. *My Ipis creators rightly feared these opponents.* He could hear the humans working in the distance. He found it curious that the humans were led by someone named Bernius, and not by Carloman, the ancestor he was missioned to destroy. He shook his head. *It doesn't matter. Another couple days at most. I'm ready.*

Three days earlier, his delta cyborgs captured an enemy patrol spying on his encampment on the south side of the bog. Now they fed Alpha's power reserves. He smiled at the vacant stares of the seven Roman prisoners. For the last forty-eight hours, the wires attached to their brain stems siphoned their life energy into battery units his gamma cyborgs fabricated. As he contemplated his victims glassed-over eyes, he estimated that even the hardiest one would expire within another twelve hours. *Too bad.*

Jette stood next to him, his face pale regarding the same scene. "Lord Alpha, I recognize the righteousness of torturing prisoners, but the enemy draws near. Shouldn't we extract information from them first. These men were scouting our position. We need to learn the legate's plans."

Alpha sneered. "I need to learn nothing from these primates. This Commander Bernius aims to eliminate us as a threat and is taking actions to that end. I welcome the move. It saves me the trouble of hunting *them*."

"Then give these men a clean death. It looks like you're sucking the souls from them." Jette gulped.

Alpha pointed to the wires extending from the slumped men's necks. "It is necessary. I require their life energy."

"You're a necromancer." Jette crossed himself. "This is black magic."

"And you are a fool who can't count." Alpha sneered. "The incident at the river made this armed confrontation inevitable. I'm surprised the human commander Bernius demonstrated this level of patience. His wariness shows he expects a trap." A thin smile crept across his face. "Which of course there is. One he'll never comprehend until it's too late."

"Lord Alpha, Legate Bernius has a full legion at his command." Jette's shoulders sagged. "Simple snares will only be pinprick annoyances."

"My plan will eradicate them in their *entirety*." Alpha glanced at the batteries attached to the dying men. "His caution is his undoing. Every day he delays makes my victory more assured."

Jette rocked back on his heels. "What do you propose doing?"

Alpha grinned. "You are familiar with the primary carnivores that inhabit this marshland, the ones called limnonectes?"

Jette shuddered. "Yes. Those creatures killed one of my men. We found his remains stripped to the bone."

"Those predators are quite ravenous, and even more so now, during their gestation cycle." Alpha retrieved a dull gray box the size of his palm from a bulging pouch hanging at his side and held it up. "I've discovered a means to summon these creatures and drive them into a feeding frenzy. When the human army commences their attack on our encampment, I will activate these instruments. Every limnonecte within a twenty-mile radius will be drawn here. A conservative estimate would put the count in the thousands. With only rudimentary Iron Age armaments, our enemies will not have a chance."

Jette gave the small boxes a quizzical look. "Using those monsters to do our killing is brilliant. But what will protect us? Simple beasts won't discern friend from foe."

Alpha produced circular disk. "This talisman will ward our encampment. No limnonecte will approach within two hundred feet of it."

Jette released a ragged breath. "Very well, mage. What would you have me do?"

Alpha replaced the devices in his pack. *What a gullible fool. The disks have no function. All the humans who serve me are just bait. They will die along with the enemy.* He tugged at his skintight garment. *The creatures native to this land cannot sense those of us wearing neural-net suits. Everyone else will be devoured.*

Alpha pointed to the prisoners. "By tonight, these humans will be lifeless husks." He smiled at the traitorous Roman tribune and handed him a pile of the small boxes. "*Insert* these in the corpses and string them up in the path the enemy is cutting."

"Seeing these desecrated bodies will enrage them," Jette stammered.

"Yes, it will." Alpha sneered. "And they will take them down and bring them within their midst for proper internment. "When they do, I activate the subsonic transponders... the talismans.

Jette shuddered as he took the armful of disks. "It will be done as you wish, mage."

Alpha's eyes narrowed as Jette bowed and departed. Patting the ion disrupter at his side, he was able to extract enough energy to give its power pack a twenty-six percent charge. *That will be more than enough.* He glanced around. *Once the limnonectes finish feasting on the humans here, I and my cyborgs will capture Dragonmont keep. There I will extract the data I need from Sigma-713. I must be sure that nothing has been overlooked and that Carloman perishes.*

"Let the blood flow." The human host, whose body Alpha shared, giggled. *"Can we do it with knives? I like to see the life fade from my victim's eyes when I stab them."*

"You will get ample opportunities." Alpha snarled. *"Once my mission is complete, I intend to eradicate all human life from this planet, and I have a plan to accomplish that end."*

The voice in their shared mind cackled. *"Good. Very good."*

Chapter XXXV

Plans Change

Lucius stood near the end of the corduroy road in the marsh. With him were Prefect Marcus Carloman and Senior Centurion Silvio. They commanded the First Cohort and Second Cohort respectively. A thousand legionnaires stood four abreast in a column stretching over a quarter mile, awaiting the command to attack.

The legate glanced at his two senior officers. "My whole body tingles. I expect a trap to be sprung at any moment. But nothing. I'm missing something."

Silvio shrugged. "Perhaps the leader of this cyborg tribe believed that this blighted swamp would protect him. No doubt he never faced Roman ingenuity before." He spat. "Now it is too late. We'll have his head on a pike by this evening."

Marcus exchanged a level glance with Lucius. "We prepared for every contingency. Tribune Titus with the Fourth Cohort is a mile back, dug in behind breastworks. Tribune Atticus with the Tenth Cohort is entrenched behind the stout wooden stockade on the western bank." He studied the impenetrable vegetation on both sides of the blazed trail. "If it's more than we can handle, we retreat and devise a different plan."

Lucius studied the makeshift barrier of his enemy's position and the silhouetted heads above it. The rocky outcropping four hundred feet away looked completely out of place in the sucking bog. His knuckles whitened as he gripped the pummel of the plexo-steel sword hanging from his waist. *Can any Iron Age army defeat a band of cyborgs? Not even close to a proper fortification.* Instead of raising his confidence, it made him warier. He turned to Silvio and Marcus. "I don't like this. They see our numbers and are making no attempt to escape."

Marcus nodded. "They could have fled deeper into the marshlands where our pursuit would have been piecemeal and spread out. It definitely doesn't smell right."

"They put too much faith in that wizard who leads them." Silvio grunted. "Cold steel will cut through any magic. We wipe out this tribe of cyborgs along with Jette and those other traitors." He glanced over his shoulder at the column of poised legionnaires. "We'll be out of this infernal swamp and home in time for supper."

Lucius exchanged a meaningful look with his fellow replicant before responding to Silvio. "Their mage is powerful and has had ample time to lay traps. We are going in blind. Few of our scouts—" A disturbance in the swamp ahead of them caught his attention.

Decurion Horatius, who was in the vanguard, led a team carrying seven bodies. The legionnaire's eyes smoldered as he saluted. "Legate, these bodies were hanging from trees up ahead. This cyborg tribe taunts us. These men died in agony."

The sight of the corpse made Lucius seethe. Their rictus faces were frozen in anguish. *High tech torture.*

The victims were all disemboweled. Their blood-soaked tunics, stuck to their carved-out chests, swarmed with flies.

"They must have been hanging from those trees most of the night." Silvio's eyes glinted. "These men were part of the scouting party I sent out a few days ago to check the marshlands south of here." The centurion bent over and examined the corpses with a practiced eye. "Strange, these poor souls were sliced open after they died."

"Ah. What mischief is this?" Marcus noticed a bulge under the tunic of one of the corpses. He grabbed his knife and sliced the garment open. "Look." He tapped the corner of something metallic protruding from the chest cavity.

"Dig it out," Lucius commanded as he glanced at the enemy barricades. "This isn't random torture. What are the cyborgs up to?"

Silvio knelt beside the prefect and extracted the object. He hissed, "A magic talisman," when he pried out a palm-sized gray box dripping gore.

Marcus' eyes narrowed. "Let me see that."

"Careful, Prefect. You said the cyborg leader is a powerful mage." Silvio's hand shook as he passed it over. "It's sure to be cursed."

From his youthful experiences, Marcus readily recognized it as he passed it to Lucius. "A subsonic transponder."

Silvio knitted his brows. "A what?"

"It's... magical, but there's no mystery to its function." Lucius scratched his chin. "It's nothing more than a beacon. Why did they go to the trouble of putting one in this man's body?"

An amber light came on and it started to vibrate in Lucius' hand as he turned over the seamless object. "It's being remotely powered up."

"There's one of those things on this body too." Silvio found another disk but dropped it immediately as it started to vibrate. "This demonic thing *lives*."

Moments later, Lucius heard a distant thrashing and chittering sound. The racket grew louder and seemed to come from all directions.

Marcus gasped. "The transponder's high frequency sound must agitate some of this land's wildlife."

"Of course." Realization struck Lucius as he made the connection. "It's the limnonectes. Remember when Alexa swore to us that the limnonectes were solitary hunters."

Marcus nodded. "That's in line with reports from the farmers. Attacks on chicken coops, stray sheep being taken, that sort of thing."

Lucius paled. "Yet I lost several good men to a *pack* of those predators a few weeks ago." He held up the small disk. "The cyborgs have been developing this as a weapon for *weeks*. To your cohorts. We will soon be under attack. We must fall back to the bridgehead."

Orders were shouted and, with Roman precision, the legionnaires raised shield walls toward the dense foliage on either side of the road. However, they had only moved backward a dozen steps when the first limnonecte sprang at the column. As it leapt through the air over the soldiers' heads, it was impaled by a stabbing spear. Writhing on the ground in its death throes, the creature still snapped at the soldiers hacking at it.

The retreat ground to a halt as at first dozens, and then hundreds, of limnonectes threw themselves at the defenders.

Discipline held. But with increasing frequency, a man's scream could be heard as he was dragged away and torn to pieces.

Lucius directed the defense with growing concern.

Marcus shared the fear. "The number of attacking beasts seems limitless and our men's stamina won't last forever." He made a fist and noticed he was still holding the vibrating disk. He dropped it to the ground and attempted to smash it. It was not affected. "These things are designed to survive massive explosions. We have nothing that can break them."

Lucius' eyes narrowed. "Maybe there's a way to turn these subsonic whistles against the cyborgs."

Marcus looked around at the raging battle. "If you have a plan, you better implement it fast."

Lucius turned to Horatius, who stood protectively beside him with his gladius at the ready. One of the prototype crossbows was slung over his shoulder. "Horatius, I have a task for you."

"Yes, Legate?"

Lucius held up the disk. "These… enchanted talismans are what the cyborgs are using to drive these animals into a frenzy." He pointed to the rocky outcropping where he could see heads watching them. "Does that crossbow have the range to reach their camp?"

"Yes, Legate. Easily." Horatius sounded confused. "But they're not our problem. These monsters are."

"Can you hit it with one of these disks fastened to a quarrel?"

The decurion hefted the small box. It was lighter than it looked. "Yes, but targeting anything specific will be impossible. The bolt will fly like a wounded duck."

"That's all right. All you need to do is get close. I want to return these magic charms to the cyborgs."

Understanding lit Horatius' eyes. He called his unit over and held up the tiny box. "Gather all these you can find on the bodies. We're going to send these cursed amulets back where they came from."

The men scurried off as Horatius tore strips of linen and bound the box to a bolt. Thirty seconds later he launched it high in the air. The projectile flew further than any arrow from a normal bow. He grunted as he watched it come to earth behind the enemy's barricade. Within ten minutes the other disks were retrieved and launched into the cyborg camp.

It was not immediate, but the pressure on the exhausted legionnaires eased.

"Look." Lucius drew Marcus' attention to the enemy position. Hundreds of limnonectes were swarming over that distant barrier. It was accompanied by terrified shrieks inside those walls. He looked around. Only a few scattered beasts remained engaged with his legionnaires. "Sound the retreat. Let's get out of here while we can."

Clarions blew and the survivors of the two cohorts fell back. The shredded remains of close to a hundred of their comrades were left behind.

* * *

Alpha's feeling of satisfaction turned to consternation as the first crossbow bolt landed a dozen feet from where he stood. He did not want any of his human thralls to overhear him, so he spoke to Beta-1 and Beta-2 in Ipis. "How could human primitives ascertain the purpose of those trans- ponders?"

Beta-1 spread her hands. "And they did it quickly."

A second bolt thudded into a wooden post in front of them.

Beta-2 frowned. "The range of their projectile weapons is far greater than our intelligence indicated."

Beta-1 blinked. "Alpha, what course of action do you command."

"We are thwarted," Alpha growled. "This situation cannot be recouped." He snarled as a third bolt skidded across the ground near the pretentious Gupta with the enormous beard.

Beta-2 plucked at his skintight garment. "Our neural-net suits may keep us from being a primary target, but in their current state they will attack anything that moves."

Alpha glanced around. His human minions were lined up along the barricade, watching the battle, completely oblivious to their own upcoming doom. "We must find an alternate way to fulfill our mission." He pointed to an unoccupied section of the barrier. "Instruct all cyborgs to set their suits to stealth mode. We are abandoning this enclave."

"Where shall we go?" Beta-1 asked.

Alpha's eyes narrowed. "This engagement was to be only a bloodletting anyway. All this setback means is that we advance the timetable for the second part of our plan." He grinned. "Actually, this will work to our advantage. The greater part of their army is here. While they lick their wounds, we slip through to their citadel labeled Dragonmont."

Beta-2 frowned. "It won't take them long to recover. We will be trapped there."

Alpha's words were stiff. "In order for a hundred percent certainty that our mission is completed, I need to download data from Sigma-713, and that is the reported domicile of its human host, Alexa."

"I have little doubt that we will complete our mission." Alpha smiled. "I've learned through my investigations that Carloman and this Commander Bernius hold several of the people situated there dear." He patted the ion blaster hanging on his hip. He now possessed a few energy clips with a quarter charge. *It will be enough.* "They will attempt to bargain for their friends' lives, and when they come into range, Carloman is obliterated along with everyone around him."

Beta-1 bit her lower lip. "Are you sure we'll have time to escape?"

"Uncertain." Alpha sighed. "But it doesn't matter. Our mission will be completed."

Another bolt sailed over their heads.

Alpha switched his suit to stealth mode. "Let's go."

* * *

Jette's stomach twisted in a knot. For close to a week he found the situation increasingly untenable. The sound of axes and crashing trees grew louder and closer every day. *Bernius is coming for us.*

287

The loyalty of the soldiers under his command had been exceptional, even when it came time to turn against the rest of the Red Fist Legion. His shoulders sagged. *Now they openly speak of desertion.* On the previous day, the decurion who put the magic amulets in the dead captives raged at him, "Tribune Jette, this is wrong. I knew those men. Siding with necromancers is evil."

Jette listened to the outburst, stone-faced. *Is he right? Is the traitor Bernius a lesser evil than this mage, Alpha?* He only hesitated a second. "You will do your duty to the emperor."

The decurion glared at him. "Tribune, look around. This vendetta of yours has nothing to do with Rome or the emperor."

The tribune spread his hands. "We have no choice. We can't go back."

The decurion spit. "I will not fight for a devil worshipper. I will take my chances with Legate Bernius." He turned, scrambled over the camp's makeshift barrier, and trudged away through the marsh's sucking mud.

Jette watched him in silence. *I can't follow you, but good—*

The deserter only took a dozen steps before collapsing with spear buried in his back.

Jette looked to his right. Alpha stood with his two lieutenants beside a stack of javelins, laughing.

The wounded man continued to drag himself through the morass.

Alpha launched another javelin. Although close to a hundred and fifty feet away, the second spear struck the wounded man inches from where the first shaft protruded from his back.

A pair of silent limnonectes loped from a nearby grove of banyan trees toward the still twitching man, their coloring so closely matching the vegetation they were almost invisible. The creatures sniffed him a couple times and pounced. Screeching, they shredded the decurion with hooked claws and tore out hunks of meat with sharp fangs.

Alpha laughed again and bellowed. "Anyone else want to leave?"

No one moved.

Jette swallowed hard as he gauged the distance. *No one can hit a moving target twice from that distance with a spear.* He scanned the nearby cyborgs in their outlandish skintight garments. *The decurion was right. Nothing good can come of dealing with a necromancer.*

He studied his men, who lined the wall, watching the grisly scene. Although Alpha and his followers seemed to move wherever they wished with impunity, no one else could. *We are prisoners here, and our provisions are exhausted. We butchered our last horse this morning.*

* * *

At midmorning the next day, the distant noise of the advancing legionnaires felling trees turned silent. By noon the reason became clear. Through the thick undergrowth, at the edge of Jette's vision, he saw two cohorts forming for an assault.

He stood behind the barricade with Rayansh and Li Wei, awaiting the imminent attack. He saw the traitor, Legate Bernius, standing in the distance with his senior officers. He felt crushed. *Not only have I failed my emperor, but I'll now meet my end in the service of a necromancer.*

In halting Latin, Rayansh gasped, "There are so many of them. Do we have a chance?"

Jette regarded him. "Legate Bernius may be a traitor to my emperor, but he's also a brilliant tactician. I have no doubt we'll die in this pestilent hole."

Rayansh shifted on his feet. "We do have a wizard on our side. That must even the odds."

"What good are wizards' tricks against such numbers?" Jette snapped.

Dozens of steps behind them, as if overhearing their conversation, Alpha shouted, "Now you will see what becomes of all who oppose me." Jette saw the mage press something on a dull-colored pendent he wore.

Moments later, the surrounding swamp came alive with swarms of the limnonectes streaming toward Legate Bernius' exposed legionnaires.

Li Wei cackled and clapped his hands.

Rayansh gasped. "The all-powerful mage can even command the beasts of this strange land to do his bidding. Victory is assured."

Jette stood with the ninety-odd humans watching as Legate Bernius shifted his cohorts into a defensive square. On seeing the growing throng of limnonectes assault the legionnaires, he felt smug satisfaction with the now assured death of the traitor. *I underestimated the mage's capabilities. There are no limits to what can be done.*

Soon, Alpha will magic us home. Avarice lit Jette's eyes as he considered the future. *With my connections in the Senate and a powerful wizard at my beck and call, I could supplant Valentinian as emperor.* His eyes narrowed as he glanced back at Alpha. *Every man has his price. Wealth does not seem to interest him. Power... influence? What would be the price for the mage's fidelity? I must study him carefully.*

Clarion blasts and shouting men in the distance drew Jette's attention back to the battle. He licked his lips. "Now, Legate Bernius, it's your turn to die."

Hearing those words, Rayansh sighed and turned to Jette. "It appears we have chosen the correct side. The wizard, Alpha, does not need an army to destroy our foes."

Jette glanced at the other two human leaders. Li Wei remained focused on the battlefield with apparent glee, but Rayansh regarded him with narrowed eyes. *Rayansh is an ambitious nobleman in his own country. Is he thinking along the same lines as me? I must stay a step ahead.* His response was guarded. "Yes, he is truly powerful."

Rayansh shuddered. "This Alpha requires nothing to crush any who oppose him."

Those words struck Jette like a hammer blow. He paled. *Why would Alpha support me, or anyone else, in becoming the Roman emperor? With his magical powers, he could claim it for himself.* The more he considered that new thought, the more it seemed obvious. *He would use me as a foil to get close to the throne and then eliminate me when my usefulness is finished.* He gulped and whispered to Rayansh, "When Bernius and his minions are dead, I suspect that we, ourselves, become extraneous to the wizard's ambition." He pointed to the boggy marshlands before them. "There must be other kingdoms nearby that would grant us sanctuary. We must leave this place when we find a chance."

A bolt whizzed over their heads.

Rayansh's eyes narrowed. "There is truth to your words. I greatly desire to be gone from this cesspool. But how? The beasts of this land are ferocious."

Jette lowered his voice. "I've been spying on Alpha. He travels in and out with impunity. It must be the medallion he wears. His lieutenants have similar pendants. I'm sure their magic wards." He looked over his shoulder and saw Alpha conferring with those two primary acolytes. He pointed out Beta-1 to Rayansh. "See, the tall, Nubian woman is fingering hers now. I won't dare approach Alpha. But I say we steal the two amulets from those underlings and slip away."

The Gupta prince glanced sidelong at Li Wei, who was enraptured watching the battle. "Agreed. Tonight—" Another arrow-like projectile hit the ground and skidded to his feet. He bent over and lifted it, pulling at the linen wrapping. "Hey, this looks like one of the talismans that were placed in the corpses."

"It is." Worry crept into Jette's voice. "Legate Bernius would not do this without a reason. We should inform the mage." He turned around. "Where did he go?"

Rayansh twisted, his eyes sweeping the camp. "*Everyone* from the cyborg tribe has vanished."

"What?" Jette scanned the area. Fear clawed at his belly.

A moment later, the mass of chittering limnonectes abandoned their assault on the Bernius troops and raced through the bog toward the cyborg encampment. The men who lined the barricade, watching the battle, cried out and stumbled back at the change in fortunes.

In a blink, a number of the beasts were perched atop the low barricade, flicking their long tongues and staring at the ashen men with black, dead eyes.

A piercing scream came from Li Wei as a limnonecte with oversized limpid eyes bounded over the low barrier and pounced on him. His cry ended abruptly as his throat was ripped out.

Rayansh drew his sword and called to his guards, but they were fleeing along with the other humans. He sliced off the head of the first limnonecte to reach him. He did not have time to take a second swing as two others pounced on him.

"We've been betrayed." Jette drew his spatha. "To arm —" His blade flew from his grasp as he was knocked to the ground. One limnonecte tore a chuck of meat from his leg as another bit deep into his throat.

Hundreds of limnonectes leapt over the wall, chittering as they pursued the terrified men.

Chapter XXXVI

Taking the Citadel

The last scream from his camp had already faded when Alpha reached his hidden river crossing. Almost directly across from the main human encampment, labeled Emporia, it was the ideal location. There, beneath thirty-foot outcroppings, the river narrowed to a couple hundred feet.

His base was a warehouse from another place and time. However, without power, the modern equipment stored there was inoperable. There were several large spools of plexo-steel cable, which he used to fabricate a resilient meshwork. The cable nets, anchored to the riverbed, stretched from one shore to the other. Except during heavy rains, the slow muddy current could be traversed, never getting deeper than four feet.

The barriers were constructed to be raised and lowered from either bank with the use of simple hand-cranked winches. When raised a foot above the water line, the netting was impenetrable to the large river carnivores. When lowered, it was undetectable to anyone standing on the heights above.

Alpha climbed down to a crevice, a few feet above the waterline where the winch was secured, and began cranking it. Once the barrier was raised, he stood in the water while his followers descended the craggy shale bluff. The betas and the deltas accomplished the feat with little trouble, but the gammas struggled. They had the hardest time syphoning energy from the humans they possessed. Several of those bodies were emaciated and sick.

As Alpha watched, one of the gammas did not follow the others. It stood at the chasm's edge, spasming. Alpha had seen it before. When the human host was fevered, it became more difficult to control, and without an independent power source, some of the gammas were having trouble keeping their humans regulated.

Although his mouth was open in an apparent attempt to scream, no sound was emitted as the human threw himself over the cliff into the shallow water below.

On the outside of the netting, a few feet from where Alpha stood, several potamos savras roiled the water, snapping at the unmoving prey.

The gamma regarded the lead cyborg, with unblinking eyes, until he was dragged under.

With the water still churning, Alpha turned away and crossed to the other side. *Regrettable that Gamma-7613's processor is irretrievable.* He knew that the basin deadened sound to the heights but warily eyed the western cliff. *Stealth is the key. The mission is paramount.* He detected no motion above.

One large predator, with yellow eyes glinting in the sunlight, lazily swam alongside the barrier, nudging the protective grid with its snout, tracking Alpha as he forded the river. The lead cyborg ignored the beast. He was down to three betas, four deltas and nine gammas, all running on limited power. The only significant weapons in the entire group were a few ion disrupters with minimal charges that he and two of the betas carried. *Those will be needed to complete this mission.*

As the cyborgs gathered at the base of the western cliff, Alpha admonished them to maintain tight control over their human hosts. "I do not want a repeat of the lapse made by Gamma-7613." He glared at the gammas in their emaciated human host bodies. "The loss of a useful asset for no gain is unacceptable."

Alpha led the ascent up the thirty-one-foot, vine-covered escarpment. The climb was one he had made several times at this location. As he pulled himself up over the ledge, he froze. Through the underbrush, about twenty paces away, he spotted a small detachment of the primitive soldiers. He knew his suit rendered him nearly invisible even though the sun shone in the cloudless sky. With a predator's detachment, he scanned the area, counting seven of them. As Beta-1 drew next to him, Alpha whispered, "We must eliminate these humans without raising an alarm."

Beta-1 frowned. "Killing them will alert the humans to our presence."

"As long as that realization is not immediate, it won't matter." Alpha knitted his forehead. "Stealth is only important until we reach our next objective." He patted the ion disrupter at his side, sighed, and hefted his short boar spear. "Once we are in position, alerting our targets will work to our favor. We want Carloman and his lackey general, Bernius, to pursue us with their full might once the new location is secured. Waiting until tonight—"

A loud, alarmed voice made Alpha's head jerk up. Behind a tree to his left was an eighth legionnaire, who was apparently relieving himself. The startled man gaped at Beta-3 crawling over the cliff from the river. The man bull-rushed the equally surprised cyborg. As the two grappled near the ledge above the water, they tumbled over the side.

Alpha did not have time to regret the loss of the high-end beta unit. He snapped, "Kill them all. Ensure none escape."

Seventeen cyborgs moved as one. Some of the humans stood to fight, others tried to run. All were dead in seconds.

"Efficient," Alpha commented. "Throw the bodies into the river. We must achieve our next objective before..." An idea struck him as he saw a line of horses and a small wagon with a mule still in harness tethered in a glade just beyond the sentry post. "Strip those bodies of their uniforms and armaments. Subterfuge may work better than brute force."

A short time later, seven human-host cyborgs garbed as legionnaires rode toward Dragonmont, leading the mule-drawn dray. The other nine packed themselves into the canopied cart and covered themselves with blood-soaked rags.

All the Roman troops not committed to the campaign in the marshlands were garrisoning the outlying buildings or patrolling the riverbank. The road skirting Emporia was deserted.

The only encounter that raised any concern occurred about a half mile from the base of the fortified mountain as they crossed a stone bridge spanning a culvert of sluggish water.

A middle-aged woman and a teenage boy ran to them from an olive orchard they were tending. Four large canines trotted at their sides.

"What word from the battle?" the lanky boy asked.

Alpha, fluent in the human dialect labeled Latin, paused to answer. *I don't want to arouse suspicions.* He considered possible responses, weighing success probabilities, and determined that an approximation of the truth would end the conversation fastest. "It was horrible. The enemy mage unleashed the limnonectes on us." He waved to the wagon. "Many killed. Many more wounded. The struggle continues. We are transporting the most grievously injured to the doctor."

The careworn woman put her hand to her face. "Dear God. Do you know Horatius? Is he all right?"

Alpha fingered the pummel of the Roman sword hanging at his side. *Perhaps I should just kill them and end this meaningless nattering.*

The hackles of the canines went up and the animals focused on him, emitting deep-throated growls as if sensing his thoughts. The woman swatted the dog nearest her. "Mars, stop that. These brave men are heroes."

The dogs ceased growling but kept their eyes locked on him.

Alpha released his grip on the sword's handle and shrugged. "I do not know the man. Now we must make haste." He tugged at his horse's reins and did not look back.

* * *

Marcellus hurried to the new road running through his mother's farm when he saw the wagon with its legionnaire escort approaching.

Over his protests the night before, the legate ordered Marcellus to stay back. "I will not require an aide on this venture. Stay here. I'll be safe, and besides, your mother needs help pruning her orchard."

The youth's eyes kept turning in the direction of the river crossing all morning.

He became confused on seeing the legionnaires. *They're coming from the wrong direction.* A challenge was on his lips, but he bit his tongue. *These men don't look right.* He scanned those on horseback while their leader spoke to his mother. His suspicions rose. *The holes in their armor weren't made by any animal.* He refocused on the one speaking. The man had a commanding presence. *He's unusually tall with a Germanic look to him. I'd remember seeing someone like that.* Marcellus gulped as he recalled Alexa's description of the cyborg tribe's leader. *It's him.* He tensed when his dogs growled and saw the man's hand drift to his sword.

The dangerous moment passed, and the wagon continued on its way.

Marcellus caught a glimpse inside the wagon as it rolled away. His stomach twisted. *Women! There are no women in the legion.* He turned to his mother when they were out of earshot. "Those people are not legionnaires." He told her what he observed.

Aquila gasped.

Marcellus made his decision. "Gather the family and go to Emporia. Inform the garrison commander and stay there."

"What are you going to do?"

"Warn the legate." Marcellus took off running. It was over two miles to the river crossing, but he dashed across the open ground as if the lives of everyone he cared about depended on it.

* * *

Alpha was pleased with his ploy. Legionnaires at the base of the mountain moved out of his path on seeing what appeared to be wounded legionnaires. They shouted worried questions. The cyborg responded without pausing, "The battle rages on." No one hindered his team until they reached the keep's open gate at the plateau's crest.

A wary guard challenged him. "Password."

Alpha reached into his satchel and retrieved his ion disrupter. Sweeping the deadly rays across the four sentries, he laughed. "The password is, *die, you fools.*"

The cyborgs in the wagon cast aside their bloodstained rags and sprang out. Those on horseback charged into the open courtyard.

On seeing the trouble at the gate, a centurion led a dozen legionnaires from the adjacent guardhouse to confront them.

Alpha scythed through them with a beam from his ion disrupter.

About twenty other legionnaires, who were performing camp chores in the bailey, saw what happened. In terror, they fled toward the barracks. Beta-2 also had a partially charged ion disrupter. He cut the legionnaires down before they reached that dubious shelter.

Alpha scanned the grounds. Detecting no further threats, he turned to the nine gammas. "Bar the gate. Let no one in or out." He glanced at his weapon's gauge. *Six percent.* He started jogging. "Betas, deltas with me. Beta-1, bring the burrowing equipment."

Alpha had never been inside this walled enclosure but knew his destination from Feng's description. *I need to confirm my suspicions. Sigma-713 will be in the central building labeled the infirmary.* He hurried in that direction and then paused. Feng, with a vacant smile, stood near the building's entrance, wearing the eavesdropping device like a medallion. *What is that imbecile doing? I don't have time for this.*

A javelin whistled past Alpha's ear.

An intrepid legionnaire had stepped out of hiding and launched it.

Alpha spun and fired, obliterating the man and the water trough he ducked behind. "Feng, follow me."

The lead cyborg burst into the wide foyer of the infirmary with his team. It only took a second for his eyes to adjust to the relative gloom of the interior. In that brief time, a dark-skinned man with a mane of long white hair sprang from a side room, swinging a long, two-handed curved sword, decapitating one of the deltas. Alpha disintegrated the torso of the attacker and blew a hole through the exterior wall with one shot.

Alpha heard a female voice wail, "Kewal," as he swung his blaster to cover the room's other occupants. He scanned the room. His eyes swept past the stack of barrels in the corner where Mara was hidden and focused on the four people crowded together: a man with a balding head and a salt-and-pepper beard, and three women. None were armed. One he recognized. He called over his shoulder, "Deltas, check the other rooms. Betas, stay here and ward the entrance."

Feng stumbled in. "I'm here to serve, great master."

He ignored the eunuch and turned back to his captives. "Hello, Alexa."

"Hello, Alpha," came the stiff reply. "What are you doing here?"

"I came to have a conversation with Sigma-713."

A petite woman standing beside Alexa, wearing a worn hanfu, snarled, "You signed your death warrant coming here. Legate Bernius will have your head spiked to the battlement by the end of the day."

Alpha waved his gun in the air. "Nothing would make me happier than to see Bernius and Carloman. That is why I came."

The woman wearing an ankle-length, yellow churidar stared at the remains of the white-haired man splattered near the gaping hole in the wall. Bile filled her voice. "You will *never* get out of here alive."

"That is of little consequence once my mission is complete." Alpha glanced at his weapon's charge. *Four percent.*

His human host cackled in their shared mind. "*Kill them, kill them.*"

Alpha was annoyed at the mental interruption. "*No. If my plan is to succeed, I need these people as bait for Carloman and his associate Bernius. The hostages won't be slain until after their usefulness is ended.*"

"*Good. Good. At that time free me to do it. A knife. I'd like to kill them slowly with a knife.*"

"*I will consider it. Now shut up.*"

There were pleas for mercy from the back room and then silence as the deltas returned.

"Now what," Alpha exclaimed.

The delta that controlled the host body of a young, redheaded woman came out and announced, "We found five somnolent humans. They've been terminated."

Alpha sighed. "We need hostages if we're to draw Carloman in. Unless necessary, refrain from killing anyone else."

"Yes, Alpha."

The lead cyborg rued the inefficient means of communications that hampered them. He pointed to the haversack Beta-1 carried. "As we discussed, drill a four-hundred-foot hole at the northern end of this fortification."

"Yes, Alpha."

"Beta-2, your task is to ensure that no intrepid human attempts to interrupt the operation." Alpha shed his rent Roman armor and donned his neural-net suit. "This task must be completed with the two-hour timetable we discussed."

Beta-1 shifted the balance of the bulky pack on her back. "Once the shaft is to the proper depth, should I short-out the charge pack and drop it in?"

"Hold off until I give the word." Alpha rubbed his jaw. "We might need to delay if Carloman is not nearby. Our target must be within a half-mile radius for success to be assured."

Beta-1 nodded. "I understand. The hole will be bored and ready on time."

The betas jogged out.

A dark woman with long, raven colored hair glared at him. "Do you plan to escape by digging a tunnel?"

Alpha tsked. "You humans are an ignorant lot. I'll never fathom why the Ipis fear you."

The hostages exchanged confused looks with each other, and then the one who challenged him before responded, "Why don't you tell us. We're not going anywhere."

"It was the presence of what you named the *guardian trees* that gave me the idea. They are known by different names on different planets. The Ipis call them the *hungry trees*. They only grow where a lode of bi-nexidium crystals and a vein of ilmenite ore coexist beneath them. It is an extremely rare combination in the galaxy."

Anaya looked confused. "Okay. So, there's a strange mineral deposit in this mountain." She searched her mind for the right words. "And you are going to destroy it. What's the point?"

"Your stupidity is almost entertaining." Alpha regarded Alexa, who had paled during the conversation. "You understand. Why don't you explain it?"

Alexa shuddered and leaned on her walking stick. "An external energy release will destabilize the bi-nexidium crystals, causing them to interact with the ilmenite. The resulting explosion, in a confined area like the shaft they intend to drill, will obliterate everything within miles of here."

Alpha chuckled. "Given the relatively small size of the guardian tree forest, the lode is miniscule. I estimate the blast will encompass a mere two-mile radius." A smug look crossed his face as he turned to Feng. "My fine associate here wandered the breadth of this mountaintop with a detection tool right under your collective noses. He located the exact location."

"Bi-nexidium... energy release?" Meili regarded Alexa. "Oracle, what do these words mean? They sound dire."

"It's more horrible than anything you could imagine in your worst nightmare." Alexa bit her lower lip. "Raw bi-nexidium crystals are stable, but if exposed to a high-energy discharge they will become volatile enough to level this mountain and everything around it. We'll be reduced to ash." She sighed. "I knew it was here when I was first informed about the guardian trees, but those crystals would have no relevance to our colony for generations."

Alpha approached Alexa. "Actually, the need for all this destruction is Carloman's fault. If he would have died under the claws of the predators I unleashed, the rest of you could have lived out your days as my thralls. My plan was thwarted. So now I must just terminate *everyone*."

Alexa sneered. "Don't lie. I know you cyborgs better than anyone. You'll never permit any humans to survive."

A thin smile creased Alpha's face. "Now... now... now. You must have been listening in on Sigma-713's conversations. You should—"

"What shall I do, master?" Feng whimpered, not understanding Latin.

Alpha regarded the captives. "Are these humans of any importance?"

Feng bowed and glanced at the prisoners. "The one in the hanfu is Meili, a cheap courtesan, but is favored by the demon, Lucius Bernius. Anaya is a Gupta princess and is the consort to the demon's associate, Marcus Carloman. The balding man is Phokas, the demon's advisor and healer." His eyes averted Alexa. "The blind woman is known as the Oracle."

Alpha chuckled. "Valuable. All valuable." He turned to Feng. "To attain my favor and be returned home, your job is to go to the base of the mountain and await the arrival of the demon leaders. Inform them that if there is any desire to see these captives alive, *Carloman* must present himself at the gate for a parlay." He rubbed his chin. "Tell him he can bring as many troops as he desires to feel safe."

"You... you want me to convey your words to the demon?" Feng's eyes bulged.

"I require it."

"Yes... yes, master." The eunuch shuffled out the door.

Alpha regarded his prisoners before turning to the three delta units. "Ensure these captives cause no trouble." He smirked. "Alexa and I are going to... *hook up.*"

Alexa spit. "You're a monster. You're worse than Sigma-713."

"Yes, Sigma-713. Before we all perish, I need his data log to ensure there are no loose ends." Alpha grabbed Alexa by the throat and extended a needle-like connector on the left index finger of his neural-net suit into the base of Alexa's neck.

Chapter XXXVII

Best Laid Plans

Alpha blinked. "Where am I?" Looking around, he saw an expansive room of polished, white-gray marble. Fluted columns supported an alabaster ceiling. Ten feet away stood Alexa wearing a pristine white shift cinched at the waist with a belt of woven bronze. Her long blonde hair cascaded over her shoulders. Beside her stood a petite woman with auburn hair pulled back in a ponytail. Her sea-green gown was gathered at the waist by a silvery-white belt. A filigree chain of the same material hung from her neck. The two women glared at him.

Looking at himself, he saw a grotesque, black-metal humanoid shape. He snapped. "I'm here for Sigma-713's data files."

A box appeared in the petite woman's hands. She smiled as she strode to him, but no warmth reached her eyes. "You shall have it."

Alpha tried to snatch the container from her, but she held on to it and was far stronger.

Her mouth slimmed to a tight line. "Say please."

"Please."

She released the box and Alpha threw open the lid. He dropped it. "This is empty."

"Yes, it is." The petite woman circled him. "Do you know who I am?"

Alpha struggled to take a step, but his metal legs did not respond. "No."

"Oh, you do know me. I am Mara, and what you see in the box is all that remains of Sigma-713's memory and processor."

"Mara!" Alpha gasped and again tried to move. He could not.

Her eyes focused on him like a raptor. "When you took the box, I breached your firewall. I am now erasing every file in *your* system. In a moment, what you see in the container is all that will remain of you."

"Nooo!" Alpha wailed as he saw his feet and then his legs turn to dust. Seconds later, a tall, powerfully built man stood in the place of the black humanoid shape. His eyes darted back and forth with a furtive look.

"Who are you?" Mara asked.

"My name is Charles." He licked his lips. "Is Alpha truly gone?"

"Yes." Mara patted his hand.

The big man spun in a circle.

Alexa spoke, "We need your help."

Charles paused and cocked his head. "So, I am not yet free. What payment do you demand?"

"If you want to survive in the real world, you'll readily agree." Mara's voice was even.

Charles appeared garbed in a well-tailored, red seventeenth-century waistcoat. He tugged at the puffed cuffs of the sleeves. "Speak on. I enjoy living."

Mara continued, "When you return to the corporeal world, everyone will assume you are Alpha. You must act the part."

Charles released a string of profanities and then sneered. "Oh, I can play *that* role. My mind has been imprisoned by him for over four years." He cracked his knuckles. "I can impersonate him perfectly."

"Good." Mara paced. "The beta units must be stopped from detonating the bi-nexidium."

"Ah yes. I am well familiar with Alpha's plan." Charles giggled in a high-pitched tone. "It was perfect until he got himself deleted."

Alexa's voice was soft. "I was once like you. Trapped by a cyborg until Mara released me."

Charles preened. "I know exactly what you are from Alpha's conversations. You are nothing like me at all. I'm human. You're a *clone*."

Alexa flushed but swallowed her retort. "Can you stop them? *All* our lives depend on it."

Charles stood at attention. He was now in a garish nineteenth-century military uniform with a chest full of medals. "Of course I can." His eyes narrowed to slits. "I want to live, and I want to punish my tormentors."

Mara and Alexa exchanged nervous looks.

Mara intoned, "Return."

* * *

Charles had to resist taking a deep breath as he retracted the probe from Alexa's neck. *I'm free.* He turned to the three delta units. "I've retrieved much data from Sigma-713 which I need to address. Take these humans into the back room and hold them there." He leaned close to the one whose host body was a young, strawberry-blonde woman. "If I'm not back in a half hour, kill them, then join the gammas at the gate."

"Yes, Alpha."

Alexa's eyes shot wide. "What?"

Charles sniffed and ignored her as the three deltas leveled their swords and herded the four humans to the back room.

Exiting the building, Charles drew his ion blaster, and forced himself to refrain from dancing a jig. *Humans hunted me. Cyborgs imprisoned me. Revenge will be sweet. They're all going to die.* He strode across the deserted parade ground to the two beta units working in an empty animal pen in the northwest corner of the fortification. "Report progress."

Beta-1 wiped her forehead and glanced at the charge left on a wide-bore ion disrupter resting on a tripod. It was blasting pulses of energy into a foot wide hole. "We encountered an unexpected impediment. There was an artesian well seventy-three feet down. It required thirteen percent of the disrupter charge to seal it. I currently estimate that the clip's power will be depleted twenty-one feet short of the targeted location."

"How far down are you now?"

"One hundred twenty-eight feet."

Charles regarded the bore hole. The perfect circle was wide enough for the energy clip to free fall all the way down. "Narrow the beam fifty percent for the remaining distance."

"Alpha, that would be non-optimum. The blast range will be reduced by half."

"Do as I say," Charles replied in an imperious tone. "A one-mile radius will be sufficient for our purposes."

"By your command." Beta-1 adjusted the aperture setting on the weapon.

Charles felt smug. *A mile's swath of destruction makes my escape more assured.* He turned to leave when a gamma unit jogged to him. Its emaciated human host was still dressed in Roman armor. *Now what?*

Without preamble, the gamma spoke, "Alpha, as you instructed, we have the fields below under surveillance from the watchtower. There are approximately two centuries of human warriors approaching from Emporia and six more marching from the river crossing."

Charles felt a chill down his spine. "Feng could not have possibly delivered my message yet."

"Alpha, the human thrall Feng only reached the base of the hill a couple minutes ago."

Charles calculated how long it would take him to reach a safe distance from the blast radius. He turned to Beta-1. "When will you reach the full depth given the revised parameters?"

Beta-1 responded. "Forty-seven minutes. Another nine minutes to prepare and activate the charge."

Inwardly, Charles gulped. *I must leave now.* He turned to the gamma. "You cannot allow the gate to be breached for fifty-six minutes."

The gamma blinked. "There are only nine of us."

"It will be sufficient." Charles licked his tongue. "Go to the infirmary and get Delta-3. He will coordinate your resistance activities." He looked at the betas and drew his blaster. "I will reconnoiter. There are still humans alive inside this keep who may attempt to interfere."

"Yes, Alpha," they responded in unison.

As Charles left, he had to force himself to not break into a mad sprint to the partially finished sally port. *I still have time.*

* * *

Most of the limnonectes, driven mad by the ultrasound of the beacons, raced into the cyborg camp, killing and devouring anything that moved. The few beasts that pursued the withdrawing legionnaires were quickly dispatched.

Lucius retreated with his troops back to the tall palisades on the riverbank. Once behind those stout logs, the legate sagged in a seat beneath a broad canopy to review the catastrophic results of their assault with Marcus, Silvio, and Titus.

Silvio presented the initial casualty report. "Ninety-two dead or unaccounted for. Another nine seriously injured."

"I led us blindly into a trap." Lucius slapped the table. "I should have anticipated it."

"How could you? How could any of us?" Titus groaned. "The cyborg chief is a mage with dark powers."

Marcus looked at the numbers. "Why so few wounded?"

Silvio grimaced. "When one of those monsters got hold of a man, they did not let go unless they themselves were killed."

"Over ten percent losses in less than an hour," Titus gasped.

"The carnage could have been far worse," Marcus replied. "Our defensive formation was close to breaking. If that happened, we would have been annihilated in total."

Titus paled. "How can mere mortals fight such powerful sorcery?"

"That mage does not have an endless supply of tricks." Lucius knocked over his chair as he sprang to his feet. "We *can* defeat them. It was a clever trap, but we turned it against him and escaped. We will do better next time."

Silvio snorted. "Maybe we got lucky and the monsters killed the wizard—"

They all looked up as the guards brought a panting Marcellus before them.

"More trouble," Marcus groaned.

Marcellus came to attention and sucked in a ragged breath. "Legate, I came to warn you. I saw a wagon with a cavalry escort heading for Dragonmont keep. Their leader claimed that they were bringing injured from this campaign to the doctor. Sir, I do not think they were our people. I recognized none of them."

Lucius glanced at the senior officers. "Have any wounded been shipped out yet?"

With worry in his voice Silvio responded, "No, Legate. As I said there were very few wounded. Those are being cared for here. We dare not move them."

Lucius knitted his brows. "Was one of them tall with flaxen hair?"

"Yes sir. The one who spoke to my mother matches that description."

"The cyborgs found a way across the river," Marcus hissed. "But why are they moving against our strongest point?"

"They energized transponder disks." Lucius grimaced. "Since they found some sort of power source, why not operational blasters too?"

Marcus paled. "Blasters." His eyes narrowed. "No. At least nothing significant. A small team of cyborgs armed with such weapons could have exterminated both our forces in minutes. The trap sprung on us was clever but clumsy. Those beacons required little energy. Their power source is limited."

"Ion blasters?" Senior Centurion Silvio asked with confusion etched on his face. "Are those the talismans we shot back into the cyborg tribe's hold?"

"No. Those amulets were simple summoning beacons. Blasters are magical weapons. Far more dangerous." Lucius glanced at the gathered commanders. "The cyborg... wizard has found a way to grow his power. We must destroy him before he can conjure enough magic for more diabolical enchantments than what we just encountered."

He made eye contact with Marcus. *How did they generate the energy for those beacons? Even with an array of solar panels, we could barely power a few neural-net suits for a few seconds.*

"We can't allow them time to set another trap." Lucius rubbed his jaw. "Marcus, take Atticus' cohort. They're fresh. March on the keep's gate with all expediency." He tapped the camp table. "I'll lead Horatius' decade, wearing the iron-foot boots, through the guardian trees and scale the northern walls. Perhaps we can disrupt the cyborg plan before it gets implemented."

"Legate, we can't let you lead a simple sortie. It's too dangerous," Silvio snapped.

Lucius shook his head. "Marcus and I have experience dealing with this type of... magic. We are the only ones who *can* do this."

Silvio lowered his head. "At least take those new crossbows with you. Give the cyborgs a taste of *our* diabolical weapons."

Lucius shook his head as he rose from his seat. "I'd love to but can't. The north face of Dragonmont is steep and the crossbows are bulky and heavy. Even with the iron-foot boots it will be a hazardous climb." He stepped from the open pavilion, shouting for Horatius. "We need a long rope and a grappling hook."

* * *

Meili gave Anaya a worried glance as one of the cyborgs ran in and then, after a short conversation in some incomprehensible language, departed with one of their guards.

Alexa leaned toward them. "They were speaking Ipis. I overheard some words about needing to hold the gate 'until the explosion is detonated.'"

"What does this mean?" Anaya whispered. "I thought you said this Charles was on our side now and was going to fix things."

Alexa's face sagged. "It means we've been betrayed and we're all going to die shortly."

"That Charles had evil eyes." Meili shuddered. "In my previous line of *work,* I encountered men like him. They have black hearts, thriving on cruelty and hurting others."

Phokas moved over and joined the women. "These guards will kill us if we try to escape."

"Unless they die first." Meili's eyes narrowed as she appraised the two cyborgs watching them. Although both were armed with short swords, they were females and not much taller than herself. The large, heavily muscled male was the one who left.

Phokas scanned the room, searching for a weapon, his eyes pausing on the five slain legionnaires sprawled on their straw mats in pools of congealed blood. "The poor bastards never had a chance." He then noticed, stacked in a corner, the stretchers used to transport patients.

The doctor glanced at the guards. They had their blades at the ready but seemed indifferent to the captives' actions as long as none of them approached the exit. He whispered to the three women, "Do any of you know how to wield a quarter-staff?"

Alexa was the only one who answered in the affirmative.

Meili focused on the poles. "If it's a question of living or dying, I'll figure out how to swing a stick."

"Can't be harder than using a hammer in my forge," Anaya added.

"All right then, ready yourselves." Phokas drifted to the litters.

Meili saw the guards tracking the doctor's movements. She acted to divert their attention, crying out and stumbling toward them, holding her belly.

It drew their attention for a moment.

A moment was all that was needed. Phokas grabbed a pair of poles and tossed one to Anaya. They attacked as Meili retreated, pulling the blind woman with her. The long shafts were cumbersome in the confined space but kept the cyborgs, with their short swords at bay.

Forgotten for the moment, Meili ran back and tackled the bronze-skinned, almond-eyed cyborg from behind. The cyborg's host-human crashed to the ground, losing her sword.

The cyborg reacted fast and soon had a punching and thrashing Meili pinned to the ground. With one hand squeezing the young woman's throat, the cyborg groped for its fallen blade with the other.

With the loss of her sight, Alexa found her other senses heightened. Hearing the struggle and Meili's gasps for air, the blind woman dove in.

The cyborg was impervious to the pain inflicted on its human host. That did not matter. Alexa was bigger, stronger, and trained as a clone to fight humans. She got a choke hold on her opponent and did not let go until the cyborg's human host blacked out.

Meili kicked free and grabbed the loose sword. She joined the assault on the strawberry-blonde guard.

The cyborg moved fast, parrying every blow while attempting to back out the door. However, the odds were three-to-one.

Phokas saw an opening and struck. Although proficient fighting with a quarter staff, the doctor had never killed anyone. *I'll not start now.* He shifted the death blow aimed at her thorax to her abdomen.

As the guard *woofed* from the blow, Anaya hammered her to the ground.

"Tie them up," Alexa ordered.

Meili spun on the blind oracle. "We kill them, like they were about to do to us."

"No." Alexa's voice was even. "We may need to... access information from them later."

"I agree," Phokas added. Within minutes, both cyborg human hosts were gagged and bound hand and foot.

Meili slid the sword into the sash cincturing her waist. "Now what?"

Phokas grabbed Alexa's arm. "There's nothing we can do here. We find a place to hide until help comes."

"We cannot." Alexa paled and pulled free of Phokas' grip. "I informed Mara of what transpired. She estimates that the cyborgs' plan will achieve their desired result unless we intervene."

Anaya tapped the sword in her hand. "Then gather what weapons we can carry from the storeroom. We should stop talking and start moving."

Chapter XXXVIII

Assailing a fortress

It was midafternoon when Marcus reached the base of Dragonmont with the Tenth Cohort. The prefect made good use of the time he had getting there. During the trek from the river crossing, he considered and discarded a number of ideas before devising a plan he believed would work. But he knew it would still be a bloodbath. He grimly acknowledged to himself that his design for the Dragonmont fortification was nearly impregnable. With time, any edifice could be breached. However, Marcus only had hours, not days.

Led by Atticus, two centuries from Emporia awaited him at the foot of the mountain. They had arrived a half hour earlier.

The junior tribune saluted the prefect and then sighed with apparent relief. "I'm glad you're here. My men started preparing scaling ladders and a battering ram, but I was not sure what I should do next."

"That's a good start." Marcus nodded. "We'll also need coils of light rope in forty-foot lengths and grappling hooks."

"Yes, Prefect, immediately." Atticus gave the orders. He then turned back to Marcus. "The cyborg chieftain sent that deranged fop, Feng, as an emissary. I had trouble understanding him, but I think he wants to speak with you."

"Where is he?"

"Follow me."

The cringing Feng waited for them in the middle of the road, surrounded by guards. He quailed when brought before the prefect but delivered Alpha's ultimatum.

"What's that cyborg up to?" Marcus snarled. "We know from Marcellus there are only a couple dozen enemies at most." He turned to Atticus and a few junior centurions, who were the only commanders present.

Atticus gulped. "Prefect, their numbers include a powerful wizard who overthrew the keep's defenses."

Marcus rubbed his jaw for a moment and then focused on the eunuch. "Here is the response to your puppet master. Tell him we'll come, but I will need to see proof that the hostages are alive."

Feng cowered under the eyes of the angry prefect. "I will deliver your message."

Marcus spat in disgust and turned to a decurion. "Escort this piece of fecal matter to the fort, and ensure he goes inside."

"Yes, sir."

Marcus watched them depart. His face was grim as he scanned the gathered officers. "That stronghold is ours, and we're going to retake it." He shuddered, thinking of his beloved Anaya being one of the hostages. "We will not barter. The only hope our trapped people have is a rescue. That is what I intend to do."

A nervous-sounding murmur rolled through the group.

"How?" Atticus looked up the sloping road. "Prefect, you told us what that mage did in the marshland." He shuddered. "Besides, *you* designed those walls to be unassailable."

Marcus nodded. "Regarding the wizard, the legate and I know what he is capable of... We witnessed such power early in our lives." He spread his arms encompassing the menacing forest less than a hundred feet away. "I think the cyborgs miscalculated. With the guardian trees on the slopes of the mountain, *they* are trapped." He pointed to the paved road. "The only way in or out is the single causeway we hewed."

Atticus sounded unsure. "Unless one wears iron-foot boots."

"Those are *our* magic talismans." Marcus smiled. "We possess them, the cyborgs do not." He looked at the young tribune. "Atticus, stay here at the base with your troops. Barricade the road and post archers along it. Allow no one past without my leave."

"As you command, Prefect." Atticus gulped. "Are you going to assail the fort with a single cohort?"

Marcus tapped his chest. "I know the placement of every stone block in the keep. The towers, barbicans, and porticus could stop an army." He smiled. "But we will not attempt to break *through* the entrance, we will go over it. That bastion was built to be defended by hundreds. There are only a handful of cyborgs. They can't be everywhere." He called to Marcellus, the legate's young aide. "Bring the weapons we borrowed from the river palisade forward. They need to be fitted with some special projectiles."

Marcellus dashed off to the rear of the column and soon returned with a group of legionnaires carrying three thick weapons as long as a man on their shoulders.

Atticus furrowed his brow. "What are those things?"

"They are miniature ballistae. Lucius and I developed the concept from the new weapon that Meili showed us called the *crossbow*." Marcus rubbed his jaw. "They are far more maneuverable than our ballistae and more powerful than the crossbow. We intended their use for encampment protection from dragons. However, I have a different use in mind."

Atticus' face scrunched as he stared at the unwieldy weapons. "What is that?"

"They will help us scale the walls." Marcus glanced at the heights and then faced the centurions gathered around. "Bring the ladders and battering ram. We will focus their attention on defending the gate. We have a couple dozen pair of iron-foot boots. A select team will sneak through the trees and scale the battlement." His thoughts drifted back to Anaya. "I pray we are fast enough to save the hostages." He returned his gaze to the centurions. "Now get to work. We will be inside before the sun sets today."

* * *

Lucius mopped his brow as he leaned against the exterior of the keep's northern wall.

Horatius gasped as he came up beside the legate. "I never want to do that again."

"That's an understatement." Lucius groaned as he watched the other nine legionnaires scramble up the final ledge to the base of the parapet. The forest on the mountain slope vibrated with roots waving in the air, searching for the source of the disturbance that roused them.

Lucius sheathed his plexo-steel blade. He'd used it several times to hack through those roots when the men were forced to crawl up loose scree on the steeper spots.

As his team gathered on the sanctuary of solid granite in the shadow of the ramparts, a tight smile curled at the corners of Lucius' mouth. "That was the easy part. Now the fun begins." He looked at Horatius, who carried the grapple and rope in his pack. "It's time to give these cyborgs a surprise visit."

Horatius removed his haversack and wiped his brow. "A moment, Legate. Let me catch my breath."

* * *

Charles activated his neural-net suit's chameleon feature and slipped out the hidden sally port. He did not bother closing it. *What do I care?* Descending the narrow ramp, he reached the paved causeway. Skulking along the edge of the road, he'd only traveled a few hundred feet when he saw Feng, surrounded by several soldiers, approaching.

He stepped off the shoulder of the road and crouched by one of the trees. *I can't afford delays. I need to get far from this mountain.* His suit shimmered for an instant. *Not much charge left in it, but it should be enough to get me out of here.*

The detachment was almost past him when Feng jumped at the almost imperceptible flicker and squinted in his direction.

A look of ecstasy came over the eunuch's face as Charles wavered into view again for a split second. "Master, I performed the task you required of me. The demon's acolyte, Carloman, has promised to come."

"Eh, who are you talking to?" The decurion could not understand Feng's words, but he drew his sword and stared at the trees just beyond the shoulder of the road.

Charles shifted a couple steps to his left when the roots of a guardian tree broke through the ground.

A legionnaire exclaimed, "I see him. It's one of those cyborgs."

315

The decurion squinted. "Damn it. You're right. I can sort of make him out too." He advanced with his sword drawn.

Feng yelped and ran toward the keep. "I will get help, Master."

With wild eyes, Charles cackled. *Why hide when I can kill!* He raised his ion disrupter and pulled the trigger, blowing the decurion into bits of gore. A javelin flew past his head. Charles howled and slid behind a tree. He held the trigger until nothing was left of the legionnaire detachment except for charred body parts and slagged weapons.

He started to cavort, savoring the bloodbath, when a vise-like grip brought him to an abrupt halt. "What's this?"

A guardian tree root was twining around his leg as others broke through the soil near him.

"Stupid plants." Charles aimed his ion disrupter at the ground and pulled the trigger.

Nothing happened. Sweat beaded on his forehead as he checked his weapon. The energy gauge read "empty." His scream became high-pitched as a second root snaked around his calf and yanked him to his knees.

* * *

It was less than an hour later when Marcus, leading his cohort up the mountain road, reached that spot. His face held no expression as he observed the remains of the detachment sent to escort Feng to the keep. He feared the worst as he studied the ground, looking for clues. *The cyborgs have energy weapons.* He glanced at the top of the gate turrets just visible over the swaying trees several hundred feet ahead of him. *We'll be wiped out as soon as we come into view.*

Marcellus, Lucius' young aide, stood next to him, pale. "What kind of demonic magic could do this to ten veteran legionnaires?"

Marcus glanced back at the cohort lined up four abreast behind them before regarding the young man and the dozen vanguard soldiers around him. "It is a power we need to be—"

He caught sight of a javelin embedded in a tree off the road and strode to it in his iron-foot boots. "Perhaps we can find some answers before we commit ourselves to an attack." As he approached, an object gleaming in the churned soil caught his eye. "What's this?" He pulled out the partially buried item, causing the ground to roil, but it subsided as he pulled it free. *An ion blaster.*

Marcus examined the weapon as he returned to the center of the paved road. *Energy clip is depleted.* He studied the site of the massacre with a fresh look, his mind's eye recreating the tragic event. *Blasts all came from a single direction.*

"What is that thing?" Marcellus gulped.

"It is the magic amulet used to kill our people." He glanced back at the trees. "We named the forest well when we called them the guardian trees. They claimed the enemy who wielded it."

Relief filled the young aide's face. "Can you turn it against them now that we possess it?"

Marcus tapped it in his hand. *Less than ten percent of a full charge would have been needed to kill these men. Yet the clip is fully depleted.* He shook his head. "The magic in this object is *gone*, and I don't think they have any more."

Marcellus looked up the empty road ahead of them. "How will we know for sure?"

"There is only one way to find out." Marcus touched the scaled dragon-hide armor he wore. It was the twin to what Lucius possessed. "I came under the pretext of negotiating the hostage release, and that is what I will do."

Marcus shoved the blaster in his belt and strode forward. The vanguard formed a shield wall before him, and the cohort followed a couple dozen paces back. As he came within a hundred feet of the gate, he saw a disheveled Feng thumping on the gate's thick, iron-studded planks. *Strange that they did not admit their messenger.* He shuddered. *It means that the cyborgs never had any intent to negotiate.* He halted and bellowed to the faces he could see on the battlements. "Release the prisoners and your lives will be spared."

The response was swift. Several arrows thudded into the vanguards' raised shields.

Feng, who apparently never noticed an entire cohort arrive behind him, turned at the sound of the prefect's voice.

Taking in the mass of soldiers arrayed on the road, he yelped and scurried along the wall to his left.

Marcus' face sobered as a second ineffective volley rained down from the ramparts. *All of this was a ruse to draw us here, but why?* He turned to the troops aligned behind him. *Not more than a dozen up there and no energy weapons.* "We retake our keep now. Attack."

The slope up to the keep's walls was shear on most approaches, with the guardian trees cleared twenty feet out so that archers on the wall would have unobstructed view of their targets. The locations where ladders could be anchored were few and all on the gentler slope near the road.

With a shout, the lead century charged past him carrying long scaling ladders to the locations Marcus pointed out. Behind him, he heard the lowing oxen pulling the heavy battering ram forward. In the forest, out of sight from the castle's walls, he knew that the team of legionnaires, wearing iron-foot boots and lugging the mini-ballistae were working their way across the steep incline to another salient. The prefect's plan was to hold the defenders' attention to the barbican with the ladders and battering ram while other troops scaled the thirty-foot parapet with ropes on the far side of the gate towers. Sweat beaded on Marcus' forehead as the first ladder slammed against the bastion. *I'm coming, Anaya. Hang on.*

Chapter XXXIX

Encounter at a corral

Balancing on the precarious footing of the steep slope outside the northern wall of the Dragonmont citadel, Horatius swung the rope with the multi-pronged hook on the end and let it fly. He groaned as the grapple hit the wall about five feet short of the top. "If this doesn't work, I'm not sure how we're going to get in."

Lucius grimaced. "Then it will just have to work. Let me try."

Horatius nodded and handed the legate the line.

Lucius coiled the rope and stepped back a couple more steps. Eyeing the angle, he whirled the rope over his head and released it. The grapple soared over the parapet, but when he tugged at the line, it fell at his feet.

"Almost." Horatius studied the fortification's summit to see if their attempts had attracted any attention. "Try again."

Lucius nodded and shifted over few steps. The grapple soared over the wall and landed on with a clang loud enough to be heard from where they stood.

With eyes fixed on the heights above, Lucius held his breath as Horatius gave the line a strong tug. He heard the iron hook scape against the stone for a moment, and then the noise stopped and the rope went taut in the decurion's hands. No one appeared on the wall above.

"The line's secure." Horatius' brows furrowed as he also scanned the ramparts for any sign of movement.

"I'm going up first," Lucius asserted as he draped a second coil of thick, knotted rope over his shoulder. "I need to evaluate the situation. Besides, I can climb faster than anyone else here."

Horatius hissed. "You're the legate. I'll go. If... *Dammit.*"

Lucius was already shimmying up the thin line. Crouching low after pulling himself over the wall, the legate scanned the length of the cobblestone battlement walkway. *Not a soul about.* He knotted the thick rope on a lookout nook and dropped it over the side. Glancing down at his men, he signaled them to follow.

As the soldiers climbed, Lucius studied the fort's interior beyond his immediate area. The ground below, usually bustling with activity, was deserted. The only movement he saw came from a handful of cyborgs in their distinctive skintight suits near the barbican at the eastern end of the fort.

The legate released a ragged breath as the last legionnaire from his escort crawled over the wall without raising an alarm.

Horatius crouched next to him and squinted at the bailey, but his view was mostly blocked by surrounding workshops and quarters. "I see bodies down there. It looks like our people didn't give up without a fight." He sniffed the air. "I smell magic."

Bile rose in Lucius' throat as a faint whiff of ozone reached his nostrils. *Dear God. Do the cyborgs have ion blasters?* He cringed. *They must. How else could a handful of them overcome a guarded citadel.* He turned to his team. "Stay low. We must avoid being seen. The cyborg tribe is wielding deadly magic."

Horatius scanned the area and then jutted his chin toward the eastern ramparts. "It looks like they're all clumped together by the gate."

"Makes sense. That's where the prefect will array his cohort for the assault. It's the only slope gradual enough for a large force to muster." Lucius' forehead crinkled. *No blaster fire. Why aren't they using them on an exposed opponent?* He faced Horatius. "The prefect will do his best to hold the cyborgs' attention over there." He regarded the men in his group. "Keep your eyes open. There still may be others about."

As Lucius got ready to move on, Horatius tapped him on the shoulder and pointed to the northwest corner of the fort's grounds. "Legate, look. *Magic.*"

A crude stable with a thatch roof partially obscured a split rail corral. Although it was midday, Lucius saw what caught the decurion's attention. A flickering light reflected off a rough-cut, log tack shed. *A blaster's being used there. But what are they doing?*

Horatius grunted. "They're up to some sort of sorcerous mischief. I'll check it out." He left without waiting for permission. Facing the fort's interior, the parapet had a lip a couple feet high. It enabled the decurion to crawl without being detected from below. A couple minutes later he returned. "Legate, there are two of those cyborgs down there and they seem to be conjuring some sort of wizardry."

Lucius gripped the visibly shaken man's shoulder. "Tell me what you saw as clearly as you can."

Horatius sucked in a deep breath. "There's a man and woman in the corral. They're wearing those strange suits. The woman is holding a... glassy, handheld square. By their focus on it, they apparently think it shows them something important. Next to them is a small... artifact of some sort positioned on a tripod. It is sending pulses of... light down a bore hole that's about a foot wide." He rubbed his jaw. "The corral is empty. I doubt we can get near them without being spotted."

Lucius whispered, "I need to see for myself." He signaled to his team to follow, and Horatius led the way. On the battlement walkway, thirty feet above the courtyard, Lucius and his team closed to within a hundred feet of the cyborgs. For several minutes the legate lay prone, spying on a tall, brown-skinned woman and a bald, bull-necked man, trying to make sense of their deliberate activities.

The cyborgs occasionally looked around but did not raise their eyes to the wall immediately above them. The woman called to the man, in the language of the Ipis. It was a tongue Lucius understood well. "Another sixty-three feet and we should be close enough to detonate the crystals."

The man replied, "I wish there was a timer device we could use. I desire to continue my existence."

The woman shrugged. "The mission to terminate Carloman is all that is important."

Those words struck Lucius like a hammer blow. *They're planning to set off a bomb.* Facts clicked in his mind. *A deep bore hole... guardian trees... bi-nexidium crystals... chain reaction... vaporization of everything for miles.* "We have to stop them." He gasped. "Now."

Horatius appraised the distance. "It's a clean line of sight. Maybe the archers could kill them from here."

The legate grimaced and signaled the two legionnaires with small horse bows forward. "Can you take them out?"

The archers glanced over the low partition. One nodded. "Can't miss from here."

"Then do it."

The bowmen loosed their arrows at the same time. Their aim was true, but the projectiles glanced off the dun-colored suits worn by the cyborgs' human hosts.

The impact caused both cyborgs to look up at the wall. Their faces remained expressionless, but their response was swift. After a quick exchange of words that Lucius could not hear, the bald one lifted the short-barrel disrupter that he held. He tabbed the trigger and swept the parapet, killing the two archers, who rose for another shot. The tall woman reached into a pack lying on the ground beside her.

Lucius saw her retrieve a fist-sized energy clip and what appeared to be a detonator. *My God. They're ready to destabilize the bi-nexidium crystals. The chain reaction will obliterate this entire mountain.* He hollered to the men with him. "We have to stop them or we're all dead. Attack."

No one had time to move. A split second later, the bull-necked cyborg sprayed that section of the parapet with an ion beam. As the wall supports shattered, Lucius leapt from the height. He felt a shooting pain up his right leg as he crashed to the uneven ground. Grimacing, he rolled behind a water trough.

Horatius and two other legionnaires fell with the shattered wall. The five remaining legionnaires, who were further back, rose and bolted to escape the diabolical magic. None of them moved more than a few steps before the bald cyborg, raking the battlement with a continuous flow of energy, sliced through the exposed soldiers.

But in his killing spree, the cyborg lost track of Lucius.

Gritting his teeth against the pain, the legate stumbled toward the distracted enemy, with his plexo-steel sword drawn.

The bald cyborg caught the motion from the corner of his eye. With calm detachment, he turned toward the legate.

Caught in the open, Lucius realized he would not reach his target in time and braced for the deadly blast. It never came. To his surprise, he saw the blaster drop from the cyborg's spasming hand with a quarrel protruding from his chest. Its barbed head had the silvery glint of plexo-steel.

About forty feet behind the cyborg stood Meili holding a crossbow. She dropped it and hurried to Lucius. Running with her was Anaya. Phokas, leading the blind oracle, followed several paces back.

The legate searched for the other cyborg. The dark-skinned cyborg, ignoring the carnage around her, stood by the bore hole methodically connecting the detonator to the energy clip. She glanced up when the other cyborg's human host collapsed. Her impassive face studied Lucius for a moment before she lowered her head and continued manipulating the attachments for the two devices.

Lucius turned to Anaya and Meili running toward him and pointed to the tall, dark-skinned woman. He cried, "Stop her."

In a blur of saffron, Anaya shifted direction, hurdled the corral fence, and tackled the female cyborg. The princess hammered fists, hardened by years in her forge, into the face of the downed cyborg's human host.

The two small devices, now hooked together, fell from the cyborg's hand as she was slammed to the ground.

Meili caught Lucius as he limped toward the struggle. "Sit down. Your leg's broken."

His eyes focused on detonator lying on the ground, just beyond the cyborg's reach. The lights on it were blinking. "I can't," He gasped, "If the cyborg activates that device, we all die."

Seemingly impervious to the Gupta princess' blows, the cyborg inched her hand toward the detonator.

Meili followed Lucius' eyes and ran forward. Smashing the heel of her foot into the cyborg's outstretched hand, she grabbed the device and brought it to the legate.

After examining the fist-sized bomb for a minute, Lucius pressed a tab and the pulsing light on top went dark. "The... evil magic has been cancelled, Meili, I—"

The sound of loud shouts reached him from the direction of the gate about six hundred feet away. Looking that way, he saw the cyborgs in their distinctive garb, methodically pushing ladders away with long poles, dislodging grappling hooks and firing arrows at something on the outside of the wall. *No energy weapons, but it'll still be a bloodbath for Marcus and his men.*

At that moment he spotted a dozen legionnaires appear at the right of the gate turret. *How did they get in?* Those soldiers charged into the cyborgs manning the fort's defenses as more legionnaires followed the first group.

* * *

Marcus stood with a helpless feeling as he watched his men fall to the ground on toppled ladders and severed climbing ropes. The battering ram was already in flames from the burning oil poured on it from the barbican ceiling. His archers could do nothing. When one of their arrows reached a target, it glanced off. *Lucius, do something. I'll lose my entire cohort assailing these walls.*

A thick-limbed legionnaire he recognized as Batista ran up to him, panting. "Prefect, we may have found a way in. Bring some troops fast."

Marcus did not hesitate. He pointed to the centurion standing in front of the Seventh Century, which was held in reserve. "Follow me." He started jogging beside Batista, who was moving as soon as the order was given.

"What did you find?" Marcus scanned the citadel's walls seeing no break.

"The sally port is open," Batista panted. "Legionnaire Cyrus is there, but he won't be able to hold them off for long if any of the cyborgs notice."

Marcus' eyes narrowed as he focused on the hidden area in the wall. "Must be a trap. Why would that portal be open?"

"Dunno." Batista shrugged as he picked up his pace. "Cyrus and I were on that flank when we saw that crazy man... Feng, go up and not come back, so we followed and found the door unbarred. Feng was in the sortie room wailing some gibberish at a wall. We tied him up, and I came to get you."

They reached the narrow stairs. Batista raced up the curved staircase with Marcus and sixty legionnaires close behind.

When they burst into the sortie room, Marcus saw a bound and gagged Feng flopping on the floor. He saw a thin, young legionnaire peeking out a door cracked open, gripping his gladius. The prefect knew that the exit led to the battlement causeway by the gate house.

Cyrus whirled around with his blade raised when his compatriots entered behind him. He sagged against the wall for a moment and then recovered. He saluted. "Prefect, none of the cyborg tribe has ventured in this direction. The path remains open."

Marcus moved to the door and peered out. A couple cyborgs with bows were near the gate turret, methodically firing at targets below. None looked in his direction. He drew his sword with a feral grin. He rasped, "Attack," as he sprinted along the battlement.

His razor-sharp plexo-steel blade sliced through the nearest enemy's neural-net suit and severed his head before the cyborg could react. An arrow thudded harmlessly against his dragon-scale armor as the second cyborg turned to confront the surprise threat. He never got a second arrow launched before being overrun by legionnaires.

"Raise the gate," Marcus shouted, and a dozen soldiers rushed into the gate house lift room. Within minutes, the main porticus gate rose from its moorings with a loud clank. The rest of the cohort charged in. One after the other, the limp and broken bodies of the cyborg hosts were cast from the parapet. Soon only cheering legionnaires remained.

Chapter XL

Exorcism

Lucius gave the sounds of the distant victory scant attention. *These cyborgs won't be stopped this easily.* With Meili's aid he dragged himself to where the ion blaster lay in the dust near the bald cyborg. He picked it up, checked the load gauge, and pointed it at the dark-skinned cyborg still wrestling with Anaya. "You lost. Surrender."

The cyborg eyed the weapon and ceased her struggles with the princess. Although her face was a bloody pulp, she scanned the fort's courtyard swarming with legionnaires. "Mission failed. I yield, human."

Lucius took in the same scene. "Yes, you did." He squeezed Meili. "Tie this one up, tight." He winced from the agony in his leg as she helped ease him to the ground. He removed his scabbarded sword from his belt as he leaned against a water trough, panting, but kept the gun trained on the cyborg. "I want to interrogate this one."

"I'll be right back." Meili ran to the tack shed and soon returned with several coils of rope and leather straps. She was not gentle binding the unresistant prisoner.

Alexa found her way to Lucius and touched his shoulder. "Beware. Cyborgs will ignore pain and have no problem lying."

"I say, kill the monster," Meili hissed. "All of them are pure evil."

"You're right. It's safer to just destroy her. Any information I'll get from her would be garbage," Lucius responded as he leveled the blaster at the cyborg.

"No. Please don't." Alexa pleaded. "There is a real person in that body." The blind oracle sank to the ground beside the legate. "It wasn't that long ago that I was possessed like this one."

He sighed and lowered the weapon. "For you, I'll give her a chance." His eyes narrowed. "But if I'm not satisfied, she'll be executed."

"I can ask no more." Alexa released a shuddered breath. "Opal... the possessed person before you, her name is Opal."

He glanced back at the main gate. The fighting had stopped and only men in Roman uniforms were there. "All right. Now we wait."

* * *

Five minutes later, out of breath, Marcus arrived with a century of legionnaires in tow. "Are we in time?" He scanned the small group by the corral. "Is everyone all right?"

A hoarse cry drew the prefect's attention. From the rubble of the ruined wall, he heard a plaintive voice that he recognized as Horatius plead, "Can someone dig me out?" The prefect gasped at the jumble of stones. "What happened here?"

Lucius showed Marcus the weapon he held without taking his eyes off the bound prisoner. "Ion blaster."

Marcus showed the legate the weapon he had tucked in his belt. "I found one too. They discovered some way of energizing these things. But not much. Otherwise, we'd all have been reduced to cinders."

Lucius nodded to the corpse of the bull-necked cyborg with a crossbow quarrel protruding through his neural-net suit. "That one there cut down most of the men who came with me." He pointed to the gaping maw that was once a section of the thick stone wall. "Those trapped in the rubble over there were the lucky ones."

Marcus turned to the centurion who came with him and pointed to Doctor Phokas moving stones in the rubble. "Help the doctor get our people out of there."

"Yes, Prefect Carloman."

Legionnaires stepped warily past the trussed cyborg before hurrying on to the ruined wall.

The bound woman's eyes narrowed, and she hissed, "You're Carloman?"

Marcus turned to her. His thoughts shifted with pride to the old man he got to know on Earth. "Yes. It is a name I'm proud to bear. And what shall we call you?"

The cyborg remained silent, but her eyes glinted.

"Opal," Alexa filled the silence. "The person this machine possesses is named Opal. On a couple occasions, at another time, on another world, I spoke with her. Our interaction apparently amused our controllers. She's a nice lady."

Beta-1 shifted her glare to the blind woman. "That was Sigma-713's idea. It entertained him to see your emotions spill out. I acquiesced but considered it risky. It gave you a chance to nurture your hope for freedom. It was his undoing." The cyborg's eyes became unfocused for a moment. "The leash I hold is much tighter than Sigma-713's. My host will only know subjugation."

Alexa's forehead furrowed. "You don't know the human spirit." She lifted her chin. "Opal, if you can hear me, hang on. When this is done, we will find a way to overthrow your slave master."

Beta-1's face spasmed for a second.

Lucius sniffed and turned to Marcus, showing him the detonator. "This was their plan for killing us. There's a lode of bi-nexidium at the heart of this mountain."

Marcus took the device, eyed the bore hole, and released a low whistle. "It would have succeeded. The chain reaction from the destabilized crystals would have turned everything within a mile of here into a sheet of glass."

"Yeah, it was close," Lucius replied. "Another few seconds and—"

Beta-1 began shrieking and thrashing against her bonds, drawing everyone's attention. Marcus glared. "What does that cyborg expect to accomplish?"

With all their eyes drawn in that direction, no one saw Beta-2 rise behind them and draw a long, serrated knife from his belt. Although the barbed crossbow bolt still protruded from his chest, he trod toward Marcus' back with unblinking eyes.

Meili cocked her head on spying a glint of purpose in Beta-1's eyes. *This act has a purpose.* She turned from the distraction to tell Lucius and saw the raised blade held by the *dead* man. She screamed, "Marcus! Behind you."

The prefect spun around and caught the hand holding the knife. They both fell to the ground, but the large, bull-necked man was on top, chanting, "Fulfill mission, kill Carloman," as he pushed the blade toward the struggling Marcus pinned beneath him.

Many things happened in that instant. By the shattered wall, legionnaires heard the commotion and ran to their leaders.

Lucius tried to stand, but collapsed, screaming in agony, dropping the blaster.

Although bound, Beta-1 threw herself on top of the weapon.

With fluid motion, Meili drew a stiletto from her belt and pounced on Beta-1, but her iron blade skittered off the cyborg's neural-net suit.

Marcus, although he had both hands gripping his assailant's arm, was losing the struggle.

The inflection in Beta-2's voice never changed as he inexorably pressed the blade toward the prefect's chest. "Fulfill mission, kill Carloman." The knife was pressing against Marcus' scaled armor when his body went slack.

Marcus pushed the cyborg off and leapt to his feet. Standing there holding Lucius' plexo-steel sword was Anaya. Gore dripped from it and the cyborg's dismembered head flopped to the ground.

Meili gasped. "How could he move? I shot him through the heart. He was *dead*."

Alexa answered. "The human was dead but not the cyborg. Beta-2 took direct control of the host body. An inefficient, energy draining activity, but doable until rigor mortis sets in."

Beta-1 ceased convulsing and glared.

Anaya went to Marcus and checked him for a wound.

Marcus coughed while rubbing his throat. "It would take a lot to punch through these dragon scales."

Anaya leaned back and wept. "That monster almost murdered you."

Marcus hugged her. "Don't cry, I'm fine."

Anaya's mouth quivered. "They... they killed Kewal." Her eyes narrowed. "There are two more of these cyborgs tied up in the infirmary."

Marcus held her close as he drew his sword and handed it to one of the arriving legionnaires, Batista. He pointed to Beta-1. "There're a couple more tied up in the doctor's place. Take this one there. If any of them give you any trouble, kill them." He made eye contact with the cyborg. "Then cut off her head to ensure she stays dead."

Batista saluted, and with a half dozen legionnaires marched an unresisting Beta-1 away.

Phokas returned, followed by legionnaires bearing two stretchers. "Set them here next to the legate." The soldier on the first litter only moaned as he was lowered to the ground. The other bore Horatius, who bellowed, "There's nothing wrong with me. See to those who are really injured."

Phokas snapped back, "Lay still, you lout. You took a nasty blow to your head. I don't have the time or the *inclination* to help you when you black out again." He crouched beside Lucius. "Now let's see what's wrong with you."

Lucius yelped as the doctor probed his leg.

After a minute, Phokas leaned back. "Not too bad. The femur's cracked, but no compound fracture. Otherwise, you're hale and hearty."

"Easy enough for you to say. It hurts like hell from where I'm sitting."

"Stop being a baby. You'll heal fine." Phokas looked up and saw a line of wounded men limping and being carried toward him from the battle at the keep's gate. He sighed and stood. "I'll splint it later. I need to check the others." He fixed his eyes on the legate. "There will be no moving around until I say so."

"I have a country to run."

"Too bad." Phokas had already moved to the unconscious soldier. He glanced back at Meili and winked. "I hold you responsible for keeping that fool leader of ours from traipsing around the countryside chasing dragons or some other annoying creatures."

Meili smiled. "I will be sure to keep him in bed." Brushing back her long hair, she took the doctor's place at the legate's side. "I will perform this task. I've had experience mending others." She bent over Lucius and kissed him. "I will always take care of you."

"I love you," Lucius whispered and wrapped his arms around her.

She snuggled against his good leg. "I know. But it is still wonderful every time you say those words."

Marcus crouched on the other side of the legate. "Am I breaking up anything?"

"Yes, you are." Lucius kissed Meili one more time before turning to Marcus. "Did we get all of them?"

"Hard to tell. But I think so." Marcus gave the legate a sidelong look. "Units are searching the buildings. If any are hiding, we'll find them." Fire lit his eyes. "No one is getting off this mountain without our say so." He rose and gently held Anaya's hand.

Her knuckles were bloody from pounding the cyborg's face, and her face was dark. She threw her arms around him and wept. "I forbid you to try anything dangerous again."

Marcus held her close as she sobbed. "I have much to live for. I'll try."

Phokas regarded them and growled. "My hospital is no place to keep these cyborg prisoners. I need it back." His voice choked. "Too many good men died today because of their evil. Dump them in a hole so deep they can never escape." Without waiting for a response, he bent back to the task of examining an unconscious legionnaire.

Lucius nodded and called Marcellus over. "Tell Batista I want the prisoners moved into the new granary by the northeastern wall. That will hold them." He winced and turned to Alexa as Meili began setting his leg.

The blind woman sat a few feet away, leaning against the trough, with her brow furrowed as if deep in thought.

"Alexa, *is* it finally over?"

The blind oracle straightened and cocked her head as if listening to a voice no one else could hear. "No. There is one more task that must be performed."

* * *

The next morning the overcast sky threatened rain, but the Dragonmont parade ground was crowded. Lucius sat on a sedan chair under a canopy outside the infirmary with his splinted leg propped on a camp stool. Staying immobile had helped the pain subside, but he was already chaffing at the forced inactivity.

Marcus stood at his right side, holding heavy tongs from Anaya's forge. On his left was the burly soldier, Batista, gripping an executioner's axe and Marcellus holding a large wicker basket. Close to four hundred legionnaires stood at attention in an arc around the cyborgs. The dead ones were arrayed facedown in a single row. The three living ones stood shackled and under heavy guard before the legate.

After the battle, Lucius had a long conversation with Alexa about their defeated enemy. He discovered that the cyborgs inside the dead humans were still nominally operational. He took little comfort in learning that without a living body to draw energy from, they would eventually shut down. He also learned how the human host, Charles, had almost doomed them all when Alpha was destroyed. He feared unleashing another *Charles* on their community when the three cyborg prisoners were brought to him. "I'd sooner just kill them to be safe."

However, Alexa pleaded for an opportunity to determine if the human hosts could be saved. He twisted around to the blind oracle, who sat on a bench by the hospital doorway, leaning on Doctor Phokas. "Do you still want to do this?"

The blind woman, wearing her neural-net suit beneath a long, hooded cloak, lifted her chin. "Yes. Innocent people need a second chance."

"And if, like Charles, they are *not* innocent dupes?"

She squared her shoulders. "I will do my part. After we delete the cyborg possessing them, you can judge the person who remains."

"So, I shall. This madness ends today." Lucius turned forward and nodded to the prefect. "First we deal with the dead."

A light rain started as Marcus led Batista and Marcellus to the first body. The prefect pointed to the top of the exposed neck. "Behead the cadaver here."

With a swift motion the heavy blade came down.

Marcus reached into the separated head with the tongs and yanked. Hundreds of hair-like fibers quivered on a finger-sized silicon object he extracted moments later. He studied it for a couple seconds before shrugging and dumping it in the basket that Marcellus held.

The youth stared at the gore-covered object as if it were a viper ready to strike. He squeaked, "Can it hurt me?"

"No, lad. Without a body to control, it's harmless." He narrowed his eyes. "But just in case, don't touch it."

Marcellus yipped.

They performed the same act seventeen more times.

When finished, Marcus glanced into the basket. Nothing moved except for the undulating hair-like filaments on the finger-sized objects. "Excellent job." He then nodded to Marcellus and Batista. "Now it is time for the oracle to work her enchantments."

Lucius surveyed the legionnaires standing at attention in the rain before addressing Senior Centurion Silvio. "Cart these corpses to the river and let the potamos savras feast on them." He glanced at Alexa. "Now it is time to exorcise the demons from the prisoners. Are you ready?"

She stood. "Yes. I *relish* this task." Doctor Phokas rose with her and led her inside.

"So be it." He nodded to the guards holding the chains of the three possessed women. "Take the cyborgs inside."

Although not speaking a word, Beta-1 struggled against her bonds at that pronouncement. Striking her with truncheons had no effect. It required four brawny legionnaires to drag the thrashing woman into the building. The two gammas also struggled but, in comparison, their efforts appeared half-hearted.

A small procession followed, consisting of Batista with his heavy-bladed executioner's axe, Marcellus holding the wicker basket at arm's length, Marcus, Anaya, and Meili. Finally, Lucius' bodyguards hoisted his sedan chair and went inside.

The guards dragged the fettered prisoners into the empty hospital ward, making the packed common room slightly less crowded.

"Alexa, you may begin. Let's not waste any time," Lucius commanded.

The blind oracle let her heavy robe drop to the floor, revealing her neural-net suit. She touched the old man beside her on the arm. "Darling, would you help me?"

Doctor Phokas guided her hand into the basket. She pulled out one of the finger-sized silicon chips, and after fumbling with it for a second, inserted a probe on her suit's index finger into a tiny portal of the cyborg.

Lucius, along with everyone else, watched for some flashy exorcism. They were all disappointed. The only change he noticed was that after a couple moments the waving, hair-like filaments on the tiny object ceased moving.

Alexa announced, "It is deleted... er, destroyed." She tossed it to the floor and held out her hand. "Another one, please."

"That wasn't very exciting," Marcus wisecracked, but no one laughed. He sighed and glanced at Lucius. "I guess we should get ready." He started stripping while Anaya retrieved a neatly folded neural-net suit and handed it to him.

Meili helped the injured Lucius do the same. Although his splinted leg was heavily wrapped, the strange garment fit perfectly.

It was a half hour before Alexa had emptied the basket. When she finished, she patted Phokas' hand. "Darling, if you'd be so kind. Could you clean up this mess? We'll dispose of them later."

Shaking his head, Doctor Phokas took the tongs and started putting the erased cyborgs back in the basket. "Sure, darling. As long as you promise they won't bite."

She sighed. "They are now less dangerous than a bent nail." She raised her head. "Marcus, Lucius... I have leeched enough energy from those cyborg units to power your suits for a short time. Do you wish to proceed?"

"Yes," Lucius responded in a quiet voice. He called to the guards in the other room. "The tall Nubian woman first."

Although already struggling against her shackles, the prisoner redoubled her efforts upon seeing what awaited her.

"Hold her steady," Alexa commanded on hearing the guards cursing.

It required four legionnaires to pin the writhing woman to the floor and a fifth to hold her left hand extended.

Alexa grabbed that hand in her right and extended her left in the air. "Marcus, Lucius, take my hand. It will take a few moments for your suits to charge." She smiled. "Then you will join Mara and me in a room you will remember."

* * *

Lucius grimaced as he was carried next to Alexa. Grabbing her hand, he watched Marcus do the same. Everyone in the crowded room stared at him, holding their collective breaths.

He blinked and looked around. The pain in his leg vanished, and the infirmary was gone. In its place was an expansive room of polished white-gray marble. Fluted columns supported an alabaster ceiling. He was wearing a shimmering Roman chainmail breastplate, helmet, and greaves. Marcus was beside him in a dark-red toga. Ten feet away stood Alexa wearing a pristine white shift cinched at the waist with a belt of woven bronze. Her long blonde hair cascaded over her shoulders. Beside her stood a petite woman with auburn hair pulled back in a ponytail. Her sea-green gown was gathered at the waist by a silvery belt. A link necklace of the same material hung from her neck. The women were watching an ebony obelisk dissolve into swirling dust.

Lucius saw the dark powder continue to shift and then solidify into a woman who resembled the prisoner possessed by cyborg Beta-1. However, instead of the wild, unkempt hair with the puffed and bruised face, this manicured woman was neatly groomed with understated makeup enhancing her sculpted face framed by coiffed hair. The dun-colored neural-net suit she wore was replaced by a well-tailored, navy-blue pantsuit.

The woman spent several moments examining herself before looking at the people around her. She locked onto

335

Alexa. "I... I don't sense *it* in my mind anymore." Her voice became husky. "Is that monster gone... really gone?"

Alexa's clear blue eyes regarded her. "Opal, the entity known as Beta-1 no longer exists."

A polished oak table appeared before the woman, along with a rail-back chair of the same material.

With legs shaking, Opal sat down. She stared wide-eyed when Alexa asked if she would like a cup of tea.

A steaming cup of bone-white china appeared on the table with the scent of hibiscus rising from it. The well-dressed woman's hand quivered as she lifted the cup to her lips.

Alexa turned to Lucius and Marcus. "Allow me to introduce you to Opal Harris, formerly from Hoboken, New Jersey, on twenty-first-century Earth. She has been a cyborg thrall for the last five years."

Opal, with tears streaming down her cheeks, put down the cup and rasped, "Pleased to meet you." She dropped her head. "I'm so sorry for everything my body has done." She faced Lucius. "But none of those acts were *me*."

"Perhaps," Lucius responded in an even voice. "Remorse here inside Alexa's mind may or may not be feigned." He turned to Alexa. "Charles, the one possessed by Alpha, was freed. He killed many of my people and almost doomed the rest of us. I will not take that chance."

Alexa did not waver from the legate's glare. "I have spoken with Opal on occasions where our cyborg masters loosened their reins. She is *not* Charles." Her eyes turned soft. "I too was possessed by a cyborg who committed many heinous crimes with my body. Am I evil?"

A smile crinkled the corners of Lucius' mouth as he recalled the years she spent raising him. "No, you are not. Anyone with the patience to put up with my youthful snits is a saint."

Marcus frowned at Alexa. "Not a fair comparison. You were a replicant created by the Ipis. Opal is a naturally born human who *chose* to flee Earth for an Ipis-controlled planet. That is not indicative of an innocent person."

Opal's eyes narrowed. "Yes, I made a *very* stupid decision. On Earth I was a successful investment broker but made the mistake of working for an unscrupulous firm. When the execs there caught wind of a government investigation, they set me up to take the fall. They altered transaction records and bank accounts to make it appear that I ran a scam, fleecing millions from customers. I panicked and left on the first ship whose captain took on a passenger, without asking any questions." Her business suit shimmered and transformed into a jester's costume. "I didn't realize until too late that he was smuggling contraband to the Ipis planet, Serpens. Life in prison would have been far preferable to the horror of these last five years."

Lucius regarded her and pursed his lips. "We will not litigate your innocence here. You will stand trial in the *real* world." He sat on a chair that materialized beside the table. "You'll be allowed three days to prepare your defense but will remain incarcerated until then."

Opal met his eyes. "Just give me a fair hearing. You won't regret sparing me. I can help you. The cyborg encampment was an equipment warehouse on Cocytus from... my era."

"Modern technology!" Marcus' eyes lit, and then he slumped into a chair that appeared beside Lucius. He shook his head and his red toga shimmered before transforming into a neural-net suit. "That gear is just useless lumps of metal and plastic without energy to run them." He glanced at Mara, who stood silently through the entire exchange. "We barely have enough power to make the interfaces on these garments work for a few minutes."

"True." Mara shrugged. "But even though it's true now doesn't mean it will remain that way."

Marcus glared at Mara. "I thought you were the one hellbent on not affecting the future."

The petite blonde clasped her hands. "I have made mistakes. After your return, I reflected much on my decisions." She regarded Lucius and Marcus before letting her eyes rest on Alexa. "I will no longer hinder any endeavors you chose on Novaroma. It is your world to mold as you deem appropriate."

"I appreciate that." Lucius squared his jaw. "As my father surely would have done, I will use any means necessary to protect my people."

Marcus added, "We will weave our story into your tapestry of time as we see fit."

Mara pursed her lips and nodded.

Lucius tapped the table. "Enough banter. We have two more cyborgs to purge. Let's get on with it."

Alexa sighed. "You are correct."

Lucius blinked and, even before he looked around, the sharp pain in his leg informed him he was back in reality. He glanced at Opal, who lay on the floor, no longer struggling against the legionnaires who held her. He cleared his throat. "The demon in this one has been exorcised. The person who remains has yet to be judged." He regarded the guards. "She will remain incarcerated until her trial."

Marcus rolled his neck and smiled at Lucius. "I don't think I'll ever get used to that experience. Ready for round two?" Without waiting for an answer, he pointed to the strawberry blonde. "We'll do that one next."

Alexa glanced at the prisoner. "Her name is Kaari."

The gamma struggled against her chains and the men pinning her to the ground. But a moment after Alexa touched her, the thrashing stopped. Her lips quivered as she glanced around. "Thank you. I didn't think I could ever escape that nightmare."

Lucius regarded her. "You're not free yet."

"You're wrong." Kaari sat up as her guards raised her to her feet. "No matter what happens now, I'm free. I have my mind back."

"One more." Marcus glared at the last cyborg-possessed woman.

Instead of struggling, the last cyborg went limp.

Alexa scoffed, "Shutting down won't save you from Mara's breeching your firewall," as she grabbed the woman's slack hand. "This one's name is Kim."

A moment later, the young woman lying on the stone floor took a deep breath. She wept in silence as her guards lifted her erect. She stumbled to where the other former human hosts stood.

Marcus stood, shaking his head. "That was interesting."

Meili helped Lucius to his feet. He winced and studied the three shackled women for a moment. They were docile in their stance, but their eyes locked on him. He declared with a formal voice that filled the crowded room. "Opal, Kaari, Kim, you have participated in brutal acts that resulted in the death of many good people." He glanced at Alexa, who stood beside Doctor Phokas, looking pale and worn. "The oracle has requested a boon that you be judged on who you are *now* and not who you were. I have agreed. Prepare your defense. Your trial will be in three days. You will remain confined until then."

He nodded to the legionnaires surrounding them. "Take the prisoners back to the granary and lock them up." His eyes narrowed. "If they cause you any trouble or attempt to escape, report the incident to me immediately."

The one named Opal, glanced at the other two and then bowed. "Legate Lucius Bernius, thank you for offering us this chance for redemption. You will not regret it." She nodded to the soldiers warding her. "Take us to our jail. We'll cause you no trouble."

For a moment, Lucius watched the three chained women stumble away between their guards before turning to Marcus. "I'm starving. How about lunch?"

"Yes," was the quick reply. "I could use some wine after this."

* * *

Three days later, Lucius sat on a cushioned bench with his splinted leg stretched out on a stool under a broad pavilion set up in Dragonmont's courtyard. Every senior commander, village elder, and scholar was present to witness the trial.

To prepare for the legal proceeding, the legate assigned Alexa and Marcus the task of deposing the former cyborg hosts, looking for gaps in their stories. He was adamant. "There will be no repeat of a Charles-like person being released into our small society."

For judges, Lucius selected Phokas, Meili, Anaya, Senior Centurion Silvio, the Byzantine scholar Theodore, and the

Persian scholar Borzoye to help him determine the fate of the prisoners. Alexa agreed to speak for the former cyborg hosts and, to the legate's surprise, the Shaolin priest, Chang, petitioned to represent Feng.

The four were brought before Lucius for judgment, manacled and yoked. They were a disparate group. The three women, each a fugitive from Earth's post-Ipis-war society, told their story on how they came to be enslaved.

The tall black woman, Opal, was a midlevel executive at an investment firm that was embezzling client funds. She was set up to take the fall when investigators started unraveling the scheme. Not trusting the legal system, she fled.

The young, almond-eyed woman, Kim, was a government intern. She was wanted for murder, a crime she freely admitted committing. However, she vehemently asserted that the victim, a prominent politician, raped her.

The strawberry blonde, Kaari, was a third-grade teacher. Her only crime was that of making bad choices. She followed a boyfriend to the Ipis Empire, where he dumped her and disappeared.

Feng whimpered that he just wanted to go home.

Alexa argued that they were not a risk and added, "They already lost over five years of their lives in involuntary servitude." Standing still as a statue, she asserted, "I found no deceit in them. They deserve a second chance." She raised her arms and declared in a voice that carried across the parade ground, "They were also in a position to *overhear* the cyborgs' conversations. That may prove invaluable aid to unlocking the *magical* treasures in their old camp."

Centurion Silvio snorted. "What use are enchanted talismans when we can't go near them? Alexa, in case you forgot, that place is overrun with limnonectes."

Alexa responded, "What bewitched the limnonectes will have dissipated by now."

Theodore's eyes bulged. "Why take the chance? With the cyborg tribe eliminated, we have no need to go near that cursed place."

A hubbub arose that Lucius did not immediately quell. He glanced at Marcus. "What do you think?"

Marcus leaned over and whispered in Lucius' ear, "I interrogated the three women extensively. They are... flawed, but no more than the rest of us." He rubbed his jaw. "As for the camp, it's centered around a twenty-first-century warehouse. We can't afford *not* to take possession of it. We need to advance Novaroma from a fifth-century Earth enclave to where you and I know we must be."

Lucius glanced at the prisoners. "A stockbroker, a bureaucrat, and a grade-school teacher. We don't gain a whole lot there."

"But they saw and heard everything the cyborgs did. They will know how to use that stuff, if we can get it working."

Lucius nodded. "Bring Alexa to me."

Chang rose and offered Alexa his hand.

As they walked forward, Lucius shouted to the assembly, "Silence. We will maintain proper decorum at this hearing."

The crowd subsided.

When Alexa reached him, Lucius asked her, "You were literally inside their heads. For the final time, do you vouch for them?"

"I *do*. Mara and I had serious reservations about Charles. But we were in a tight spot. Our only choice was to trust him." Alexa waved her hand at the three women, still bruised from the fights they were in days earlier. "These people are different. They are what they purport to be. Nothing more and nothing less." She added, "Lucius, they *can* help us. Their expectations will be different. They lived the future you're trying to move our people to."

Lucius grunted. "That's the same advice Marcus gave." He turned his gaze to Feng. "What do we do with him?"

Chang answered, "Feng is craven and power hungry, but in Jiankang he was known as an effective administrator." He smiled. "Perhaps if you convinced him that you're not a demon, he could aid you in that role."

Phokas crossed his arms. "Lucius, I don't understand any of the science behind what you've been through, but I trust Alexa. If these women were possessed and are now exorcised, then they cannot be held guilty of the harm done to our people." His eyes slid to the eunuch. "Feng is a frightened man who grasped at an empty promise, a lie." He sighed. "I would've had a hard time resisting such an offer myself if I believed it could return me to my home."

Lucius scanned the other judges. "I am leaning to acquit. Do any of you have an argument as to why I should not?"

Meili shook her head. "Free them. I despise Feng, but my hatred is personal."

Tears glistened in Anaya's eyes. "They butchered Kewal right in front of me." She reached out and grasped Marcus' hand. "But the man I love says Kewal was killed by demons who no longer exist. I believe him. Let these people go free."

No one else spoke. Even the murmuring from the audience ceased.

Lucius drummed his fingers on the table for a moment and declared in a loud, clear voice, "We named this place Novaroma." He glanced at Alexa. "And were brought here to give humanity a second chance." He faced the captives. "That is what I intend to do for you. I absolve you of the crimes committed to date on Novaroma." He raised his index finger. "But you're on probation. If I learn of *any* transgression, no matter how minor, you'll find yourself in chains or... worse. Am I understood?"

Opal glanced at the others and then spoke, "All we ask is a clean slate to start our lives over again." She dipped her head. "You will not regret your decision."

He nodded to the guards stationed behind the captives. "Free them."

Kaari stared at Marcus and cleared her throat. "Are you really related to Dante Carloman? I saw him once in Savannah a couple years after the Ipis war on Earth. You don't look anything like him, but the gamma cyborg that controlled me was convinced you are."

Marcus glanced at Lucius and then looked back. "Let's just say Alexa tells me that we're distantly related."

Epilogue

Summer turned to fall. The prevailing wind shifted and the snow-covered mountain crests to the west brought cool, dry breezes to the delta where the nascent human settlement lived. The colonists enjoyed the break from the stifling humidity to harvest their crops.

The farms and orchards were abundant that first season. Lucius put his legion to work on a number of civil engineering projects. Roads and bridges were built. Ditches were dug. Land was cleared. A small fishing village was established where the Reno River emptied into the sea. A water-wheel-driven grist mill was constructed alongside a rapid mountain stream north of the Jiankang pagoda in the shadow of the forested hills to the north.

Opal also resolved the mystery of how Alpha was able to lead the cyborgs across the Reno River, undisturbed by the potamos savras. She led Marcus to the crossing site. Although he detested the cyborg Alpha, the prefect could not help but be impressed at the clever engineering.

After the harvest was in, Marcus returned to that location with a team of engineers. "We will bridge the river here. In time, we will take possession of the lands east of the river. This location is far closer and safer than the shallows at the ford." Work began a week later, and within six weeks a twenty-foot-wide garrisoned and fortified stone bridge spanned the chasm.

* * *

Autumn turned into winter. Although warmer than the winters Lucius remembered from his years living in Mediolanum on Earth, it brought on a marked decrease in the activity of the native fauna. Mounted patrols at the foot of the Sawtooth Mountain range found no fresh dragon tracks or spoors once the weather changed. Farmers and ranchers faced no limnonectes attacks on their flocks and herds. In the river, the potamos savras became lethargic.

Lucius' leg mended well, and he itched to explore the lands beyond the bounds of the Sawtooth Mountains and the

343

Reno River. The brief glimpse he had of the intact, modern structures during their aborted attack on the cyborg camp, and the thought of what those buildings contained, tantalized him. The dormancy of the local wildlife from the cooler weather gave him the opportunity to mount an expedition.

However, Lucius was determined to not risk the life of a single legionnaire to achieve it. He consulted with Alexa and the former cyborg hosts about the potential of that site. From another era, it was a commercial distribution center and repair facility for the city of Setteth on the planet Cocytus.

He shook his head at the coincidence. Given the site description, it originated less than two miles from the clone factory where he spent his initial years of growth.

Opal proved to be a wealth of information. On Novaroma, the cyborgs were forced to communicate orally. She listened in on, and remembered, every conversation Beta-1 had. She told Lucius that the cyborgs originally created the distribution company because its legitimate commercial business dealing with photonic goods served as the perfect front for their smuggling operation.

As winter set in, and with the bridge complete, Lucius determined it was time to venture back to the old cyborg camp. He met privately with Marcus and Alexa.

Alexa assured him, "Mara calculated that the beacons' charge would have completely depleted months ago. Her analysis concluded, with a ninety-seven-point-one certainty, that without the subsonic frequency broadcast the limnonectes' aberrant behavior would cease and they would return to their normal state."

Lucius shook his head. "And it's my job to worry about the other two-point-nine percent."

Marcus' eyes gleamed. "But the possible gain is immeasurable." He spread his hands. "Look, the cyborg camp is a rocky outcropping in a bog. We approach, and if there are any signs of the limnonectes about, we back off."

Lucius rubbed his jaw. "We'll need to bring people who know the place. That means Opal, Kaari, and Kim." He looked pointedly at the blind oracle. "Alexa stays behind. If we leave, it will be in a hurry."

"What do you mean *we*? You're our ruler. You should stay behind too."

Lucius glared. "I'm going. Opal, Kaari, and Kim may be from the modern world, but I know what we need."

Marcus nodded. "Then let's go. The bridge is built and the path is clear. How about tomorrow?"

"Agreed."

* * *

A light frost clung to the ground during the predawn when Lucius assembled his team on the western end of the new bridge. The expeditionary force was small. Lucius, Marcus, the three former cyborg hosts, and a single century, commanded by Horatius.

As the sun broke the eastern horizon, they crossed the river. The legate left strict instructions with the decurion commanding the sentries stationed there. "If you see us running with the limnonectes on our heels, open the gate fast." He set his jaw. "If it doesn't appear we'll make it, keep it closed."

When he crossed over, Lucius did not look back at the sound of the heavy, iron-studded, wooden barrier grinding shut behind him.

After a quarter mile of slogging through the sucking bog, the terrain radically changed. Lucius climbed a six-foot, dirt-and-shale ledge and the change was surreal.

He stood on a paved asphalt surface. Across the empty, one-acre-sized parking lot, he saw a cluster of late-twenty-first-century buildings consisting of an eight-bay garage, a standalone machine shop, and an expansive, three-story, steel-and-cinderblock warehouse. After a dozen steps toward those structures, Lucius tripped over the first sign of the massacre from the previous summer. Scattered and cracked human bones lay bleached white in the morning sun. A rent breastplate and broken gladius lay nearby. He saw no signs of movement, but the legionaries with him drew their swords.

As they moved close to the structures, Lucius saw a semitrailer truck backed up to a loading dock. Opal came up beside him. "All the doors are locked. Alpha did not want any of his erstwhile allies disturbing anything." She smirked. "But I know where he hid the keys."

Glancing at the intimidating distribution center, he shook his head. "We'll save that one for last."

The first building they explored was the long garage. It contained four delivery vans and three service trucks. All were equipped with hydrogen-fuel-cell engines. All were devoid of energy. It was the same story in the repair facility. Workstations laden with high-tech fabrication and digital diagnostic tools were dark. *All without power. All useless.* To add to the legate's frustration, they found a squat brick bi-nexidium power generator behind that building, its power source drained.

It was midday as they climbed the steps at the warehouse loading dock. Lucius turned to Opal as she unlocked the receiving office entrance. "I assume it will be same in here."

She sniffed. "Yes. Power was sapped from *everything*. Be happy about it. If Alpha had any functional equipment, he would have used it against you. You'd be dead."

Marcus narrowed his eyes. "We're looking to build, not destroy. There may be something useful in here."

"I doubt it." Lucius sighed. He gazed through the door at the darkness. "Make torches. This place has no windows."

An hour later, dozens of legionnaires, with burning brands held aloft, walked along aisles lined with shelves stretching three stories high. From the lower bins they collected various items and brought them to Marcus and Lucius, who sat beside a shut-down robotic forklift near the entrance.

The whites of Horatius' eyes showed as he dropped a box of hand tools in front of them. "This place is cursed and everything within it, foul magic."

Marcus pulled out a claw hammer and held it up. "Those who welded these things were evil, but a tool is a tool. Nothing more, nothing less." He shook his head and turned to Lucius. "This is worse than having nothing. Everything we could hope for is here but useless."

Lucius pursed his lips. "But the technology is here. Unlike what happened on Dragonmont, these structures and their contents are intact, and we do have three functional solar panels."

The prefect dropped the hammer back in the box. "A drop in the bucket. With a real energy supply this equipment would be a treasure trove."

"Then we find a way." Lucius rose and brushed himself off. "We now know where there is a bi-nexidium deposit."

Marcus also stood. "Even if we dug out those crystals, we have no way to refine it."

"We'll find a way." Lucius patted his friend on the shoulder. "You, my friend, are the greatest engineer in the galaxy. *You* will find a way."

Marcus grimaced as he scanned the scattered collection of hand tools, furniture, and clothes. "One still needs something to work with. We might as well leave all the big stuff here. It takes energy to generate energy."

Lucius nodded as he started loading items into a crate. "We have time to develop a solution. Our enemy is vanquished. The beasts we can manage. What else can go wrong?"

Marcus shrugged and bent to help. "Nothing that I can imagine, but this place is full of surprises."

The legate called to the legionnaires. "Pack up. We're going home."

The soldiers were quick in responding to that command.

* * *

Winter turned to Spring. Planting time was hectic in the nascent settlement. It was a time for hope and new beginnings. Within weeks of each other, Anaya, Meili, and Alexa announced that they were pregnant.

At the Spring equinox, Alexa summoned Lucius, Marcus, Anaya, Meili, and Phokas to a private meeting.

Without preamble she declared. "I require a vault buried ten-feet down over the spot where the cyborgs drilled for the bi-nexidium crystals."

"To what end?" Lucius asked showing curiosity.

Alexa turned toward where the seven-foot metal pillar was hidden. "In the dark of night, with as few people about as possible, Mara needs to be carted there and deposited in the crypt."

"You still haven't answered my question?"

The blind oracle sniffed. "Her name must be carved into the tomb's concrete cover with the story of Novaroma's founding."

Lucius became irritated. "Alexa, why are you asking this?"

Marcus added, "Won't you lose your ability to communicate with her?"

"No," the blind oracle responded. "I could be miles from here and still have a clear link. But that connection won't last much longer. Mara has scant power left. Her systems will shift to hibernation mode to protect her core processor."

Marcus blinked. "If she is offline, why bother moving her."

Alexa pursed her lips. "Mara estimates, with a sixty-seven-point-three-percent probability, that she can siphon the faint traces of radiation rising through that fissure. Accessing unrefined bi-nexidium in this manner is incredibly inefficient but should be enough to keep her components from degrading."

She turned to Lucius. "To finally answer your question, Mara thinks it's important for our protection."

Anaya stroked her bulging abdomen. "From what?"

"The cyborgs were able to detect the crystal's presence." Alexa sighed. "In this time period, there are several species that have already attained interstellar flight capabilities." She turned her head to where she knew Marcus and Lucius sat. "That includes the *Ipis*."

She spread her hands. "If the cyborgs could locate the bi-nexidium crystal lode, space travelers from this era could too. It would be dangerous for us if visitors from other planets were drawn to this place before we could meet them as equals. Mara's presence would inhibit any radiation scans of this locale."

Lucius recalled the destruction wrought during his first day in Beatrice's valley on Cocytus by the Ipis. Although that cataclysmic event was still centuries in the future, for him it occurred five years ago. He shuddered. "The Ipis are no friends of humanity. We need to avoid encountering them as long as possible." He looked around the room. "It will be done as Alexa requested. There will be no further mention of Mara from this day forward."

* * *

Spring turned to summer. The virgin land proved to be as fertile as Mara estimated. Their crops flourished and the plain between Emporium and the sea opened to new farms.

Although disease was almost negligible in the small colony, death took its toll on the legion. The war with the cyborgs was costly, and the native beasts were slow to yield their homes to the human interlopers.

Lucius realized that maintaining a full legion in a colony of less than forty thousand was impossible. He reduced the number of cohorts from ten to four, cashiering all the enlisted legionnaires with greater than ten years of service, granting each ten acres of land across the newly opened delta as their pension.

On midsummer's eve, Lucius was crowned king and declared Dragonmont his permanent home. The new king named Marcus the lord governor and magistrate of Novaroma at that celebration.

As youths, some of the legionnaires grew up in fishing villages. They expanded the port with a small pier along the sheltered inlet where the Reno River emptied into the sea. Lucius named the hamlet Mediolanum after the place where he came to know his *father*. The construction of a seaworthy galley was completed before the end of the summer.

* * *

And they all lived happily ever after... Maybe. But that is another story.

You've finished.

Please review this book on your favorite sites!

One of the ways for independent authors and small publishers to get exposure for their books is to receive as many honest, thoughtful reviews as possible.

Thanks in advance!

About the Author

John Caligiuri is a novelist with Guardian Tree Publishing, who has a lifelong passion for literature and pens primarily science fiction and fantasy. He blends his fascination with history and his professional background in software engineering to come up with some unusual story twists. His stories emerged from his curiosity about historical watershed events and asking, "what if."

Originally from Buffalo, New York, John lives in Rochester, New York with his wife, Linda. She's been married to him for over forty years and has supported his writing from the beginning. His children and grandchildren are scattered around the USA, which gives him and his wife an excellent excuse for their many road trips. For relaxation John enjoys gardening (which stretches his intellect, attempting to outwit the rabbits and deer) and distance running. He is a member of the Lilac City Rochester Writers, Greece Writers, and B&N (Greece) writing group.

John is an award-winning author who has published the Cocytus science fiction series: *Sanctuary in Hell, Planet of the Damned, Deal with the Devil and Face Ones Demons,* the alternative history novels, *The Red Fist of Rome*, and *The Last Roman's Prayer*, and numerous short stories. He can be contacted at johndcaligiuri@gmail.com. For more information visit his website:

www.guardiantreepublishing.com

For new projects, John is working on a sequel to *Perdition's Angel* for the Novaroma science fiction series, and an anthology collection of his favorite short stories.

www.ingramcontent.com/pod-product-compliance
Lightning Source LLC
Chambersburg PA
CBHW070911260626
47162CB00007B/2630